Praise for k   ls

"Wonderful, terrific storytelling, with a real sensitivity
for ' e past and a violent world with so many different
     ⸍ies and preconceptions. It has a visceral quality
     ⸍nly enhances the jealousy and betrayal afoot. There
     ⸍ething mesmeric about it too, for it powerfully
     ⸍res a world of spirit-belief, which is a great
     ⸍vement when we are living in a secular age. In
   t, it is a real triumph of historical imagination."
   ⸍ortimer.

   ⸍aman heroine's spirit-haunted romance . . . The bone
   ⸍ of her skull fiddle winds through battles, betrayal
   ⸍evenge. A great read." *Susan Price.*

   ⸍ghis Khan is a byword for brutality and military
   ⸍ance. But in this fascinating book, Katherine Roberts
   ⸍ates the layers of legend and seeks out Temujin, the
   ⸍ Genghis: the child abandoned by his tribe but
   ⸍ ⸍mined to survive. In a sweeping narrative, she tells
th ⸍le of his tangled relationship with his blood-brother
ja ⸍ha, and with Borta, the woman they both love."
S: ⸍rkiss.*

"⸍   ⸍citing and imaginative re-telling of a little-known
1ʹ   ⸍, this story brings ancient Mongol society to life."
      ⸍rnbull.

I AM THE GREAT HORSE

"A wild, surging, enormously readable narrative . . . Bucephalus joins Anna Sewell's *Black Beauty* and Richard Adams' *Traveller* as one of the great equine storytellers." *Books for Keeps*.

"A marvellous book . . . Her Alexander is complex, driven, alternately coldly ambitious and warmly generous – arguably both hero and villain . . . A rich, rewarding and propulsive read that deserves a wide audience." *Coop Renner, School Library Journal*.

"A major work of historical fiction." *John Newman, Bookseller's choice, Publishing News*.

"A funny, informative and highly original historical novel." *Amanda Craig, The Times*.

"Roberts wears her considerable research lightly and you never question for a moment that this was how Alexander came to rule the Mediterranean and the east." *Guardian*.

"A truly epic adventure story with masses of factual detail and sympathetic insights, not least into the psychology of warfare." *School Librarian*.

"A great read . . . romps along through plots and battles and sieges, rather like Bucephalus himself." *Tony Bradman, The Times Educational Supplement*.

"The author knows both her history and horses." *Historical Novels Review*.

"A huge, action-packed war novel with echoes of today's conflicts . . . questions what Alexander calls the 'liberation' of the people he conquers." *Booklist*.

BONE MUSIC
THE LEGEND OF GENGHIS KHAN

BONE MUSIC

THE LEGEND OF GENGHIS KHAN

Katherine Roberts

The Greystones Press

First published in Great Britain in 2018 by

The Greystones Press Ltd
Greystones
37 Lawton Avenue
Carterton
Oxfordshire OX18 3JY

A CIP catalogue record for this book is available
from the British Library

ISBN 978-1-911122-21-0

3 5 7 9 10 8 6 4 2

Designed and typeset by Nigel Hazle

Printed and bound in Great Britain by Clays Ltd, St Ives plc.

CONTENTS

PART THREE: BLOOD OF WOLVES: JAMUKHA'S STORY

- PART ONE -
PRINCE OF WOLVES: TEMUJIN'S STORY

WHEN THE MONGOL clans were numerous, Lord Heaven summoned Blue Wolf and Fallow Doe to Holy Mountain.

"My people are as many as blades of grass," he said. "But they have no leader. When enemies attack, they are torn from the earth as if by horses' teeth, their blood is spilled so their spirits cannot return, and their ashes blow in the wind. I shall choose a boy from among them to make my people strong. You, Blue Wolf and Fallow Doe, will guide him. This boy will have the fire of the wolf in his eyes and a girl who runs with deer for his wife, and his people shall name him Khan."

YEAR OF THE HARE

WE'VE A SAYING on the steppe that wars start with a single stone. When a sharp piece of flint came whizzing out of the trees and almost hit the girl Father had chosen to be my wife, I should have gone after the idiot who had thrown it and sorted him out there and then. Growing up with three younger brothers and two half-brothers, I'd learnt to hold my own in a fight. It might have saved us all a lot of bother later.

But the shaman had tied my wrist to Borta's wrist with a chain of flowers for the betrothal ceremony. Breaking that link would have dishonoured my family and my clan, which Father had warned me not to do unless I wanted to feel his bow across my back. This was more than mere discipline. My father was Yesugei the Brave, leader of the Mongol Alliance. If his plans worked out, I would be khan when I was old enough and Borta would be the mother of my heirs.

We were already a legend. Borta's father, Dei the Wise,

had dreamt of our match the night before we rode into his camp. He claimed a white falcon had flown down from Heaven and told him some spirit tale about a wolf lying with a deer to give birth to a new nation. I'm pretty sure Father only went along with this prophecy because he'd stolen my mother while she was on her way from Dei's clan to her wedding with a Merkid chief, and wanted to bind Dei the Wise's people to the Alliance by marrying me off to one of Dei's daughters. Borta had a pet fawn that trailed after her everywhere, even during our betrothal ceremony, which meant she was the obvious choice for the deer.

That made me the wolf.

Since I was only nine at the time and knew nothing of the spirits, I quite liked the idea. Encouraged by the way everyone smiled at us, I even stood on tiptoe to give Borta a kiss – though she was taller than me so I could only reach her chin, and the stone ruined it anyway.

The shaman's eyes were half shut as he brushed our hands with his horsehair staff, and nobody else was close enough to see what had happened. Borta frowned at the trees. I pulled her out of harm's way and scowled at the lithe form running off towards the river. I did wonder briefly if my pain-in-the-backside half-brother Begter had followed us across the steppe to throw stones at my betrothal ceremony, which was just the sort of thing he'd do as the jealous son of a second wife. But Begter didn't have the balls to follow us across Tartar territory alone. One of the camp lads, no doubt.

I watched to see which tent he dived into so I could deal with him later. Then Borta's pet fawn started eating the flowers linking our hands, and she giggled. "No, Whisper!" she scolded. "You'll break the prophecy." I had to push the silly deer out of the way, and by then the stone thrower had vanished.

Father left camp straight after the celebrations, saying he had to get back to the Alliance before the other chiefs started squabbling among themselves. An unexpected lump rose in my throat as I watched him gallop away on his silver-bay gelding. I'd never been away from my family before and had to stop myself from running after him.

I never did find out who had thrown that stone at our betrothal ceremony. Three days later I was leading Borta along the riverbank on my silver-bay gelding, teaching her how to hold the reins, when two dusty warriors from the Alliance galloped into Dei the Wise's camp yelling my name.

"Temujin! Temujin! Where's Temujin?"

The gelding plunged in excitement, and Borta fell off. She wasn't hurt. Our Mongolian horses are small, and the ground by the river was soft. She sat up and frowned after its disappearing tail. With her long braid coming undone, she looked prettier than she had done at the ceremony, dressed up like a woman. She had gone pale, though. I realize now she might have had some kind of premonition, but back then I was too eager to find out what Father's men wanted to notice. I paused long enough to brush the mud off Borta's trousers and pick the leaves out of her hair, before she told me to stop fussing and hurry.

By the time we got back to camp, Dei's warriors were clustered around Father's men muttering in low voices. They fell silent as we approached and separated to let Borta and me through.

As soon as I saw their faces, I knew it was bad. Dei the Wise drew his daughter to his side, while one of Father's men caught my gelding and led it across to me. The rest of Borta's clan gathered around us, whispering uneasily. The boys I had not yet had a chance to get to know stood in a group, staring at me.

Nobody was throwing stones that day. They didn't have to. Dei the Wise's words hurt more than any missile, striking straight at my heart.

"Temujin," he said, his tone sympathetic but firm. "I'm sorry to tell you your father met with enemies on his way home across the steppe, and they poisoned his drink. He's dead. You'll have to get to know my little deer some other time. Your family needs you now."

- 2 -

YEAR OF THE DRAGON

YESUGEI THE BRAVE'S death changed everything. One moment I was playing with Borta's pet fawn and trying to teach my future wife how to ride a horse. The next, I was head of my clan, in charge of the entire Mongol Alliance. Any fool could have seen it wouldn't work out. A boy who hadn't yet learnt to bend a bow, ordering about battle-scarred warriors like Chief "Fatface" Kiriltuk and the rest? Probably I was stupid to go back there at all.

I found Mother being sick behind the tent (pregnant again, as it turned out, though at the time I thought it was because she was upset about losing her husband), and my little brothers in tears. Everyone blamed the Tartars for Yesugei's murder, but it made little difference who had killed him. As we galloped our horses nine times over Father's grave to hide his bones, I promised his spirit that when I was old enough to lead the Mongol horde I'd hunt down his murderers and send their ashes blowing in the wind.

That winter passed in a miserable blur. Mother dragged me around the yurts reminding everyone I was Yesugei's heir and asking for the clans' support to avenge his death, while Chief Fatface strutted about camp giving orders of his own. If our paths crossed, he ruffled my hair and told me not to worry because he would look after us now. I knew he didn't mean it, because he had hated the lot of us ever since we gave him his nickname – before that he used to be Kiriltuk the Large, which he'd quite liked because he thought it sounded like "the Great", but our name had stuck. I wanted to tell him to get lost. But Mother warned me I had to be on my best behaviour as next leader of the Alliance, so I could only clench my fists and scowl behind his back.

The other chiefs were sympathetic, but told us they couldn't risk avenging Yesugei the Brave until they had asked our ancestors' advice on Red Circle Day. This sounded to me like the sort of excuse people make when they're scared but, having only just turned ten, there wasn't much I could do about it. So I waited impatiently for the moon to rise red in the sky, while Mother's belly grew bigger and bigger, and Second Mother tried to keep us boys quiet without much success.

When the melting snows finally brought Father's old shaman to our yurt, my heart thudded in excitement. At last, some real action!

"Are we going after the Tartars now?" I said, hoping I would be allowed to ride with the horde.

Mother sighed. "Hush, Temujin. We don't even know which clan they were from. If we're going to avenge his death, we need to find out who the murderers were first."

"Let's ask Temujin," the shaman said smoothly. "Do you want me to try summoning Yesugei's spirit, little wolf? His blood wasn't spilt, so there's a good chance he's still nearby watching over his family. Shall I ask your father if he knows who poisoned him?"

Mother looked upset. "My husband's spirit is with the ancestors now," she said. "It shouldn't be disturbed."

I didn't really understand the spirit stuff, either. "Why can't we just kill all the Tartars?" I said.

It seemed a simple enough solution to me. Father had told us they were our biggest enemies, after the Merkids and the Naimans.

My half-brother Begter snorted. "Don't be stupid, Temujin! Do you know how many warriors the Tartars have? We can't just make war on them."

I didn't see why not. We had a lot of warriors, too.

"At least let me try," the shaman said, looking at Mother now. "If Yesugei's spirit doesn't come, I promise you I won't try to force it."

Mother bowed her head. She got tired easily, being so close to giving birth. "If we're going to keep the Alliance together, Temujin's going to need your support," she said. "Do what you think best."

The shaman smiled. "What do you say, Temujin? There's no need for a leader who has his people's welfare at heart to fear the spirits." And he turned the full force of his shaman gaze on me.

What could I say, with Begter leering at me, and my little brothers clamouring to see their father again? Reluctantly, I nodded.

We waited until after dark, when the magic would be at its strongest, while the shaman fetched his violin made from the skull of a stallion. Although part of me wanted the magic to work, a deeper part of me cringed at the first wail of that bone. Outside, the other clans were feasting as usual on Red Circle Day, but in a subdued manner because of Father's death. As far as I could tell, we were the only ones asking for any sort of advice from the spirits.

We sat in a circle in our yurt, Half-Brother Begter and me on opposite sides of the fire because our mothers knew what we were like. Begter glared at me as the shaman played, and I glared back. No doubt that's why neither of us noticed the door felt lift slightly behind the shaman's back. A cold wind blew in.

"Father's spirit!" gasped my brother Khasar, pointing.

Even as my neck prickled, a spear hissed through the flap and thudded into the shaman's back. His violin let out a final screech and fell into the fire, while our shaman crumpled to the ground. Second Mother screamed. Mother grabbed Khasar and the little ones. Begter went pale and pulled his younger brother Belgutei clear of the door.

It wasn't Father's spirit, of course.

Chief Fatface filled our doorway. I could smell the airag on his breath. As we all stared at him in shock, he jerked his spear out of our shaman's back and prodded the body with his toe. Blood stained the earth.

"I forbid such magic in my camp!" he roared. "Who gave permission for this?"

Mother recovered first. She straightened her shoulders and glared back at the chief. "You've no right to bring death into our tent! As Yesugei's heir, this is Temujin's camp now and he gave the order."

Fatface's lip curled as he looked at me. "A boy who can't even bend a bow? I am chief of the Alliance now. I thought you understood that. Your yurt is already tainted by death, and now a shaman's blood has been spilt in it. From this night, you're outcasts. We're moving on in the morning. Don't try to follow us, or your sons will feel my spear, too."

He aimed the blood-stained point at me.

Mother froze. "Temujin," she said. "Get behind me, quickly."

Half-Brother Begter sneered, but I didn't move. I suppose it might have looked brave, but the truth was my legs had turned to sour milk, so I couldn't have run even if a bear had lumbered into our tent. Our shaman's blood pooled beside my foot making me feel sick. Then a wolf howled outside, and I remembered the taboo among our people against killing an enemy who has not yet grown tall enough to peer over the wheel of an ox-cart.

"If you kill me, Father's spirit will curse you," I said. "He's behind you now, watching us." In a rather wobbly voice, I'll admit, but it worked. Fatface's spear lowered slightly.

"That's true," Mother said, giving me a peculiar look. "Temujin's still a boy, and our shaman summoned Yesugei's spirit to protect us."

Fatface paled and glanced over his shoulder. He eyed the smouldering violin, as if he thought Yesugei the Brave might spring out of it fully armed to avenge the shaman's death. Then he thrust his spear into the ashes and laughed. "Then maybe Yesugei the Brave's spirit will feed you and protect you from the wolves, because no one else is going to!" He laughed again and lurched out into the night, leaving us with a second body to bury.

We should have gone after him then. Maybe if Half-Brother Begter and me hadn't always been at each other's throats, we might have done. Fatface had been drinking. We might have had a chance of sticking a dagger into his belly if we'd caught him while he slept it off. But right away Begter started blaming me for the mess we were in, saying it had been my idea to try summoning Father's spirit, and Yesugei the Brave's death had been my fault in the first place.

He had a point, I suppose. If we hadn't crossed Tartar territory to find me a wife, Father might still be alive. But, of course, I never let on I agreed with my half-brother about anything, so I told him to shut his mouth or Father's spirit would get him. Then Second Mother started wailing worse than the shaman's violin had done, asking who was going to look after us now? Mother ordered us to pack our things, catch the horses and be ready to leave, in case Fatface changed his mind about us being too short to murder and sent his men to finish us.

The following morning, using the excuse that the Ancestors had told him to do it, Fatface broke Father's standard and cast us out. What could we do? Heavily pregnant, Mother couldn't fight them, and none of us boys was strong enough yet to bend a bow. We retreated up the River Onan with our eight silver-bay geldings and a handful of scrawny sheep that had been left behind in the confusion when everyone rode off. It seemed like a bad joke. Yesugei the Brave's family, who had been princes among our people, reduced to grubbing in the dirt for onions!

As for my betrothal and becoming khan, my half-brother Begter said (in a rather gloating tone) that I could forget the whole thing, since Dei the Wise's daughter would hardly want to marry me now. In fact, he added, if her father had any sense he'd give her to the Tartars to stop them from raiding his camp now the peace was broken.

Since I no longer had to be on my best behaviour, I punched him for saying so. Begter punched me back, and we rolled in the mud taking out a whole winter of frustration on each other, while our little brothers cheered us on. I'm not sure who came out best – we were both a bloody mess after – but I felt better for defending my promised wife.

I swore to Heaven no one would take Borta away from me as the Tartars had taken Father. My wild deer-girl and Dei the Wise's prophecy were my best chance now of reclaiming my birthright.

- 3 -

YEAR OF THE SNAKE

AT FIRST OUR exile wasn't so bad. The summer is a good time to be alive on the steppe, and it was quite a novelty to be camping up in the forest with no one to order us around. Mother gave birth to our little sister without much trouble – after all, she'd had plenty of practice by then – and we gave the baby a boy's name, Temulun, to stop evil spirits from stealing her away in the night. The two mothers found plenty of berries for us to eat, while we boys spent the long, hot days attempting to catch fish from the Onan with our clumsy hooks.

But when the berries shrivelled and the first snows came, things began to get more serious. I knew we'd be in trouble if we couldn't hunt for meat, so I struggled to master Father's huge bow, hidden by tall pines where the river raged loud enough to hide my grunts of frustration. My arrow-making skills improved (they had to, since I kept breaking the stupid things). But, no matter how hard

I tried, I couldn't draw that string far enough to send any of my arrows after a deer – or even, most times I'll admit, hit the trunk of whatever tree I'd chosen that day to take the place of Chief Fatface.

Before you get the idea I'm some kind of weakling, bending a Mongol bow is not as easy as you might think. We curve them both ways so that our arrows will fly twice as far, and it takes a man's strength to draw one. It's what turns a boy into a warrior. I would have died if Half-Brother Begter had bent his bow first. Out of desperation, I prayed to the Ancestors for help.

I never expected my prayer to be answered so quickly. When a lanky boy swaddled in furs stepped out of the forest and smiled at me, the surprise froze me to the spot like some fool marmot caught with its head out of its hole. He was the first stranger we'd seen since Fatface abandoned us and he seemed vaguely familiar, although I couldn't think where he'd come from. He caught me red-faced, bow half bent, trembling and sweating with the effort, my toes poking through the holes in my boots and going numb in the melting snow. Hardly an impressive sight.

"You're doing it all wrong, you know," he said.

"Wolf piss in Blue Heaven!" I yelled as Father's bow sprang back into shape, twanging my finger with its string on the way.

It was the foulest curse I knew, but it didn't impress the boy from the forest. As I sucked my finger, hoping the nail wouldn't go black, he brushed snow from his squirrel-fur collar and held out a hand. "Here, give it to me. I'll show you a trick."

I put on my fierce look – the one I'd been practising for when I went to claim Father's people from Chief Fatface and led them to war against the Tartars. "Who are you?" I demanded. "How did you get here?"

He didn't seem to have a horse. But he had a bow, I noticed, slung over one shoulder next to a quiver of black-feathered arrows. Again I had the feeling I'd seen him before, only I couldn't remember where.

The boy smiled again. "You needn't be afraid of me, Temujin."

My spine prickled. "How do you know my name?"

I wished I hadn't ventured so far from our yurt. I even wished Half-Brother Begter would turn up to see what was going on, which shows how much the stranger's sudden appearance had scared me.

"Everyone's heard of Temujin, forced into exile to protect his family." The boy coughed into his hand, and I realized he was thin under his furs and not much older than me. He looked hungry and cold.

"Do you need food?" I said, remembering my manners. I might not have been able to bend Father's bow yet, but I was head of our clan now, and there are certain codes to follow. "My little brothers are fishing. They might have caught something. Sometimes they do."

The boy spat out phlegm and eyed me. "It'd be easier if you let me show you the trick to bending that bow. Then you could shoot some marmots and squirrels to feed your brothers. Deer, even, like your future wife's pet maybe?" He gave me an amused look.

That was when I realized where I must have seen him before. I'd more or less forgotten the boys in my promised wife's camp. It seemed a different world, stuck up the Onan with my little clan. The thought of impressing Half-Brother Begter with my new hunting skills tempted me almost as much as the thought of eating real meat again. But I was still wary. I remembered that stone at our betrothal ceremony.

"You're from Dei the Wise's camp, aren't you?" I said, staring a challenge at him. "Did he send you up here to find me? Is Borta all right?" For all I knew he could have been sent by Borta's father to murder me as a way of breaking off the marriage treaty. Or maybe something had happened to Borta? My heart gave an uneasy thud.

The boy smiled. "Don't worry, your Borta is growing up fine, but she's not going to want to marry you until you're back in charge of the Alliance. I can help you with that. I'm Jamukha. My father was chief of the Jadaran clan – you might have heard of them? They're one of the richest clans north of here."

I hadn't, but didn't want to show my ignorance.

The boy tilted his head. "You left us so suddenly I never had time to introduce myself, so I thought I'd come and find you. We heard what happened. You're Yesugei the Brave's rightful heir, but fat old Chief Kiriltuk of the

Taychuit clan decided he'd like to lead the warriors your father had assembled and took advantage of Yesugei's death to steal them from you, didn't he? So here you are, hiding up the River Onan with your family like frightened deer. Not a bad hiding place, actually. You took some finding."

This lad who could have only just learnt to bend his own bow calling me, the wolf of the prophecy, a frightened deer made me furious. "I'm not afraid of Chief Fatface!" I said. "Nor of the Tartars, neither."

Jamukha laughed. "You looked afraid enough of me when you thought I was one of them."

"Did not."

"Did."

"Did not!"

We glared at each other. If he said "did" again, I swear I'd have thumped him, dishonour to my clan or not.

He gave me another teasing smile. "What's the matter, Temujin? Don't you trust me? I've come a long way to find you. The last good meal I had was my horse. So if you're not going to let me show you how to bend that impressive bow of yours, then at least take me back to your camp. I like the sound of those fish you say your brothers are catching."

"*Might* be catching." I couldn't help a smile, too. "They're not very good at fishing."

"Get bored, do they? Prefer to play at warriors, like you?"

His words got my back up again. "I haven't time to fish. I've got to learn how to use Father's bow so I can . . ."

I decided against telling him about my plans to lead my father's warriors to war on the Tartars so that when I returned to claim Borta as my wife she'd be proud of me, and said instead, ". . . feed my clan."

"Yes, you need a weapon if you're going to hunt properly." Jamukha gave me that sly look again. "Why don't we swear anda? If we were blood brothers, you'd trust me, wouldn't you?"

I thought of Half-Brother Begter, whom I wouldn't trust with anything more than a fish hook, and sometimes not even that. But *anda* . . . anda was different. It was a spirit-bond made before Heaven.

"Up to you." Jamukha shrugged. "It just seems to me we're both in need of friends at the moment. You've lost your father to the Terrible Tartars, and I lost my parents to the Murdering Merkids. If we become anda, we'll be bound by blood and spirit. Then we can help each other get revenge on our enemies. We Mongols ought to stick together."

So the Merkids had killed his parents? It sounded believable enough. They were nearly as bad as the Tartars.

Jamukha spread his coat on the frozen needles and laid down his bow. He took out his dagger and bared his arm as far as the elbow. He paused with the blade glittering in the sunlight, and his teeth flashed a challenge at me.

Alarmingly close, a wolf howled.

"Not scared, are you?" Jamukha said.

That did it.

I propped Father's bow against a trunk. I took out my knife and crouched by Jamukha, hoping he wouldn't notice the state of my clothes. They were patched to death and I was growing out of them fast – we all were – but Mother could hardly make new ones for us out of fish scales and onion skins, could she? She needed deer hide for that. Deer that I would be able to kill, just as soon as Jamukha showed me how to use Father's bow.

I rolled up my sleeve and made the cut quickly, brave and deep, to show him that blood didn't scare me. I kept my knife sharp, so it didn't hurt very much. There was rather more blood than I'd expected, though, and it stained Jamukha's coat. He didn't seem to mind. His eyes gleamed as he cut his own thumb, took my hand in a firm grip and pressed his wound to mine.

"Before Heaven, we two are anda," Jamukha said. He sounded pretty pleased with himself.

"Before Heaven, we two are ANDA!" I shouted, proud at the way my voice echoed in the mountains: *DA . . . DA . . . DA!*

The world spun around us. For perhaps ten heartbeats we let our blood flow together, dizzy and fierce. My legs wobbled and stars fizzed before my eyes. I felt shaky yet strong at the same time, as if I'd run up Heaven's Holy Mountain.

Beside me I heard Jamukha panting, and thought for a moment he was the wolf I'd heard in the forest. I lurched off his coat, grabbed Father's bow and fumbled for an arrow. Then Jamukha laughed, my vision cleared, and I saw my new friend holding out the anklebone of a sheep in his blood-smeared palm.

"Here, Anda Temujin," he said. "My first present to you. Now we'll have something to do when the river's frozen over."

I stared at the bone, my head still roaring with the blood we'd shared.

"Knucklebone dice?" Jamukha prompted. "Surely you know how to play? Or hasn't civilization reached you up here yet? Good job I came, if you ask me."

The traditional friendship gift cleared my head, and I started to think again. "First, show me your trick with the bow," I said.

We were anda now, so I was not afraid Jamukha would shoot me with it. I felt pretty clever, tell you the truth, because I'd just increased our clan by as many warriors as my new blood brother would one day command.

It never occurred to me to wonder why Jamukha would want to swear anda with an outcast like me.

- 4 -

YEAR OF THE HORSE

AS SOON AS we older boys could bend our bows, Mother sent Half-Brother Begter with Jamukha and me into the forest to hunt. At first, I resented her for destroying the happiness I'd found that winter with my anda. But she was clever. The three of us were so keen to outshoot one another we brought back enough meat to feed an entire camp, let alone one small clan. For the first time since we'd moved up the Onan, our bellies were full at night and our clothes did not have holes in them. With enough meat to see us through the winter months, we spent the days inventing new tricks on horseback that would come in useful when we went to reclaim Father's people from Fatface.

Then the snows melted, and Begter ruined everything by bringing up the subject of girls.

"I say we ride downriver and carry off that girl Dei the Wise promised Temujin the summer Father died," he said one day, leering at me. "She'll be thirteen now, won't she? All filled out in the right places . . . bet she's hot for it."

I knew then that he'd been spying on Jamukha and me, because my anda was the only person I'd ever discussed Borta with. But that summer of the Horse, with our randy geldings trying to mount each other, and fat marmots popping their heads out of holes left, right and centre, reminded us of what we were missing exiled up here.

"Don't talk about my future wife like that!" I said. Begter's gestures, demonstrating what he'd like to do to Dei the Wise's daughter, made me sweat under the collar.

"Oh, don't be such a stuffed marmot, Temujin!" Begter grinned. "She'll go round more than one of us. Tell you what, I'll help you break her in if you like. Don't expect you've done it yet, have you?"

"Nor have you!" I pointed out with a frown.

Begter had been stuck up the Onan with us ever since Father's death. In all that time, we'd not had any visitors except Jamukha.

"I know what to do, though," Begter said, giving my anda a sly look. "I've been practising."

"On what?" I felt pretty sure he was lying. "I don't see any girls up here." At least none except for my baby sister, and Temulun still had a boy's name so she didn't count.

"We've got sheep, haven't we?"

"That's disgusting," I said, even as an image came into my head of my half brother hopping after our scrawny sheep with his trousers round his ankles. I couldn't help it – I snorted with laughter.

Begter scowled. Jamukha smiled and carried on whittling away at an arrow he was making.

"I know more about girls than you two, any rate," Begter said. "If my mother had been Yesugei the Brave's first wife, Dei the Wise's daughter would have been promised to *me*. And I'm telling you now," he added. "I'd not have wasted my time in his camp trying to teach the girl how to ride . . . I'd have been too busy teaching her how to be ridden!"

It was all just talk. Three years ago, Begter would have been a boy same as me. But I was fed up with my eldest half-brother trying to make me look stupid in front of my anda.

"Borta's mine," I growled. "Hands off."

Begter chuckled, seeing he had touched a raw spot. "What about sharing her with Jamukha, then? You blood brothers are supposed to share everything, aren't you? I've even heard andas comfort each other under the furs when there are no girls to be had."

There was not a grasshopper's breath of truth in this as far as I was concerned. But I'd heard such rumours too, and it wasn't something I wanted spread across the steppe. "That's a lie," I growled.

Jamukha had gone very still. He eyed me, and then blew through the hole he had made in his arrowhead, making it whistle as it would when it flew through the air after a deer. "I don't need to share Temujin's wife," he said. "I've a queue of girls back home, waiting for me."

"What are you still doing up here with us, then?" Begter said, giving my anda a jealous look.

In those days, Jamukha's hair was always escaping its braids to float around his face in a girlish way. But he was taller than both of us, and didn't have my current trouble with his voice going up and down all over the place. If he hadn't been camping with us since he was eleven, I might have believed him about the girls, too.

"I'm making them wait, of course," Jamukha said with a shrug. "A man's got to show his wives he's boss. Otherwise, before you know it, they get their tall headdresses on and start strutting around as if they own your whole camp."

Begter scowled again. He never liked being reminded that, as a son of a second wife, he'd never be in charge of any camp.

"We can't just go riding off to Dei the Wise's camp to collect Borta without any lads to back us up," I said, a bit relieved about that, since I doubted her father would exactly welcome me with open arms if I turned up before I'd got my people back from Fatface. When she had been promised to me, I'd been heir to half the Mongol herds and clans. Now I was fighting just to lead my small family.

"Even if we did get some girls up here, the Terrible Tartars or the Murdering Merkids would only raid our camp and steal them from us as soon as they found out," I added. "And what about the mothers and little ones? They rely on us, you know that."

"We can't hide up here all our lives!" Begter said. "I'm tired of hunting deer."

For once, I agreed with my half-brother. As Jamukha had pointed out to me many times, marrying Borta would remind people of the prophecy and make them believe in me as their next khan. It might be a good idea to start making plans to get Father's people back now I could bend my bow. But there was still the problem of Fatface having a thousand warriors and us having only seven, and that was counting my little brothers armed with stones.

"We'll get some girls," I promised. "But first we have to get more lads and horses to join us so we can protect them—"

"My point entirely!" Begter interrupted. "So how are we supposed to find all these brave warriors, when we're still hiding up here like frightened rabbits?"

I clenched my fists. I wanted to punch the smirk off my half-brother's face, because he was right, damn him.

"I know where I can get us some more lads," Jamukha said, unfolding his long legs. "If you lend me a horse, I'll try to persuade some of my friends to come up here and join us." He paused and added, offhand, "I can visit Dei the Wise's camp on the way and let Princess Borta know you're safe."

"I'll ride with you," Begter said eagerly. "Temujin can stay and look after the mothers and the little ones until we get back. I want to see if this girl he's planning to marry has any pretty sisters."

I couldn't think of a good enough reason to stop Jamukha going. I didn't want to lose my anda, but at least I trusted

27

him. Begter, I didn't trust at all. The thought of my half-brother and wild little Borta – not so little Borta any more, I supposed – in the same camp together made my head spin.

Things might have cooled down if we'd gone back to the yurt and discussed our plans with Mother. But while I was still trying to think of how to keep Begter well away from Borta, my younger brother Khasar and Begter's little brother Belgutei rolled into the clearing, fighting over some fish they'd caught. It was a harmless tussle, but Begter seized my brother by the collar and thumped him viciously on the nose.

At the sight of that blood, the rage that had been building inside me ever since my half-brother had insulted Borta burst free. I grabbed my bow. Jamukha, seeing my quiver lay out of reach, thrust his newly made arrow into my hand. I hauled back on the string and took aim at Begter.

"Let Khasar go." For once, my voice didn't play up.

Begter stared at me, my brother's blood still on his knuckles.

"If you don't let him go right now, I'll put this arrow in you," I said.

Belgutei picked himself up out of the mud and scurried out of the way. He wasn't nearly as stupid as his older brother.

"Oh, so Temujin's decided he's got the right to order us all about now, has he?" Begter said with a sneer, shoving Khasar away. "Funny how people get big-headed with a weapon in their hands. You'd best put that bow down, little khan, before you shoot yourself in the foot."

He must have noticed my arms trembling with the effort

28

of keeping the bow bent. I hauled the string tight again and set my jaw against the strain in my back. Jamukha raised an eyebrow at me. He wanted to know if I needed help. I shook my head.

"Khasar, pick up Begter's bow," I ordered, seeing Begter's gaze slide to his own weapon.

My brother did so, and Begter pulled a frustrated face.

"See if you can bend it," I said.

Khasar grinned, took an arrow from Begter's quiver and bent the bow quite easily.

Jamukha gave me a wary look. He joined Belgutei in the trees, leaving Begter trapped between Khasar and me like an angry bear between two hunters.

"See, Half-Brother?" I said, prolonging the moment. "Khasar is strong enough to bend a bow now. And Jamukha can bend his bow, too. That leaves you a bit outnumbered, doesn't it?"

"You wouldn't dare," Begter said. "You need me to help you look after the mothers and little ones, remember?" But his voice squeaked, giving him away.

"I don't need people who think it's funny to beat up my younger brother. Besides, you were going girl hunting with Jamukha, as I recall."

I could see the fear on my half brother's face. "All right then," he said. "I'll stay and look after the camp. Whatever you say. I don't care." He cast a nervous look over his shoulder at Khasar. "Come on, Temujin! A joke's a joke. Put the bow down now, huh?"

"And what you said about Borta?"

"Borta . . . ? Oh, that. I don't want your girlfriend, don't worry! She'd be no fun. Everyone knows Dei the Wise only promised her to you because he couldn't get anyone else to take her. What sort of man wants a wife who'd rather run with deer than lie with her husband? Only someone who's scared of her laughing at him between the furs, I'm thinking . . ."

It might have been all right if he had just said "sorry". But Begter never knew when to stop. My arms were half dropping off, keeping that bowstring taut for so long, and I had terrible cramp in the backs of my legs. I'd only meant to scare my half-brother. But a movement in the undergrowth distracted me, and Jamukha's arrow had a smooth shaft. Before I could stop it, the arrow was flying through the air.

Begter's mouth opened, his cry cut off by the whistle of the arrowhead as it pierced his throat. Khasar's eyes widened, but he followed my lead and let his arrow fly as well. I heard the thud as it hit Begter in the back.

Ever since Father's death, I'd been trying to imagine what it would feel like to kill someone. Not in a cowardly way like the Tartars, poisoning Father so that he collapsed on the ride home. I'd promised myself that when I killed my first enemy, I'd do it face to face with an arrow shot from my own bow.

Well, I'd done it all right, and it felt unreal. As if my half-brother would jump up with a scowl at any moment, saying he didn't want to play any more, that he was too old for stupid games. He wouldn't play games with me any more, that was for sure.

Belgutei gave a cry of horror and rushed to his brother's side. Jamukha fingered his anda scar, staring at me uneasily. Maybe what the shamans say is true, and the anda bond links us more closely than the blood we exchange when we swear to be brothers for life.

"You *killed* him!" Belgutei said, staring at the bow in my hands with undisguised fear.

Part of me wanted to put my arm around my remaining half-brother and say I was sorry. I didn't, though.

Another heartbeat passed, and the moment when I could have weakened slipped further away. If Belgutei was afraid of me, I decided it would be a good thing, because then I'd never have the same trouble with him as I'd had with Begter.

Khasar stepped forward for a closer look at the body. "Belgutei's right, Temujin. He's dead." He sounded no sadder than if he had discovered a dead horse.

While we all stood there, not knowing what to do next, Begter's blood trickled down a channel into the river and swirled red in the water. Fish gathered to feast on it.

Part of me said we were missing a trick. We ought to have had the nets out. There were still mouths to feed back at camp. But there was a strange roaring in my head. I saw black patches over the water, and the trees on the far bank sparkled where the undergrowth had moved. Still a bit dizzy, I thought I saw a large silver-blue wolf standing there, watching us. But even as my spine shivered, the creature vanished into thin air.

Khasar touched the feathers of my anda's arrow, glanced at Jamukha, and finally looked at me. "What are we going to tell the mothers, Temujin?"

What would you say if you'd just killed your half brother and had to explain his death to his mother, your mother, your two little brothers and your baby sister? *A spirit distracted me?* I needed a better excuse than that.

"We'll say he insulted Princess Borta," I said. "You all heard him."

Jamukha nodded. He pushed Belgutei aside and plucked his arrow out of Begter's body. Watching him rinse off the blood in the river, I wondered if the fact an arrow made by my anda's hand had killed my half-brother made Jamukha partly responsible for the death.

Who could I ask? We had no shaman in our camp. One thing I did know. I couldn't tell my family Begter's death had been an accident. Khasar would never respect me again. Nor would Belgutei. I couldn't even bring myself to admit the truth to my own anda. But I learnt one thing that day.

Killing a man was easier than I'd thought. And, if you did it for a reason they understood, it made people respect you. Or fear you. Which amounts to much the same thing on the steppe.

Jamukha left camp as soon as he'd caught his horse. I didn't blame him. I wouldn't have wanted a lecture from someone else's mother, either. And lecture we got, big time.

After we'd buried my half-brother, with Mother insisting we gallop our horses nine times over his grave to hide his bones the same way we'd hidden Father's (as if anyone would find them all the way up here), she yelled at me and Khasar like we were still in our first year cycle. I suppose Khasar was still a child, being a few moons short of his twelfth summer, but only just. Firing that arrow into Begter's back had made him grow up all at once. Then later, after we'd eaten some berries the mothers had found, we got the old bundle-of-arrows lesson.

"Snap it!" Mother said, handing Khasar one of my arrows.

Khasar gave me an apologetic look, but obeyed. The shaft broke at once, and I groaned inwardly at the thought of having to whittle another one.

Then Mother took five of my arrows and held them together in a bundle, which she passed to me. "Now you, Temujin," she said, knowing very well I wouldn't even if I could, because making good arrows to replace them would have taken me ages.

I shook my head and passed the arrows to Alchidai, who struggled so hard to break them his face turned bright red. All the time, Mother just looked at me with those steady eyes of hers, which made me feel worse than the sound of Begter's mother wailing over her son's grave.

Alchidai gave up, and handed the five arrows to

33

Odchigin, who nearly ruined the whole thing by letting the bundle fall apart. Well, he had little hands back then, so you couldn't really blame him. Belgutei took them next, eyed me, and passed the arrows back to Mother without even trying to break them.

She pressed her lips together, and we braced ourselves.

"I'm quite sure I don't have to tell you the broken arrow is Begter. These five are the rest of you, strong only if you stick together. Up here, we have no friends except our own shadows and no whips except our horses' tails, so you ungrateful horde of savages had better stop fighting each other if you want to live to see your children grow up! Now get out of my tent the lot of you. You're keeping your sister awake."

Temulun lay in her cradle behind Mother, giggling and trying to reach the feathers on the ends of the arrows. She didn't look as if she minded being kept awake. But Mother was angrier than we'd ever seen her, and part of what she said was true because Jamukha, my only friend in the world, had gone.

That night, curled up in my blanket near the horses, I couldn't sleep. I felt bad – not about Begter, who had insulted Borta and deserved his fate – but thinking about my brothers sharing my punishment, and how there had been seven of us when now there were only five. Heaven knows it wasn't a good start for my clan.

- 5 -

YEAR OF THE SHEEP

I SHOULD HAVE realized old Fatface would get to hear about Begter's death. Second Mother had stolen one of our geldings and ridden off downriver soon after we buried him, wailing about me being a disgrace to Yesugei the Brave's name. I just didn't think the fat chief would be that bothered, considering he'd exiled us all up the Onan to die in the first place.

That was my first mistake.

When he came for me, he brought a hundred of his warriors in leather armour, their quivers bristling with arrows. He led them on the gelding Begter's mother had stolen, his legs sticking out and his enormous stomach swaying from side to side. I knew at once he was going to use Begter's death as an excuse to break up our little clan for good.

Belgutei, Khasar and I held them off with our arrows long enough for Mother to get away with little Temulun and my younger brothers. Then I told the other two to look after the family until I got back, jumped on one of our geldings and rode like the wind.

The whole troop came after me as I'd planned. I went up the deer paths into the forest and lost them in the thickets where Anda Jamukha and I had hunted the morning before I'd killed Begter to defend Borta's honour. Then I set up my shelter and waited, too afraid to light a fire in case Fatface saw the smoke.

It went quiet on the fourth day. Aware of being a single snappable arrow, I stuck it out for four more. All right, so maybe I wasn't as cautious as I should have been. After nine nights alone in the forest with only the spirits for company, you wouldn't be either. By then I was cold and wet and hungry and I'd started seeing things that weren't there, such as Borta's pet deer bounding through the trees and the wolf that had watched me kill Begter lying outside my shelter.

Thinking Fatface had long ago given up and gone home to the comfort of his own yurt, I hacked a path out of the forest. Cutting the last of the branches, I dragged my horse through without checking first to see if anyone was waiting for me on the other side – and something cracked down on the back of my head. There was a sickening lurch as the earth spun away.

"Stupid," said the big silver-blue wolf, looking down at me. "Didn't we warn him?"

"Stupid," agreed the beautiful doe standing beside the wolf spirit.

Then nothing for a long while.

*

Sensation returned painfully. All my limbs prickled, as if I had fallen into a patch of nettles. There was a heavy weight around my neck, fixing my wrists in a wrestler's hold. The world seemed to be upside-down, and something hard kept hitting my groin. The jolting became a horse's trot, bouncing me painfully on its saddle with every stride. It was no wet dream, I can tell you.

"Boy's awake, chief," said a voice, and to my relief the jolting stopped.

"Good, then he can walk the rest of the way."

Fatface rode his horse up beside mine. He loosed some ropes that had been keeping me in place and his foot connected with my backside. I fell from that saddle like a dead deer, and the thing around my neck twisted like a pair of oversized antlers, cutting off my air supply. Choking, I struggled to my knees.

They had put me in a cangue, a good strong one made of wood that locked my wrists to my chin. While I knelt there, gasping helplessly, one of the men dismounted and tied a rope to the side of the contraption then tied the other end to his saddle.

Chief Fatface leant on his horse's withers and peered down at me, as if trying to decide how dangerous I was. "Get up, Temujin," he said. "Or we'll drag you the rest of the way."

I'd been lucky not to break my neck! Anger filled me, and then fear at the thought this might have been what my enemies intended all along. I tried to get to my feet and fell over again. The fat chief made an impatient sound and told one of his men to give me a drink.

While I gulped the water, wanting to spit it into my captor's face but too desperately thirsty to waste a drop, Fatface explained a few things to me. "This is how we treat criminals," he said. "And you're a criminal now, Temujin. You killed your own flesh and blood."

My breath returned then, and hatred rose in me so fierce it overcame the pain of my bruises. "You're a murderer, too," I said, raising my head as far as possible wearing the cangue to stare him in the eye. A tense silence came over the men, only broken when I added, "You killed our shaman. The spirits will punish you for that."

The man holding me laughed. "The boy's still got life in him, Chief! Better watch him."

Fatface regarded me with narrowed eyes. "You're getting too big for your boots, Temujin. You're not with a bunch of women and children now. Since your father's dead, it's up to me to teach you some manners. I've had to ride all the way up here after you, so I'm warning you now I'm not in the best of moods. You'll wear that cangue as long as I say so, which means you'd better watch your mouth from now on."

He wheeled his gelding – *our* gelding – and trotted to the front of his troop. The man who had watered me remounted and urged his horse after the others. The rope attached to my cangue tightened, leaving me no choice but to stumble after him. I didn't know if they would really drag me as they'd threatened to, but I didn't want to find out the hard way.

I'd forgotten how noisy and smelly a big camp could be. Obviously Begter's mother had been bad-mouthing me all winter. As I was led through the clans my father used to rule, small boys ran after us throwing stones and the women spat in my face. Locked in my cangue, I could do nothing to stop them.

Chief Fatface ordered me passed round the yurts, a different one every night, so everyone in his camp could have a good laugh at me. Each morning he had me hauled out and measured against the wheel of his ox-cart to see if I had grown tall enough to be counted a man so he could kill me without risking the curse of our Ancestors. There was only a hand's breadth in it that year, so I bent my knees and sagged in my captors' grip and gave silent thanks to the spirits that had made me short for my age. And all that time I wore my cangue, which grew heavier and more uncomfortable with every day. The skin around my wrists and neck rubbed raw, and whenever I wanted to pee I had to ask the family I was staying with to help me. Humiliating was not the word.

My hatred for the fat chief grew until I felt sick with it. But what could I do – me, a single arrow locked in a cangue? I worried about my family up in the forest on their own, and wondered if my anda had found those warriors he'd gone to look for. If so, I hoped he'd have the sense to keep them and my family safe until I got back.

To make things worse, most of the yurts I slept in had girls in them. Not babies like my little sister, but girls my own age who reminded me of what Borta must look like now. Their mothers usually made sure one of the minor wives took on the task of helping me with my bodily functions and kept their daughters well out of the way. But I saw the girls glancing at me and giggling when they thought I wasn't looking. They seemed fascinated by me and made excuses to visit whatever tent I was being kept in at the time. Fatface probably meant the embarrassment to be part of my punishment, but pretty soon I realized those girls were my best chance of escape.

I tried my grin on every girl I caught looking at me, but they were all too afraid to talk to me. Then one day I ended up in a yurt where the women were making airag by churning bucketfuls of mare's milk. As usual, my guard led me to a corner and tied my cangue to one of the poles holding up the roof. We didn't have any mares up at our camp in the wilds, so I hadn't tasted airag since the sips I'd been allowed on feast days before Father's death. The smell of the churned milk turned my mouth sour. To make things worse, I'd been tied in the tent so long I had an urgent problem.

"Excuse me!" I called. "Can someone help over here?"

One of the girls unfolded her long legs, wiped her hands on her trousers and came over. She squatted down just out of reach and studied me. She was tall for a Mongol and had muscular arms. From all that churning, probably.

Not wanting to scare her away, I said, "Are you sure you want to do this? Usually one of the older women comes."

Her dark eyes regarded me in amusement.

"They're all too busy making airag for the feast," she said, and I realized with a start I'd lost track of the days and Red Circle Day was almost upon us. "Father says I'm supposed to look after you tonight. You're Temujin, aren't you? The one who murdered his brother?"

"*Half*-brother," I corrected. "And he asked for it." I gave her a level stare to show I wasn't ashamed of what I'd done.

She did not lower her gaze. "Why don't you just apologize to his mother?" she asked. "Then Kiriltuk might stop punishing you."

"She betrayed us," I said. "She doesn't deserve an apology. Besides, it won't make any difference. Fatface has been looking for an excuse to kill me ever since Father died. He's just waiting for me to grow tall enough so he can do it without risking the wrath of our Ancestors."

The girl frowned. "It's true that when Chief Kiriltuk heard how you'd killed your half brother, he was worried you might ride downriver and put an arrow in *him*. But he's too scared of your father's spirit to kill you, so if you pretend to have learnt your lesson, he'll probably just let you go."

As if.

When I didn't say anything, she added, "So why *did* you kill your half-brother?"

So far, no one had thought to ask why I'd killed Begter.

41

"He said something rude about my wife," I told her, embarrassment making my voice rough.

The girl blinked. "You're married already?" she said, surprised.

My flush must have given me away. "No – at least, not yet. But we've been betrothed for ages. Her name's Borta. She's a princess of Dei the Wise's clan, and as soon as my anda gets back with some warriors we're going to ride to her camp and collect her."

"Princess Borta's lucky," said the girl, giving me a wistful look. "To have a boy love her so much he'd fight to the death over her."

This made me feel stronger than I had since the wolf had made me kill my half-brother. My brain started to function again. I grinned at the girl, rather enjoying the way she kept blushing, even while I felt like a louse under the collar for being nice to her just so I could trick her into letting me escape. "Don't suppose you can take this thing off me?" I said hopefully. "I'd be able to do my business by myself then."

She hesitated. Then she nodded, and struggled with the fastening at the side of the cangue.

One wrist came free, raw where the wood had rubbed – such bliss to be out of the thing! But I was still in the middle of Fatface's camp, surrounded by a thousand of his warriors. I'd need a bit of a head start. So I grinned at her again. "Thank you, uh . . . ?"

"Khadagan," she supplied, smiling back.

42

"Khadagan," I said in my most seductive tone. "My wrist's sore. Don't suppose you've got something to help?" She examined the raw skin and mumbled something about getting her mother's ointment from the medicine chest. I prepared to leg it.

Then, as if from nowhere, two lads appeared.

"Hey, what are you doing?" said one, staring at my half-open cangue.

"Stay away from our sister, kin-murderer!" said the other, pushing me back against the felt wall of the tent. "How'd you get loose, anyway?"

Khadagan told them angrily that Yesugei the Brave's son would not kill his half-brother for nothing, and they were fools if they couldn't see that, while I fought them as well as I could with one wrist locked to my neck.

We were attracting too much attention. If I tried to run, I knew I wouldn't get halfway to the river before they caught me again. I had to let them lock my other hand back into place before they would listen, but in the end – after I'd explained how Fatface had killed my father's shaman and exiled my family and was just waiting for me to grow tall enough to kill too – Khadagan persuaded her brothers to help me.

We planned my "escape" for Red Circle Night in the dark time before the moon rose. On feast days there's always a lot of airag flowing, but it was stronger than usual that night because Khadagan's family was in charge of making the stuff. By moonrise, most of Fatface's people were staggering about the camp with sore heads.

My guard led me round the yurts like a sacrifice, flexing his puny muscles and gulping down a cup at every fireside. I followed him meekly, biding my time and trying to ignore the wail of the horse-skull violins that reminded me of the night our shaman had died. I waited until we were passing through the shadow between two yurts. Then I clouted him hard on the side of the head with my cangue. He went down like a stone. I ran for the river and jumped in.

The cangue acted like a float. The plan was for me to hide in the reeds and wait for Khadagan's brothers to come and free me once everyone else was sleeping off the airag. But my guard must have woken up and raised the alarm, because the stupid dogs started barking. I remember wishing I had hit him harder. Then the moon grew very bright and red, something tugged at my spirit, and everything went blurred for a while.

I thought I saw a silver-blue wolf running along the bank, being chased by the dogs. Then Borta's deer raced past crying something like *Help him!* Or that might have been Khadagan's voice, calling faintly to her brothers in the night.

The next thing I knew, I was lying on the riverbank free of the cangue and Khadagan was dragging an old yellow mare towards me by the bridle. She stared down at me, pale-faced. It was very quiet in the grey time just before dawn. I'd lost half the night to the spirits.

Her hand trembled on the reins as she led the horse forward. "Father says you can take this mare," she said. "She's barren but she'll carry you. There's food in the pack, and a bow and some arrows. If I were you, I'd not stop riding until you reach Holy Mountain. You might have friends in this camp now, but old Kiriltuk's going to be furious you've escaped."

"What happened?" I had too many questions and not enough time for the answers.

"Just *go*, Temujin!" she begged. "Nobody's going to follow you. The dogs ran off after a spirit, and the men are so spooked they're refusing to set foot in the forest. The Ancestors must be angry with Chief Kiriltuk for capturing you. You're lucky . . . you nearly got us all killed."

Her lips parted slightly. She looked as if she wanted me to kiss her. Nobody was around, so I did. She tasted sweet and warm, and I wondered if her father might agree to give her to me as a second wife. But then she pulled away, reminding me I still had to fulfil the prophecy by marrying Dei the Wise's daughter and get Father's people back before I'd be in a position to protect any extra wives.

As I cantered away on the yellow mare, I swore to Heaven that the first thing I'd do after I found my clan was recruit enough warriors to take over the Alliance and send Fatface's ashes blowing in the wind.

- 6 -

YEAR OF THE MONKEY

THE YELLOW MARE proved slow as a yak, giving me time on the ride home to imagine all the horrible things that might have happened to my family while I'd been gone. At one point I heard a twig snap behind me and thought Fatface's men had followed me. But it was only Second Mother, her feet blistered and her clothes in rags, begging me to take her back with me. She claimed it hadn't been her who had told Fatface about me killing Begter, but that everyone blamed her for bringing the spirits down on his camp and had cast her out.

I felt tempted to leave the lying bitch to the wolves, but she clung on to my ankle sobbing that she'd do everything I said from now on, if only I'd let her stay. I knew the silly woman would die if I left her on the mountainside alone, which would upset Belgutei again, and I was too weary and sore after my captivity to argue. So in the end I let her hold on to the mare's tail and stumble along behind me.

To my relief, the worst thing that had happened in my absence was that a small party of raiders from over the ridge had stolen our herd of silver-bay geldings. I promised my tearful little brothers I'd get our horses back, and we moved our camp further upriver to the foot of Holy Mountain, hiding it as best we could among the rocks and branches. If Jamukha looked for us at our old camp, it was just too bad. I couldn't risk splitting our small clan at such a perilous time, not even to send a message to my anda.

We couldn't raise an army without horses. In the spring, when I was sure Fatface hadn't sent anyone after me, I set out on the trail of our stolen geldings, all too aware of being a single snappable arrow again. I asked everyone I met if they'd seen any horse thieves in these parts, and in the end my patience was rewarded. A trapper told me he'd seen a herd of silver-bays with a scruffy group of raiders who had passed that way not long ago. He directed me out on to the steppe.

As I hesitated at the edge of the trees, cautious in case it was a trap, I saw a lad of about my age milking a fat mare surrounded by a large herd of horses. Thinking our geldings might be among them, I put an arrow on my bowstring, stuck my heels into the yellow mare's sides and charged him. But the lad didn't run. He shaded his eyes to see me better, grinned and said, "You must be Temujin."

The yellow mare pulled herself up to greet the other

horses – it hadn't been much of a charge, to be honest, and when I got closer it became obvious our geldings weren't there. "How do you know my name?" I demanded.

"Oh, everyone's heard of you in these parts," the lad said. "You're famous for putting the fear of Heaven into fat old Kiriltuk! I'm Boorchu. What are you doing riding that old nag?"

It seemed news of my capture and escape had travelled faster than the mare. I explained, and his face hardened.

"Merkid bastards, I bet. Some idiot's been carrying out moonlight raids on their camps so they've been raiding up here in revenge. Don't worry, I'll help you get your geldings back – but you'll need a faster horse if you're going to keep up with me."

Just like that, I had a friend. We swapped my saddle from the yellow mare to a grey gelding with a dark stripe down its back. Boorchu hid his bucket in the grass, swung up on his horse, and we galloped off after the thieves without wasting any time to call at his camp and let his family know where we were going.

This meant we had only one bow between us. But we had two fast horses, and I felt much better with a friend beside me. We slept rolled in our blankets under the stars, and on the way Boorchu showed me a warrior's trick for survival when crossing a barren steppe – how to drink my horse's blood.

You make a small hole in the vein at the throat with your knife, and then suck out the blood before the wound heals. The warm, sweet liquid filled my mouth and coated my tongue. I could feel it clotting on the way down, filling me with strength. My heart pounded and my legs trembled. We were crouched in the long summer grass under our horses' necks so I couldn't see if the blood was having the same effect on Boorchu. But afterwards he gave a great groan and flopped on his back with his arms spread wide as if to catch the sky.

"Better than any girl I've ever had!" he said.

I licked Grey Stripe's wound clean of blood so the flies wouldn't bother the horse and flopped down beside him. "Um," I agreed.

Boorchu rolled on his elbow and chewed on a stalk of grass. His eyes, the pupils still wide, considered mine. "So, how many girls have you had, Temujin? Tell!"

"Lots," I lied, flushing.

My new friend laughed. "Word is you haven't any girls in your clan apart from your little sister."

So I told him about Khadagan, exaggerating our farewell kiss a little bit, and his pupils – which had started to shrink in the strong sunlight – expanded again.

"Really?" he said. "Nine times in one night?"

"At least."

"And she didn't complain?"

"She loved it!"

More likely, Khadagan's brothers would have murdered me if I'd tried it so much as once with their sister on that riverbank under the red moon. Not that I'd have had the energy, after swallowing half the Onan and spending most of the summer in Fatface's cangue. But what would you have said? It seemed I had a reputation to live up to.

Boorchu spat out his grass stalk and leapt to his feet. "Then let's hurry and get those geldings of yours back so we can raid old Kiriltuk's camp. I want to meet this girl Khadagan!"

Drinking my horse's blood had aroused me in a way even kissing Khadagan had failed to do. My nervous sweat at the thought of our first real fight and the mad gallop across the steppe did the rest.

When we finally came across the thieves' shelters pitched for the night and I saw my family's geldings grazing among their horses, I had no caution left in me. Without waiting for Boorchu, I dug my heels into Grey Stripe's ribs and charged the herd yelling war cries. Boorchu followed my lead, and we raced back across the steppe with the geldings galloping flat out before us and the other horses following.

The thieves staggered out of their tents, hopping about and tripping over each other as they pulled on their trousers. We weren't close enough to see who they were, but without their horses they didn't have a hope of catching us. I snatched the bow off my shoulder and dropped my reins on Grey Stripe's neck so I could fit an arrow to the string. Grey Stripe proved an excellent mount and went on galloping even when I turned round in the saddle to take aim. The arrow went wide and didn't hit anyone. Well, it was the first time I had tried the trick, and it was dark.

It stopped them following us, though. By then, night had truly come. By the light of a quarter moon, Boorchu and I fled across the steppe with our herd, whooping like maniacs.

"That was brilliant fun, Temujin!" he said when we eventually pulled up, slapping me on the back. "So are we going to raid Kiriltuk's camp and carry off that girl who helped you escape now?"

This reminded me of Borta and what Jamukha had said about Dei the Wise giving up on me and marrying his daughter off to someone else if I didn't hurry up and claim her.

"When my anda gets back and we've got enough lads to challenge Fatface," I said. I'd learnt my lone arrow lesson the hard way. The next time I visited the Alliance camp I intended to have a fat bundle of warriors at my back, and the more the better. "I've another girl to marry first."

Boorchu's face fell a bit. "Another one? Nine times a night *each*? Isn't that a bit much, even for you, Temujin?"

Even as I laughed with my new friend, I couldn't help wondering how many times Borta would agree to do it in a night, and if nine were even possible. I was looking forward to finding out, but we had some work to do first if I wasn't to lose her the same way my brothers had almost lost our geldings.

Boorchu and I spent the rest of that summer riding out into the hills seeking more warriors to join us. With our successful two-man attack on the thieves' camp to boast about, we found several isolated camps with lads our age eager to follow us, and quite a few more who said they would be happy to join us when we needed them. But since raiders were active in the area that year, they asked to stay with their families for now. Understanding this only too well, I added a notch for each potential warrior to one of my arrows, and our small troop rode back to check on the mothers and little ones before setting out in a different direction.

It's pretty tedious work, building an army one or two lads at a time. But by the end of that summer of the Monkey, I had a small horde of fighters at my back, as well as nine arrows with neat lines of notches strung up in my yurt – a good strong bundle of warriors, if not exactly an army. My little brothers Alchidai and Odchigin got excited about being generals, jumping on and off their horses and yelling at the tops of their voices. Temulun trailed after them, yelling too. I'm sure she thought she was a boy.

Snow blocked the passes, and there was still no sign of Jamukha – which made me pretty annoyed to tell the truth. By now, my anda must surely have heard about my escape and know where to find me. Spirits began to trouble my dreams again, and I knew I could wait no longer. I had to do something to turn all those notches on my arrows into flesh and blood warriors, and the only thing left was the prophecy.

The wolf will lie with the doe and give birth to a new nation.

Once they heard I'd taken a wife, I felt sure all those

lads we'd recruited would come to join us, and Anda Jamukha would return with his promised recruits too. In the meantime I'd just have to rely on Boorchu and my little brothers to protect Borta, and pray to the Holy Mountain spirits that she still wanted to marry me.

YEAR OF THE HEN

MY MAIN MEMORY of Borta was of her falling off my gelding when it had been startled in the woods. It had been a bit of a joke back then – a Mongol girl who didn't know how to sit a horse! But now it might be a big problem. Without enough warriors to defend her honour, I knew the best thing would be to take a small group of lads with a spare horse for my wife and gallop back to our camp as fast as possible before any raiding party noticed us. But if Borta still couldn't ride very well, we'd be vulnerable on the journey back. I couldn't take all my recruits with me to protect my wife, though, or my family would be vulnerable while we were away.

In the end, I left Boorchu and Khasar in charge of half our recruits to guard the camp, and mounted Belgutei and the others on our silver-bay geldings. I rode Grey Stripe, and we took the old yellow mare as a spare. At least she was steady. Maybe Borta would stay on her if we had to gallop back.

Our route lay close to Tartar territory, and as we rode across the steppe all my helpless boyhood anger at the way they had murdered Father resurfaced. I clenched my fists on the reins, making Grey Stripe dance and toss his head.

Belgutei chuckled. "Looking forward to seeing your promised wife, Temujin?"

His words made me flush. "I'm thinking of raiding the Tartars, actually," I said. "They killed Father. They should be made to pay."

"Now?" Belgutei looked over his shoulder in alarm. "Just the eight of us?"

I had to laugh. Riding Grey Stripe alongside his gelding, I slapped my remaining half brother on the thigh. "No, you big marmot-hunter! Not until Jamukha gets back with some more lads, anyway, and then we're going to practice on Fatface's camp first and get Father's people back, you know that."

Belgutei looked a bit relieved. "*Are* you looking forward to seeing Borta again?" he asked, genuinely curious this time.

I was nervous as a newborn foal, but I grinned. "What do you think?"

Honest to Heaven, as Belgutei and I stood in Dei the Wise's yurt awaiting my promised wife, I had never felt so terrified in all my life. Knowing I would have to persuade him of my suitability as a husband now that Fatface had stolen Father's people, I'd rehearsed all sorts of fine words on the journey. But to my surprise, Borta's father welcomed us with open arms and said *of course* he'd give me his daughter in marriage as he'd promised my father six years ago. For the life of me, I couldn't work out why he seemed so delighted. I even wondered if he might have made a deal with Chief Fatface and planned to hand me over to my enemy in a cangue as soon as we laid down our weapons. That shows how out of my depth I felt.

Then the flap of the yurt lifted, and two women came inside. The older one I recognized at once as Borta's mother. The younger woman had glossy dark hair braided up in loops and wore a shimmering summer deel. A scent came off her like the smell of the forest after rain, and green light shone out of her eyes as she looked warily from me to Belgutei and back again.

I thought at first the younger woman was a female shaman, come to bless our marriage, and looked behind her for my wild little Borta and her pet fawn. But, of course, there was no wild girl. As I returned my gaze to the poised young woman with the light in her eyes, something brushed against the felt outside the yurt and I saw the shadow of a full-grown deer.

Belgutei's mouth hung open. He virtually drooled. I elbowed him. He straightened his shoulders and cleared his throat.

"Temujin, eldest son of Yesugei the Brave of the Borjigin clan of the Mongol people, comes to claim his wife Princess Borta of the Ungirad clan," he announced, exactly as I'd told him to. One thing about Belgutei, he knew how to follow orders.

I felt exactly nine years old again. My back stiffened. My palms sweated. My groin shrivelled. "Er . . . hello, Borta," I said, forgetting everything I had been going to say about her being the mother of my heirs, the first wife of my new clan, and all that impressive stuff.

Her lip trembled. I noticed then she was holding a tuft of white horsetail in her hands, clasped tightly under a fold of her deel.

"Hello, Temujin," she said. "You look different."

"So do you." Understatement of the year.

We fell silent. With Belgutei and Borta's mother in the tent watching us, it was awkward to say the least.

Then Borta's mother gave a little cough and said, "I'm sure Borta and Temujin would like to be alone for a bit. I expect they've a lot of catching up to do." She pushed her daughter further into the yurt, held up the door flap so Belgutei could duck out, and gave us a bright smile.

"Take your time, you two. There's no rush. We'll have the wedding on Red Circle Day so you've time to get to know each other again first. Then, after you've sealed the marriage bond, we'll all ride back to Temujin's camp." Borta didn't see because she had her back to the door, but I caught the look she gave her daughter and wondered at it. Then she winked at me and was gone.

Leaving me alone with a shaman.

I knew it straight away by the shivering power that

rippled off my promised wife, and the way her eyes lit up green when she looked at me.

I took her hand – sweaty as mine – and gently eased the horsetail out of it. Then I led her to one of her father's couches. A bucket of milk in the corner reminded me of Khadagan but there was no answering heat in my groin. Not yet. I was almost afraid to touch this tall, strange girl.

"I didn't think you'd come back," Borta said, watching the deer shadow move around the outside of the yurt.

"Is that your pet fawn?" I asked to avoid saying all the things I really wanted to say. "She's grown."

"Yes, she has." Her voice was tight. She seemed determined to talk about me. "We heard about your capture and how you escaped. Everyone's saying you can change into a wolf – is that right?"

I grinned at her. It seemed the wolf story had grown in the telling on its way across the steppe. "What do you think?"

She frowned. "I think you're dangerous. You killed your brother. Why?"

"*Half*-brother," I corrected, wondering if every girl I met would demand an explanation for Begter's death before they would let me touch them. If so, I was going to get more tired of Begter dead than I'd ever been of Begter alive. But in this case, I could at least be sure of a sympathetic ear.

So I told her how Begter had insulted her, and how

I'd only meant to scare my half-brother but the arrow had slipped in my hand. Her light-filled gaze stopped flickering after the deer and steadied on me. "*Truth*," she breathed.

"Of course it's true!" Her doubt made me angry. "You don't think I'd lie to my first wife, do you?"

Borta bit her lip and looked at her hands, which she'd clasped in her lap again. "They're saying you don't have any other girls in your camp."

"Not unless you count my little sister," I agreed. "And she's still got a boy's name."

She frowned. Then she got the joke. Her cheeks reddened. "What about when you were in Chief Kiriltuk's camp?"

This was straying into more dangerous territory. I wondered what she'd heard. "Locked in a cangue, you mean? It's difficult to get up to very much wearing one of those, especially when everyone thinks you're a wolf."

She stared at me uncertainly. Then her lips twitched into a small smile. "And none of Chief Kiriltuk's girls run with deer, do they?" she said.

I grinned, too, and suddenly it was all right again.

Borta poured us cups of milk, and we talked about my stay at her camp six years ago, how she'd fallen off my horse, how funny Whisper the fawn had been, and other such safe things we remembered sharing back then. She asked about my father's death and, though she had been the reason for his journey across the Tartar steppe, I could not blame her for his murder any more than I could blame myself. And then, somehow, we got on to planning the journey back to the Onan without ever mentioning our forthcoming marriage and the night in-between.

"I've brought a yellow mare for you to ride," I said. "She's old and slow and her tail is going bald, but she's sweet-tempered and has a broad back so she should be comfortable enough. Belgutei usually takes her hunting marmots."

Borta bit her lip. "Horses still don't like me much," she admitted. "It's probably better if I ask Papa to give us a cart and one of his yaks."

A cart would be useful, I supposed, but yaks were notoriously slow animals. I must have looked doubtful, for she smiled and added, "Then Whisper can run behind it and won't spook your horses."

At which point I had visions of a full-grown deer in our marriage yurt, getting in the way of things. "Maybe Whisper will be happier if you leave her here with her friends?" I suggested, ruining everything again.

Borta stiffened and re-clasped her hands, sitting up very straight. "You don't understand, Temujin," she said. "I'll be your wife because Papa says I must marry you to forge links between our two clans as he promised your papa, and because the Ancestors wish it. But Whisper comes with me so I can continue to speak with the spirits, or I won't let you touch me. Ever."

It was just as Half-Brother Begter had warned me. I had a wife who preferred to share her tent with a deer.

*

60

Our wedding turned into the biggest Red Circle feast I'd seen, with buckets of airag for every family and ten whole oxen roasted for the occasion, as well as the tough old sheep whose meat we had to chew in public to show our marriage would be strong. Borta's giggling half-sisters decorated the yurts with flowers and hung lengths of silk from Dei the Wise's clan banners until the whole camp looked like a brightly fluttering festival.

As he blessed us, the shaman gave Borta the same sort of look her mother had on the day we arrived, and I wondered at it. But I got a quiverful of fine arrows fletched with eagle's feathers from Dei the Wise, and Borta's mother gave us a long deel-coat made of black fur so soft and sleek it shimmered in the firelight as if it were alive. So everything seemed proper.

That fur aroused me, big time. By then I'd drunk a bit too much airag, and all the sweating Borta was doing under her ceremonial deel made me hot under the collar. I could hardly wait for everyone to leave us alone.

As the traditional clods of dung hit us, showering us with brown powder, I grinned in relief. I'd been a bit worried the stone thrower of our betrothal ceremony might be there and take advantage of the tradition, but if the disgruntled lad was still around he'd obviously grown up a bit since then.

I clawed down the strings of flowers Borta's sisters had used to tie shut our door flap and put my hand on my new wife's back to encourage her inside. Sable, I realized as I ran my fingers through the fur. Black sable, rarer than gold. My wife's dowry would buy us many warriors.

Inside the yurt, Borta's family had been busy. A bed awaited us, strewn with petals and branches of pine and piled high with sheepskins. A jug of airag, two cups and the rest of our marriage feast had been placed nearby in case we got hungry or thirsty during the night. Even though it was high summer, a fire crackled in the central pit filling the yurt with scented smoke that had me tugging at the neck of my tunic.

Borta, however, clutched her sable coat close as if we had married during a freezing winter in the high mountains. She stared at the bed and chewed her lip. "Temujin," she whispered. "I'm not sure if—"

I wrestled her down into the sheepskins before she could say any more, both of us tangled in the sable fur, and kissed her hard on the mouth.

Khadagan had quickly melted under my kiss. Borta, however, wriggled out from under me and slapped me on the cheek. The blow stung. I stared at her in surprise, wondering what I'd done wrong. Maybe she was just shy, and I should kiss my new wife again and show her how things were to be between us?

Something stopped me. That light in her eyes. Anger, yes . . . but something else, too. As if the spirits were spying on us. It embarrassed me. Of course Borta was not Khadagan. She was a princess of her clan and, as my first wife, would be empress of our people one day. I told myself we'd only just been married, and she would be with me for the rest of my life. There would be plenty of time for kissing and we had the whole night. The first time should be done right.

We were both panting from the struggle. Neither of us said anything. Borta wriggled the rest of the way out of her fur, pulled the hem from under my foot and folded it neatly, taking her time. With her back to me, she laid the sable coat on a couch at the side of the yurt and said, "We shouldn't use my dowry as a bedspread."

"No," I agreed, a bit relieved she hadn't run straight to her father to complain about me. "You're right. It'd be a shame to stain such a valuable fur."

She gave me a quick look, then perched on the edge of the bed and clasped her hands in her lap. "I'm not ready for this, Temujin," she said in a small voice. "I'm sorry. You took us all by surprise, turning up here after so long. I haven't had time to get used to being married yet. When we heard about your poor papa's death and how you'd been exiled, I thought I'd study as a shaman and not marry anyone. Now you're back, and suddenly I'm expected to be your wife as if nothing's changed." She chewed her lip. "I like you, Temujin, I really do. Only . . . can you give me some more time, please? At least wait until we get back to your camp?"

I didn't know if I could wait that long. On the journey, true, we'd have little chance to seal our marriage bond. But tonight it was expected of us and we'd not be disturbed. I wondered how loudly Borta would have to scream before one of her family came to see what was wrong. Perhaps they would even expect her to scream a little? I could have had her down in those sheepskins, and the whole thing over with in less time than it took to swallow a cup of airag. But what then? Would Dei the Wise be likely to lend me any of his warriors to reclaim my people, once he heard how I had forced his daughter?

"It's supposed to take away a girl's power to speak with the spirits," Borta whispered, as if she felt bad about refusing me and needed to explain. "You haven't got a shaman in your camp, have you? I could be useful to you, maybe find out who killed your papa?"

"No!" I said, with a vivid memory of Fatface's spear plunging into our old shaman's back. I wouldn't risk such magic in my camp again.

"It feels wrong to do it on Red Circle Night," she said, her voice growing fainter still. "With the spirits among us . . ."

"You don't have to make excuses," I told her, my voice emerging rough. "I'm not an animal. I can wait until we reach my camp." At least none of her family would hear her scream up there.

She sighed and removed her hand. "I won't forget your kindness tonight, Temujin. Thank you."

Kindness? Is that what she thought it was?

We didn't speak again that night. Borta curled up behind me, while I got busy working off my pent-up frustration the only way left to me. To be fair, I tried to imagine it was

Khadagan I was forcing in the sheepskins. But before long Khadagan changed into Borta, and I was holding her down the way I used to dream about up in our Holy Mountain camp. Beautiful, curvy, deer-girl Borta, who acted stiff and cold at first but soon melted under me . . . and then she was squirming, all soft and hot and deep, and I . . . and I . . .

Honest to Heaven, but I hoped my new wife had gone to sleep.

We took Borta back to our camp in a cart drawn by a yak, exactly as she'd said we would. It spooked me a bit, because telling the future is a shaman power. As part of her dowry, we also took a good-sized flock of Dei's sheep and goats. Her entire family came as escort, their quivers bristling with arrows, so at least I didn't have to worry about anyone stealing her on the way back. That would have been humiliating, losing my new wife to a rival clan before we'd even sealed the marriage bond.

By then the frustration of our wedding night had cooled, and I was glad I had not forced Borta when she refused me. I didn't know whether to believe all the spirit nonsense she'd spoken of, but neither did I want an unwilling wife between the furs, and it kept things simple between us. We slipped easily back into our childhood friendship and laughed a lot on that journey home. What with Whisper the deer frightening the horses, Belgutei's mouth falling open every time he looked at Borta, Borta's mother giving us knowing winks, and Borta's father lecturing me on all the things a young clan chief ought to be thinking about apart from making sons, it was pretty funny, I suppose.

Not one of them suspected how we'd actually spent our marriage night in that flower-strewn yurt. In the morning, Borta took the precaution of cutting her arm and staining the sheepskins with her blood, which alarmed me a bit until she explained that was what the servants would expect to see when they took out the bed coverings to wash them. She kept her mouth shut, too, and it became our secret, binding us as close as the traditional marriage bond would have done. Maybe closer.

On the way back, I started making serious plans for taking over the Mongol Alliance now that I'd fulfilled the prophecy in everyone's eyes except my wife's and mine. The tricky bit would be how to persuade all the extra lads Boorchu and I had recruited over the past year to leave their clans and join us, when I could offer them no guarantee of success. To take over Fatface's camp completely rather than simply raid it, I needed a decent horde. But to raise a horde of that size, I needed to prove myself a good leader on a raid first, and I couldn't risk losing any of my lads by raiding rival camps.

I was still thinking about my problem when we reached the valley where we'd left Mother and the others. Borta's cart creaked beside me, while her deer frisked in the edge of the forest, investigating the unfamiliar smells. Boorchu had ridden out to meet us the previous day with some new lads who had turned up to join us while I'd been away, so the last thing on my mind was being attacked.

Luckily, Belgutei proved more observant.

"Where have all those horses come from, Temujin?" he said, pointing.

Finally, I noticed the makeshift tents pitched around ours, simple forest shelters like the one I'd slept under while I'd been on the run from Fatface's men. A whole lot more of them than were needed for Boorchu's lads. A hollow sensation lodged itself below my stomach. Some impression I was going to make on my new wife's family if, the moment I left my camp, enemies moved in and took it over!

In a flash, I had an arrow on my bowstring. Belgutei fumbled for his bow, too.

Borta stuck her head out of the yak cart. "What's wrong?" she asked.

"Get back inside!" I yanked the felt closed across the window, already picking out the best places to take cover . . . where to park the cart . . . how to make sure no one came close to my wife without getting an arrow in him . . .

But Boorchu was laughing at me, and I realized he already knew about the extra tents and had been saving them as a surprise. The last of my fear vanished as I recognized the lad who ducked out of the nearest shelter and came striding towards us with a grin. He'd grown, but his hair still escaped his braids to float girlishly around his cheeks. He looked even more handsome than I remembered.

"Anda Jamukha!"

I tossed my bow and arrows aside and leapt off my horse. We hugged each other fiercely, oblivious to Borta's shocked face peering out of the yak cart, oblivious to the whole world.

I took the sable fur and Anda Jamukha into my yurt, while Mother took my new wife and her family into the women's tent. Borta cast me some backward looks as I went off with Jamukha, but the way I saw it *she* could wait this time. Maybe it would make her more eager the next night we were alone together.

Meanwhile, I summoned my brothers and we discussed the best place to find more warriors for the attack on Fatface's camp.

"How many men do you want, exactly?" Jamukha asked, sounding a bit irritated. I suppose he thought me ungrateful. But even if all the notches on the arrows hanging in my yurt turned up to join the two hundred or so lads my anda had brought me, we'd still be struggling to raise enough warriors to challenge Fatface's Alliance.

"A division at least," I said. "A thousand men."

"I don't know where you're going to find that many lads, Temujin," Boorchu said, frowning. "We've already tried all the camps who haven't joined the Alliance."

I smiled. Jamukha's arrival had raised my spirits. Now that I was officially married with a rich dowry, it seemed a good time to remind the other tribes of the prophecy. "We've been thinking too small," I said, stroking the sable

68

fur. "I'm not poor any more. Mercenaries don't have to come from Mongol clans, do they?"

"You're not thinking of going begging to the Tartars after they murdered your father?" Jamukha said quickly. Too quickly maybe, but I was too full of my new plan to notice.

"Don't be silly," I told my anda, grinning at his alarm. "We're going to raid the Tartars as soon as we've got my father's warriors back from Fatface, remember? But the Kereyid Khan has a thousand men to spare. More like five thousand, I'd say."

"The *Kereyid* Khan?" My anda frowned. "Why would he help you . . . ?"

"He was my father's anda," I said.

Jamukha stared at me, a flush spreading under his collar. He hadn't known that, obviously.

Boorchu grinned. "That makes him your spiritual father, doesn't it? And if some fat chief with ambitions beyond his breeding had put a spiritual son of mine in a cangue and paraded him around his camp like an enemy captive, I know I'd be bloody angry . . . it might work, Temujin!"

"Of course it'll work," I said, wrenching another leg off the sheep we were devouring while I considered my options. "I was just wondering who I can leave here to look after my camp while I go to find the Kereyids."

Which was the truth, because I'd have to go in person on such a mission. Take Borta's sable fur as a gift for my father's anda, and just hope the powerful Kereyid Khan didn't box my ears for my insolence and boot me straight back to Holy Mountain.

The Kereyid Khan's name had caught the others' imagination. They gathered round, eyes bright with interest.

"Can I come with you to see the Kereyids, Temujin?" Belgutei said. "Please?"

"You'll need someone to watch your back," Khasar said. "I'd best come, too."

"And me!" Boorchu wasn't going to be left out.

We all looked at Jamukha.

My anda had recovered his composure. He smiled and glanced at the women's tent. "No problem, Anda Temujin! I'll look after things here for you until you get back. Your Lady Borta will be safe with me, don't worry. I'll care for her exactly as you would yourself."

You should understand I trusted Jamukha more than I would have trusted any of my brothers. The anda bond is formed of blood and is sacred before Heaven so I knew Borta would be in safe hands. I hoped my visit to the Kereyids would not only buy me an army, but also give my new wife the time she needed to adjust to being married.

When we said goodbye in my yurt, we kissed with more passion than we had so far. "Please don't go," Borta begged.

"You know I have to find us some more men," I told her, rather pleased by her reaction.

"Then take me with you." She cast a nervous glance at the door flap.

"No, Borta – it's too dangerous, and we'll be riding fast. Don't worry. Anda Jamukha will look after you."

She caught her breath, and something unreadable flickered behind her eyes. "Be careful, Temujin," she whispered, giving me her shaman look. "I'll speak to the spirits for you."

She looked so brave standing there with curls of hair escaping from her braid, that I kissed her again. Borta even clung to me a fraction longer than I clung to her. I can tell you, I had high hopes for my welcome home!

- 8 -

YEAR OF THE DOG

A THOUSAND MEN for a coat of midnight sable. Maybe I expected too much. But at first all went smoothly enough.

We weren't killed on sight, but escorted through the Kereyid yurts that covered the steppe like a human sea. The Kereyid Khan welcomed us like lost sons, and I managed to make my speech and present the sable fur to him, watched by two long lines of his bodyguards, without making too much of a fool of myself. He accepted my gift graciously, passed the sable to one of his servants, and rested his arm across my shoulders. The muscles under the sleeve of his deel felt hard and strong.

"You see, Temujin, I can't let you ride off with a thousand of my men just because you have a whim to raid a rival camp," he explained. "They pledged their families to follow me, not a Mongol lad, and this camp you're thinking of raiding belonged to my late anda. Even though you've reason enough for the raid according to what I've heard,

I can't break my vow of peace with the Alliance and send my men to attack their camp. But I appreciate the gift, and if ever you're in genuine need of an army I'll remember it. Meanwhile, you're welcome to stay the winter. You were still in the cradle when I saw you last – it'll be good to get to know Anda Yesugei's son."

I tried to talk him round, of course. But I'd never had Jamukha's talent for clever words, and for once my grin didn't seem to be having much effect. It occurred to me then that I should have brought Anda Jamukha along to do the talking and left one of my brothers to look after Borta, but I wasn't going to ride all the way back for my anda's help now. What would that make me look like in the Kereyid Khan's eyes? Like a right marmot, that's what. Besides, the well-ordered camp with its air of luxury interested me. This was how a khan's people were supposed to live! I'd been too young when Father was alive to take much notice of camp organization, but this seemed the perfect opportunity to complete my education.

So I decided to accept the Kereyid Khan's invitation to stay the winter, and see if I could get an army out of him in the spring once I'd had a proper chance to explain why I needed it. Besides, what did I have to go back to? A cold yurt in a poor mountain camp and a wife who wasn't ready for marriage, compared to a winter in the rich camp of the Kereyids surrounded by girls who were already eyeing us up with interest . . . I'm only human, despite what half the Mongol people seem to think.

Boorchu and Khasar soon had a contest going, notching their arrows each morning to keep count of the girls they'd tumbled in the furs, in much the same way Boorchu and I had kept count of the lads we'd recruited on the mountain. It was just as well my arrows were already full of warrior marks, because otherwise my reputation might have suffered. Boorchu teased me for being so madly in love with my wife I'd forgotten how to have fun, and said whatever happened to nine times a night? But if you want the truth, every Kereyid girl I bedded that winter made me think of Borta, and in the end I found it easier just to send them away.

The Kereyid Khan made noises about me taking a second wife from his clan but I couldn't imagine any of those Kereyid girls roughing it with us in the forest, and whenever I thought of Borta waiting for me in the furs with her wild deer expression, my groin tightened with anticipation. That winter, in addition to my lessons on camp administration, the spirits taught me a thing or two about desire.

When the passes opened, I made one last attempt to talk the Kereyid Khan into loaning me some of his warriors – even a hundred would have made a difference, because where a hundred ride another hundred will soon follow. But he shook his head. "No, Temujin," he said firmly. "I can't risk my men's lives in a raid on a Mongol camp against warriors trained by my late anda. But if you ever need my help to defend your people from an enemy tribe, all you have to do is send word."

We had no choice but to thank the Kereyid Khan for his generosity over the winter and ride back to our camp, empty-handed. The sable coat had bought us nothing but another promise. A promise of a thousand men, true, but still a thousand puffs of empty air at our backs.

The way I'd bungled things with my father's anda put me in a bad mood. Even when one of the Kereyid blacksmiths and his son galloped after us, riding double on a skinny mare, I felt no triumph. The lad, Jelme, must have been about Belgutei's age. He gazed at me in awe, and my heart sank. Another one who had heard the wolf transformation story from Boorchu and my brothers that winter!

So instead of my hoped-for division of a thousand men, we had merely two extra mouths to feed when we reached Holy Mountain, and Alchidai and Odchigin came running to meet us yammering so fast I couldn't hear what they were saying.

My little brothers waved their arms at the ridge, the words tumbling out of them *forest . . . cart . . . raiders . . .* while I frowned at our three patched yurts, which looked scruffier than ever after our winter in the Kereyid camp. The rest of our horses grazed nearby, mixed with the sheep and goats Borta's father had given us. I couldn't see the yak that had pulled my wife's cart up here. Nor could I see Jamukha's horses or shelters.

A cold lump lodged itself in my belly.

"Where's Anda Jamukha?" I said, still not understanding.

"Where're the Kereyids?" Alchidai demanded in return,

peering behind us at Jelme and the old blacksmith. He obviously didn't think much of our reinforcements, for he clenched his fist and whacked the ground with his bow, making mud fly.

"Don't treat your bow like that," I said. "You'll break it. What happened to the yak and the yellow mare?"

My brothers glanced at each other.

"Lady Borta was riding her when the raiders came," Odchigin said, and burst into tears.

"We couldn't stop them, Temujin!" Alchidai said defensively. "But we hid in the forest, like you taught us to, so they didn't find the rest of us—"

A cold sweat bathed me. Leaping off Grey Stripe, I ran to Mother's yurt. Little Temulun grabbed my legs at the door and hugged me fiercely, while Mother stared at me over my sister's head with tears of relief in her eyes. "Thank Heaven you're safe, Temujin!" she said. "You were gone for so long, we were sure the Kereyids had killed you."

Fear made my head spin.

"Where's Borta?" I demanded, holding Temulun away from me.

Mother's silence told me more than words could.

"The raiders took her, didn't they?" I said. "Fatface's men sneaked up here while I was away and stole my wife! I'll kill him. I'll hang him up by his hairy balls and cut off his pecker! I'll . . . I'll . . ." I couldn't think of a harsh enough punishment. Then a fresh sweat came over me. "Where's Anda Jamukha?"

Mother frowned at my crude language and sent little Temulun outside to help my brothers. "He's gone."

"I can see that! Where? Did he go after Borta?"

"He said he was going to meet you. You must have missed him. He left before the raiders came, Temujin. It wasn't his fault."

"He left you here *alone*? With only little Alchidai and Odchigin to look after the camp?"

Mother avoided my gaze. "He was worried about you so he took his lads with him in case you needed help with the Kereyids. Borta sent her spirit with Whisper into the forest to keep watch so we would have warning and time to hide if any strangers came. We almost got away, only Borta couldn't ride well enough to keep up and there were too many of them . . . I'm sorry, Temujin," she said. "Without Jamukha's lads, we couldn't stop them taking her."

I could see it all. My little brothers and the women galloping into the hills to escape the raiding party, the old yellow mare trailing behind, poor Borta terrified and wobbly in the saddle, clinging on to the mane, unable to make her go any faster . . . Honest to Heaven, I didn't know who to blame. I couldn't understand my anda's desertion.

"Which way did they go?" I said, clenching my fists. "How many days? We might catch them before they get back to their camp – Boorchu, get your lads!"

"Wait, Temujin!" Mother ran after me, clinging to my tunic like an annoying bramble. "It's nearly dark. You've just ridden across the mountains. You need to eat and rest your horses. You might be as tireless as a wolf, but your brothers and the others aren't. Remember the bundle of arrows, Temujin!"

This brought me back to my senses like a slap. I knew if enemies caught me alone on the mountain again, I'd be no use to Borta or anyone else. I took a deep breath and told myself that at least Fatface's men were Mongols. If they had taken my wife they would look after her, she being a Mongol princess. They'd probably kidnapped her because of the prophecy. Then I imagined Fatface with Borta between the furs and felt a bit sick.

"I'm sure Jamukha's lads will be back as soon as they hear what's happened. The more of you there are when you catch up with the raiders, the better," Mother went on. When I said nothing, she asked gently, "You did get some men from the Kereyids, didn't you?"

"Two," I told her in a rough tone. "A lad called Jelme and his blacksmith father, which should at least be useful when we want to make spearheads and stirrups for my army of spirits!"

She frowned. "Don't joke about the spirits, Temujin. They have sharp ears."

The last thing I needed was another lecture from my mother.

"Do you think I'm *joking*?" I snapped. "Now Jamukha's vanished again, we're nearly back to where we started. The blacksmith's too old to fight, Jelme is convinced I can change into a wolf, and Boorchu doesn't have enough imagination to feel fear. At this rate, I'll be relying on my little sister to lead my army!"

Temulun looked up from her work and stared at me uncertainly.

"That's not true." Mother put an arm around my sister and looked me in the eye. "Even if Jamukha doesn't come back, you've recruits of your own to call upon now, and I'm sure Dei the Wise will lend you some warriors as well to help rescue his daughter. The Kereyid Khan has a reputation for being careful. That's why your father swore the anda bond with him. He's probably afraid that if he helps you raid the Alliance camp, Kiriltuk will treat it as a declaration of war and make alliances with the other tribes against the Kereyids."

"Things are different now," I insisted. "Fatface took my wife!"

"We don't know who the raiders were, Temujin," Mother reminded me gently. "I didn't recognize any of the men. They could have been anyone. Even if it was Kiriltuk, he might have kidnapped Lady Borta precisely *because* he'd heard you were planning on raiding him. I think he's scared of you after you led that wolf spirit into his camp. He's probably taken her as a hostage. We'll have to be careful not to annoy him. He's already punished you once for killing your half-brother, and you've grown taller than the wheel of his cart since then. Next time he'll be able to kill you without angering the spirits."

79

"I suppose Second Mother told you to say that," I growled.

Mother shook her head sadly. "The raiders took Belgutei's mother, too."

Good riddance, I thought, though I'll admit this confused me slightly. Fatface had already turned the stupid woman out of his camp once. Right then, with my head spinning with anger and guilt and fear for my wife, I couldn't see what was right before my nose. I blamed myself for abandoning my family and Borta up here for so long, while I feasted and bedded the girls in the Kereyid camp.

I told Jelme and his father to take Mother and the little ones further up the mountain and find a new campsite, while I took Khasar, Belgutei, Boorchu and the others after Borta. The raiders' tracks were easy enough to follow, since they had stolen our yak cart too, though it bothered me that they led in the opposite direction to Fatface's camp, and we wasted quite a bit of time checking behind us in case it turned out to be a trap.

By the time we realized the raiders had not been Fatface's men after all, it was too late. We found the yak cart abandoned in a circle of hoof prints with a Merkid banner fluttering beside it as a message for me. The sheepskins my wife had brought with her from her father's camp lay trampled in the mud nearby. I shouted Borta's name until the mountains echoed and my voice grew hoarse, but there was no arguing with the evidence.

My wife, the wild deer-girl of the prophecy betrothed to me since we were children, had been stolen by an enemy tribe.

I could hardly think straight. It's true what the shamans say, and you don't realize how much you care for something until you lose it. Even if Borta refused me in the furs for the rest of her life, she was *mine*. No one else was going to have her, least of all the Murdering Merkids!

Leaving Boorchu's lads and Jelme to look after Mother and the younger ones, I took Khasar and Belgutei on the fastest gallop of their lives, straight back to the Kereyid Khan's camp. I suppose I had some vague hope that, if we were quick enough, the Merkids wouldn't have time to make Borta their own. But, of course, it all took a lot longer than that.

Although sympathetic, the ever-careful Kereyid Khan said we needed an army large enough to finish off the Merkids properly, and it mustn't look like his idea. He'd raise two divisions from the Kereyids, if I could find two from the Mongols.

I set my jaw and thought of Jelme and Boorchu. "I have two lads back at camp," I said.

Oh, I knew the Kereyid Khan meant two *divisions* of a thousand men or more each, not two untried lads who had never seen a real battle. But I couldn't resist rubbing in the fact that if he'd given me some of his men to reunite my people when I'd asked for them last year, I might have those two divisions by now armed and ready to ride.

The Kereyid Khan didn't think much of my attempted humour and folded his arms, waiting for me to be serious again. Not that I felt much like laughing, you understand. It tore my heart, thinking of what those Merkid bastards might be doing to my wife. But shrieking and wailing doesn't help very much when you intend to be the next khan. Not if you want people to respect and follow you, that is.

So Khasar and I counted up all the warrior marks on the arrows we'd been promised during our recruitment ride, and it came to about three hundred in all. Not nearly enough. Even with Dei the Wise's warriors as well, I'd be struggling to raise a single division let alone two. I needed Jamukha and his lads.

"We'll get them," I promised.

We headed back to Holy Mountain, collecting up our recruits on the way. Strange how the Kereyid Khan's promise had them all racing to grab their bows and catch their horses! It made me wonder if they were joining me or the Kereyids, but this was no time to split hairs. The important thing was that they were eager to fight.

When we got back, I set Jelme and his father the task of making lances for my army. Then I sent Belgutei and Khasar off on fresh horses to find Jamukha, while I headed out with Boorchu to break the bad news to Dei the Wise.

Despite what Mother had said, I wasn't at all sure Borta's father would trust me with any of his warriors, considering I'd lost his daughter to a rival tribe less than a year after

I'd married her. But fortunately he proved wise enough to realize questions would only delay her rescue, gave me some of his best men and promised to send reinforcements as soon as their families could spare them.

By this time it was almost the end of summer. Borta had been captive for several months and there was still no sign of my anda. I sent Boorchu's lads over the ridge to spy on the Merkids, wondering if we could get away with a quick raid to rescue my wife the same way we'd rescued our geldings from the horse thieves, but they brought back news I'd been dreading. While I'd been busy recruiting an army, the Merkid Khan had been doing the same. He'd put his camp on a war footing and appeared to have summoned his entire tribe to guard my wife.

Even if we did manage to rescue Borta and get her out of there alive, I knew the Merkids would simply come straight after us and steal her back again, and probably murder us all into the bargain. I still didn't have nearly enough lads to protect her properly. I ground my teeth in frustration, moved my camp to more open ground, and told my generals to teach the newcomers the shooting-backwards trick Boorchu and I had used on the horse thieves, before I got married and everything had seemed so simple.

If Jamukha didn't turn up and the Kereyids didn't come, I'd at least have a well-trained horde behind me when I rode to rescue Borta in the spring.

- 9 -

YEAR OF THE PIG

TOWARDS THE END of winter, my brothers discovered Jamukha camping in the Khorkonag Valley. He sent a message back saying of course he'd help us rescue Lady Borta from the Murdering Merkids. He had half a division with him already, and would try to find some more lads before we met up. We'd all meet in the spring on the ridge at the head of the Onan on Red Circle Day so we could attack the Merkid camp by moonlight, and don't be late.

I thought it a bit of a cheek my anda ordering us not to be late, when we'd already wasted months last year looking for him. So I left that part out of the message I sent back to the Kereyid camp, and suggested that our two forces should meet up first and ride on together to join Jamukha's forces on the ridge. Then I took Belgutei and Khasar into my yurt.

They devoured the meal I offered them and sank back gratefully on the couches, while I passed round the airag.

"How was my anda?" I asked them.

They sat up a bit straighter and glanced at each other.

"He looked fit," Khasar said carefully. "And he really does have five hundred warriors in his camp. More, I'd say."

I wondered where Jamukha had got them all from.

"All Mongol lads?"

"Well, it's difficult to tell from a distance . . ."

"Don't give me that!" I scowled at my brother. "Has he got fighters from any of the other tribes with him?"

"I didn't see any Tartars or Merkids," Khasar said with a grimace. "If I had, I'd have gutted them with a blunt knife."

"What about girls?"

"There were a few families and their herds, of course . . ." Belgutei blushed. I could always tell when my half-brother was trying to hide something from me.

"What?" I growled. "Tell me."

"He's got Borta's deer," Belgutei mumbled. "He keeps it in a cave."

"Whisper?" I almost laughed. I'd never imagined my anda to be so soft. "Never mind the deer. Has he taken a wife?"

Khasar rolled his eyes and punched me on the shoulder. "Is that why you think he abandoned you, Temujin? No, your anda hasn't taken any wives. There's no need to be jealous."

"Don't be ridiculous!" I rubbed my shoulder – even being playful, my younger brother packed a punch. Of course I wasn't jealous of some girl my anda might have taken into his yurt. It had just occurred to me as a possible explanation for Jamukha leaving Borta unprotected last year and hiding from me in the Khorkonag Valley, that was all. A wife would have meant an alliance, one Jamukha might not want me to know about.

I didn't like to think of the other reason, but I had to ask. "And is he making any plans to join Fatface's Alliance?"

"No," Khasar said, looking more serious. "Even if he does, Jamukha's your anda, isn't he? If he gets Father's people back, then so do you."

"Only if we're still camping together," I pointed out.

But the news reassured me. As long as we joined up with the Kereyid Khan before meeting Jamukha, there would be no worries about my anda's warriors outnumbering ours. I was pretty sure that once we'd had a chance to talk, everything would be all right again. After all, I could hardly blame Jamukha for the Merkid raid on our camp. They'd murdered his parents so he hated them as much as I did, and together we'd have an army capable of building a new nation!

Hope returned. Though I hated to think of her spending the winter in a Merkid yurt, Borta's capture just might be the best thing that had happened to our people since Yesugei the Brave united the Mongol clans under a single banner.

"Hold on, Borta," I whispered. "We're coming."

We were three days late at the ridge valley. The Kereyid Khan wanted to hold a special Red Circle feast to ask the

Ancestors' protection in our forthcoming battle. This gave his men sore heads, so we lost half a day at the start. Then, before we set out, he insisted on sacrificing a lamb to his standard and sprinkling mare's milk the traditional nine times over it. Also, he needed to bring camels to carry his war-drums, and they were slow on the narrow paths under the trees. But I must admit the Kereyids looked impressive in their leather breastplates and helmets tooled with their khan's insignia, their lances balanced on their stirrups, and their quivers bristling with arrows.

By comparison, my lads were a motley crew, armed with arrows they'd originally made for hunting deer and riding mismatched horses. We didn't even carry a banner, since Father's standard had been smashed by the Merkid raiding party, and I'd been too concerned that winter with making sure we had enough weapons to rescue Borta to remember to ask Jelme's father to mend it. That was a mistake, I realized too late. Next time we rode to war, I'd make sure I had a proper spirit banner carried proudly at the front of my army.

At least my lads seemed keen, bawling battle songs at the tops of their voices and practising the horseback tricks they'd need in battle. Going to war against the Merkids obviously excited them a lot more than simply raiding another Mongol camp. Boorchu told me they were looking forward to a *real* fight.

The sheer number of horses and warriors excited me, too. Our massed hooves throbbed like a gigantic heartbeat, as if

I led a two-headed Mongol-Kereyid monster. The thrill of being in charge of a real army made my blood pound, and the thought of seeing Borta again made me sweat under the collar and in another place, too.

Jamukha was waiting impatiently for us on the ridge, as promised. A surge of joy went through me at the sight of my anda. He looked very handsome in his battle dress with his hair blowing loose and all his young warriors behind him. But he was thinner than when I'd last seen him, and there was a wary look in his eye.

Ignoring the Kereyid Khan, he marched up to my horse and grabbed my reins. "What time do you call this, Temujin?" he demanded.

I grinned down at him. "Time to attack the Merkid camp!" He really did have an army of his own, a division at least, camped around the cliffs. I imagined them joined with our forces and leapt down to hug my anda. "Thanks for coming."

"I've been up here three days already, waiting for you." Jamukha stiffened in my arms. He seemed very edgy. "The Merkids aren't blind."

"The Kereyid Khan had to make his prayers," I explained.

"I told you not to be late! I had a plan and now you've ruined it. The moon's three nights past full."

"We'll still be able to see well enough to kill Merkids," I said. Remembering that I had cause to be angry as well, I held my anda away from me so I could stare hard into his eyes. "What's wrong, Jamukha? So what if we're a bit late? A few more days isn't going to make much difference to Borta after so long. Were you afraid the Merkids would attack you up here? You seem to have found enough warriors to hold them off, and my army's here now. What I'd like to know is why you left my wife and my camp unprotected in the first place."

Jamukha's gaze slid away from mine. "Your mother didn't tell you?"

"She said you'd gone to meet me and bring me your lads."

"Which, as you can see, I have!" My anda relaxed a little and indicated his camp with a sweep of his arm. "Don't let's argue, Anda Temujin. I've been busy, you've been busy. We've both made mistakes. As you say, you're here now. We're all ready to ride. Don't worry, we'll get your Borta back tonight." Then Jamukha gave me a sly smile and added, "That's if you want her back, after the Merkids have finished with her?"

I wanted to punch that smile right off my anda's face. But the Kereyid Khan sat his horse nearby, watching us with an amused expression, and andas do not fight in public.

I unclenched my fists and made myself grin back. "Of course I want her back! She's my wife, and I love her."

"Of course you do," Jamukha said, hugging me close again. In my ear, he said in the same tone he'd used when he'd surprised me trying to bend Father's bow by the Onan, "What's the matter, Temujin? Don't you trust me? Were you afraid I was raising this army to attack *you*?"

He had guessed my thoughts so accurately I stiffened.

Jamukha squeezed me harder, and his voice had a choke in it. "You are a marmot sometimes, Temujin! We're andas, aren't we? I can't spill your blood without spilling my own. All I want is to unite the Mongol clans so we can be together, always."

"Then help me rescue Borta from the Merkids." My voice came out harsh, too. "And we'll forget this stupid argument and start over."

"Swear it?" Jamukha said, stepping back to look warily into my eyes. "You won't blame me for anything that's happened to Borta in the Merkid camp?"

"Honest to Heaven!"

My anda had a point about us being three days late and leaving him exposed up here. But, to my mind, it made up for him leaving my wife and camp unprotected while I'd been visiting the Kereyids. We were even – or so I thought.

When the moon rose, we lit torches and swept down on the Merkids with our battle drums thundering, our lances lowered, our arrows hissing like rain, yelling and setting fire to the yurts as we went. In the smoke and confusion I soon lost sight of my anda, but it didn't matter. All I wanted was to find my wife.

The wolf just appeared. I've no idea where from. I urged my horse faster, faster, faster . . . until I rode up near the front, out of the smoke, the speed bringing tears to my eyes. With everyone galloping at breakneck speed, and Jamukha's lads with us as well, the Mongol-Kereyid monster roared! I couldn't have stopped it, even if I'd wanted to. No one could have done, not even Heaven himself.

"Borta!" I yelled as shadowy figures ran out of the burning yurts in panic. "Borta!"

Merkids kept getting in the way. I galloped through them without bothering to waste my arrows, scattering them as a wolf scatters sheep. Enemy weapons stung me like flies but none scored much of a wound and I barely felt the pain. The moon shining through the smoke, even three nights past full, seemed to make the camp run with blood. The noise of the fighting faded, and although men were dying all around me they didn't seem part of the real world. Spirits howled at my back. Rage filled me at the thought of what the Merkids might have done to my wife. I honestly don't know how many Merkids I killed that night. I wanted to kill them all.

When Borta scrambled out of the back of a cart with her clumsy splint stuck out in front of her and flung herself at me, I thought at first she was some crazy Merkid warrior maid trying to spear me. Then the moonlight brightened around us, and relief washed over me.

"BORTA!"

As I caught her in my arms, the red mist finally left me. Plunged back into the world again, I hugged my wife with all my remaining strength, only easing off when she made a little sound of pain.

Her old servant clambered out of the cart, too.

"Temujin!" she sobbed, grabbing my hand and kissing it. "Oh, Temujin *Khan*!"

At the edge of my vision, the wolf spirit watched us with blood dripping from its jaws. Then it turned and vanished into the smoke.

Our combined armies scattered the Merkids across the steppe and sent their ashes blowing in the wind. It was the usual stuff . . . slaughtering the enemy wounded, piling up heads, capturing women, ransacking yurts, rounding up stray horses and sheep . . . but it was my first experience of a real battle, and I knew I'd remember it for the rest of my life.

Suffice to say that the rumour about me being able to transform myself into a wolf spread like wildfire through a summer-dry forest, until just about every lad in our army believed it. Some even claimed to have seen me kill the Merkid Khan in my wolf shape, which made me laugh because everything that night had been a blur, and his death had been just one of many at our hands. Only Borta's old servant had any sense. She took my wife into an abandoned yurt and ordered everyone out, saying she needed to check the splint on her mistress's arm.

I ached to be alone with my wife. But she clearly needed time to recover from her ordeal. Not only had the Merkids stolen her from me, it seemed they had used her in some sort of barbaric ritual on Red Circle Night and killed her pet deer too. I wondered how they had got hold of the poor creature, since I remembered my brothers telling me how Jamukha had kept Whisper in his camp after the Merkid raid. But spirit magic works in strange ways. I knew only that, as we hugged behind the cart, Borta trembled and cried on my shoulder. I'd not seen her cry until that night. It did peculiar things to my insides.

The Kereyid Khan and Anda Jamukha eventually returned from chasing the fleeing enemy, and we shared out the spoils. Horses, furs, sheep, yaks, gold, girls, servants . . . the list went on and on. After all those years of hiding in the forest and struggling to raise enough warriors to get my father's people back from Fatface, I'd become both rich and a feared war leader in a single night. But the Merkid treasure bored me, and even being called "Khan" at last did not give me the thrill I'd thought it would. While Fatface still controlled the Alliance, I was only the Mongol Khan in name. I should probably have led my army straight to the Alliance camp and claimed back my people right away, but all I could think of was Borta over in that yurt.

When Belgutei finally showed some backbone and rounded up the surviving Merkids who had raided our Holy Mountain camp, I couldn't even get excited about revenge. "You take care of it," I told him. "They stole your mother as well as my wife."

Belgutei had the prisoners bound hand and foot, then ordered his men to fire blunt arrows into them until they died – slowly and painfully, as they deserved. I suppose that showed he must have cared for his mother, though the crazy woman had chosen to run off with the Merkid refugees rather than be rescued by us.

I didn't care. Borta filled my thoughts. I had to know.

Finally, I could stand it no longer and marched into the yurt where she lay resting on a couch with her eyes closed. Old Khoga had washed and re-braided her mistress's hair and dressed her in a clean deel. My wife's arm had been freshly bandaged, and the awkward splint she'd been wearing on it when we found her was gone. Burning in the fire, I hoped. According to the old servant, Borta had broken her arm falling off the yellow mare when she'd been captured – but that had been eight months ago, so I knew she must have hurt it again since.

I didn't want to startle my wife. I sat beside her and touched her cheek. "Borta?"

Her eyelids flew open. She stared at me in terror, clearly not recognizing me at first, then shuddered and reached for me with her good hand.

I took it in mine. She trembled, though not as much as before. That was good.

"Borta, did they . . . ? Did those Merkid bastards hurt you?" My tongue kept sticking to the roof of my mouth. The words I wanted to say wouldn't come.

Her hand wriggled out of mine. She put a finger across my lips.

"Borta, did they force you in the furs?"

She shook her head.

"TELL ME!" I grabbed her shoulders and shook her.

Maybe I was a bit rough. But not knowing the truth was eating me up inside. "Because if any Merkid so much as *touched* you I'm going to hunt him down, and if he's not dead already I'll soon make him wish he was!"

Borta curled up on the couch, clutching her knees with her good arm. Silent tears rolled down her cheeks.

"Honest to Heaven, Borta." I knelt beside her and took hold of her braids, one in each hand. I squeezed them tight but without pulling. I wouldn't hurt her again, whatever had happened. "I'm not angry with you. Just tell me who it was and what they did to you."

"She hasn't spoken since the night they broke her spirit-bond with her deer, Temujin Khan," said a voice behind me.

I whirled, my dagger half out. But it was only the old servant, come to rescue her mistress from my anger.

"They tried to take away her shaman powers so she couldn't warn you of their plans to destroy the Mongol Alliance," old Khoga went on, glancing at Borta. "They took me to another part of the camp on Red Circle Night so I didn't see what they did to her, but I know they kept her in Chilger the Athlete's tent. He's the younger brother of the Merkid Khan. He was with the raiders when they attacked your camp, but he wasn't among the prisoners Belgutei killed. Maybe he died in the fighting?"

My stomach turned as I remembered the excuse Borta had given me on our wedding night. *It's supposed to take away a girl's power to speak with the spirits.* Of course, she'd been captive almost a year. It had been too much to hope for that the Merkids hadn't touched my beautiful wife in all the time they'd kept her in their camp. "I'll murder this Chilger!" I roared, leaping up. My dagger had leapt into my hand. For the first time, I noticed the dried blood on the blade. Merkid blood. "I'll hunt him to the ends of the earth!"

"It may not have been Chilger, Temujin Khan," the old woman said, holding me in the yurt with a claw-like hand. "He seemed scared of Lady Borta. He thought she was a shaman."

"She *is* a shaman! She speaks to the spirits!"

I frowned at my wife. She didn't look much like a shaman now.

"Give her time, Temujin Khan. When she's ready, I'm sure she'll tell you everything."

Borta's gaze flickered to mine. She blinked away her tears, uncurled slightly and reached for me again. I thought she was trying to speak, but no words came out of her mouth.

Instead of arousing me, something inside me shrivelled. Battle weariness hit me like one of Belgutei's blunt arrows, bringing as much pain. I sheathed my dagger, folded Borta's hand away and kissed her gently on the forehead.

"Never again," I promised. "Never again will another man get close enough to touch you. Until we find the Merkid who took you from me, you'll be guarded night and day and have the best care my people can give. I'll leave you in peace until you've recovered your tongue. When you're ready to tell me what happened, I'll return."

Her tears twisted my heart. But no way could I have stayed in that tent a heartbeat longer. I'd have gone raving mad, imagining her with the Merkid they called Chilger the Athlete. I'd make sure he lost the "Athlete" right away once I found him!

The old woman frowned at me as I pushed past her. Let her frown. Ordering Boorchu and Jelme to guard my wife's yurt, I went in search of my anda.

- 10 -

YEAR OF THE RAT

ONE GOOD THING came of that time. After rescuing Borta from the Murdering Merkids, Jamukha and I became best friends again. Drunk on victory and rather too much airag – well, what were we supposed to do when everyone who visited our tent expected to celebrate with a drink? – we renewed our anda vows, giving each other bigger and better presents from the spoils . . . golden belts, horses, weapons, furs, and other riches we'd seized from the Merkid camp. It was all pretty childish, I suppose, but it made up for our stupid argument earlier.

That winter, we all camped together in the foothills, where high cliffs sheltered our yurts and herds from the worst of the snow and bitter winds. Word had got out about our victory over the Merkids, and hardly a day went by without lads riding in to join us from the outlying camps. They came in ones and twos, icicles hanging from their horses' manes and their braids crusted with snow, but with bows slung across their backs and fire in their eyes. Even after the Kereyid Khan led his men home, our combined clans made an impressive camp at least twice the size of Fatface's Alliance. Our young warriors told stories around the campfires about their bravery in the battle, which grew more and more dramatic every night, while my little brothers Alchidai and Odchigin galloped about camp on captured horses wearing gold and furs, pretending to be khans. We let them have their fun. There isn't much fun to be had in winter, otherwise – not when you're still in your first year cycle, anyway.

Mother took Borta into her yurt, while Belgutei and Khasar took the prettiest of the captive Merkid girls into theirs. The girls' bellies soon swelled with new life, and as the months passed it became obvious the Merkid captives were not the only women in our camp expecting a war-baby in the spring. Although I'd not tumbled her in the furs since we'd rescued her from the Merkids, my wife was expecting one too.

When Khoga told me the news, I instructed the women to keep Borta's condition quiet for as long as possible until I decided what to tell everyone. Meanwhile, Jamukha and I spent a lot of time sitting beneath an ancient tree, talking. We'd take flasks of airag and roast meat, spread sheepskins over the carpet of pine needles, and huddle together for warmth. The branches of the tree, heavy with snow, kissed the ground around us sheltering us like a green-shadowed yurt. The forest smell reminded me of being back on Holy

Mountain in my shelter, only this time I had my anda at my side, and no one was hunting me. It should have been a happy time. But, inevitably, our conversation turned to my wife.

"Do you love Borta?" Jamukha asked one day out of the blue.

We'd had some airag to warm our bellies, and my reply came quickly. "Course I love her! She's my wife, isn't she?"

"Your father and her father arranged the marriage, didn't they?"

"So? What's that got to do with it?"

"I'd say it's got everything to do with it." Jamukha stretched his legs under his fur and propped himself on one elbow to gaze at me, less than an arm's length away in the green-scented shadows. "I'd say it's got everything to do with the fact Borta sleeps in your mother's tent, while you sleep in mine."

I could feel the earth throbbing in response to my heartbeat. I'd been putting off telling my anda about the baby, but soon it would be so obvious that the whole camp would know. Better he hear it from me, than from one of my tactless brothers.

"She's pregnant." Somehow I got the words out past the lump in my throat.

Jamukha went very still for maybe a heartbeat, and I saw a flash of something in his eyes that scared me. Then he looked at the snow falling outside and laughed.

"It doesn't matter, you know! Just because there's one

child in her belly doesn't mean you can't try to put another one in there. I bet it didn't bother the Merkids." His eyes glinted, teasing me. "Hey! Maybe that's why some girls have twins, like sheep have twin lambs?"

I'd killed Half-Brother Begter for less. But we didn't have any weapons in our tree shelter, because there was no need with all our people camped outside to defend us from attack. Just as well for Jamukha.

Deep breaths calmed me enough to say, "Mother says it's best if I leave Borta alone until after the child is born." I told him, "Because of it being her first babe, and all the upset with the Merkids, and everything."

My anda laughed again. "She's having you on, Temujin! Women are stronger than you think. They just try to confuse us with their girl talk. We're big chiefs now, you know. If Borta's being difficult, you could easily take a second wife from among the Merkid captives – according to your brother Khasar, half of them would cut off their own braids for a roll in the furs with the handsome Temujin Khan, the hero of the steppe who can change himself into a wolf!"

Jamukha always could make me feel like a marmot. He could do it when we were ten, and he could do it still. Honest to Heaven, the last thing I wanted was some over-eager Merkid girl in my furs to remind me of what Borta was not ready to give. I'd had enough of that from the Kereyid girls, the winter I'd foolishly left my family in Jamukha's care.

"I don't like any of them enough," I said, to change the subject. "Anyway, what about you? I've never seen you with a girl. You could take one too."

"I haven't even got a first wife yet," Jamukha said.

"Take one of the captive girls as your first wife, then," I said, still annoyed with him.

Jamukha frowned. "First wives are important for a chief. I don't want some scrawny Merkid girl to bear my sons. I need a Mongol wife to bear my heirs."

Of course Jamukha would want a Mongol wife. I'd insulted my anda and owed him an apology. But I still couldn't forgive him for what he'd said about Borta.

"I was thinking of your sister, actually," Jamukha said into the silence that had fallen between us and threatened to divide us again. "She's strong and pretty, rides well too."

I'd been thinking of the Merkid bastard Chilger the Athlete, whom no one had yet managed to find. He'd been spotted running away from the battle in the smoke, and that was the last anyone had seen of him. Jamukha's gaze fastened on me, intense in a way that made my stomach crawl.

"Be serious!" I said, realizing what he meant. "Temulun's only nine!"

"You could bind her to me with a chain of flowers. Borta was promised to you when you were only nine."

"That's different. You're nearly old enough to be Temulun's father! It's disgusting."

Protectiveness surged through me at the thought of my

little sister in Jamukha's furs. Then I felt confused, because I wasn't sure whether it was my sister I wanted to protect, or my anda.

Jamukha sat up and hugged his knees, staring out through the latticework of branches at the river that had mostly turned to ice.

"It'd make sense, Temujin. Think about it. We're andas, aren't we? Me marrying your sister would bind us even tighter, so that when I—" He grinned at his slip of the tongue. "—when one of us becomes khan, the other can never desert him. She's got your bloodline, all the way back to Blue Wolf and Fallow Doe, hasn't she? And I can trace my ancestry back through the Jadaran clan to Blue Wolf, too . . ."

He kept talking. I heard none of it. I could only stare at my anda's profile in the green shadows. *When I become khan.* Had it just been a slip of the tongue? Or did Jamukha honestly believe he could fulfil the prophecy by bedding my little sister? Was that why he had kept Borta's deer after her capture, in some misguided attempt to confuse the spirits into supporting him as the wolf who would lie with the deer?

"No," I said. "You can stop thinking about it right now. You're not marrying my little sister, and that's an end to it."

Jamukha held up his hands and chuckled. "All right, Temujin, get off your high horse! It was only an idea. You're right, anyway. I'd have to wait too long for her to grow up. I need a wife who can give me sons now, and it seems you've already got a head start on me in that department!" He bared his teeth at me in a knowing grin.

I eyed him sideways. So far, everyone who had found out about my wife being pregnant seemed to have accepted the story that Borta's unborn child was mine, sired during a night of passion on her return. She hadn't been showing when we rescued her. As far as I was aware, only Borta and her old servant knew any different – and the real father, maybe. Which got me back to thinking of Chilger the Athlete. The Merkid rat was probably dead, eaten by wolves or frozen on some icy steppe, but I ought to have been out hunting for the fugitive, not camping in this snowbound valley with my anda. Then I'd know for sure the reason for my wife's silence.

"If you really loved Borta, you'd spend more time with her," Jamukha said, scattering my thoughts like ashes on the wind. "I know I would, if she carried *my* son in her belly."

I'd had enough of this conversation. I burst out through those branches like a bear with a sore head, shedding snow and leaving my surprised anda sitting there with ice melting over his fur-clad knees.

"Touchy today, Temujin!" he called after me, laughing again. "Don't let's argue. I know how you feel. I hate winter, too. All this sitting around – talk, talk, talk, like gossiping women. It does a man's head in. Come back and finish the airag! We should make plans for spring, decide what to do about old Kiriltuk . . ."

I strode quickly away until his words faded behind me. He was right. We should make plans for dealing with Fatface's people in the spring. Only I didn't like the plans my anda seemed to be making. Marrying my little sister, becoming khan . . . he had it all the wrong way around!

My father had been Yesugei the Brave, leader of the Alliance. The prophecy said *I* would become khan of the new nation. I needed my anda to support *me*.

I slept alone for the rest of that winter. My wife's tent was busy with women waiting for Borta's baby to come, and my anda's tent was no longer the welcoming place it had been following our victory over the Merkids.

In the spring we packed up our yurts and led our warriors slowly towards the Alliance camp, while their families followed with our herds and captured riches. My gelding's summer coat showed through the remains of winter fluff. Its silvery hairs stuck to my trousers as Jamukha and I rode at the front of our people, knee to knee. A whole winter of talk, and you would have thought that we'd have made some firm plans. But we still hadn't decided what to do about Fatface, and the closer we got to the Alliance camp the quieter my anda became.

We'd just found a good place by a stream to water the animals, when Jamukha said, "Maybe you should ride on to Chief Kiriltuk's camp in the morning, and see what he does when he realizes everyone's calling you khan now? I'll stay here with my lads to look after everyone, where there's good grazing for the horses. You can easily send a message if you need me."

I stared at my anda, confused. "But I'd only have half our warriors!"

"That's still more than fat old Kiriltuk has, even if your father's people in his camp don't support you as they promised. This is your argument, Temujin, not mine."

"You're my anda," I pointed out. "That makes it yours, too."

"Kiriltuk's people are Mongols, not Merkids," Jamukha reminded me. "The Kereyid Khan wouldn't give you his warriors to fight against his anda's people, and neither will I."

So that explained his coolness since our argument under the tree. Or did it? Jamukha's face gave nothing away.

"So you're not coming with me tomorrow?"

Jamukha shook his head.

"Fine!" I said. Furious, I wheeled my horse and left my anda to supervise the unloading of the carts, while I went in search of my wife.

I still couldn't decide what to do. Lead my half of the army to attack Fatface's camp, while my anda kept his half here with my captured riches and my pregnant wife? That sounded suspicious to me. What was Jamukha up to? He'd been in a strange mood ever since we left our winter camp, deep in thought about something. Not helping me reunite the Mongol people and establish a new nation, obviously!

By the time I reached my family's wagons back along

the column, the sun was going down. When I pulled aside
the felt and peered into the cart, Mother's head was resting
against the wood and snores came from her open mouth.
Borta sat opposite her, her belly so big it looked as if it
might burst. My wife's eyes were very green as they stared
at me from the shadows. The old servant knelt on the boards
at Borta's feet with a basin of water and a cloth.

All at once, I wished I'd stayed at the front of the army
with Anda Jamukha.

"Is the child . . . ?" Staring at Borta's swollen belly
brought a rush of unwelcome feelings.

"Soon," said the old woman, tight-lipped. "Maybe
tonight."

Leave her alone, that meant. After seeing my younger
brothers and little sister arrive amid screams and blood, I
knew what a dangerous time this was for a woman. Would
Borta survive it? Would the baby inside her come out alive?
Did I even *want* it to live?

"Borta?" I wet my lips and leant into the cart, reaching
for her hand. It felt clammy and cold. "Be brave. I'll make
everything right again, I promise."

Her fingers squeezed mine. For a heartbeat, I squeezed
back. Then, unable to bear the sight of my wife's belly
swollen with another man's child a moment longer, I
dragged my hand free and spurred my horse further down
the column to find Boorchu and Jelme. But before I'd gone
two strides, a cracked voice behind me called, "*Tem . . .
u . . . jin.*"

107

A shiver passed down my spine. That voice reminded me of when Father's warriors had come to Dei the Wise's camp to summon me home. I wheeled the gelding again and galloped back, my heart thudding like hoof beats during a raid.

Mother had woken up. She blinked about her in confusion, while Borta sat up straighter and gazed at me with the shaman light back in her eyes.

"Anda Jamukha doesn't want to fight, does he?" my wife said quite calmly. Her voice still sounded a bit cracked, but she was speaking again . . . speaking! "He's betrayed us before. You can't trust him. The spirits say we should load up our carts again and travel through the night, leave Jamukha and his people behind. We'll be better off on our own now."

Mother nodded, as if she agreed. Tears sparkled in the old servant's eyes. "Oh, Lady Borta!" she whispered. "You *spoke*!"

I had so many questions for my wife! But Borta closed her eyes and moaned as the child in her belly moved, and if we were to leave Jamukha behind I knew we must act fast. Borta's words, the first she'd spoken since her rescue, had confirmed my suspicions. The last thing I would do was leave my wife in Anda Jamukha's care again.

Since not everyone had unloaded yet, it was a simple matter to give my lads the order to ride on through the night. In the confusion of making camp, no one noticed if we were unloading, like Jamukha's people, or reloading our half-unloaded carts. By the time my people were moving again, Jamukha's camp was too well established to follow us. His women had already lit the fires, and his men had killed sheep for supper. A few of his people called after us and began to remount their horses. I told my lads to let them come if they wanted. We had to leave most of our captured Merkid herds behind in the interests of speed. But with the moon lighting our way, my half of our army travelled across the Mongol steppe as fast as we could have by day.

Fatface must have been wetting himself all winter, because he'd posted sentries on every rock. I gathered my warriors and mounted them on the fastest horses. We left the women and children by the river with the wagons under guard, and reached the Alliance camp in the spirit hour just before dawn.

I told Jelme to carry my father's banner with its tails of dark yak hair blowing proudly against the eastern sky, and ordered my lads to light the torches. Up until then, I think my lads had been a bit worried about splitting our forces now we no longer had the Kereyids behind us. But Boorchu grinned at the thought of meeting nine-times-a-night-Khadagan at last, and the others cheered when they recognized Yesugei the Brave's war banner. I gave them a bit of a speech about how Fatface had betrayed my father, abandoned my family to die on Holy Mountain and paraded me around his camp in a cangue like a common criminal. Then I couldn't think what else to say, so I howled like a wolf and led them down into the valley to take back Father's people.

The sentries had spotted our torches and galloped off to give the alarm. By the time we fired Fatface's yurts, breaking their doorposts and scattering his herds, his women had loaded up their carts with their children and belongings and were already fleeing across the steppe. I half expected the wolf to appear, as it had during our attack on the Merkids, but obviously the Ancestors didn't think I needed any extra help this time. Fatface's warriors didn't even try to stop our initial charge. They hung around long enough to give the carts a head start, then turned tail and fled after their women like the cowards they were.

We galloped after them a short way, yelling insults. "Camel dung!" "Sons of yaks!" "Lice under the collar!" That sort of thing. I put three arrows into Fatface's backside, knocking him off his horse so that he had to flee in a wagon with his women, then told the lads to let them go. Our horses were too weary after carrying us all through the night to chase across the steppe after the fugitives, and I had Borta to think of. Although I felt a bit frustrated we hadn't captured the fat chief, Fatface was on the run. He was scared of *me* now. We could finish him off later, once we'd rested and eaten. I'd got Father's people and herds back, and that was the main thing. It felt good.

It felt even better when several of Jamukha's clans turned up at our camp the next morning, bringing news that Fatface had limped straight to my anda to beg protection from me. When I heard this, I couldn't help but laugh. With all Fatface's herds, my lads, my father's people, Jamukha's clans who had changed sides, and the stray children and servants who had got left behind in the panic, the sun rose over a camp almost as impressive as the Kereyid Khan's.

But the Ancestors had not finished with me that day. Even as I stretched the kinks out of my shoulders and thought about where to pitch my yurt now I was khan in more than name, a scream like an injured animal came from the women's tent.

Honest to Heaven, I thought the wolf spirit had returned to attack our camp! My stomach gave a peculiar jolt. Then I was running, my head full of unnamed terrors.

"Borta!" I shouted, leaping into the yurt with dagger in hand to keep the wolf away from my wife. But there was no wolf, spirit or otherwise. I spun full circle and saw Borta sitting up on the couch with something gore-splattered in her arms.

As I stared, it wriggled tiny arms and legs, became a baby.

"It's a boy, Temujin," Mother said matter-of-factly, helping Borta's old servant rinse the bloody cloths in a basin of water. "Congratulations. Your first son."

Not *my* son.

Thinking of Chilger the Athlete, my fist tightened on my dagger. Then my rage cooled, and I lowered the blade. If I killed the child, everyone would know why. If I let it live, they would be more inclined to believe it mine. Whatever happened now, my people had to believe Borta's firstborn to be the son of their khan.

I crept forwards for a closer look. The baby clenched its bloody little fist and waved it at me. Then it screwed up its eyes, opened its mouth and screamed loud enough to wake the entire battle-weary camp.

There was no help for it. I laughed as loudly as when I'd heard about Fatface running to my anda for protection.

Borta gave me a wary look, guided the small mouth to her breast (which at least stopped the screams) and put her arms around the baby as if to hide it from me. Her gaze met mine over its head of sticky black hair, challenging me.

"Well done," I said, and immediately felt stupid.

What were you supposed to say to a girl on occasions like this? Especially when the fierce little boy sucking at her tit is not yours, could no way be yours. Tell you the truth, I was a bit relieved my wife had produced just one baby, and not the twins Jamukha had teased me about under our snow-laden tree that winter.

I reached out to touch the baby then drew my hand back, afraid of hurting such a small spirit.

"We'll call him Jochi, a good *Mongol* name." I said. My gaze challenged her in turn. Borta's eyes widened, and for a heartbeat I saw confusion in them. Then she relaxed slightly and nodded. "It's a good name," she agreed.

Time to find out the truth.

Ordering Mother and the old servant out of the women's

yurt, I took the baby from my wife's arms and put it gently in the cradle. Then I pulled Borta close and kissed her on the lips, no messing.

She went rigid, as I had been half expecting her to. But very soon her lips softened and her body pressed against me. Warm, fatter with motherhood than it had been before, but all mine now the child had gone from it. And that kiss . . . well, let's say it put my red moon kiss with Khadagan in the shade.

I pressed my wife against me long enough to let her know how it would be between us from now on, and then stepped back for air. Taking her hands, I held them firmly and looked deep into her green eyes. "They're calling me khan now," I said.

Borta smiled. "I know. They're very loud. I heard them."

"As my first wife, you'll be the mother of my heirs."

"I know." Fainter.

"So no one must know the truth about little Jochi, except us."

Borta just nodded this time, looking at her feet.

I let go of her hands so I could lift her chin.

"Who's the father?"

A trembling silence stretched between us, like the rope on a wild horse. Borta's chin quivered in my grip. Her whole body stiffened. The green light in her eyes flickered, trying to escape, but I would not let it. I held her gaze, as if I could make her tell me by reaching deep into her with my spirit and dragging out the truth.

"I don't know," she whispered, though I could tell from the look in her eyes that she did.

"You must know!" I said. "Was it Chilger the Athlete? Or was there more than one, is that it? Tell me all their names. Because, honest to Heaven, I'll not rest until every last one of those Merkid bastards has paid in blood for what he did to you!"

Borta's eyes filled up with tears. She made a half-hearted attempt to pull free. Then she jerked her chin up so suddenly my hand slipped, and gave me a fierce look.

"You don't understand, Temujin," she said. "They were scared of me cursing them, so they took precautions. They blindfolded me so I wouldn't see who came to me that night, and tried to trap my spirit in my body so I couldn't use my shaman powers. But I couldn't stay to feel . . . feel that . . ."

She sucked in a ragged breath before continuing.

"I only saw him with my spirit-eye, so I can't be sure. But I think he was a Mongol. The one with the wolf spirit in him, the one the prophecy says will found a new nation." I must have looked blank because she gripped my hand again and said, "Oh, Temujin, don't you *see*? When Yesugei the Brave came riding across the steppe seeking a wife for his son and heir, we all wanted to believe Papa's dream meant I'd marry you and we'd live happily ever after. But the spirits must have been angry that day because they made sure your papa would not survive the ride home and took your father's people away from you. Then they gave me to the Merkids and took Whisper away from me so that when the wolf came I could do nothing to stop him . . . and he wasn't you! Papa's dream didn't mention any names, did it? What if the Ancestors meant someone else to be khan?"

"Who is this traitor?" Losing all control, I grabbed her by the arms and shook her. "You know, don't you? Who are you protecting? Give me a name!"

My beautiful, brave wife stared at me for so long I thought a spirit had stolen her tongue again. Then she sighed and lowered her dark lashes. "The wolf told me his name was Genghis," she said. "I don't know any more."

Well, that threw me completely! I tried to remember if I knew anyone called Genghis. I'd never heard the name before. He mightn't even be a Mongol as my wife obviously thought, though I couldn't imagine any Merkid founding a new nation, especially since we'd just wiped out most of their tribe.

In the furs that night, I made Borta tell me everything. It amazed me that so much could have gone on behind my back, though it did explain certain things that had been puzzling me. I also saw that if I was to keep the Mongol people together, the killing wasn't over yet, not by a long stride.

I vowed to hunt down this "Genghis", whoever he might be, and make him wish he'd never been born.

- 11 -

YEAR OF THE OX

THE TROUBLE WITH hunting a spirit across the steppe is that people tend to take it literally. Shamans visited my camp offering their help, and word got around that I was on a spirit quest for the wolf that appeared beside me in battle. Some impressionable idiots like Jelme and Boorchu even started to call *me* Genghis, which meant I was effectively hunting myself. I might as well have been, because nobody else would own up to the name. Of course, I couldn't tell anyone the real reason I wanted to find the wolf, or they might suspect little Jochi was not mine.

The following spring, I took a break from chasing spirits and avenged my father's death. Even without Jamukha's lads, I had more than enough warriors to challenge the Tartars. Seeing Yesugei the Brave's war banner at the head of our yelling horde put the fear of Heaven into them, and their khan surrendered before we could destroy his tribe as we had destroyed the Merkids.

The prisoners we took claimed they had not been responsible for poisoning my father, so I had every male carefully measured against the wheel of a cart before executing only those who stood tall enough. I would not risk the curse of our Ancestors as Fatface had done. The smaller boys were too young to have been involved in my father's murder in any case, so I sent them back to my camp to be raised as Mongol warriors.

The shamans officially crowned me Khan of the Mongol people on Red Circle Day. Borta's father Dei the Wise came with his family to congratulate us on our first son, and I invited all the chiefs of the Mongol clans to a great feast.

Now that I'd got my people back from Fatface and avenged Father's death, I hoped Anda Jamukha might come to congratulate me too. I was feeling generous after our victory and planned to make my anda a gift of some of the Tartar gold and horses in apology for leaving him behind last year. Also, I wanted to ask Jamukha if he knew this "Genghis" Borta had told me about. I hoped he might help me hunt down the traitor, as we'd hunted for food on the banks of the Onan in our first year together. But my anda did not turn up and, a few days later, a long line of horses and carts arrived from his camp with the news that Fatface's remaining clans had crowned *Jamukha* the Mongol Khan.

All thoughts of a reunion with my anda fled. I ordered Khasar and Boorchu to line up the hostages we'd taken from Fatface's clan and make them kneel. Then I took an axe and walked down the line of terrified men and boys, asking each one straight out: "Is your name Genghis? Tell me who he is, and I'll let you live." But none of them would confess, so I executed every last one of them and sent their heads to Anda Jamukha's camp as a warning of what would happen if he dared challenge me for the leadership of our tribe.

Needless to say, this ended the celebrations. The other chiefs made their excuses and rode off home, while my people disappeared into their tents. When she saw me with my axe dripping blood, Borta took little Jochi off with her sisters, leaving me to sleep alone again.

Tossing and turning in my furs that night, a horrible suspicion dawned on me. I thought of how Borta had refused to answer my questions about Jochi's father, claiming that the Merkids had blindfolded her so she wouldn't see who came to her that night. I remembered how Jamukha had kept my wife's spirit deer in an effort to change the prophecy. Then I thought of the ten-year-old boy from Dei the Wise's camp who had travelled across the steppe in winter to swear anda with me, when I'd barely had an arrow to my name.

Seemed I'd been the blind one, not my wife.

- 12 -

YEAR OF THE TIGER

THE PEOPLE COULD not have two khans. Jamukha knew it, and I knew it. We had put things off long enough. Not even the shamans' warning that the blood bond we shared extended beyond death could make me forgive my anda. So I told Jamukha I'd meet him on the Donkey-Back Steppe, and we'd settle the matter once and for all.

I didn't expect him to accept my challenge, to be honest. But Jamukha found a glimmer of courage from somewhere and sent a message back promising he'd be there on Red Circle Day with his army, by which I guessed he meant to spend the winter recruiting warriors from the remaining tribes to strengthen his small force. I had nothing to fear now that so many people had flocked to my banner and the spirits were on my side. So I ordered my troops to make camp for the winter and set my brothers to training all the new lads and horses ready for the coming battle.

Borta spent most of that winter in the women's yurt,

fashioning a skull-bone violin when she wasn't nursing little Jochi. I left her to it. After what I'd done to the prisoners, she had been very quiet. Although we'd kissed and cuddled a bit while Jochi slept, I'd promised not to take her to my bed until she told me she was ready. I didn't want to upset her again and have another spirit steal her tongue, so I found other ways to scratch that itch when I needed it scratched. The Alliance girl Khadagan, who had come in with the last line of carts, proved willing enough and asked nothing in return.

Besides, there's a lot to do when you're khan – judging disputes, meeting envoys, organizing equipment for my growing army – and I still had to decide how to punish Jamukha. My anger had cooled slightly since last year, but I could not let my anda get away with challenging me so openly. He would have to be made an example of in public. I just had to work out how to do it without dishonouring our anda bond and risking the curse of our Ancestors by spilling his blood.

My generals had their own ideas.

"Boil the bastard alive," Boorchu urged.

"Put him in a cangue and parade him round our camp, like Fatface did to you," my brother Khasar suggested. "Then leave him out on the mountain for the wolves."

"Break his arms and give him to Lady Borta," Alchidai said. "Let her punish him for abandoning her."

"Let me fire blunt arrows into him," Belgutei said eagerly. "I can make his death last a long time, very painful."

I knew he could, too.

"Do all of them!" Odchigin said. "The two-faced snake deserves it!"

I looked in surprise at my youngest brother and wondered where the little boy had gone. But none of us had been little boys since the day Fatface abandoned us up the Onan to die.

"The coward probably won't show up, anyway," Boorchu said. "We'll have to hunt him down like an animal, come spring." My friend's eyes gleamed at the thought, and the others started arguing about how best to smoke Jamukha off the mountain.

I was inclined to agree with Boorchu. If Jamukha had any sense, he'd be using the winter to put as much distance between our two camps as possible. I just hoped we wouldn't have to waste years chasing after him, because I had plans to make for my new nation.

Then the flap of my yurt lifted, and Borta ducked inside. Her presence silenced them all.

"He'll come," she said.

My brothers glanced at one another, avoiding her gaze.

Borta looked different. At first I didn't realize why, until I saw her hand gripping her new violin. She had strung the instrument with gut and carved little animals into the bone, one for each year of the spirit cycle. It was the most beautiful violin I had ever seen. It must have taken her all winter. Her green eyes held mine. Her hair, unbound and smelling of flowers, aroused me. I ordered the others out and they went without a word, eyeing my wife warily.

My gaze strayed to the violin again. "Is that . . . ?"

"Whisper's skull," she said. "Khadagan brought it for me last year."

I hadn't realized until then where the skull she'd been working on so hard had come from. She stroked the strings with a fingertip. As the sound shivered down my spine, my thoughts spun back through the years to when I'd first seen her, a wild-eyed girl with twigs in her hair staring at me over her pet fawn's back. Shaman magic . . . was it possible she still had her power?

"I thought they had to be horse skulls," I said.

Borta's lips twitched. "Horses still don't like me very much."

I started to laugh, then had a vision of her falling from the yellow mare at the Merkid Khan's feet. The laugh stuck in my throat.

"Come here." I reached for her other hand, but it slipped out of mine.

"Not now, Temujin," she said. "I've more important things to do. Listen." She raised the violin to her shoulder.

I wasn't sure she would be able to play it with her twisted arm, but of course she'd found a way. The music sounded wilder than that made by the horse skulls. The notes danced around us like sunlight dances through the forest.

I relaxed back on the couch to watch my beautiful wife, imagining her dancing too. Then the door flap lifted in a draught, and a ghostly spotted deer trotted inside, exactly like her pet fawn used to do all those years ago.

I blinked, but the ghostly deer did not vanish. "It's true, then?" I said. "The spirits are real?"

She nodded. "They're real if you believe in them, Temujin."

Borta let the music fade and rested a hand on the deer's head until it faded from sight. Smiling, she set down the violin carefully on a pile of furs – the latest gifts from envoys anxious for peace and alliances with me. Then she knelt beside the couch and touched her lips to mine. I tasted the forest on them.

"Your deer's still here, isn't it?" I said, awed.

She nodded. "Whisper's spirit lives in my violin now."

"So you've got your shaman powers back?"

"Some of them, yes. I can't spirit-travel any more, but I should be able to help you on Red Circle Day."

"I don't need your help to defeat my anda." My voice came out rougher than I had intended, and she wriggled free.

"Yes you do," she said. "You need me to bring him here."

The smell of her unbound hair was driving me half crazy. "Borta . . . please! Hasn't it been long enough? Jochi's old enough to be weaned now. Don't let Jamukha come between us now. I want to love you properly. I promise I won't hurt you like Genghis . . . like the wolf . . . like he did."

The silence stretched between us. Now I would find out if my suspicions held any truth.

Borta went very still. "First promise me one thing," she said.

"Anything!" I said rashly. "I'll give you anything you want, you know that. We're rich now, richer than my father ever dreamed of. You're my first wife, the one I destroyed two tribes to find, the one I love more than any other. You know you only have to ask."

Her eyes flashed with the same shaman light I remembered from our marriage night, and my stomach twisted with unease. Would she ask the impossible? That I not touch her again, in case I took away her remaining powers?

I didn't know if I could keep such a promise. I could take other wives, of course. As khan it would be expected of me to sire sons and secure alliances. Khadagan, maybe . . . but I couldn't see myself wanting any of them as much as I wanted Borta right then.

I was worrying about the wrong thing. She smiled, her green gaze fixed on my face.

"Jamukha," she whispered. "When you catch him, let me decide his punishment."

Honest to Heaven, how could I refuse her request?

What can I say about that battle? Later, people would compose great songs to tell how bravely we fought, how many men flocked to our banners, and how Anda Jamukha and I led our armies until the bitter end with curses on our lips and the spirits at our heels. It's always better to sing about such things than live through them.

As the sun rose, our two armies assembled on the steppe. I suppose we must have made an impressive sight. The nine black tails of my war banner hung motionless in the heavy air. Huge, yurt-shaped clouds were building on the horizon. Glancing across the slope I saw my shamans at work, playing their horse-skull violins to call down a storm. The wail of those skulls sent shivers up and down my spine.

I'd have preferred to fight my anda without the help of the spirits, but Borta had insisted. Behind the white-bearded old men, my beautiful wife stood on a rock against the sky, her black hair loose to her waist, holding her delicate deer-bone violin. As my breath caught, she raised her hand and pointed up at the ridge.

A lone horseman sat up there, silhouetted against the rising sun, staring down at us.

Jamukha.

I wish I could tell you Anda Jamukha rode down from his hill, that we fought a duel for Borta's hand and he died bravely and with honour. But that would be more of a lie than the stories about me changing into a wolf. The truth is we had to fight our way through his men to reach him, and even then he hid from me. But he came in the end. He had no choice.

Suffice to say that, by the end of that battle, Jamukha knelt at my feet wearing a cangue. He begged me to kill him cleanly with my axe, as I'd executed Chilger the Athlete, Fatface, and the other cowardly traitors who had brought my anda to me when all seemed lost in the hope of bargaining for their lives. It was a better death than they deserved.

I almost swung my axe one last time to cut off Jamukha's head and end the whole sorry prophecy. But, mindful of the spirits watching us, I kept my promise and gave my anda to Borta.

When you've heard her story, you will understand why.

- PART TWO -

BRIDE OF WOLVES:
BORTA'S STORY

BLUE WOLF LAY down beside Fallow Doe and licked his paws.

"Lord Heaven has given us a difficult task," he said. "We must decide how to carry it out."

Fallow Doe thought quickly. "We can't mate in these bodies and create a human child. We'll have to borrow human forms."

"Clever," growled Blue Wolf. "But for how long? How long can a wolf and a deer live in the same tent?"

Fallow Doe did not like the idea of sleeping in a tent with a wolf in the furs beside her. "Only for the night of the red moon," she said.

Blue Wolf smiled. "I agree. Then in the morning I can eat you."

- 1 -

YEAR OF THE HARE

THE FIRST TIME I saw Temujin, I remember thinking how proud and happy he looked. A boy riding across the steppe with his father, free as the wind. They rode matching silver-bay geldings and carried a white standard, which meant they came in peace. Nobody warned me that the next time I saw that standard it would be hung with the black tails of war, and I would be the cause of it.

If I had known what lay ahead, would I have run? Maybe. I'm not that brave. I might have gone up the secret deer trails with my pet fawn Whisper and hidden in the forest. But when the spirits are involved running does no good, so probably I would not have escaped for long. Besides, I was just as curious as everyone else to see what Yesugei the Brave and his son wanted. Visitors out here are rare.

When Papa summoned me to his yurt, I left Whisper to graze on the riverbank and went straight away – smelling of deer, my tunic grass-stained, my twig-ridden hair hanging loose around my knees. Our shaman was already there. Nervous, I stopped at the door.

Papa beckoned me over. "I had a dream last night, little deer," he said, picking a leaf out of my hair. "A white falcon flew down from Heaven, bringing me the sun and the moon in its claws. When I took them into my yurt, the moon turned into a doe and the sun turned into a wolf. Then the two creatures lay down together and loved each other. Tell my daughter what this dream means, Shaman."

The shaman stroked the white horsetails hanging from his staff. "A powerful dream, wise chief. The falcon is clearly Lord Heaven, bringing you a gift. The wolf and the deer are our first ancestors, Blue Wolf and Fallow Doe, who joined their spirits to give birth to the Mongol people. I'm wondering if this has anything to do with Yesugei the Brave and his eldest son riding into our camp to claim hospitality of the steppe?"

"Of course!" Papa said, slapping his own forehead, pretending to have only just seen the connection. "Yesugei the Brave is on his way to find a wife for his son, and our enemies call his men wolves. As for the deer . . ."

They both looked at me, and unease rippled down my spine.

"I think your dream means Yesugei the Brave's son will wed your daughter, and they will give birth to a new nation," the shaman said, nodding in satisfaction. "Both are descended from Blue Wolf and Fallow Doe, so Heaven will bless the match."

Papa gave me a fond smile. "This is wonderful news, isn't it, Borta? I must tell Yesugei the Brave about my dream as soon as possible! Meanwhile, you go and ask your mother and sisters to help you get ready. Brush your hair and wear something nice for young Temujin. He'll be khan one day and you'll be his first wife. You can do no better."

I knew he spoke the truth. Everyone had heard of Yesugei the Brave, leader of the largest clan alliance this side of Holy Mountain, who had driven off the Terrible Tartars and the Murdering Merkids and brought peace to our people. It was an excellent match. I should have been happy, but the thought of leaving my family and friends behind to live with a strange clan made my knees go weak. What if I had to leave Whisper behind, too?

My panic must have shown on my face. As the shaman left to prepare for the ceremony, Papa gave me a quick hug and whispered, "Don't worry, my little deer. I'll make sure Temujin stays with us for the rest of the summer so you can get to know each other before you marry. I won't pack you off to a strange camp with a lad you barely know like a bride snatched from her father's tent!"

This made me feel a bit better. My empty-headed half-sisters said it would be romantic to be kidnapped by a handsome khan, but I'd never liked those stories. Getting to know my future husband first seemed much better. Anyway, Temujin was only nine at the time and shorter than me. How much carrying off could he do?

Yesugei the Brave proved easy enough to convince. No

doubt our airag, fermented from mare's milk, helped since Papa instructed the women to make it strong and sweet in his guests' honour. As the two chiefs linked our hands together with a chain of flowers, a strange shiver went through me and I wished they would let me have a drink, too. Our shaman blessed the union with his horsetail staff, which tickled, making me want to giggle. Apart from that idiot Jamukha throwing a stone at Temujin when he tried to kiss me, we got through it without too much embarrassment.

I was afraid Temujin's father would be insulted and withdraw from the treaty, but Jamukha ran off before anyone else saw him so I pretended nothing had happened and scuffed the stone away with my foot. Afterwards, I took Temujin to meet my half-sisters, Altani and Orbei, while the two chiefs got down to some serious drinking.

The next morning nobody got up very early, and the sun had climbed high into the sky by the time we waved Yesugei the Brave off. My head was spinning, even though I was too young to have drunk any airag at the feast, so I closed my eyes. When I opened them again, the wolf was there. Huge and silver-blue, it loped after Yesugei the Brave's horse like a ghostly shadow, windswept grass showing through its body. No one else seemed to see it. But as I stared, it turned its head and looked straight at me, death in its gaze.

I put my arm around Whisper's neck with a shiver. "Temujin's papa must be very brave to cross Tartar territory on his own," I said.

"One man doesn't attract attention," Papa explained. "A horde of warriors would raise dust. Besides, Yesugei the Brave's people are going to meet him halfway. Don't worry, little deer. Heaven will look after him until then."

"But the wolf . . . !" I whispered, pointing.

Papa chuckled and tweaked my braid. "Given you nightmares, have I? Forget about my silly dream, it's served its purpose – look, here comes young Temujin! Go and show him where you found Whisper in the forest. It'll take his mind off being homesick."

The wolf had gone by then, and I decided I must have imagined the whole thing. But the spirits had shown me the truth that morning.

Three days later, Yesugei the Brave lay dead on the Tartar steppe, and the Mongol Alliance scattered like ashes in the wind. Temujin galloped off home with the messengers who brought the bad news, his face pale as a skull-bone violin.

Me, I breathed a sigh of relief. At ten, being married seems an eternity away. If I thought of our coming wedding at all, it was only in a vague, romantic kind of way. All I wanted in those days was to be left alone to run with Whisper up the secret trails into the forest. I was actually quite glad my future husband had gone, because it meant I would not have to worry about leaving my family and friends for a while.

- 2 -

YEAR OF THE DRAGON

I CAN SEE now how everyone tried to protect me from the truth for as long as possible. But Whisper and I spent so much of that year exploring the forest I'd scarcely have noticed a raid on our own camp, let alone worried about bad news from anyone else's.

My half-sisters never stopped telling me how lucky I was to be betrothed to the future khan. All winter they talked about my wedding and practised braiding my hair into loops and coils – which was quite a feat in those days, since it collected tangles and twigs the way sheep collect burrs from the steppe. Giggling, they told me every Mongol alive would come to see us wed. But our fantasies stopped at the flowers tied across the door of the marriage tent, while in my dreams Temujin became a handsome prince from a fireside story instead of the small boy who had galloped off home in tears when he heard his father was dead.

Then my innocence ended.

I had a stomach ache that day, so I had escaped my morning chores and found a quiet place on the riverbank to doze in the sun. My half-sisters rode off into the forest to collect berries, but for once I didn't feel like going up the deer trails with Whisper.

At first, when Jamukha sauntered over and started to talk to me, I merely felt annoyed because his shadow blocked the sun. The boy had joined us from the Jadaran clan after his parents were killed in a Merkid raid. He had a silly crush on me, though we both knew Papa would never marry me off to an orphan without warriors to protect his tent. Since Temujin's departure he had kept his distance, which was a bit of a relief because he'd grown taller than me that winter, and the way he stared at me whenever our paths crossed made me feel uncomfortable. Now I realized he'd just been waiting for the right moment to pounce.

He tried to stroke Whisper, but my pet sprang away. Then he put his hand on my arm, and I saw his intentions as if his spirit had touched mine.

"Leave me alone!" I sprang to my feet exactly as Whisper had done earlier. "You know I'm promised to Temujin!"

He gave me a sly smile. "You know your precious Temujin will never come back, don't you? Maybe you'd better start being friendlier to people in your own clan."

"Maybe you'd better be careful what you say to the chief's daughter," I told him in my haughtiest voice, though I couldn't help wondering what he meant. "I know you threw that stone last year at our betrothal ceremony. I wonder what Papa would say if I told him that?"

Jamukha scowled. "Maybe the chief's daughter should forget about stones and ask her papa why her promised husband has not been in touch for almost a year."

"His father died, everyone knows that. Temujin's still in his first-year cycle. He can't marry me for ages . . . why? What do you know?"

I decided Jamukha was just trying to upset me because he was jealous, but that didn't stop me imagining Temujin married to someone else . . . disgracing our clan by dishonouring his papa's promise . . . leaving me touched with shame so no one would want me as a wife.

"I know your Temujin will never be khan, for one thing," Jamukha said. "And if he can't look after you properly, Dei the Wise won't let you marry him."

"That doesn't matter, because I'm not sure I want to marry him, anyway," I said.

As soon as the words were out, I regretted them. After all, Temujin had been nice enough to me during his short stay in our camp. He'd even tried to teach me how to ride, when just about everyone else had given up on the idea of me and a horse going in the same direction at the same time. I remembered his grin, and I knew he'd make me a much better husband than someone like Jamukha. But a spirit had control of my tongue that day.

Jamukha's lips twisted up at one corner. "Oh? Then maybe you won't mind giving *me* a kiss, proud deer girl?"

He'd grabbed me before I knew it. He might have been skinny, but he was strong. His breath stank of the sheep he'd eaten for breakfast. My stomach cramped in revulsion.

"Get *off* me!"

The kiss went nowhere near my lips. It landed on a corner of my mouth and left slobber down my cheek. I kicked Jamukha as hard as I could on his shins and twisted out of his grip. Then I fled blindly after Whisper.

Oh, I know I should have run towards our camp. I would have been safe as soon as I got within shouting distance of the yurts. But in my panic the forest with its deer trails seemed the best place to hide.

My head filled with green shadows. Blood pounded in my ears. Don't ask me how it happened. All I know is that, when Jamukha caught up with me and grabbed my arm again, something inside me snapped. My spirit bounded onwards with Whisper, leaving my body an empty husk in my attacker's hands.

To a deer there is no past or future, just blurs of green and gold. We crash out of the trees, making my half-sisters' horses shy in alarm. The girls shriek as they nearly fall off, and then laugh.

"It's Whisper!" says Orbei, letting go of the mane. "Borta must have decided to come riding with us, after all."

They turn in their saddles to look past Whisper for a horse and rider.

"I can't see anyone," Altani says with a little frown. "Maybe she's fallen off again? We should go back and check."

"And ruin our ride?" Orbei sighs. "We can't always be looking out for her. When Yesugei the Brave's son returns to carry her off to his camp, she'll have to learn to look after herself."

"But what if she's hurt?"

Orbei hauls angrily on her reins. "Her silly pet almost got us hurt! Don't worry so. She's probably fallen asleep by the river, and her deer got bored, that's all."

"We should check," Altani insists. "Whisper looks as if she wants us to follow her."

"You're imagining things!"

"Maybe, but it's unusual for Whisper to leave Borta's side for very long. Let's go back, Orbei, huh?"

I don't know how long I stayed out of my body. Long enough to feel my pet's surprise and hear my half-sisters talking about me. Then my spirit plunged back through the darkness. When I realized I was lying on the ground with Jamukha bending over me, the shock of it made me scream.

My half-sisters came galloping back through the trees. "What are you *doing*, Jamukha? Let her go!" Altani sprang off her horse in mid-stride and wrapped her arms around the boy's neck, pulling him off me.

I stumbled to my feet in relief, ran to Whisper and hugged her tightly.

"I didn't touch her!" Jamukha protested.

"Why did she scream, then?" Orbei demanded. "Borta? Are you all right?"

I managed a nod.

"He didn't hurt you?"

Not wanting to make a fuss, I shook my head.

"There, see!" Jamukha pushed out his jaw. "She just went crazy and ran into the forest after her deer. I came after her to make sure a wolf didn't eat her, that's all."

Altani looked from me to Jamukha. "Why did she run?"

"I don't know, do I?" Jamukha scowled at me, daring me to tell. "There's something very wrong with your sister, if you ask me. Her eyes lit up green, and then she fainted. Just like that, for no reason at all."

Fainted? All I could remember was the wrench of my spirit leaving my body. It wasn't something I wished to repeat in a hurry.

The journey back to camp took ages. I stumbled along, clinging to Whisper's neck, while my half-sisters led their horses on each side of us, watching me closely as if I might faint again the moment they took their eyes off me.

Jamukha trailed behind, whacking at bushes with his bow and scowling. He kept muttering about the green fire in my eyes, and how some things weren't worth the bother. I didn't have the energy to tell my half-sisters what he'd said earlier about Temujin. All my strength had gone, leaving only confusion. Blood trickled down the insides of my legs. I didn't have the first idea of how it had got there.

Papa treated the reports of my screams very seriously. He took Jamukha off to his yurt, and I suppose he must have given the boy a real ear burning, because that same afternoon Jamukha saddled his favourite horse, took his bow and a quiver of arrows and rode out of our camp. Sent home in disgrace to the Jadaran, we heard later, as an example to any other boy who might think that sort of behaviour clever.

Meanwhile, I had to endure Mama's probing questions and my sisters' attempts to explain what had happened. Since I couldn't tell them what Jamukha had done to my body while my spirit had been out of it, the old woman who brought babies into the world was called in to examine me.

It was *so* embarrassing.

But afterwards she smiled, patted my head and reassured Mama that nothing had, in fact, happened to ruin me as a marriage prospect. I was having my first moon-blood, that was all. It was something of a relief, though of course that didn't mean Jamukha wouldn't have tried to do more, if Whisper hadn't brought Altani and Orbei back from their ride in time.

I thought that would be the end of it. But after the birthing woman had left, Papa came in with our shaman. By this time I was sitting up on the couch wearing a clean tunic and trousers with a pad of moss inside them to catch the blood, and Mama was combing my hair to remove all the twigs and leaves that washing never seemed to shift. Freed from its braids, it hung around me in a thick black curtain. When the shaman came in, I had a sudden urge to pull it across my face and hide from the world.

He carried his staff hung with white horsetails and bells, and the first thing he did was shake it over me. The way the horsehair tickled my nose and cheeks reminded me of the betrothal ceremony, and my skin prickled with unease. I wanted to knock it away but didn't quite dare. Outside the tent, I could hear Whisper trotting around in agitated circles. My spirit whirled around with her.

"Hmm," said the shaman. "I thought so."

"You thought what?" Mama did not like our shaman much, and made no secret of it.

"Your daughter has recently sent her spirit into an animal," he said.

I couldn't stop trembling as he hitched up his white robe, knelt in front of me and peered into my eyes. "I'm guessing she travelled with her pet deer. Am I right?"

I wasn't sure if he expected Mama or me to answer, so I stayed silent.

He pursed his lips and tapped my head with the end of his staff. "You can't hide these things from me, child. I can sense the echoes of power in you, and the boy's story confirms it. You sent your spirit into your pet deer's body to call on your friends for help when Jamukha attacked you in the forest, didn't you?"

Mama stared at me, aghast. Papa frowned. "Is this true, little deer?" he said.

"I didn't mean to," I said, feeling guilty and proud of my talent at the same time.

The shaman sat back on his heels with a satisfied sigh. "She'll need proper instruction," he told Papa. "She ought to come to my yurt every day from now on. Her moon-blood brought it on, of course. The boy must have been put off by it just long enough, lucky for us . . . I should have seen the signs earlier. Not every girl adopts an orphaned fawn as a pet, does she? My guess is she's been seeing spirits for some time. Am I right, child?"

I nodded, thinking of the wolf I'd seen when Yesugei the Brave rode out of our camp.

The shaman chuckled and stood, the bones of his knees cracking. "She must be watched carefully from now on! No more boy nonsense of the sort that went on today. It's a nuisance, but girls lose their ability to spirit-travel once they seal the marriage bond."

Mama flushed, making me wince. Any moment now she was going to tell our shaman to get lost, which was never a good idea.

To my surprise, Papa stepped protectively in front of me and shoved the shaman's staff away. "Borta's promised to Yesugei the Brave's eldest son. We can't break the treaty, just because it turns out my little deer-girl's got shaman talents."

"The way I understand it, that particular treaty isn't worth much now," the shaman said.

"It's still a treaty," Papa insisted.

The shaman frowned. "Yesugei's son is unlikely to be khan now. It's a waste of your daughter's talents to marry her off to a fatherless boy with no warriors to support him and barely a horse to his name."

This reminded me of what Jamukha had said earlier

about my promised husband. A chill crept over me. No warriors . . . what had happened to his father's men?

"Dei the Wise does not break his promises!" roared Papa, making me jump. "My Borta will marry Temujin when the boy comes back to claim her, and that's an end to it."

"*If* he comes back," Mama muttered, eyeing our shaman, "once he hears of all this spirit nonsense."

"Which he won't," said Papa. "Because my little deer is not going to train as a shaman. I don't want anyone breathing a word about what happened today."

Curiosity overcame my fear of the shaman.

"Why won't Temujin be khan?" I asked. "I thought he was Yesugei the Brave's heir? Won't his father's warriors support him . . . ?"

Mama sighed, sat down beside me and put her arm around my shoulders. "Now look what you've done!" she said, scowling at the men. "You'd better tell the poor girl. She'll find out sooner or later."

So, on top of everything else that day, I learnt how, after the Tartars had killed Yesugei the Brave, one of the minor chiefs – Kiriltuk of the Taychuit clan – had taken the opportunity to seize power for himself and abandoned Temujin's family. Now Yesugei's two wives and their children were all on their own, a very small clan hiding in the forest with no hope of inheriting any real power, let alone the Mongol khanship.

The relief of it washed over me like warm milk. If

Temujin wasn't an important prince any more, then it wouldn't matter if I married him or not. And since there seemed a good amount of doubt as to whether my promised husband would return for me, I might not have to upset Papa by telling him I'd changed my mind. He might even be glad of an excuse to get out of the marriage treaty. Then I tried to imagine what it would be like to lose your papa, your herds and your friends, all in one day. It made me feel guilty, because I still had mine.

"Don't fret, Borta," Mama said. "I'm sure it won't change anything. Temujin will come back for you when he's ready. What boy wouldn't, when you're growing into such a beautiful princess?" She smiled and picked another twig out of my hair.

"She can easily train with me for the time being," said the shaman. "Then, if Yesugei's son doesn't come back for her, she'll be useful to us in other ways. You'd like to learn how to speak to the spirits, wouldn't you, child?"

Another shiver went through me. Being a shaman would be a lot better than being a wife to someone like Jamukha, true. But what if I trained as a shaman, and Temujin did come back? A promise broken between two clans meant war, although it sounded as if marrying Temujin wouldn't be much safer than speaking to the spirits.

Papa didn't give me time to answer.

"Temujin will return," he said in his most confident voice. "Heaven sent me a dream of this match – and you yourself interpreted it for me, Shaman. The wolf will lie with the doe, as did our very first ancestors, and they will create an empire whose sons and daughters will rule the world. Temujin is the wolf and Borta is the doe. So, you see, there's no point in my little deer learning how to speak with the spirits. It'll only make her miserable, one way or another."

Mama squeezed my hand. "I agree," she said. "Borta will be much happier bearing Temujin's children."

The shaman narrowed his eyes. "Dreams are strange things," he muttered.

But he knew when he was trapped. If he admitted his interpretation of Papa's dream had been wrong, then he would be questioning his own skill as a shaman. If he'd been right, then Mama had a point, and there was no sense in training me to speak with the spirits, because I was destined to be the mother of our future khan's heirs.

As the men left the yurt, a chill went down my spine exactly as if a spirit had whispered the truth in my ear.

"What if it means something else?" I said.

"What if what means something else?" Mama was distracted by Whisper, who had pushed her head under the roll of felt at the door. She patted my hand in sympathy. "I know the Taychuit chief stole Yesugei the Brave's people, but that doesn't mean you and Temujin can't have a good marriage. Being the wife of a khan is not easy. There's less pressure being married to a minor chief as Temujin will be if he's sensible and accepts Kiriltuk's leadership. You're a woman now, Borta, so we need to talk about certain matters—"

"The dream Papa had, that says the wolf will lie with the deer and create a new nation," I insisted, my tongue under the control of the spirits again. "What if the wolf isn't Temujin? What if it's someone else?"

Mama hadn't thought of that. I could tell by the peculiar way she looked at me. But she forced a laugh as she finished off the braids in my hair with loops of red wool.

"Like who?" she said, making a joke of it. "Jamukha?"

The idea of skinny, girlish Jamukha leading the Mongol clans was so silly, it made me smile. None of us suspected treachery back then.

Mama smiled, too. "Forget dreams and spirits, Borta," she said. "You're destined to be a mother of sons one day, and there are more practical things you need to know."

So I didn't escape the mother-daughter talk, after all. And as I listened in growing discomfort, Jamukha's attack became confused with the unfamiliar feel of my moonblood trickling out of my body and Papa's dream of the wolf lying with the doe. Now that I had been in Whisper's body and experienced her deer thoughts, the prophecy sounded violent, an unnatural act.

If Temujin came back for me, I would honour Papa's promise and do what I could to help my husband become khan. But in the meantime, I knew I had to find a way to protect myself.

- 3 -

YEAR OF THE SNAKE

IT TOOK ME a little while to summon the courage to defy Papa. But one winter's night I woke with a start, my heart thudding like a shaman's drum and a triumphant shout echoing in my ears.

ANDA...DA...DA!

Were we being raided? I hugged my knees in the dark until my sweat cooled, listening for more, every nerve as tense as a bowstring. Wolves were howling in the forest, but the camp seemed quiet enough. I relaxed slightly. Nobody raided in winter. The shout must have been part of my dream. Then I felt stickiness between my thighs and knew I'd started another moon-blood, which brought back all the fear of what Jamukha might have done to my body while my spirit had been gone from it. So that very night – may the Ancestors forgive me – I pulled on my warmest deel and crept across camp to the shaman's yurt, taking Whisper with me.

I found the shaman sitting on a stool facing the door flap with his violin resting across his knees, waiting for me. "So, little deer!" He sounded satisfied. "You've decided you want to be a shaman after all, despite what your wise father said."

I couldn't take my eyes off that violin. It had been fashioned from the skull of a horse using horse-gut for its strings, and I'd always been wary of it. Inside lurked a stallion's spirit, captured during a sacrifice to the Ancestors on the night of the red moon. As a little girl I'd seen it disappear into the skull, one of the very first spirits I remember seeing. When the shaman softly plucked a string, the sound raised all the hairs on the back of my neck and I almost turned and fled. Whisper, however, pricked her ears and walked fearlessly into the yurt. The shaman silenced the string and reached out to stroke my pet.

"I'm not sure yet," I managed at last in answer to his question.

He stopped rubbing Whisper's forehead and narrowed his eyes at me. "A shaman can always tell when someone is lying," he snapped.

"I have to obey Papa, of course," I said quickly. "I just want to find out more about my talent . . . so I . . . can control it next time." I couldn't even control my silly tongue, which kept tying itself in knots.

"And?"

"And what?"

"There's another reason, isn't there?" He pushed Whisper

away, laid his violin carefully on the stool, and took hold of my wrist. As he pulled me closer to peer into my eyes, my heart started to pound all over again. "Ah, I see. That boy frightened you more than the spirits do, didn't he?"

I bit my tongue.

"Have you thought about what you'll do if I train you, and this son of Yesugei's does come back for you?" the shaman asked.

"I'll tell him I can't have his children because I'm learning to speak with the spirits. That doesn't mean I can't still marry him, does it?"

I'd thought and thought about it, lying under my furs during the long cold nights, until my head spun with the agony of it all. How to honour Papa's promise, yet still carry out my plan. I'd more or less convinced myself that Temujin wouldn't come back for me anyway, so the chances were I'd never have to explain such an awkward thing to my promised husband or anyone else.

The shaman chuckled – a sound that made my skin prickle as much as the violin had done earlier. "I wonder what red-blooded Mongol lad will accept a wife on those terms. Still, that's your problem, not mine. You have talent, but you need to learn to control it. You might see things you don't want to see while you're in the spirit world. A shaman's life is not an easy one. I'm wondering if you're strong enough for it, a sensitive girl like you."

My stomach churned. I lifted my chin. "I'm a woman now. I can do anything I want."

And in my twelfth year on this earth, after learning how to cope with my moon-blood, I really believed I could.

The shaman sighed and pressed his lips together. "It's partly my fault for missing the signs when you were younger. You hide things too well, child. Sometimes it's a good idea to keep these things to yourself, but at other times it can be very dangerous. Yet it appears the spirits have given you a second chance and sent you to me to complete your education. Let's make the most of it, shall we?"

So I got my first lesson as a shaman. There was no speaking to the spirits that night, though. All we did for ages was practice sending my spirit out of my body and into Whisper's and back again, while keeping the doe inside the yurt until she learnt not to be frightened by my visits. Don't ask me to explain how I did it, because you either have the talent for it or you don't, and if you don't then no amount of training will help. All I can tell you is that being inside a deer's body means sensing other deer, everywhere, flickering at the edges of your thought like flames in the forest. I felt their nervousness and their fear of being caught by a wolf or a hunter's arrow, and it made my legs twitch in sympathy.

But the shaman gently plucked his violin to guide my spirit back each time, so there was no helpless spinning in darkness, as there had been when I'd left my body in Jamukha's hands. After the first few times, once I knew what to expect, I lost my fear. In fact it got rather boring, repeating the same lesson night after night, until I could make Whisper do just about anything I wished while I was inside her deer body.

And tiring! I'd never dreamt how tiring it would be. Although I'd felt weak on my return from the forest the first time my spirit had left my body when Jamukha had scared me, I was not prepared for the heaviness of my limbs and my aching muscles in the mornings afterwards. I staggered about my chores, keeping one eye out for the wolf spirit, relieved when it didn't appear.

Mama decided I must be sickening and mixed potions for me, making me drink them with warm milk so I would sleep at night. That meant I missed some of my lessons with the shaman, yet my powers swelled inside me like my moon-blood every month, vibrating to the music of the lesser violins the men played carelessly around the campfires after supper.

Unseen, half trained, longing for the freedom of the forest . . . I'm not sure even our shaman realized what a dangerous game we were playing.

- 4 -

YEAR OF THE HORSE

SPRING BROUGHT FLOWERS to the steppe, but no word of Temujin. I could tell Mama was a bit upset, but she hid her feelings behind a cheerful face and said I was still rather young for marriage, and that Yesugei the Brave's son would return for me when he was ready. The shaman smiled, while I made the most of my freedom because I knew my childhood would come to an end, one way or another, very soon.

After the business with Jamukha, Altani and Orbei had appointed themselves guardians of my honour. Not that any of the other boys dared to come near me after the example Papa had made of Jamukha, but I could feel their eyes on my body whenever I walked past and the looks they gave me made me shiver. So when my friends suggested a foraging trip to dig for roots and find the leaves our mothers needed for medicines, horses seemed the lesser threat and I agreed.

We packed food for several days and a rolled-up deer

hide to make a shelter at night. Then Altani led out an old mare called White Mouth, and Orbei boosted me into the saddle. Riding was still quite an effort for me, so it took all my concentration just to stay on. Added to which, I was watching Whisper frisking in the forest and trying to sense the green shadows with my spirit as the shaman had taught me, so I didn't take much notice of where we were going.

When Altani leant out of her saddle and gently prodded me on the arm, I saw they'd brought me to our favourite swimming lake. Whisper was already drinking from the blue water. The forested slopes reflected in its surface with little fluffy clouds scudding above them. *Moist green scents . . . water beautifully cold . . .* In danger of slipping into my pet's body, I caught myself just in time to make an ungraceful dismount.

"For Heaven's sake, Borta!" Orbei said. "No wonder horses throw you off."

My friends took the bridles out of the horses' mouths and tethered them under the trees to graze. By the time they returned, the tension of the ride had worn off and I was glad I'd agreed to come. It was good to be out in the mountains, away from the shaman's choking smoke for a few days.

Remembering our excuse for the outing, I pulled my digging stick out of the pack and began to search for roots. But my half-sisters showed no rush to get started.

"So!" Orbei said brightly. "What do you learn in the shaman's tent, then?"

My joy at the simple task fled like a wild deer. "Who told you?"

Altani laughed. "Oh come *on*, Borta! You can't hide it from us! It's obvious you've been training with the shaman. You've got the look."

This made me wonder what "the look" was, and if my disobedience had been as obvious to everyone in the camp.

Orbei giggled at my expression. "Don't worry, we won't tell anyone."

"Papa mustn't know!" I said in sudden fear.

"It's all right, he won't find out." Altani squeezed my hand. "Men don't notice these things the way we do."

I felt tempted to point out that Jamukha had noticed. But Jamukha had seen my body when my spirit had fled from it. The memory made me shiver, and the lake darkened as the sun went behind a cloud.

"I think we should get on with the digging," I said.

Orbei frowned. "Oh, Borta, don't be so pathetic. We didn't bring you all the way out here just to dig roots. We want you to speak to the Ancestors for us and ask them who we're going to marry."

Altani frowned and mouthed something at her sister, but Orbei shook her head. "She'll do it, you'll see."

At last it became clear why they had brought me this far into the forest on horseback. They knew if I wanted to get back to camp without them to help me with the horse, I'd have to go on foot and wouldn't make it home before dark. The way they'd tricked me made me angry – though I didn't know if I was angrier with them, or with myself for being so easily tricked. And me meant to be shaman-trained!

"You don't understand the first thing about speaking to the Ancestors," I told them. "I don't know how to do that yet, anyway. All I've done is send my spirit into Whisper's body inside the shaman's yurt."

"Then now's your chance to try!" Orbei said, her eyes shining. "I bet that old shaman has no intention of letting you and Whisper loose in the forest. He's probably too scared of Papa finding out he's training you, and that's why he's making you stay inside all the time. I can't believe you haven't even tried to send your spirit to spy on your promised husband yet. That's the first thing I'd do, if I had your talent."

It's probably just as well people like my half-sister don't have shaman talents, or there would be spirits whizzing about all over the place snooping on boys. But her words made me think. Could it be true about the shaman keeping Whisper and me safely inside his tent because of the danger of Papa finding out he was training me? Whisper certainly seemed excited to be out in the forest. She kept lifting her head and sniffing the breeze, trotting a few steps into the trees and then looking back at me, as if to say, *Come on, what are you waiting for?*

A little thrill went through me. Spy on Temujin . . . could I do that? No, the whole idea was silly. I didn't even know where his family was camped, and it was bound to be too far away for Whisper to get there and back in a day.

"Just this once, Borta? Please?" Altani said, touching my

arm. "The silly old shaman won't speak to the spirits for such things. He says it's a waste of energy."

"You're lucky," Orbei put in. "You already know you're going to marry Temujin. But we're only half-princesses. There won't be any handsome young khans coming to claim *us*." She giggled.

"Temujin's not khan yet," I reminded them, wondering if he ever would be after what had happened to his poor papa. "Anyway, I told you I don't know how to speak to the spirits."

Would the Ancestors even know such a thing? It seemed unlikely to me. And it wasn't the red moon, so even if I did take Whisper's body out into the forest there probably wouldn't be any ancestor spirits around to ask.

"If that idiot Jamukha's going to come back here looking for a wife, I want to be warned so I can make sure I marry someone else first!" Altani smiled, making a joke of it, though her words chilled me because I too had been thinking of Jamukha and how he'd scared me the first time my spirit had escaped into the forest with Whisper.

"We'll watch over your body as the shaman does," Orbei said, pulling out her knife to show she meant business. "Promise we'll guard it with our lives!"

I sighed. They obviously weren't going to be satisfied until they at least saw me try, and I was curious to know what it would be like out in the forest, free as a deer. After all, I'd learnt how to control the spirit transfer, hadn't I? What harm could it do, if there were no ancestor spirits around to see us? And if I managed to send my pet far

156

enough, maybe I could even find out whether Temujin intended to come back for me, like Orbei said.

Still, the lack of a horse-skull violin to call my spirit back to my body made me hesitate.

"The shaman usually . . ." I began, then caught the glance my half-sisters exchanged. They thought me afraid.

"All right," I said, my heart pounding with sudden determination. "I'll do it."

The forest is so beautiful! It's as if I've never seen it properly before. Green and gold with dappled shadows and damp pine scents. Every so often, Whisper pauses to nibble a few leaves or take a drink at a stream. This feels strange, since I cannot taste what she swallows, but I don't try to stop her. I want her to have enough strength to get back to the lake where we left my body.

When it grows dark, I get a bit anxious and wonder if we should turn back. But Whisper can see well enough where we are going, and the forest takes on a new beauty in the moonlight. I decide to let her go on until morning. A deer cannot get lost, and I am so enchanted by the glades seen through her eyes I do not even think of wolves.

Morning finds us in a part of the forest I have never seen before. As I am about to try turning her back, Whisper stops with her head high. She has heard human voices.

A gangly boy with long dark hair stands with his back to us, holding the reins of a silver-bay gelding. It looks so much like the horse Temujin rode when he came to our camp with his father, I think I've found him on my first try. Joy sparks through me, catching me by surprise. I'm relieved he's alive. Then I realize the lad is too tall and slender to be my promised husband, though I can't help thinking I've seen him somewhere before. Whisper flares her nostrils to catch his scent, and I feel her trembling. Something is wrong.

"My Anda Temujin has just killed his half-brother," the dark-haired lad says. He is talking to a fat man, who is flanked by several armed guards. "I can take care of Temujin for you, but I'll need some warriors. Ten or so should be enough. He's only got his little brothers to support him now."

At the sound of his voice, my spirit prickles in fear. If I let Whisper move, I know he will recognize her. I use every bit of my training to keep my pet standing motionless in the leaves.

The fat man throws back his head and laughs. "Ten warriors against your anda's little clan? Ah, I see . . . you're scared of him, aren't you? Go home to the Jadaran, boy. Don't worry, I'll take it from here. When I've finished with young Temujin, he'll be no threat to anyone."

My spirit begins to spin exactly as it did the first time it left my body, and not only because of what I've just heard. Because I know now who the dark-haired boy is. Instead of finding my promised husband, I have found Jamukha! My panic transfers to my pet, and I cannot keep Whisper standing still a heartbeat longer. My deer leaps into the air and flees.

I expect the men to come crashing after us, so I do not try to stop her. But there is no sound of pursuit. Only the leaves falling all around us, a blur of sunlight and shadow, and my deer's wild leaping speed.

When my spirit returned, I felt as if I had been running along the deer trails for a month. My entire body trembled with weakness and hunger. "At last!" said a worried voice, and Altani crouched beside me with a flask of water.

My throat was so dry I finished it in three enormous gulps. "What happened?" My voice scraped like an old woman's. "Where's Whisper? Did Jamukha—?"

"It's all right, Borta, you'll be all right now. Jamukha's gone, remember? And your deer's perfectly safe, see?" Altani pointed to Whisper, drinking from the lake as if she would drain it dry.

Orbei put her arms around me and hugged me tightly. "We're sorry we made you try. You scared us! You've been gone all night! We didn't know what to do. I wanted to put your body back on the horse and take it back to the shaman, but Altani said your spirit might return and not be able to find it. We dug plenty of onions while we were waiting, though. Here . . . eat."

The food tasted wonderful. They had also caught some fish, which they watched me devour with frightened eyes. They must have been more scared of the shaman than I'd thought; more scared of taking my body back to him and admitting what they had asked me to do, than they were of losing my spirit in the forest.

It seemed we'd got away with it, though. At least Whisper seemed all right, tearing leaves off a bush at the edge of the lake, none the worse for our recent journey. A shiver went through me as I tried to remember exactly what I'd seen.

Had I really seen Jamukha with those men in the forest and heard him call Temujin his anda? How could that be? Had the two boys sworn the blood bond while Temujin had been staying with us that summer before his papa died? I didn't think he had stayed long enough to make friends with any of the camp boys, let alone someone like Jamukha. Temujin obviously had no idea Jamukha had thrown that stone at our betrothal ceremony . . . I should have warned him straight away, instead of trying to hide it. Who was the fat man? And what if my promised husband had really killed his half-brother, as Jamukha claimed?

Something twisted in my stomach, and suddenly I couldn't eat any more.

"Did you speak to the Ancestors for us, Borta?" Orbei asked. She'd been waiting impatiently for me to finish my meal. "What did you see?"

Altani frowned at my half-sister. "Not now – can't you see she's exhausted?"

"I think I saw Jamukha," I told them, irritated that Altani thought me so weak. What had the fat man said? *When I've finished with young Temujin, he'll be no threat to anyone.* I had to warn my promised husband somehow. Could I risk another spirit journey? But how would I find his camp? And how would I speak to Temujin from inside my deer's body, even if I did find him on one of my spirit journeys?

My half-sisters glanced at each other in equal confusion. "Jamukha?" Orbei said, looking round nervously. "He's not coming back here, is he?"

"No . . . at least, I doubt it. He seems to have found some new friends." My spirit echoed with swirling leaves and shadows, as if I were still leaping through the forest in Whisper's body.

"What else did you see, Borta?" Altani asked gently.

"I don't want to talk about it," I said. Had I really seen Jamukha betraying Temujin to the fat man, or just imagined it? Already it was becoming muddled, like trying to remember a dream. "Let's go back now, please. I need to talk to the shaman."

Altani frowned, but Orbei scowled and looked at me sideways. "I bet she didn't go on a spirit journey at all! I bet she's just been pretending to be in a spirit trance, laughing at us while we dug up all those onions. Either that, or she went to spy on her promised husband like I suggested and she didn't like what she saw. What's wrong, Borta? See your Temujin with another girl, did you? Make you jealous, did it?"

Unable to believe Orbei could be so simple-minded, I glared at my half-sister. "No, I did not see Temujin with another girl. I didn't see him at all, if you must know. And even if I had seen him with a girl, it wouldn't bother me because I'm training to be a shaman. I don't care what Temujin does. I wish I'd never met him!"

This wasn't true, though. I often tried to imagine what

the nine-year-old boy with the cheeky grin would be like grown into a man. The most frightening thing was that I *did* care. I cared if Temujin became the sort of man who could kill one of his brothers in cold blood, because no girl wants that sort of man for a husband. As for my promised husband and Jamukha being blood brothers, what would that mean once we were married?

My confusion took a long time to fade. My cheeks burned and I caught Altani giving me an amused look.

Orbei opened her mouth, then shut it again. "Borta, you're scary sometimes," she said in the end, and giggled.

I swore my half-sisters to secrecy on the ride back to camp, but there is no keeping secrets from a shaman. He knew at once what I'd done, and that night in the privacy of his yurt he swung his staff in an arc and slapped my flushed cheeks with the horsetails. They stung, bringing tears to my eyes. Although I'd not meant to tell him why I'd tried the spirit journey, he had it all out of me in the end.

"Foolish, foolish girl!" he snapped. "*Never* play with the spirit transfer like that again! The spirits of the Ancestors are out there, true enough, but if they find you before you're strong enough, then all my work will be undone. Your body's vulnerable when your spirit's gone from it, and what do you think would have happened if one of those men you were spying on had put an arrow in your deer while you were still in her body? I knew a young shaman once who got trapped inside an animal when it died. His spirit never found its way back, and his body withered and starved to death."

By this time, I was shaking. Both from the shock of the slap he'd given me, and from the way his words scared me. But what I'd seen in the forest made me even more determined to learn the shaman skills. "If you'd teach me how to travel with my spirit properly, I wouldn't have to experiment on my own," I pointed out, blinking back tears.

He shook his head. "Tell me exactly what you were thinking when you left your body, and then maybe we can make sense of this vision of yours," he said.

This was more difficult. Truthfully, I'd not been thinking *exactly* anything. My head had been churning in its usual way with all kinds of things. Who my friends were going to marry . . . if Temujin would return to claim me as his wife . . . if Papa's dream had been a true prophecy . . . and, most of all, the identity of the wolf who would lie with the deer to become the next Mongol khan.

I did my best to explain, because I desperately wanted to know the meaning of what I'd seen, and the shaman's brow creased as he listened. "Hmm," he grunted. "I suppose it's possible."

"What's possible?"

"That the vision was a true one, of course!" he snapped. "You say you saw our banished lad Jamukha, and he claimed to be Temujin's anda? If you were thinking of your promised husband, that would make sense since the anda bond is a spiritual one, and Jamukha was the boy who attacked you earlier . . . Hmm! I wonder if he hasn't more of a part in this than we suspected."

"But I'm not going to marry Jamukha!" I said, remembering Mama's joke and horrified by the thought.

"I admit that's unlikely," the shaman said with a smile. "But this glade you guided your deer to was obviously some distance from where you left your half-sisters. I've no idea where you found the power to do that – straying that far from your body is a risky business, especially when you leave it in inexperienced hands. I only hope you realize . . . how foolish you've been?"

I felt certain he had been about to say something else, and tentatively tried the shaman skill of looking into a person's eyes to see what their spirit is really thinking. He flicked his staff between us, making me blink, and something like a boulder rolled across the light inside my head.

"Stop that!" he snapped. "From now on, you will stay in the camp and not run wild in the forest with your friends. You'll make no more spirit journeys until I say you're ready again. A full day's journey out of your body at your age! I'm surprised you found your way back on your own! And don't even think about disobeying me, because there are ways to keep your spirit tethered, if necessary."

This was hidden in the darkness behind his eyes, so I couldn't tell what he meant. But before he blocked my view of them, I glimpsed something of his other thoughts.

"The fat man I saw with Jamukha is the chief you and Papa spoke about, isn't he?" I said with a sudden flash of understanding. "The Taychuit chief who seized power after Yesugei the Brave was killed? He said he was going to punish Temujin. Do you think that'll stop him coming back for me?"

The shaman sighed. "As for that, little deer, it's beyond my power to see. I expect the spirits will tell us when they are ready. Until then, we'll just have to wait for more traditional news."

- 5 -

YEAR OF THE SHEEP

KNOWING I COULDN'T fool the shaman, and afraid to try another spirit journey without his guidance, that winter dragged for me as slowly as a lame sheep.

I might not have been able to send my spirit across the steppe to spy on my promised husband, but my imagination more than made up for it. Instead of a determined nine-year-old boy with a grin that could persuade me on to a horse's back, Temujin grew into a thick-armed, cold-blooded murderer with a price on his head.

The worst thing was not knowing if this ugly, grown-up version of Temujin would suddenly gallop into our camp one morning, fling me across the withers of his horse and carry me away through the snow. A boy who could kill his own half-brother was unlikely to listen to anything his wife said, shaman-trained or not.

Then I'd remember the fate the fat chief and Jamukha had planned for Temujin in my vision, and become anxious in case my promised husband wasn't a cold-blooded murderer after all, but still the cheerful boy who had petted Whisper and grinned at me as our hands were joined with flowers.

I suppose I can't have been much fun to be around that winter, because even my friends avoided me. Whisper took to vanishing into the forest for days at a time. She would come back smelling of stag, which made me glad I'd obeyed the shaman and kept my spirit out of her body.

Mama, of course, got completely the wrong idea and thought I was upset because I was madly in love and Temujin hadn't come for me yet. To distract me from the waiting, we started to sew a beautiful deel for my dowry out of the furs taken from sables we trapped by the river. The coat grew very slowly, because sables are small animals and also rather clever, so more often than not our traps remained empty. I sewed as slowly as possible, and if it was my turn to check the traps and I found a sable in it uninjured, then I let it go. If my dowry remained unfinished, I reasoned, then maybe Heaven would not bring my promised husband back for me until I'd had a chance to discover the truth.

When the spring thaw opened the passes, however, and Temujin still didn't come, I knew something must have happened to stop him returning for me. What if the Taychuit chief had killed my husband?

Desperate, I tried sending Whisper out into the forest myself, each night using my spirit to guide her a bit further along the deer trails towards the place where I had seen

Jamukha and the fat chief talking, that time when Altani and Orbei had asked me to speak to the Ancestors for them. I reasoned Temujin's camp could not be far from there. Whisper soon strayed beyond my reach, but I could still sense the wild spirits of deer in the shadows of the trees. Then one night the Ancestors rewarded me with a dream.

I see a mountain surrounded by shadows. Men are waiting in the trees with arrows on their bowstrings, like hunters stalking their prey. A stocky boy in patched clothes is leading a silver-bay gelding along the trail towards them—

The dream ended abruptly in darkness. I jerked awake, my heart thumping, and lay staring at the moon shining through the smoke hole of our yurt. I paused long enough to make sure I hadn't woken my half-sisters, then wriggled out the back way and hurried to the shaman's tent.

"I think I saw Temujin!" I gasped. "He's in trouble, and I've lost Whisper." I explained my dream as quickly as I could. "You have to help me find him . . . if we can't find Whisper, then send me into a wild deer!"

The shaman shook his head at me. "It's too dangerous, my child. Not many trained shamans have the strength to control a wild animal, even after years of practice, and you are still coming into your powers." He opened the door flap. "It's nearly light. You must go now. If your father finds you here, he'll stop me training you."

"Then I'll take a horse and find Temujin myself!" I said.

The shaman smiled sadly, because we both knew this

would be a challenge even for someone who could actually ride. "If there really are hunters on the mountain where you saw your promised husband, I don't think that's a very good idea, do you?" he said. "If they catch you as well, then you'll be no use to Temujin as either shaman or wife."

Spring stretched into summer, and still Temujin did not come to claim me. Even Papa, with his faith in his dream from Heaven, started to think something had happened to stop my promised husband from returning. Worse, after the night the Ancestors sent me my dream of Temujin, I lost contact with Whisper completely. The young doe was probably just enjoying her freedom, but I kept thinking of what the shaman had said about hunters on the mountain. I didn't know what would upset me most – if they killed Temujin or my pet.

By the time our dogs set up a barking at the edge of camp, Red Circle Day was nearly upon us and my nerves were in shreds. Orbei burst into the women's yurt. "Boys!" she cried. "They're about the right age for Temujin and his brothers . . . oh, come *on*, Borta! Hurry!"

My half-sisters giggled and ducked out of the yurt. But I could not move. My heart began to pound and my mouth went dry. Whisper . . . where was Whisper when I needed her? But I couldn't risk another spirit journey into the forest to look for her now. I hardly wanted my spirit gone from my body if it *was* Temujin, did I?

Orbei tried to drag me towards the door, but Mama grasped my wrist and pushed me firmly down on a stool.

"Borta can't go out to meet her promised husband like that!" she said.

By which she meant still sweaty from beating milk, my hair frizzing from its braids, and my trousers splashed with curds. She had a point. A chief's daughter must look the part if she doesn't want her husband to think she is a common girl and take advantage of her. Besides, I needed time to prepare myself, time to stop my hands from trembling and summon my shaman powers in case I needed them.

So I put up with her fussing and took time to change into my best deel. Meanwhile, Orbei hopped up and down by the door, impatient to see if any of Temujin's brothers were handsome enough for her.

By the time we got outside, the new arrivals had dismounted and were surrounded by an excited ring of our people. Altani stood at the edge of the crowd. Seeing us, she waved. "It's not your promised husband, Borta," she said in a disappointed tone, before I'd even had a chance to see. "But I wouldn't mind being carried off by *him*!" She pointed to the tall boy in charge of the gang, who stood talking to Papa. Orbei, who had grown quite plump over the winter, stood on tiptoe to see better, blocking my view.

"Oh, stop drooling!" I snapped, still trying to understand the strange mixture of feelings that had washed through me when Altani had said it wasn't Temujin. Disappointment. But also anger that I'd got so worked up about seeing my promised husband again, and yet he had not even come to collect me himself.

Trying not to think of all the reasons why Temujin might not have come in person, I pushed past my half-sisters to see who he had sent. The lad talking to Papa had loose braids with black feathers in them. His long limbs carried his lanky frame with easy grace. He had his back to us, and something about the way he stood made my spirit prickle in warning.

Then Papa spotted me, the boy turned, and there could be no mistake.

Jamukha, now darkly handsome and wearing the same squirrel fur collar he'd worn in my spirit vision of him, searched the crowd with hungry eyes. The sky rushed towards me and the ground went soft under my feet.

"Hey, silly!" Altani caught my elbow, steadying me.

"Oh, she's not going off to talk to the spirits again, is she?" Orbei said with a groan. "Snap out of it, Borta! This is hardly the time." She pinched my arm, quite hard.

The pain brought me back to my body in time to see the crowd had parted. Jamukha was striding towards us with Papa following. Papa wore a little frown, looking a bit like our shaman had done when called upon to interpret the prophecy. Jamukha's gaze flickered over my half-sisters – who flushed as they recognized him too – and finally came to rest on me. It made my heart pound even harder for, unlike my spirit journey when I'd last seen him, this time I was not hiding inside Whisper's body.

"Borta, little deer?" Papa's voice came from far away. "Do you remember Jamukha of the Jadaran clan? It seems he's done some growing up since he had to leave us so suddenly. He's come back to apologise for what he did before, and the good news is that he's now—"

"Temujin's anda," I whispered.

Papa blinked at me in surprise. Altani and Orbei exchanged excited glances, but I no longer had any thought to spare for my family or friends. My mouth had gone dry. The way Jamukha looked at me made my legs go weak and my heart begin to thud all over again.

"What are you doing here?" I demanded, not caring if it sounded rude.

Jamukha's forehead creased a little. "My Anda Temujin sent me." His new deep voice was smooth and polished as a river pebble, and I knew straight away he had not changed one bit, in spite of what he might have told Papa. "As I've just been telling your wise father, your promised husband is fine and healthy. I left him camped with his family up the Onan river. He's head of his clan now that his half-brother Begter is dead, but he's keeping a low profile until he has enough warriors to challenge Kiriltuk for leadership of the Alliance, so he couldn't come himself."

He offered me a smile as smooth as his words. Not fooled, I raised my chin and gave him my fiercest shaman look. "How convenient for you."

"See?" Orbei whispered to Altani, apparently having decided Jamukha's charm and good looks made up for his past behaviour. "Told you Temujin wouldn't forget her, didn't I? Oh, isn't it romantic?"

Papa shushed her.

"I've just collected these lads for Anda Temujin," Jamukha continued, ignoring my comment. "So I thought I'd come and collect his wife as well on my way back . . . stun two marmots with one stone as they say on the steppe."

He stared directly at me.

My head started spinning again, and I felt the trap closing. *One stone.* Jamukha couldn't have made his message any clearer. I thought of that stone flying out of the trees at our betrothal ceremony, and wondered if he'd been aiming at Temujin that day or me.

But Papa, who knew nothing of slyly thrown stones, beamed. "You see, Borta! Yesugei the Brave's son has not forgotten you, after all."

Jamukha watched me closely. As his gaze held mine, I saw the hunger in his eyes again. My skin prickled.

"But will Temujin be khan, now his papa's dead and the Taychuit chief has stolen all his people?" I challenged him. "Because if he's not going to be khan, the treaty doesn't mean anything any more, and I don't have to marry him, so I don't have to go with you even if you are his anda now." I still hoped Jamukha might have lied about that.

Papa frowned at me. Fortunately, not many of our clan were close enough to hear, but Altani and Orbei gaped at me.

"Borta!" Orbei said. "That's hardly fair."

"She didn't mean it," Altani said. "She's just upset because Temujin didn't come to collect her himself."

My half-sister had no idea. Clearly not even our shaman could see the danger lurking in Temujin's anda.

Jamukha's hand closed possessively about mine. "I'll look after you, Borta," he said in his smooth voice. "I promise."

The place between my legs where my moon-blood came gave a throb as his finger stroked my palm. His eyes held mine a heartbeat longer, and his lips twitched into a little smile as if he knew exactly what his touch had done to my body.

It was too much. Memories, dreams and spirit visions blurred into one. Jamukha trying to kiss me that time on the riverbank . . . Jamukha betraying Temujin to the fat chief in my vision . . . Papa's dream that said the wolf will lie with the deer . . .

"I'm not going anywhere with a traitor like *you*!" I yelled.

Not caring what anyone thought, I snatched my hand free, grabbed up my deel so I wouldn't trip over it and fled into the forest.

Oh, there would be trouble when I returned! Not only had I ruined all hope of making Jamukha respect me as a princess, but I'd disgraced Papa before his visitors, and probably broken the marriage treaty into the bargain. None of that mattered. I needed Whisper. I *needed* her. So I did the silliest thing possible. I curled up between the roots of an ancient tree and sent my spirit out into the dark. Only I couldn't find my pet. And then, when I tried to return, I couldn't find my body either.

I spun helplessly in that terrifying darkness for what seemed like years. Then the shamans began to beat their drums for our Red Circle feast, and my spirit found its way out of the void and slipped into the body of a wild deer.

I see a large camp noisily celebrating Red Circle Night, obscured by drifting red smoke. At first I think it is Papa's camp, swollen in size by our visitors, but there are more tents than I have ever seen in one place before, and I can see Temujin floating facedown in the river wearing a wooden cangue.

Fearing my promised husband is dead, my spirit howls in protest. But then he begins to splash towards the bank, and hope returns. "Temujin!" I scream. "Temujin!"

Of course he can't hear me. I know I should go back to my own body while the drums are still beating to show me the way. Yet stubbornly I want to see what happens next.

A tall girl approaches, leading a horse. She releases Temujin from the cangue and they exchange a kiss. A stab of jealousy goes through me, making the deer whose body I share throw up its head, and in that moment I see the huge silver-blue wolf standing on the far side of the river.

The girl looks round in alarm and freezes. Men are poking the reeds with their spears, slowly coming closer with their dogs. Any moment now, they will see her and Temujin.

"Help him!" I order the wolf with all the shaman strength I've built up over the winter.

The wolf's eyes fix on me.

"If you don't help Temujin right now, I'll NEVER lie with you!" I add.

Maybe that wasn't a very clever thing to say. The wolf howls at the red moon and leaps across the river towards my terrified deer. The men point at it in excitement, snatching the bows off their shoulders. The dogs come racing towards us, and I remember the shaman's warning about getting trapped inside an animal's body when it dies. But just before they reach us, the distant call of a horse-skull violin curls around my spirit and tugs it back across the forest to my own body.

The drumming in our camp had stopped, and the night had given way to dawn. Early mist curled between the trees, and something rustled in the undergrowth. I felt sure it was the spirit wolf, come back to savage me, or – worse – Jamukha come to do the same. My body curled itself into a tight ball.

Then something brushed my cheek, and I saw two anxious faces looking down at me . . . Altani and Orbei. I managed a smile to let them know I was alive, but it died on my lips as my half-sisters drew back to be replaced by the shaman's scowl. He passed his skull violin to Altani and stood over me with his horse-tailed staff, brushing it lightly against my cheeks and chanting under his breath.

To my relief, my body uncramped. The shaman stepped back. "She's returned to us," he said, looking down at me with an expression that said exactly what he thought of my stupidity. "She'll be all right now. Take her back to the women's yurt, and get her cleaned up before her father sees her."

"No, wait!" I looked round for my half-sisters. "How did you find me?"

Orbei chewed her lip. "Whisper led us to you, Borta . . . we were so scared! You weren't even breathing when we found you. We had to fetch the shaman. We didn't know what else to do."

"Whisper's back?" My heart leapt in joy. Then I remembered why I had been looking for my pet in the first place.

"Has Jamukha left yet?"

Altani shook her head. "He's waiting for you at the camp. He stayed for the Red Circle feast and to help look for you, only he must have drunk too much airag, because he passed out and spent most of the night snoring by the fire. Papa's angry. He says you must apologise to Temujin's anda for running off the way you did. He took Whisper into his yurt, and says you can only have her back if you promise to stop all this spirit nonsense."

It was what I feared most – thanks to my foolishness in thinking I could control the wolf, our secret was a secret no more.

I appealed to the shaman. "Make Papa give Whisper back to me," I whispered. "Please."

"Why should I?" he said. "You've been very foolish. You've been on another spirit journey, haven't you? And on the night of the red moon, when the spirits are at their most powerful, with no one even to watch over your body! The Ancestors only know what damage you've done to your spirit." But he must have seen the desperation on my face, for he sighed and told my half-sisters to go and tell Jamukha I'd see him when I was ready and not before.

When we were alone, he pushed my hair behind my ears. "All right, what did you see this time?"

So I told him about the large camp and my vision of Temujin wearing a cangue floating in the river.

Meanwhile, the shaman paced up and down, stroking the horsetails that hung from his staff. "Hmm," he said. "Yet Jamukha told us Temujin is safe and well with his family in his little camp by the Onan, so it can't have been a true vision."

"Jamukha's lying," I said.

The shaman frowned at me. "I know you don't like the Jadaran boy, Borta, but I'm sure Temujin wouldn't have sworn anda with someone he didn't trust." He looked thoughtfully at the trees. "Considering the way Jamukha scared you when you were younger, your father says we mustn't force you to go with him if you don't want to, but you're disobedient. I've a good mind to tell the lad to take you and be done with it."

The terror of my night in the spirit world caught up with me, and I started to cry. "Please don't," I begged. "I'm sure something bad has happened to Temujin! What if Jamukha plans to take me to his own camp, instead of to my promised husband's?"

The shaman stopped pacing and tipped up my chin with his bony finger. He sighed again. "If that's so, little deer, then there's more to this business than Heaven has shown me. It's possible this wolf spirit you keep seeing hasn't decided yet which boy will lie with the doe to found a new nation. The Mongols need a strong khan, and Jamukha seems to have more lads to support him than young Temujin does right now. Sometimes a chief's daughter must swallow her own feelings and make alliances for the sake of her clan."

My stomach twisted in disgust. "No! I'll never lie with a traitor like Jamukha!" The way Jamukha had managed to arouse my body against the wishes of my spirit worried me even more than my vision of Temujin floating facedown in the river.

The shaman watched me carefully. "There are ways to scare off a boy who believes you have the power to speak to the spirits – if you want to scare him off, that is."

I sniffed back my tears. "How?"

He glanced at the camp and chuckled. "You'll work it out. You're a clever girl, despite your foolish behaviour last night."

By the time Jamukha sought me out to say goodbye, I thought I knew how to do it. By then, both Mama and Papa had told me exactly what they thought of me for acting so childishly in front of my promised husband's anda and missing the Red Circle feast. Papa didn't understand exactly where I'd been that night, of course, and Mama was too happy to have me back unharmed to be upset for very long. Altani and Orbei thought it terribly romantic that I'd gone on a spirit journey on Red Circle Night to join Temujin. If they had my talent, they said, they'd have done exactly the same. Then they started arguing over which one of them Jamukha might choose as a wife, now he was Temujin's anda and had grown so handsome.

"Maybe he'll marry both of you," I said, still out of sorts with them for being taken in so totally by Jamukha's charm. My half-sisters, of course, took this to mean the Ancestors had told me so, and raced off for another look at Jamukha, giggling as if they didn't have half a brain between them.

I took a lot of care over my appearance for my second meeting with Temujin's anda. I even threaded a bit of white horsetail into my hair to remind him I was a powerful shaman now, and not the frightened girl I'd been when he left us.

Jamukha looked at it in amusement. "Anda Temujin thinks he's getting a wife to bear his sons," he said. "Not a wife who speaks to the spirits."

My cheeks grew hot. We were beside the river, where his friends had already mounted and were holding his horse nearby. It was a public enough place, so I thought I would be safe, yet Jamukha had somehow steered me up the bank so that a pile of boulders hid us from the camp.

When we were alone, he caught my wrist and leaned

so close the feathers in his braids tickled my cheek. "Anda Temujin doesn't realize what he's missing," he whispered.

The animal smell coming off him sharpened, making my heart thump. "Keep your hands off me." I kept my voice low and, I hoped, shaman-like. But the truth was that his grip – much firmer than when he'd held my hand yesterday – made my secret place warm and moist. It was like my night in the spirit world with the wolf, terrifying and yet strangely exciting at the same time.

Jamukha smiled, as if he sensed what I was thinking. "What are you going to do, Borta? Scream for help again?"

"I . . ." My voice would not seem to work properly.

"If you were a real shaman, you wouldn't need help to get rid of me. But I don't think you want help, do you? You can feel it, too. Neither of us are children any more." He pulled me even closer, until I smelt the curds he'd eaten for breakfast warm and rich on his breath. Then his lips touched mine.

The pounding of my heart drowned out everything else. Vaguely, I was aware of Whisper's fear from inside Papa's yurt: *Flee, flee, for the wolf comes!*

With an effort, I pulled my lips away from Jamukha's and shoved at his chest with my other hand. I could hardly get my breath. "No! This isn't going to happen."

Jamukha was breathing heavily, too. His fingers tightened on my wrist. He had a peculiar look in his eye, and I was afraid he would try what he had tried before, more or less in this very place, two years ago.

But he must have realized that if he did, Papa would not forgive him a second time. His lips twisted up at one corner as he let me go. "No, you're right. After all, you're my anda's promised wife. We must do things properly. But if something were to happen to Anda Temujin, you'd be free to marry me. It would almost be expected of us. Now we are anda, Temujin and I share everything." His smile broadened. He smoothed my hair back into place, his finger lingering in the curl of my braid.

I thought of the spirit visions I'd had of him, and jerked free.

"You won't share everything for long," I blurted out. "Not when I tell Temujin how you betrayed him!"

Jamukha froze for two heartbeats. Then the fear in his eyes melted into his easy laugh. "Blue Wolf's balls, Borta! I do believe you might have a shaman's power, after all. You had me worried for a moment, there. I'll be back soon with my anda to see you married, deer girl."

He patted my cheek, then picked up his bow and strode over to where his friends waited with the horses, leaving me flustered and confused. My head was spinning so fast I could barely think. How dare he treat me like a child and then turn his back on me?

"I saw you with my spirit-eye!" I called after him. "Talking to that fat Taychuit chief."

Jamukha hesitated, then shook his head and laughed. "So? Travellers exchange news on the steppe, you know that. Been spying on me like a lovesick girl, have you?

Maybe you'd prefer to marry me instead of your promised husband?"

How did he manage to turn everything I said around?

"I wouldn't marry you if you were the last man on earth!" I said. "I'm promised to Temujin . . . *and whoever takes away my shaman powers will be cursed for ever!*" I shouted after him, making his friends glance at one another and smile.

I never meant for anyone else to hear that, not really. Certainly, I never meant for Whisper to escape from Papa's yurt, bound past me and spook their horses. Several of them shied and took off at a gallop with Jamukha's lads cursing and sawing at their mouths. Jamukha hauled his gelding around, shooed the doe away with his bow and looked down at me with those shadowed eyes of his, until I drew my deel around my shoulders and shivered in memory of the almost-kiss we'd shared.

"I don't think either of us is going to tell Temujin about today, are we?" he said.

Then he chuckled and galloped after his friends, leaving me furious and scared and feeling like a little girl again.

That hadn't gone how I'd planned. Not at all.

- 6 -

YEAR OF THE
MONKEY

LATER THAT YEAR, two young warriors from the Alliance turned up bringing news that my promised husband was alive and had taken refuge on Holy Mountain. They said their sister Khadagan had sent them to tell me not to worry, because Temujin had friends among the clans who would support him as Yesugei the Brave's heir.

When they told us how the Taychuit chief Kiriltuk had captured Temujin and paraded him about their camp in a cangue, a shiver went through me. It seemed my Red Circle Night vision had been at least partly true, and I breathed a sigh of relief that my promised husband had escaped his captivity unharmed. But the shaman's theory about the wolf having not yet decided which boy would lie with the doe to create a new nation worried me. After Jamukha's visit and what I'd seen in my spirit visions, I knew it was up to me to make sure the wolf chose Temujin, rather than his anda, to fulfil the prophecy.

I spent the cold winter nights tossing and turning in my furs, worrying at my problem as a dog worries at a bone. To be of any real use to my husband, I would need to be in his camp in body as well as spirit. That meant going through with our marriage, and yet somehow keeping my shaman powers intact until Temujin was officially named khan by his people. Would he understand this? And if his touch aroused my body against my wishes as Jamukha's had so nearly done, would my spirit be strong enough to refuse him? Somehow, I had to find that strength.

Then a daring thought came to me. I could control an animal . . . so why not a man?

Whenever I could sneak away, I quietly practised on the sables destined for my marriage deel. With just a few little nudges from my spirit, the surprised creatures kept clear of our traps. As I said before, sables are clever animals.

"Heaven obviously doesn't mean us to finish your dowry just yet, Borta," Mama told me with a disappointed sigh as she lifted yet another empty trap. "Seems you'll have to be patient for a bit longer."

I acted miserable, but secretly felt quite proud of myself. None of my clan realized what I was doing, not even the shaman.

Encouraged by my success, I tried the same trick on Papa's spirit, trying to persuade him to release Whisper. But controlling a man's spirit proved much harder than controlling the sables, and my pet stayed in an enclosure behind his yurt, where he could keep an eye on her to make sure I didn't try any more spirit journeys.

Finally, the shaman summoned me to his tent. I went by daylight this time since we no longer had need for secrecy, my heart beating fast. Whisper's enclosure had been empty when I'd passed it.

"Has Papa . . . ?" I began in sudden fear, looking round for the doe.

He raised his hand to silence me. "Thanks to your foolishness last Red Circle Night, you should know Dei the Wise has asked me to make sure you never go on a spirit journey again."

I stared at him in horror. What if Papa had felt my spirit pushing against his, and decided to punish me by ordering the shaman to kill my pet so I could never use her body again? He wouldn't understand about the wild deer and the spirits under the red moon.

"It wasn't all foolishness. I spoke to the wolf that night . . ."

The shaman's tone softened. "Don't look at me like that, child. I think you know I'm not going to do anything of the sort. Your husband will make sure enough of that when he comes to claim you, which I'm sure he will do very soon now once his anda tells him you're waiting for him. In the meantime, I suggest you confine your spirit journeys to your pet deer, and keep her close to camp so your father doesn't notice. It was hard work to call you back to your body last year, and without the red moon to boost my powers I doubt I could have managed it. I thought we'd lost you."

A shiver went through me. "You mean I can have Whisper back?"

"I told your father your little deer is pining for you." The shaman pulled aside a curtain, and I saw my pet sleeping in the back of his yurt. Relief filled me. I put my arms around the doe's neck and buried my face in her warm, musky smell.

"Thank you," I whispered, hiding my smile. My efforts to influence Father's spirit must have helped free my deer, after all.

The shaman sighed. "It's my fault for turning you into a wild animal, when Heaven clearly means you for other things. Be a good girl when Temujin comes, and make your mother happy by giving her some healthy grandchildren, hmm?"

The grandchildren would have to wait. How could I help Temujin be khan if I let him take away my powers? But to make up for my disobedience in training with the shaman and angering the Ancestors on Red Circle Night, I decided Papa would have no reason to be ashamed of me when Yesugei the Brave's son finally arrived to claim me.

Now I'd made up my mind I must marry Temujin, I needed to make sure he still liked me enough to make me his wife. The shaman's comment about me turning into a wild animal worried me. I pulled a twig out of my hair and examined my dirty fingernails. I sniffed under my armpits. Not exactly flowers.

So I enlisted the help of my half-sisters and stayed behind when the other girls went foraging in the forest. I spent that winter of the Monkey beating milk and learning the tricks women used to make their hair glossy, their skin smooth, and their cheeks glow. I found it all very boring and terribly silly, but that didn't mean I couldn't learn.

Mama was pleased and told me I was turning into a real princess at last. As a reward, she gave me one of her most trusted servants – which was just as well, really, since I found it impossible to braid and loop my hair into ladylike styles on my own. With old Khoga's help and my spirit no longer scaring the sables away, we finally finished the beautiful deel that would be my dowry.

Trusting Heaven to bring me the right boy this time, I prepared my spirit for what I must do, and waited.

- 7 -

YEAR OF THE HEN

TO MY RELIEF, Temujin had not changed very much. He had grown, of course, but not tall and lanky like Jamukha. The nine-year-old boy I remembered had become a young warrior with impressive muscles and a man's knotted braids. The way he rode his horse and ordered his surviving half-brother Belgutei around hinted that his confidence had grown to match his body, yet he still had the same grin that had persuaded me into a saddle when I'd been ten years old. The moment I saw that grin again, I knew my plan was going to be even more difficult than I'd thought.

We got married on Red Circle Day. I barely noticed the feast, though Papa had made an effort and slaughtered half of our oxen for the occasion. The food stuck in my throat, and I could not swallow my portion of the tough old sheep we had to chew in public to show our marriage would be strong. I hid the meat in my mouth and spat it out into my hand later when nobody was watching. I don't think

Temujin noticed. He was too busy trying to explain why he had killed his elder half-brother Begter for insulting me.

When the shaman blessed our union, he gave me a curious look, maybe wondering if I'd changed my mind about the grandchildren. I smiled sweetly at him around my mouthful of tough meat and let Mama place the bridal deel on my shoulders, while Papa gave Temujin a quiver full of fine arrows fletched with eagle's feathers. The black sable fur I'd spent all winter sewing was too hot for summer, but I clutched it close, wishing that the sables were still alive. Then they might have carried my spirit far away from our camp so I would not have to be in my body tonight.

As the afternoon wore on, I grew very nervous and could tell Temujin was, too. By then he'd drunk a bit too much airag, and I was sweating under my ceremonial deel. I dreaded the time when everyone would leave us alone and I had to explain to my new husband why I couldn't go any further than a kiss – and even the thought of kissing him scared me, after my experience with Jamukha.

As the clods of dung hit us, showering us with brown powder, Temujin grinned at me. Dung thrown at newlyweds often still has slime in the middle, so I suppose we were lucky. He pulled down the strings of flowers tied across the door and put his hand on my back to encourage me inside. He kept running his fingers through the sable, as if it aroused him.

Inside the yurt, my family had been busy. A bed awaited us, strewn with petals and branches of pine and piled high with sheepskins. A jug of airag, two cups, and the rest of our marriage feast had been placed nearby in case we got hungry and thirsty during the night. Even though it was summer, a fire crackled in the central pit filling the yurt with smoke that soon had Temujin tugging at the neck of his tunic.

I clutched my bridal deel close. I knew I should tell him now, before things went any further. "Temujin," I began. "I'm not sure if—"

He wrestled me down on to the sheepskins before I could say any more, still tangled in the sable fur, and kissed me hard on the mouth. It was not at all like Jamukha's kiss. It tasted different for one thing – smoky and nice – and the firmness of his grip excited rather than scared me. I grew hotter and yet more sweaty and wished he'd hurry up and strip off the fur so we could get on with being husband and wife. Then I remembered we couldn't go any further tonight if I was to keep my shaman powers.

Before I could change my mind, I wriggled out from under him and slapped him hard on the cheek.

He raised himself to his knees and blinked at me in surprise, while I lay panting in the fur thinking: *idiot, idiot*! I'd done it all wrong. I'd struck Yesugei the Brave's son, future Khan of all the Mongols! Now he'd fling me to the floor and have his way with me, and I'd be lucky if he didn't slap me, too, to teach me some manners. The look on his face just then certainly said he'd like to.

I got scared then – for him, as well as for me. In

desperation, I used my shaman powers to push at my new husband's spirit. It was more difficult than it had been with Papa, or with the sables last year, but it worked.

When I slipped back into my own body, Temujin was sitting on the edge of the bed frowning at me, and I could see his desire had shrivelled.

I wriggled the rest of the way out of the fur, got to my feet and tugged my wedding tunic straight. With deliberate care, I draped the valuable deel over a stool at the side of the yurt and said, "We shouldn't use my dowry as a bedspread."

"No," Temujin agreed in a flat voice. "You're right. It'd be a shame to stain such a valuable fur. It'll buy us many warriors."

I felt horribly guilty about what I'd done to him. Still wary, I perched on the edge of the bed beside my husband and tried to explain. I'm still not sure what I said. Some half-truth about not being ready for marriage yet, and it taking away a girl's power to speak with the spirits.

He deserved more than that.

"You haven't got a shaman in your camp, have you?" I went on. "I could be useful to you, maybe find out who poisoned your papa—"

"No!" he said with a growl that scared me. "I already know who killed my father. The Tartars did it, and when I'm khan I'm going to make them sorry."

"Don't be angry with me, Temujin, please," I whispered. "We can cuddle if you like, it's just the other thing I'm not ready for . . ."

He wasn't listening. I realized he was looking at Whisper's shadow, where my pet trotted nervously up and down outside the yurt.

"Your stupid deer's still out there, isn't it?" he said in an irritated tone.

"It's all right, she won't come inside," I told him. "I've trained her not to."

"Might as well have done," he muttered, and turned his back on me with a grunt of frustration.

We didn't speak again that night. I lay stiffly beside him, closed my eyes and pretended to sleep, while he got busy working off his pent-up frustration the only way I'd left to him. It made his smoky smell stronger, and I wanted to touch his hot flesh and say I'd changed my mind. But by then it was too late.

I'd used my shaman powers to shrivel my husband's spirit on our wedding night. No wonder Heaven punished me for my actions that day.

I'd planned to confront Temujin about Jamukha as soon as we left my father's camp, and there was no chance of anyone from my clan overhearing. But Mama and most of my family insisted on accompanying us across the steppe to see me safely to my new home. Khoga and I travelled in the yak cart with the women, while Temujin rode at the front, laughing and joking with his brothers and the other lads, so speaking to my husband in private was impossible.

Where I'd expected Jamukha to go after I'd refused to

accompany him last year, I'm not sure. I suppose I'd hoped he would stay with the Taychuit chief and his new friends in the Alliance. But the anda bond is strong. I was still trying to work out what I would say to my new husband once we were alone so he wouldn't think I was acting the jealous wife. The last thing I wanted was for Temujin to take my words as an invitation to prove he loved me more than he loved his anda, by the very means I wanted to avoid.

So I ignored the warnings from my spirit as we approached Temujin's Holy Mountain camp, putting my cold sweat down to the ghosts that were supposed to haunt this place. By the time I realized what my shaman senses had been trying to warn me about, my husband was in the arms of the last person in the whole world I wanted to see again.

While Temujin's mama welcomed me and my family to her camp, the boys disappeared into Temujin's tent. I imagined my husband telling them all about our wedding night, and my ears burned with shame and the fear that Mama would find out. I was sure my hasty attempt, the morning after, to stain our marriage sheepskins with blood from my arm hadn't fooled old Khoga. She'd given me a very funny look when she saw them, though she'd held her tongue and passed the soiled bedding to the giggling younger servants to be displayed about my father's camp in the usual way before being washed.

Whatever the boys talked about in there, Temujin emerged full of a new plan to take my dowry to the Kereyid camp as a gift and ask their powerful khan for an army to seize back control of the Alliance from the Taychuit chief. It turned out most of his brothers and his crazy friend Boorchu were going with him. Which left Jamukha and his lads to look after me.

Only once, when my family had left and Temujin came to kiss me goodbye, did I really have a chance to say anything out of everyone else's hearing. And then a spirit got my tongue, and all I could say was, "Be careful." As if the son of Yesugei the Brave, leader of his clan and master of the charming grin, was a nine-year-old boy again!

Jamukha lost no time. As soon as my husband and his brothers were safely out of sight, he ordered old Khoga out of my yurt. Then he tied the door flap shut so that Whisper could not get in and I could not get out.

He turned to me with a lazy smile and said, "So, princess! You didn't tell Temujin about our last meeting, after all. I wonder why?"

I wondered why myself. Even as my stomach tied itself in knots as tight as those Jamukha had tied in the lashings at the door, I couldn't think why I hadn't opened my mouth to warn Temujin just as soon as I'd seen Jamukha waiting at his camp.

"What? No answer, princess?" Jamukha's smile widened. He swaggered towards me, tugging at his belt. "I know why you didn't say anything. You're afraid of what your new husband will do if he finds out about us, aren't you?

I must say I'm pleasantly surprised at how you've scrubbed up. Been making yourself beautiful for me, have you?"

"If you touch me, Temujin will know about it," I said.

My tone stopped him. I'd been practising spirit control over the past year, as well as how to make my skin smell of flowers.

But Jamukha's smile did not fade. "Oh, come on, Borta! You know as well as I do Temujin won't suspect a thing, not now you're properly married. If we're going to spend all winter stuck up here together, you could start being a little friendlier. It's not as if you don't feel something for me, too. You can't hide it, you know."

Sweat trickled from my armpits. I hoped he couldn't smell it. Temujin couldn't have told on me, after all, and the thought of our shared secret made me stronger.

"We are not going to spend the winter together," I told him firmly. "You've got your own shelter. This is my yurt. Mine and Temujin's."

To be fair, I don't think Temujin had been expecting Jamukha to be waiting for us at his camp. But he obviously trusted his anda, and I supposed that meant he must trust me as well. Somehow, I had to get Jamukha to see that and respect it.

Jamukha laughed. "That makes it my yurt as well. Do you really think you can come between me and my anda? We swore the blood bond before Heaven. That's just as sacred as any marriage bond." He raised his scarred thumb to show me the proof.

"If you don't leave me alone, I'll tell Temujin how you betrayed him to the Taychuit chief," I said quietly. "I know it was you who told him about Begter's death and where to find Temujin's camp. You hoped Chief Kiriltuk would execute my husband so you could be khan yourself, didn't you?"

Now he'd either deny it, or try to convince me my spirit vision had been wrong. Either way, I'd discover if my suspicions were correct. I didn't expect him to be so confident of his position that he'd admit to the truth.

He reclined on the couch, rested an ankle on his knee and one arm along the back, and considered me.

"We'd better clear the air here," he explained. "So maybe I did pass on a bit of information to Chief Kiriltuk, but only so I could help my anda. He needed lads, so I got him lads. You don't think lads follow people for nothing, do you? They follow the brave and resourceful, who might make them rich one day. Anda Temujin understands the way the world works as well as I do. That's why he killed his half-brother Begter, and why he kept the marriage treaty his father made with your father. He doesn't care two marmots for you, princess. That sable deel of yours will buy him an army, see if it doesn't. Same with old Kiriltuk. I just used him to get my hands on some trained warriors so Anda Temujin won't get himself killed when we raid the Tartar camps to avenge his father's death."

I'd been edging towards the door, wondering if I could

get the flap untied before he grabbed me. But this made me pause.

"Temujin did *not* marry me just for my dowry!" I said. "He came back because he's honourable, and because . . . because he loves me."

Jamukha's words had put doubts in my mind, though. Was love really the reason Temujin had killed his half-brother for insulting me, and respected my wishes in our marriage yurt? Or had he respected them because, as Jamukha claimed, he had only married me to get his hands on my dowry and didn't care for my girl's heart at all? And why did any of it matter, anyway, since I hadn't married Temujin for love, only to help him fulfil the prophecy and become khan so that I wouldn't have to marry his smooth-talking anda!

As I flushed in confusion, Jamukha watched me with his infuriating smile. Then he laughed out loud. "You really believe that, don't you? I guess Temujin hasn't told you what he got up to while he was a captive in old Kiriltuk's camp?"

"What?" I whispered, remembering the girl I'd seen on the riverbank in my Red Circle spirit vision.

"Thought not." Jamukha removed his boots one by one and stood them neatly at the end of the couch. His eyes flashed in amusement. "A girl in every yurt? Not heard about that yet, have you? If you ask me, my anda rather enjoyed his captivity."

I felt a bit sick.

"So you see, princess," he went on. "You're not so special.

Temujin won't mind us getting together one bit, you'll see. Why do you think he left me to look after you? He knows you'll be lonely up here without him while he's enjoying all those Kereyid girls . . ."

Still I stood there, not wanting to believe him, yet only too able to imagine Temujin tumbling the Kereyid girls in the furs to punish me for refusing him.

Like a snake, Jamukha's arm flashed out and caught the end of my braid. He pulled me towards him and managed to jam his lips against mine and push his tongue between my teeth before I could stop him.

My body trembled. My spirit floated out of it, in danger of slipping into Whisper's. With a huge effort, I made myself stay in the yurt with Jamukha. His eyes were closed. He actually groaned with desire. Horror of what we were doing made my heart pound. I couldn't bear touching his spirit the way I had touched Temujin's, but I gave it a quick bump as I returned to my body.

He blinked at me and his lips twisted up at one corner. "You're like a wild filly," he said. "You need a leash to tame you." When he let go of my braid to fumble with the cord that held up his trousers, I seized my chance to knee him in the groin and pulled free.

"Get out," I said, drawing myself up to my full height and summoning all of my shaman strength. "Get out of my yurt and don't come back! I warned you once before what will happen to the man who takes away my shaman powers. I won't warn you again."

Jamukha scowled at me, doubled over in pain and breathing hard. For a moment I thought he might try to grab me again and braced myself for a spirit battle. Then he went very still. He gave me a wary look and said, "The man who takes your powers . . . ? Are you saying what I think you're saying?"

Only then did I realize my mistake. "I . . . we . . . what I mean is . . ."

Jamukha's eyes opened wide. "Blue Wolf's balls, Borta! I know you didn't have much time together before Temujin rode off to find his army, but I'm surprised at my anda, I must say! Even if he doesn't love a hair of your head, you're pretty enough to fire the arrows of any man on his wedding night."

His disgusting talk roused my anger all over again, and this time I gave his spirit a stinging slap. "OUT!"

"All right, all right. I'm going." Jamukha gave me a frustrated frown.

He took his time pulling on his boots and doing up his belt. Probably so he could recover his dignity before he went out to face his friends. I didn't hurry him, because I needed time to compose myself as well. My face must have been glowing like the red moon, judging by the heat of my cheeks. But maybe, just maybe, my slip of the tongue would help. With Jamukha scared of his anda finding out if he forced me to lie with him, he might leave me alone until Temujin returned.

He brushed my lips with his finger as he stood, and I

clenched my fists as my body tingled in response . . . how did he *do* that?

He gave me another wary look and shook his head in amazement. "You and Temujin honestly haven't . . . ?" He must have thought I was going to hit him again, for he raised his hands and backed off. "Don't worry, I'm not stupid. You're a princess, pure as the new snow outside, so we can't take a tumble in the furs without Temujin finding out, can we? Maybe my anda doesn't trust me that much, after all." He chuckled. "I can see it's going to be a long winter for both of us."

He shook his head at me again and ducked out of the yurt without another word. Whisper trotted inside. I let the flap drop, and all the strength ran out of me. Trembling, I put my arms around my pet's neck and buried my face in her deer smell.

- 8 -

YEAR OF THE DOG

I'D NEVER SPENT such an awful winter. I'd thought no winter could seem longer than those I'd spent in my father's camp waiting for my promised husband to come and claim me as his bride. I was wrong. I didn't know what my refusing Jamukha would lead to, or maybe I would have let him into my yurt one of those cold, snowy nights and everything would have been different. But then my husband might never have got the support of the Kereyid army, and the wolf might not have . . . oh, I don't know! It makes my head ache just to think about it.

Anyway, that winter of the Dog I dared not go on a single spirit journey. The moment my spirit left my body, I felt sure Jamukha would take advantage of it. He mostly avoided me during the day. But when our paths crossed, and he thought no one was looking, he'd brush my hand with his. Sometimes he'd simply catch my gaze and stare at me with his hungry eyes, until warmth leaked between my legs and I had to pick up the hem of my deel and flee.

I shivered under my sheepskins at night, missing my family and wondering what Temujin was getting up to in the Kereyid Khan's camp. After Jamukha's taunts, I couldn't help imagining my husband with all those Kereyid girls eager to give him what I could not. Oh, how I hated those girls! But, most of all, I hated myself for what I had done to my husband on our wedding night. The Ancestors must have truly cursed me when they gave me my shaman talents.

I don't know what Temujin's mama made of it all, but old Khoga did not spare me her opinion. "You watch that Jadaran lad, Lady Borta!" she told me. "He's a sly one, running to your promised husband the way he did after Dei the Wise banished him from our camp. I wouldn't trust him as far as a lame yak can kick."

I wouldn't have trusted Jamukha nearly that far, but it seemed we were stuck with each other until my husband and his brothers returned.

By spring I'd lost weight, and even Temujin's mama had given up all hope that I carried her first grandchild. Jamukha had kept his distance lately, and I rather hoped he wouldn't speak to me again before Temujin returned. But, one bright morning when old Khoga had gone to the stream for water, he raised the flap of my yurt and looked inside.

He had caught me undressed. Khoga's warnings about how spring made boys as randy as stags made my head spin, and my heart started banging like a war drum. I prepared my spirit for another battle. But Jamukha wore full riding gear with his bow slung across his back. When he looked at the sheepskin I'd clutched across my breasts, his fist merely tightened a little on the felt.

"I'm taking my lads up into the hills to meet Anda Temujin," he said. "If he gets back here before I do, tell him I've gone hunting and I'll return when he sends for me." He gave me a narrow-eyed look. "Though if I were you, I wouldn't tell your husband the truth about us, or you might find *your* little secret spread across the entire steppe. Where will that leave your precious husband, when he calls on our brave Mongol lads to follow him? No one wants a khan whose wife refuses to give him heirs. Even the marmots will be laughing at him." He ducked out again before I could think of a reply.

"If you're thinking of betraying Temujin again, I'll know!" I called after him, rushing to the flap with the sheepskin still clutched around me. "I'm a shaman. I can send my spirit to spy on you, remember?"

Jamukha's shoulders stiffened. But with a wave of his hand, he ordered his friends to take down their shelters. Then his whole troop went trotting off into the forest taking most of the horses with them.

The sensible thing would have been to send Whisper after Jamukha straight away to see where he went. But I was worried he might order his lads to shoot my pet on sight. Besides, we expected Temujin to come riding triumphantly into camp any day with the Kereyid army, and I wanted a chance to warn my husband about Jamukha while his anda was not around to complicate things. The only useful thing I could do was to use Whisper's eyes to watch the trails so that we'd have advance warning of any raiding parties. So I became a deer again, while old Khoga looked after my body in the patched and sagging yurt.

I felt so exhausted by my spirit journeys on top of a whole winter of fending off Jamukha, it was hardly surprising that, when the attack came, I couldn't summon a drop of shaman magic to help anyone, least of all myself. I had sent Whisper the opposite way that morning, watching for Temujin's return from the Kereyid steppe. By the time my spirit sensed something was wrong and fled back to my body in panic, a party of armed warriors was galloping towards our camp.

I sent old Khoga to warn everyone while I dragged on my clothes. Temujin's mama barely got away with the little ones, and then Temujin's younger brother Alchidai insisted on staying behind to help me on to the yellow mare, even though he knew my lack of riding skills would slow him down.

Just about everything went wrong. With Jamukha's lads gone, there weren't enough horses for everyone. Belgutei's mama and Khoga had to take their chances in the yak cart. My spirit was still weak and confused after its night in Whisper's deer body, so I didn't have the strength to protest.

"Hold on to the mane!" Alchidai shouted. "I'll lead you."

He urged his horse into a gallop. Khoga gave the mare a whack on the backside, and she leapt forwards with me clinging on to her patchy mane. She didn't feel at all steady at such a pace. I didn't even have a saddle, because there had been no time to strap one on, and it was the fastest I'd ever ridden on horseback.

The trees rushed towards us, bruising my knees as we galloped through them. Leaves whipped my face and made my eyes water. I crouched over the mare's neck in terror of being knocked off by a low branch. Even though Alchidai was still leading me, he didn't seem to be in control of either horse.

We somehow got to the top of the slope unscathed, and then Whisper came bounding out of a thicket ahead of us terrified by the yelling raiders. Alchidai's horse spooked and went one side of a tree, while mine went the other. The reins ripped out of Alchidai's hand and caught around the mare's legs. She stumbled to her knees. Leaves, sky and hooves whirled around me. Then the trunk of a tree rushed up at me, I heard a loud crack and my spirit left my body.

The next thing I knew, I lay in a patch of brambles, while Whisper trotted around me in agitated circles. The mare had already scrambled to her feet and cantered off. There was blood on the stones where she'd fallen. Alchidai shooed the doe away and looked down at me, his face white. I think he believed the blood mine.

I tried to get up, but my arm buckled in a flare of pain. I looked at it in despair. It was already swelling like a horse's leg after it has stumbled into a marmot hole. The pain made me want to scream, but I bit my tongue.

"I think I've broken my arm," I said as calmly as I could, holding it across my breasts. It's a shaman skill, to control the body when your spirit is screaming.

"You can still ride if you get up behind me," Alchidai said. But he knew as well as I did that we wouldn't have a chance of getting away double on his horse, especially if I couldn't hold on.

Old Khoga turned out to have more sense than any of us that morning. She had been following us along the track, seen me fall, and came puffing up the slope to help. She took one look at my arm, bundled me into the yak cart and pulled the sheepskins over me to hide me from the raiders.

We still didn't know who the men were at that stage. I only knew I didn't want them to find me, and lay in terror under the heavy wool, holding my broken arm and trying not to whimper every time the cart jolted it. I'd never broken anything before, and the shock of it made me feel sick. I knew Whisper was following us, but felt too weak to try a spirit journey, and I didn't want the men to find my body while I was out of it.

When the cart stopped, it was almost a relief, though we hadn't gone nearly far enough to be safe. I heard male voices. Khoga was trying to convince the raiding party she had nothing of value in the back of her cart. I held my breath, worried about Whisper. If they saw my pet, they might think she was a wild deer and put an arrow in her. I hoped she would have the sense to stay hidden in the trees.

Khoga seemed to have fooled them, for the cart jolted forwards again. Relief washed over me. Then Belgutei's mama's shrill voice called: "Don't let her go, you fools! She's got Temujin's young wife hidden in there!" and the raiders galloped after us again.

I heard Khoga yell angrily at Belgutei's mother as the men pulled her down from the cart. I wanted to tell them not to hurt my servant, but terror stole my words. I suppose I hoped they still wouldn't find me, that the Ancestors would help me like the wolf spirit had helped Temujin escape from his cangue on Red Circle Night the year before we were married. But there were no miracles that day. The sheepskins lifted, dazzling me with sunlight, and a warrior's hard face with a scar across one cheek peered in.

He looked at me in a way that made my stomach shrivel with fear, because this man was a lot older than Jamukha and not bound by any of our Mongol codes. "Ah-ha!" he chuckled. "I think I see a pretty little doe hiding in here! Come on out and say hello to your new clan, Temujin's young wife."

He grabbed my broken arm, and I screamed with pain.

You might think, being shaman trained, I could escape any time; that my spirit could just leave my body at will, and I wouldn't feel a thing they did to me. But it's not like that. To start with, all the nights I had kept watch over our camp since Jamukha left had exhausted me. Also, I dared not flee in spirit for fear of what the men might do to my body while I was gone from it. There was a third reason, too, which I was soon to learn the hard way – the dark thing Papa's shaman had hidden from me the first time I'd disobeyed him, in case he ever had to use it to control me. But there on Holy Mountain, a bride who had not yet sealed the wedding bond, I was still such an innocent.

"Stop it!" Khoga cried. "Can't you see she's hurt? Borta, my lady . . . don't worry, they won't dare harm you."

"Don't count on it, old woman!" growled the man who had hold of me, obviously the chief of the raiding party. But he transferred his grip to my other wrist, and the pain eased slightly. I sniffed back my sobs and tried to give his spirit a nudge, which wasn't easy with my hair still mussed from the sheepskins and green stains on my clothes from my fall. It didn't have much effect.

Another man trotted up with Belgutei's mama hanging facedown over the withers of his horse. She was protesting loudly at her treatment. Khoga spat at her. I couldn't really blame my servant for her anger, though it made me want to cry. Why had Belgutei's mama given us away like that? Then I remembered how Temujin had killed her eldest son before he returned to marry me. Revenge is a terrible thing.

"So you're the famous Borta the deer girl, who will lie with the wolf to found a new nation?" said my captor, beckoning one of the younger members of the raiding party across. "Here, Younger Brother Chilger, I've a present for you! Temujin's young wife in exchange for the girl his father stole from me twenty years ago. That ungrateful old mare seems to have run off into the forest with her brood, but this one's still an unbroken filly. Take good care of her. We don't want the Mongols stealing her back again."

It was only when he said this that I realized our captors must be the Murdering Merkids. I wondered at the chief's words. *Unbroken filly* . . . had Jamukha spread our secret across half the steppe already? An uncontrollable shivering came over me, and I was afraid I might burst into tears in front of them if I tried to speak.

When the young Merkid they called Chilger trotted his horse close to me, I shrank back in fear that it would knock my injured arm. "Hello, Borta," he said. At my wary look, he laughed. He leant out of his saddle to grab one of my mussed braids and clumsily tried to kiss me.

"If you do that again, you'll die," I told him in my iciest tone, though my knees felt so weak I thought I'd fall under the hooves of his horse. "You should know I've trained as a shaman."

He eyed me sideways, and the Merkid Khan laughed. "Take her back to your tent, Chilger, and teach her the duties of a wife. Someone take that old woman, too. The rest of you, come with me. Maybe we'll catch the others, and then you can have Temujin's little sister as well when she's old enough."

"You won't find Temujin's family," I said, trying to sound confident. "Heaven will hide them from you."

The Merkid Khan chuckled again. "We're not superstitious Mongols who believe boys can turn into wolves! Don't worry, my pretty Borta, if we kill Temujin you won't be without a husband for long." Still chuckling, he galloped off with his warriors, leaving the three of us with Chilger and his lads.

If we women had worked together then, we might have got away. I could have got Whisper to spook the Merkid horses, and we might have run into the forest and hidden up the deer trails like the rest of Temujin's family. But Belgutei's mama refused to even look at me, Khoga's old bones had been bruised from being pulled off the cart, and I had a broken arm that sent flares of pain and sickness through me whenever it knocked against anything, making my spirit curl up uselessly inside me.

Chilger wasn't a complete monster. He found some twigs to make a rough splint for my arm but he didn't give me a chance to run. He put one of our sheepskins on the back of a spare horse, pulled off my boots and tied my ankles together. Then he slung me over the horse, wrapped me up in the wool as carefully as if I were a valuable bow, and carried me off to the Merkid camp, while his lads hustled Khoga and Belgutei's mama on foot behind us.

Though I tried my best to send my spirit into Whisper's body so I could warn Temujin about the Merkids, the effort proved too much for me and I fainted.

*

I was so scared when I woke up in that enemy camp, you can't imagine! I lay bound inside a dark yurt with the flap tied shut. Judging by all the noise outside, the Merkids were having some sort of celebration. I felt sure Chilger was getting drunk on airag so he would have the courage to risk the "curse" and take away my shaman powers. He had left the sheepskin wrapped around me, so my arm was at least cushioned from further blows. But the pain of my injury, the smothering wool, my bare feet still tied at the ankles, and the guards I could hear exchanging crude jokes outside the door made escape impossible, at least in body.

Spirit, then, it must be spirit – while I still could.

That sort of thinking would not help. I knew the Merkids wouldn't leave me alone for long, so I closed my eyes and took deep breaths to calm myself as Papa's shaman had taught me. I planned to make a quick spirit journey, find Whisper and send her back up the deer trails to Holy Mountain. At least then I'd know if Temujin's family had escaped, and if there was any hope my husband or Jamukha were still alive and might come to my rescue.

But I couldn't do it.

No matter how hard I tried, my spirit remained stubbornly in my body. I lay sweating in terror that Chilger might have already taken away my powers while I'd been unconscious. Never to go on another spirit journey . . . I lost control then and sobbed hopelessly into the sheepskin that bound me.

I don't know how long it was before the door flap lifted and Chilger came back. At some point, I suppose I must have run out of tears and drifted off to sleep, because the sky outside showed a grey dawn. Chilger stared down at me. I stared back at him, my heart banging in my breast. At least he didn't seem to have drunk too much airag. I didn't know if that was a good thing, though.

He knelt beside me and tugged at the bindings that fastened the sheepskin. My whole body went rigid. "If you touch me . . ." It came out as another sob.

He shook his head impatiently. "I'm just letting you sit up so you can eat. You must be really hungry by now. I've brought you some meat left over from the feast. Here." He passed me a piece of cold ox-roast that made me feel sick just to look at and held out a flask of water.

I snatched the flask from him. "Where's Khoga?" I asked, watching him warily as I gulped the water. I was as thirsty as I'd been after my first spirit journey with Whisper in the forest, and this scared me, too. How long had I been asleep? "She should be the one caring for me, not a stranger like you! I'm a married woman . . ." My voice trailed off. I shouldn't have reminded him of that.

He frowned. "Khoga?"

"My servant," I explained. "The old woman your friends dragged off the cart."

Chilger looked at the door flap and gave an apologetic cough. "I'm sorry, but Elder Brother the Khan says you must be kept apart from the other captives."

Another shiver went through me.

"I want my servant in here," I said firmly. "Now! And I want to know what you've done with my husband's family. Did you catch them, too?"

"They're all dead," Chilger said in a flat tone, passing me the flask again. "Temujin's dead, too. Elder Brother's men killed him when he returned to his camp without the Kereyids." He avoided my gaze, so I knew the truth even before I touched his fingers and his spirit showed me.

"That's a lie."

All the same, in the two heartbeats I'd believed it, the news had twisted my stomach and sent me teetering on the edge of a chasm so deep and dark I never wanted to look into it again. The relief was so great – both that he had lied and my power remained – that I swayed, and Chilger reached out to steady me.

"You really care for your husband, don't you?" he said, giving me an interested look.

"What's that to you?" I pushed him away, daring him with my shaman glare to try touching me again, though I really don't know what I could have done about it if he had.

He shrugged. "It's just that these arranged marriages don't always work out. That's why Lady Hogelun didn't try to run back to her husband when Temujin's father stole her from us, isn't it? Elder Brother the Khan's going to arrange a match for me soon to make some clan alliance or another." He gave me a shy look. "I hope my wife loves me as much as you love Temujin, that's all."

I couldn't believe I was discussing love with my Merkid captor, who probably intended to ravish me just as soon as I'd finished my meal. To delay things, I chewed as slowly as I could. The greasy meat stuck in my throat just like the mutton at my wedding feast, but that didn't mean I couldn't pretend to enjoy it. The strange thing was I had never really thought before about *loving* Temujin. That couldn't be true, could it? Certainly, I liked Temujin a whole lot more than I liked Jamukha, but I'd made my choice of who to support as khan for other reasons . . . hadn't I?

Chilger's words confused me, and I felt myself flushing.

He swallowed and stroked my mussed braid. "You're very beautiful when you blush, Borta."

"Get away from me!" I stiffened again, remembering he was the enemy.

He sighed. "I'll see if I can get your servant in here. You're right, Elder Brother didn't find Temujin, and Heaven hid his family on Holy Mountain just like you said. But he told me to tell you they're dead, so you mustn't act as if you know they might not be, all right? You're our bait. If it turns out Temujin cares for you as much as you seem to care for him, he'll try to rescue you, and then we'll kill him and his crazy dream of uniting the Mongol clans under one banner. If he doesn't come for you . . ." He looked shyly at me again. "Elder Brother says I can keep you as a second wife."

"You haven't even got a first wife yet," I pointed out, ripples of relief going through me at this news. They hadn't killed my husband. And Chilger hadn't taken away my powers. Not yet anyway.

Which meant I still had that terror to face.

When Chilger wrapped me up again, I lay in almost the same misery as before. Temujin might have escaped the Merkid raiding party, but that didn't mean he'd come to rescue me any time soon. What if the Kereyid Khan refused to give him any warriors? He didn't have a hope of raiding the Merkid Khan's camp with only his little brothers and his wild friend Boorchu, even with the spirit wolf's help. And if he came to try to trade for me, he'd be killed exactly as the Merkids planned, and it would all be my fault. Even his Anda Jamukha had deserted him . . . my fault, again! These thoughts whirled round and round in my head until they made my spirit scream.

Chilger kept his word, though. That night, my Merkid guards lifted the flap of the yurt and pushed old Khoga inside. She stumbled and turned to yell abuse at them. Then she saw me wrapped in my sheepskin in the gloom and dropped stiffly to her knees beside me.

"Oh, Lady Borta! My poor child! To lose your young husband so soon."

It was such a relief to see a familiar face again, I laughed. "Temujin's not dead, silly. They're lying to us, can't you see?"

She shook her head. "My lady, I know it's hard to accept but I think they've probably killed him by now."

"Have you seen his body?" The awful teetering-on-the-edge feeling returned. What if my shaman skills had deserted me? What if Jamukha had been working with the Merkids all along, and Chilger had been lying about Temujin's escape to keep me from cursing him?

But Khoga shook her head. "No, my lady."

"Then he's alive," I said as firmly as I could. "And so are his brothers and his Anda Jamukha. He'll come to rescue us just as soon as he can find enough warriors to raid the Merkid camp, you'll see."

The old servant gave me a bleak look. "Even if he is alive, this camp is huge. He'll need to raise an army first."

"He'll get the Kereyids," I said, more to convince myself than her.

Khoga couldn't tell me where our captors had taken Belgutei's mama, or what had happened to Whisper, though she said she thought my pet had followed us through the forest for a while. She unwrapped my arm, tutted over it, and then splinted it properly – which hurt almost as much as when I'd broken it. But I bit my tongue and endured the pain because she seemed to know what she was doing, unlike Chilger. Then she nagged the guards until they brought her a comb, and started to tease the tangles and twigs out of my hair.

Having Khoga back helped a lot. Chilger spent as little time as possible in the yurt with us, so really it was little different from being up at the Holy Mountain camp waiting for Temujin to return and rescue me from Jamukha. I just had a different boy to fend off with my spirit every day, and I'd had plenty of practice by then.

I reminded Chilger I was a shaman, and that if he tried to take away my powers then he'd die a horrible death. I described this death in gory detail, borrowing from campfire tales of Yesugei the Brave's raids on the Tartars, and added that anyone who killed my pet deer would suffer the same. Chilger didn't scare me half as much as Jamukha had, actually – I even felt a bit sorry for him, because he was obviously terrified of his elder brother the khan, and he didn't look strong enough to wrestle me down in the furs without getting a few bruises in return. We were both playing a part in the story Temujin's papa had started when he'd stolen his mama Lady Hogelun from the Merkids. It brought us together in a wary truce.

But as the weeks passed, not knowing what had happened to Temujin was unbearable. Feeling safe enough from Chilger, and trusting my guards to keep everyone else out of our yurt, I asked Khoga to keep watch over my sleeping body while I tried another spirit journey to find Whisper. But still my spirit crouched in my body, trembling like a fawn. I just couldn't seem to do it. And every time I failed I lost a bit of confidence, which made the next time I tried even harder.

"Why don't you ask the Merkid shaman why you can't do it?" Khoga suggested one night, when I curled around my swollen arm after yet another failure.

"Don't be silly," I snapped, still raw from the attempt.

"If the Merkids find out what I'm trying to do, they'll stop me. You don't understand. You're only a servant. Why don't you do something useful and go pick some herbs to take away my pain so I can concentrate on the magic?"

Khoga frowned. "I'm a prisoner too, lady."

Feeling awful, I put my good arm around her and hugged her in the gloom of the yurt. "I'm sorry," I whispered. "I didn't mean to shout at you. I know they won't let you out to pick herbs. If I can't find Whisper, I'll have to try for a wild deer instead. Just don't tell anyone what I'm trying to do, all right?"

She promised she wouldn't.

The only explanation I could think of for my continued failure was that something had happened to my pet. I did try for a wild deer, but that proved even more difficult in my weakened state, and what if I couldn't get back to my body again? There would be no friendly shaman with a horse-skull violin to help me return this time.

When summer gave way to autumn, we had to accept Temujin must have failed to get the Kereyids. I worried about him riding into the Merkid trap with only his little brothers to watch his back and was frustrated I could do nothing to warn him. But even without healing herbs, bones mend eventually. As my arm became gradually less painful, I re-learnt the trick of it, sending out my spirit a bit further from the Merkid camp every night – though when I finally succeeded in finding my pet, I wished I hadn't.

Branches that will not move out of the way. A small space

like a yurt but with rocks overhead instead of a smoke hole. No stars. No herd. Alone. A rope tight around her neck. The smell of wolf—

My spirit fled straight back to my body again.

I lay trembling, my heart beating as fast as my doe's. The Merkids had caught my pet, too! They had put her somewhere dark that smelt of wolf, enclosed by rocks and poles.

My poor Whisper, a captive like me.

- 9 -

YEAR OF THE PIG

ONCE MY ARM had healed enough to have strength in it again, I turned my thoughts to escape. It wouldn't be easy. My old servant and I wouldn't have a hope of out-galloping the Merkid sentries, even if we managed to steal some horses in the first place. But carts often came and went carrying supplies – maybe we could smuggle ourselves out in one of those?

I set Khoga the task of watching their coming and goings, while I saved half of everything Chilger fed us that would keep for the journey, hiding the strips of salted meat and berries under a rug at the back of my prison. I knew we'd have to go before the snows came, or we'd never make it through the mountains. But I couldn't leave Whisper behind in Merkid hands. I might need her to find Temujin.

On my next few visits, made during the night while the camp slept, my deer was munching a pile of hay, so someone was obviously feeding her. But she remained trapped by dark rock and, no matter how hard I encouraged her to struggle against it, the rope around her neck held fast. I tried to get Chilger to tell me where they were keeping my pet, but he didn't seem to know anything about a captive deer, which suggested Whisper probably wasn't in the Merkid camp. In the end, I decided the only way was to stay with her until her captor came to feed her.

I didn't like the thought of leaving my body in an enemy yurt for very long by daylight, but by then I knew Chilger's routine and thought the risk of discovery small. Besides, I reasoned – innocent as ever – things could hardly get much worse for us, even if we were caught. So I told Khoga not to worry if I was gone for some time. Then I sent my spirit across the forest, and waited to see who would come.

When the sun rises, Whisper scents her captor. Because she associates him with food, she trots up to the poles across the entrance to her prison. My spirit shudders in recognition as a lanky lad with long hair strides up to the cave. He looks thinner, hollow-eyed and less handsome than I remember, but I know him at once. He throws over a pile of hay and cracks the ice on a dirty leather bucket. Whisper is thirsty and stretches her neck to drink. This is difficult because of the rope, but she has grown used to her tether and no longer panics at the feel of it around her neck.

"I must be soft," says Jamukha. "Silly thing! You're lucky I haven't put an arrow in you by now. It was your fault I got banished from Dei the Wise's camp and got into this whole

mess in the first place. I bet Borta wishes she'd been nicer to me now."

Whisper raises her head, and my spirit recoils as he reaches over the barrier to grasp the rope and pull the doe closer. He stares into her – into my – eyes and frowns. "Is it true?" he says softly. "Can you really talk to your mistress?"

My spirit freezes. Whisper shakes her head, pulling back, and Jamukha laughs.

"Ha! If there were any truth in it, Borta wouldn't still be a captive down there in the Merkid camp, would she? She'd have used her powers to escape by now. I reckon she made up all that curse stuff to scare me off, just like she's scaring off that fool Chilger! Merkids are stupid. Heaven only knows what crazy ritual they've got planned for Red Circle Night, but it'll be a good chance to turn things around in our favour . . . Oh, stop trembling! You're just the same as your mistress, enjoying my touch but pretending you're not."

He flicks her muzzle with his fingers. My pet leaps back, hitting her leg against a rock.

Pain—

I couldn't believe the pain!

While my spirit had been in the cave with Whisper and Jamukha – Jamukha, the traitor! – my Merkid captors had come into the yurt and caught me out of my body. Khoga was screaming at the man bending over me, but was held back by one of my guards. A second guard had lifted the rug to expose our food stash. A third man held the arm I'd broken during my capture across two blocks of wood, while the Merkid Khan pointed to it.

"Again," he said.

Chilger held a blacksmith's hammer above me. He saw I was awake and shook his head.

"Do it, Younger Brother!" the khan ordered. "You heard what the shaman said. She's gone on a spirit journey, spying on us no doubt, and we've got to stop her. Next thing you know, she'll be sending her spirit to warn her husband about the trap we've set for him. Looks like she was planning on joining him in body, too, once she got the chance. If you'd done what I told you to do when you brought her here, we wouldn't need to do this. I must say I didn't really believe the Mongol lad's claim Temujin hadn't touched her, but she's convinced me now. Hurry up, or I'll break your arm too for disobeying your khan."

Chilger gave me an apologetic look and swung the hammer. I closed my eyes and tried to send my spirit back into Whisper's body. Even being trapped in a cave with Jamukha would be better than staying in the Merkid yurt when—

Chilger brought the hammer down clumsily, but hard enough. There was a crack as the newly healed bone broke again. A scream of denial escaped me.

"There," said the Merkid Khan. "She's back with us. Quick and effective, just as our shaman said."

He pushed Chilger out of the way and rested his boot on my shattered wrist. "Hurts, does it, Lady Borta? I've only just found out about your spirit journeys, or I'd have stopped them before. Pain can keep your spirit in your body, so my shaman tells me. The other way's pleasure, but you seemed not to want that. Maybe you'll change your mind on Red Circle Night." He scowled at the hovering Chilger. "Don't splint it for her this time. We might need to bring her back in a hurry if she tries to spy on us again."

I was sobbing with the shock of what they'd just done, as well as the fear of being trapped in my body again. The Merkid Khan spoke the truth, because my spirit had clenched up tight around my damaged arm where his foot rested, braced for more pain. It couldn't escape my body, any more than my body could escape what the Merkids were doing to it. What did they plan to do to me on Red Circle Night?

A cold sweat came over me. I could only think of one thing, the thing I was still not ready for, despite being a married woman for more than a year.

"By eternal Heaven!" yelled Khoga. "Leave her *alone*, you brutes! Borta, my child . . . Lady . . . don't worry, I'll look after you. I won't let them hurt you again."

"Get that old woman out of here," ordered the Merkid Khan.

They dragged Khoga out of the yurt, and I closed my eyes as my last hope of any kindness in my captivity left with her. I tried very hard not to scream as the Merkid Khan trod down on my wrist one last time. Then, mercifully, he removed his foot and nodded to the guard. "Let her go."

I curled up around my pain and tried to control my tears. Chilger touched my shoulder awkwardly, still holding the hammer. He avoided looking at my arm. "I'm really sorry, Borta," he whispered, the worst part being he actually looked it. "I had no choice."

"Don't be such a wet marmot!" His khan clipped him round the ear. "Go take that hammer back to the blacksmith, and make sure you wash the blood off it first."

Chilger hurried out, looking relieved to escape.

"Now then, *Lady* Borta," the khan said, going down on one knee so he could peer into my eyes. "You'll stay in your body like a good girl, right? And no more hiding your food under the mat. You need to keep your strength up for Red Circle Night. If you behave yourself, we shouldn't need to hurt you like that again."

"Temujin will destroy your people for this," I said, but my voice seemed to be fading. My captor had to lean close to hear me, and the smell of his male sweat combined with the pain of my re-broken arm made me feel ill. "He'll be here soon."

"Don't count on it," he said, apparently having decided I must know they had lied to me about my husband's death. "I've had reports his army is still some way off."

Temujin had an army!

My spirit leapt in joy and almost escaped the pain. My captor must have seen the sudden hope in my eyes, for he scowled and said, "You're clever, Lady Borta, keeping my foolish younger brother at bay all this time. But he's told me all about your shaman curses and we've thought of a way to use them to our advantage. After Red Circle Night your powers will be gone, your husband will be dead, and the Mongol people will be scattered like ashes on the wind. Then you'll be my property, and I can give you to anyone I wish as a reward for their services. You're still a beautiful young woman, even with a crooked arm. Younger Brother Chilger had his chance, but maybe he's done me a favour by leaving you untouched. Seems your young Mongol friend will do anything to spend a night with you."

Something crawled through my gut. "Jamukha . . ."

The Merkid Khan laughed. "You do have some power, I see. Yes, Lady Borta, your husband's anda seems mighty eager for the chance to prove he's not afraid of your shaman curses."

Jamukha! Jamukha! Jamukha!

The traitor's name throbbed in rhythm with my pain and disgust. No one had bothered to tie me. I thought of trying to run. After all, I still had my legs. But when the khan ducked out, the remaining guard sat on a stool and stayed to watch me. Rather apologetically, he told me that he had orders to stamp on my arm again if he saw me slipping out of my body.

He needn't have worried. The first snowflakes were drifting past the banners outside. I wasn't going anywhere until spring.

*

The Merkids did not have to do very much to keep me imprisoned that winter. An unsplinted bone shattered by a blacksmith's hammer does not heal well, and is all too easily knocked in a sleep disturbed by spirit dreams, or gripped too hard by a careless guard. The khan allowed Khoga back into the yurt to tend me, and she tried to get me to eat her share of the food Chilger brought us now that we no longer had a reason to hide it. But I felt sick much of the time, and could not face even my own portion.

I think our captors must have put something in our water too, because the months slipped past before I was ready. On Red Circle Night they put me in a cangue, twisted arm and all, to keep my body helpless. They dragged the protesting Khoga out and tied a blindfold around my eyes so I wouldn't see who they had chosen to take away my powers. Then someone came into the yurt and began to play a horse-skull violin. I saw a twist of darkness with my spirit-eye and recognized the Merkid shaman who had told his khan how to control me.

My body shivered as the shaman's bow drew the stallion's voice out of the bone. On and on and on it wailed, filling my head and making my spirit ache. A white ghost-horse with a wild mane snorted and pranced around the yurt. I flinched whenever its ghostly hooves stamped too close to my injured arm, and was surprised when it shied away from me.

A crazed giggle escaped me. By taking my girl's eyes

and giving me no other way of escape, the shaman had unknowingly increased my powers.

When the flap of the yurt lifted again and the wolf came in, I felt no surprise. It was the same huge wolf I'd seen on my spirit journeys, its silver-blue coat turned the colour of blood by the red moon. Its eyes were hot and hungry as it rested large paws on my thighs and looked down at me.

The prophecy echoed in my head. *The wolf will lie with the deer and create a new nation.*

"Who are you?" I whispered.

The wolf grinned at me. "My name is Genghis," it said.

Genghis? I didn't know any Genghis.

Not some greasy old Merkid, I thought, confused and sickened. The blindfold stopped me seeing who had come. I could not escape. My wrists were locked in a cangue, my damaged arm useless. The wolf's heat moved between my legs. I felt its breath hot on my neck. The smell of the creature was overpowering.

"You can't escape the prophecy," it breathed into my ear. "The new nation starts here."

To my total disgust, an answering heat throbbed between my legs, and my spirit screamed.

No! I would not stay to endure this.

I would NOT.

I didn't care about the prophecy. I wanted – *needed* my husband Temujin to be khan.

The white stallion had reared at the sight of the wolf. It took only a small nudge from my spirit to turn it aside as easily as I had turned aside the sables from the traps back in Papa's camp. The shaman paused in his playing as the ghostly hooves smashed down on the violin that had been its skull, releasing the stallion's spirit to flee the yurt. It was the chance I needed. My spirit slipped between the notes and the heat of the wolf, and I rode that ghost-horse across the Merkid steppe under the red moon faster than I had ever ridden any horse before.

Everyone in the camp was yelling about the wolf, and I could only imagine what it might be doing to my body while I was gone from it. But I had only one thought. Escape, the only way possible.

It wasn't difficult to find Whisper. After all, I'd been here before on my spirit journeys. Something had broken through the branches at the entrance to the cave. A real wolf, maybe. My doe lay in a pool of blood, still breathing but only just. Roped in her pen, she had been unable to flee.

I slipped into her body, feeling her pain as if it were my own. Her deer-spirit recognized me and trembled in relief. I hated Jamukha then, more than I hated the Merkid Khan for ordering my arm re-broken. I'd known my pet would not live forever and one day I would have to deal with this sorrow. But not now, not like this . . . my strength wavered, and again I felt the tug of my body in the Merkid camp. I clung to Whisper's body, determined not to leave without her.

A herd of ghostly deer had gathered outside the cave, looking in at us, led by a large and beautiful doe.

"No, child," Fallow Doe said gently, seeing me. "You do not belong here."

Please take me with you, I tried to say.

But there was too much blood, too much pain. My spirit could no longer hold on to Whisper's. The fragile deer spirit slipped out of her broken body and joined the ghostly herd.

"It is over," Fallow Doe said. "You must go back now, child. Your body needs you."

Before I could protest, the herd turned and vanished into the red moon.

With nowhere left to go, my spirit whirled back through the darkness towards the Merkid camp, and I remembered what Papa's shaman had said about women losing their power to spirit travel when they sealed the marriage bond. This was the last time, the last time ever. When I got back to my body, I'd not have the strength to leave it again for as long as I lived.

Anger makes me stronger than I ever imagined I could be. When I see the silver-blue wolf bounding through the Merkid camp, snarling and howling in triumph, I follow it as I did once before on Red Circle Night and call its name.

"GENGHIS!"

It stops and stares at me in surprise.

"I have lain with you according to the prophecy," I say. "Now you must help Temujin, or my body withers in a tent without my spirit and the new nation ends right here."

It snarls and howls some more, but it turns back. I go with it and find myself in the midst of a battle. A vast horde is galloping down on the camp from the ridge, eating up the steppe like a thundercloud. Women scream as they fill carts with their children and belongings. At the head of the army, a young warrior with flying braids yells:

"Borta! Borta! Borta!"

He gallops after a cart where the Merkids have just loaded two captive women. One of them is old and in tears. The other is young and still surprisingly beautiful, her injured arm splinted awkwardly with part of a cangue. The wolf rips out the throat of the ox pulling the cart. It snarls and feasts in the middle of the battle, while the young warrior flings open the flap at the back of the cart and—

I had nowhere to go except back into my own body, which tugged so strongly I could no longer resist. I landed in the midst of a pain that went so deep I thought the Merkids had fired their arrows into me, as well. In that moment I almost wished they had.

Then I realized the cart had stopped. The moon shone through the back flap, three nights past full. That I'd been out of my body all this time gave me a jolt, but by its light I could see Temujin peering fearfully inside, calling my name. The wolf spirit stood behind him, a ghostly presence with blood on its lips. For a heartbeat I was afraid it would attack him. Then it bowed its head to me, and I knew I'd won.

My husband Temujin, betrothed to me when he was just nine years old, would be khan.

- 10 -

YEAR OF THE RAT

I HARDLY NOTICED where we camped that winter. Some valley sheltered from the winds. Temujin moved into his anda's tent, and I moved into his mama's yurt, where Khoga fed me and dressed me and looked after me exactly as she had done in the Merkid camp while my spirit had been gone from my body. It might as well have never returned. Everything moved around me in slow motion. People's mouths opened and closed, but I didn't understand their words. I didn't even feel any jealousy that my husband preferred to spend his nights with his Anda Jamukha.

Mercifully, I didn't feel much at all that winter. Everything that had happened to me in the Merkid camp had been my own silly fault for trying to change the prophecy. In punishment, Heaven had killed poor Whisper and imprisoned my spirit inside my body with the seed of a new nation. I wanted to hate the unborn spirit that kept it there, but how could I possibly tell Temujin about the child growing in my belly? He wouldn't understand about the spirit wolf, and how I'd fled my body on that terrible night and left it in the hands of a stranger.

Worse, Jamukha was back in favour again after helping to rescue me from the Merkids, and I couldn't be sure how much he'd told Temujin about us. Maybe nothing – or surely Jamukha wouldn't have stayed so long? Afraid of what my husband might do to his anda if he found out the truth, and still uncertain of that truth myself, I kept silent. If I spoke a single word, I knew he'd have everything out of me in a flash. In the meantime, I decided it would be safer not to speak at all, until I discovered exactly what had happened in the Merkid camp on Red Circle Night.

The women were not fooled by my silence, of course. After two months had passed without my moon-blood coming, old Khoga rested her hand on my belly and nodded. "Lady Borta's pregnant," she told the others in a matter-of-fact tone.

Temujin's mama thought a moment, and took my cold hands into her warm ones. "Don't worry, Borta. We'll tell everyone the child's Temujin's. You're not showing yet, so it's perfectly possible he might have sired it on your return. I'll have a word with my son. He'll soon realize it's for the best."

She and Khoga exchanged a glance. I knew then that my servant had told her how that awful night in the Merkid camp had been my first time. My cheeks flared hot with shame, and I turned my face into the sheepskins. Oh, how

I wished I'd let Temujin take away my silly shaman powers right at the start, back in our flower-strewn yurt in Papa's camp. Now it was too late. He would never love me now, and who could blame him?

Though I desperately wanted to feel my young husband's arms around me again, I couldn't bring myself to seek him out because of the shame I felt as my belly slowly swelled. I clung on to the memory of that hug we'd shared when he had found me in the Merkid camp, and consoled myself that at least Temujin had an army of his own now and would soon be crowned khan of our people. Even if his anda planned to betray us again, for now Jamukha could do little.

Our horses grew long coats. The snow fell and fell.

One morning, fed up with being treated like a baby, I took the rag off Khoga and cleaned my breasts myself. She sat back on her heels and watched me with a little smile. "I think you're going to be all right, Lady Borta," she said. "Do you want to talk about it yet?"

I shook my head and finished washing myself in silence.

But once I'd allowed myself to feel again, I couldn't return to that safe place where my spirit didn't care what happened to my body. Questions started to push their way through the fur in my head, like blades of grass pushing through the snow in spring. Had Chilger been caught with the Merkid prisoners and already executed? Or was he still out there, huddled somewhere on the icy steppe, regretting his part in breaking my spirit-bond with Whisper? I had no way of knowing. Belgutei had been in charge of the executions. I hadn't been allowed to watch the men die, and their screams had meant little to me, though now I wished I'd at least looked at their bodies. Despite the fact he'd re-broken my arm with a hammer, I wasn't scared of Chilger.

I knew I should warn my husband about Jamukha. But how could I be sure he'd betrayed us to the Merkids, if I didn't know myself exactly what had happened during those three days my spirit had been gone from my body? Who could I ask? My spirit had been galloping through the forest on a ghostly stallion looking for Whisper while the wolf was – sorry, it's disgusting I know, but my pregnancy is proof of the deed – inside me. By the time I'd found my way back to the Merkid camp, Temujin and Jamukha were attacking it with their army.

My name is Genghis.

I thought again of Papa's dream about the wolf and the deer, and the way our shaman had interpreted it to mean the boy I married would become khan of a new nation. What if I had got everything wrong, and my Red Circle wolf was a complete stranger?

Then there was the baby growing inside me, whether I wanted it to or not, its spirit curled around mine. Soon it would be ready to come out, and that scared me as well. Maybe I would die . . . maybe the baby would die and I'd regain my shaman powers and take my revenge on the wolf-spirit who had come to me that night . . .

More wicked thoughts.

Really, it was just as well the spirits stole my tongue that winter. Otherwise, no doubt I'd have said some very silly things.

In more peaceful times, I might have borne Temujin's children and grown old without ever needing to say another word. How easy it would have been! But the Ancestors did not mean my life to be easy, or they would not have given me the power to choose who would be khan.

When Khoga untied the flap of our yurt one morning to let in the first sun of spring, I opened my eyes to see a shadow falling across the felt, black and ominous. I sucked in my breath. A twisting spirit design pointed to Heaven above nine dark tails made from the long hair of our yaks . . . it was the war banner I'd seen in my nightmares.

Khoga rushed across to comfort me. "It's all right, Lady Borta, don't be scared. It's only Temujin's spirit banner." But she stared at that shadow too and shivered.

"It's Yesugei the Brave's war banner," Lady Hogelun said with pride, straightening her shoulders and adjusting her new headdress. "Temujin's mended it, at last! Now fat old Kiriltuk will have to pay attention to my son and give us our people back."

Between my own troubles and the attack on the Merkid camp, I'd clean forgotten Temujin meant to challenge the Taychuit chief for leadership of the Alliance so he could make war on the Tartars and avenge his papa's death. When the men began to cut shafts for the spearheads our blacksmiths had pounded out for them over the winter, a chill went through me. True, we had a lot more warriors now. They'd appeared through the snow like hungry wolves all winter, one by one on their shaggy horses, their braids stiff with ice. But now that the Kereyids had gone home, at least half our army belonged to Jamukha, and Jamukha had already betrayed us once. He could do so again.

Time to break my silence.

It wasn't quite as easy to spy on people without Whisper to carry my spirit around the camp, but I'd learnt to keep my ears open and discover things the way normal girls did, by listening to camp gossip. I soon discovered the special tree Temujin and Jamukha escaped to when they wanted to be alone together. I think a lot of people knew where they went, actually, but no one dared disturb them there.

I waited patiently until my husband came out of the tree alone. I heard his voice outside our yurt, and Boorchu's voice teasing him about something, and held my breath. But he strode past, as usual, without coming in to see me. A little disappointed, I pulled on my boots and a warm deel, waved my hand at Boorchu to let him know I needed to pee, and hurried clumsily around the back into the snow. They didn't suspect a thing. Pregnant women need to pee a lot.

Feeling rather giggly at escaping the yurt, I slipped and slithered across to the tree. Its snow-laden branches reminded me of the forest where Jamukha had attacked me when we were children, and I hesitated. Then I took a deep breath and pushed my way inside.

The space under the branches was dark after the dazzling sun on snow outside, and at first I thought Jamukha had gone. Then I saw him sitting with his back against a gnarled root and his arms clasped around his knees. His eyes gleamed with sudden interest as he watched me struggle through the pine needles. Doubt rippled down my spine. Those eyes looked exactly like the wolf's I had seen in my spirit vision – hot and hungry.

Jamukha offered me a wary smile. "Lady Borta! What are you doing here? Don't let my anda catch us, will you? He might get the wrong idea."

My heart was thumping so loudly it drowned out his voice. I ran my tongue over my lips, saw Jamukha's gaze follow it, and flushed in memory. Words, I needed words!

"Sit down, Lady Borta." Jamukha spread out his fur in sudden concern. "You shouldn't be running about the camp in your condition. That might be Anda Temujin's son you've got in there."

That might be . . . how much had Temujin told him? The thought that Jamukha might realize the child wasn't my husband's brought another blush, and still I couldn't find the words I needed. My hands trembled as he stared at my bulging belly with that peculiar hunger in his eyes.

It was no good. My tongue would not form the words. I had been wrong to come. We were a long way from the nearest sentry. I knew exactly what Jamukha must think I wanted, sneaking in here to meet him like this.

But being so heavily pregnant saved me. Jamukha fidgeted, pulled a face and said, "You should go back to the women's yurt, Borta. You'll catch cold out here. The baby might come."

I imagined Jamukha's panic if the baby came while we were under the tree and smiled. I half hoped it *would* come to scare him. But of course it was too early, and the new spirit inside me showed no sign of letting go of mine. I took another breath. The pine scents calmed me.

"You . . . have to leave," I managed.

They were the first words I'd spoken all winter, and they rasped in my throat like our blacksmith's file across a horse's hoof.

Jamukha flinched. The wary look returned. "Borta! You can speak!"

"The Merkids took my shaman powers, not my tongue."

The effort of saying this was almost too much. I broke into a fit of coughing. Jamukha reached across to help me, then pulled his hand back and eyed me sideways.

"Do you know who the father is?" he asked.

I thought of the lie everyone must believe and said, watching him carefully, "Why should you care?"

He avoided my gaze. "Anda Temujin wants to know, that's all. It's driving him crazy. You should hear what he wants to do to Chilger the Athlete." He studied me for several heartbeats, while I tried to work out how much he knew about last Red Circle Night. Then he said, "I assume you've already spoken to your husband?"

"Have I told him about Genghis, you mean?" I said, still watching him.

He looked genuinely puzzled. Either he was a good actor, or he really didn't know what I was talking about.

"The wolf," I clarified, my doubts stirring again.

The wary look returned. "So you saw it, too? The spirits were angry that night, for sure. Blue Wolf's balls, Borta! We thought you'd never speak another word to anyone, after what those Murdering Merkids did to you."

Now he sounded like the old Jamukha.

My courage returned with my anger. "I know you had something to do with what happened that night, Jamukha," I said, my voice croaking but my words still powerful enough to make him flinch. "I saw you with Whisper. She's dead because of you. Go! Leave our camp and don't come back. My husband doesn't need you any more. He's got his own army now."

Jamukha scowled at me. "What was I supposed to do? Leave your silly pet on Holy Mountain sniffing around your old camp? Don't let a dead deer come between us now. You don't really want me to go, do you? I'm Temujin's anda, so my lads are his to command as well."

"You betrayed him once," I said, keeping out of his reach in case my body reacted to his touch. "You can do so again. I saw you with my spirit-eye, remember."

Jamukha stared at me in sudden doubt, then sighed. "I thought we had all this out once before. Everything I've done I did for you, Borta. I helped Temujin rescue you from the Merkids – or don't you remember that bit? What more do I have to do to prove my loyalty?"

It was true he had supported Temujin in the battle, but that didn't surprise me. Jamukha always picked the winning side. "The Merkids murdered your parents," I pointed out. "You probably just snatched the opportunity for revenge. What will you do when we reach the Alliance camp and you have to choose sides?"

He was silent. I longed for my old power, to touch him and *know*. But that skill had been taken from me under the red moon. All I had left was the memory of my conversation with the wolf that night, and although it had seemed real enough at the time it was hardly proof that Jamukha had done more than imprison my deer.

I kept my chin high and out-stared him.

He waited for me to say more, the wary look lingering a moment longer. Then he smiled in his lazy way. "All right, Lady Borta, I take your point. But you look after yourself and that baby you're carrying. If anything happens to Anda Temujin when he rides to war without me, I'll be waiting."

I couldn't believe Jamukha's arrogance. I felt tempted to tell Lady Hogelun what he'd said to me, but the women didn't know I could speak yet. I was saving up that surprise for when I needed it most. Jamukha wouldn't tell Temujin about our little meeting under the tree, I could count on that at least.

The thaw finally came, turning the river into a noisy

yellow flood. Temujin gave the order to break camp, and everything suddenly started happening at once. Younger brothers galloped about bareback herding up the animals. Women packed up the yurts and cooking pans, while men loaded furniture and rugs into carts. I felt guilty sitting on a boulder and having to watch because no one would let me help.

"You mustn't exert yourself, Lady Borta," old Khoga told me, whenever I got up to try. "It's nearly your time. Heaven knows what we'll do if the child comes on the journey."

I'd been wondering that myself. So I took deep breaths and tried to stay calm, but it was hard. Jamukha's lads were breaking camp, too. It seemed he had every intention of staying with Temujin, despite my warnings.

But my words under the tree that winter must have had the desired effect, because before we reached the Alliance camp Jamukha declared he wasn't taking sides in the fight and ordered his lads to make camp. Temujin came galloping up to our cart in such a flustered state it made me want to laugh. When Khoga told him off for upsetting me and said the baby was coming, he stared at my belly as if he'd never seen a pregnant woman before. It made me feel quite powerful. And, of course, I had one more trick up the sleeve of my deel.

As my husband spun his horse to gallop away again, I called him back: *"Tem-u-jin!"*

His name came out rather more cracked than I'd planned, but it stopped him in his tracks. He rode back to us, all ears, and I made up some story about the Ancestors warning me that Jamukha was plotting something so we'd best go on alone. Khoga had a huge smile on her face and tears in her eyes, so pleased she was to hear me speak again. She's such a soppy old thing.

I could tell Temujin wanted to know everything. But he had to rush off again to make sure his lads reloaded their carts so we could ride on through the night and leave Jamukha's lads behind, so I was spared further questions.

I spent most of that moonlit journey imagining us lying together properly as husband and wife now his anda had gone and I didn't have to worry any more about keeping my shaman powers. Calm I was not – I felt as lovesick and silly as my half-sisters. That's probably why Heaven decided to separate the newborn spirit curled in my belly from mine and thrust it out into the world.

I did not die. The baby didn't die, either. Old Khoga wept with joy as she cut the cord and presented me with a healthy blood-stained son, and even Temujin's stern-faced mama smiled.

The raid on the Alliance camp – which Temujin led while I fought my own personal battle to push the babe from my body – did not turn out to be quite as awful as I'd expected. Apparently, most of the Taychuit chief's people fled when they saw Yesugei the Brave's war banner swaying in the dust clouds at the head of my husband's army, and those who got left behind were the clans who had wanted to join us, anyway. I don't even remember hearing many screams – though at the time, with little Jochi fighting his way into the world, I suppose I had other things on my mind. And as I held my son for the first time and looked into his eyes, I knew it didn't matter one sticky little hair of his head who his papa was.

I thought Temujin would stay away until Khoga had cleaned things up a bit. But he came running to my tent fresh from the battle with his enemy's blood still splashed across his face and arms. A bit frightening for a babe, I thought – except little Jochi had just as much of my blood on him at the time, and didn't seem to notice anything was wrong.

When my husband kissed me it unexpectedly aroused my aching body, and it looked as if we might finally seal our marriage bond right there in my childbirth bed. But Temujin, of course, had other things on his mind. He was khan now, and the first thing he wanted to know was who had fathered my son.

So I told him the wolf's name was Genghis, and I didn't know any more because the Merkids had blindfolded me that night and imprisoned my spirit in my body. I lied to protect us all. Chilger the Athlete hadn't been caught yet. If by any chance the Merkid lad was still alive, I assumed he'd run to join Jamukha. I didn't think either of them would dare show their faces at our camp again, considering the part they'd played in the Red Circle ritual.

Oh, if only I'd still had my shaman powers! Then I might have seen the terrible thing my lies would lead to.

That summer, Temujin sent out his generals searching for anyone calling himself "Genghis". The name quickly became a legend on the steppe and, although we couldn't tell anyone why he was hunting the wolf, word got around that it was something to do with the spirits. Shamans nodded wisely and went into trances to help with the search. Clan chiefs from all over the steppes turned up with gifts of furs and gold, silk and horses, bringing their young sons for us to train as warriors.

Our camp grew larger and richer by the day as Temujin's fame spread, and the shamans declared my husband was on a spirit quest to bring his guardian animal to join us. This was true in a way, of course, but it turned me cold inside. No one but me knew what my husband planned to do to the "wolf" called Genghis once he found him.

Meanwhile, old Khoga helped me with Jochi and watched me carefully as the days shortened. "You know who this 'Genghis' is, don't you, Borta?" she said, one night after Boorchu and his lads had returned empty-handed from yet another hunt for the wolf. "If you're trying to protect someone, it'll only end in tears. Temujin will find out eventually, and then what will you do?"

"He'll understand," I said, a shiver going down my spine. Autumn had arrived early that year, and the night felt chillier than it should have done. Temujin had not visited my yurt since the day he'd come to congratulate me on Jochi's birth. We'd barely even kissed. I longed to feel his arms around me and tell him my suspicions, but always the memory of that terrible night in the Merkid camp stopped me.

I glanced at the door flap, which we'd closed to keep the heat in and the spirits out.

"Don't worry, the guards won't hear us," Khoga said more sympathetically. "They're feasting again . . . listen."

Their laughter and shouts sounded muffled from inside our yurt. There seemed to be a feast every night in our camp that year. So many warriors, battle-ready and with nobody to fight, make a lot of noise. Also, Jochi had started crying again, missing the warmth of my breast. Khoga had tucked him up for the night, wrapped in a sable fur as soft as my dowry that had bought us an army, in the beautifully carved cradle Temujin had sent for him. It was a cradle fit for a prince, and yet – unlike my husband that year – Jochi much preferred sharing my bed.

"I can't be sure," I whispered. "They blindfolded me. My spirit was gone three days. You probably know more than me what happened during that time."

"I was too busy looking after your body when they let me back in to tend it, my lady," Khoga said. "I've already told you everything I know. Chilger came running to me jabbering that the shaman had killed you, and then there was the mess . . . men can't deal with that kind of thing. They ordered me to take care of you, and the next thing we knew Temujin was leading his army down on the Merkid camp. I never saw who was in that yurt with you on Red

Circle Night, but you know, don't you? You have shaman powers."

"Had," I corrected.

"Have," she said firmly. "Your spirit remained out of your body three nights after their ceremony. That means you've more power than everyone thinks. You can't refuse to use it, Borta. If you know who this 'Genghis' is, you must tell your husband. And if you don't know, you must find out before Temujin Khan kills every red-blooded male on the steppe."

My spirit shivered inside me. Could she be right? Could I really make another spirit journey? I hadn't tried since Jochi's birth. Did I even want to? If I found out for sure who the wolf had been that night, I'd have no excuse not to tell my husband everything.

"If my guess is right, there'll be war," I whispered. "A terrible war."

Khoga came and put an arm around me. "There already is war," she pointed out in her matter-of-fact way. "We've massacred the Merkids and broken Fatface's Alliance. You know Temujin's planning to attack the Tartars in the spring to avenge his father's death, don't you?"

I'd rather hoped my husband had forgotten about the Tartars in his search for the traitor. But, of course, that must be why he had been training up so many warriors that year. I took a deep breath, summoning the shaman strength I'd once known. "Of course." I nodded. "He has to show the other tribes he's strong enough to rule our people."

Khoga frowned at me, and then taking my hand said gently, "You think it was Jamukha, don't you? That's why you sent him away last year."

And although I hadn't planned to tell anyone my suspicions, let alone an old gossip like Khoga, her hug broke my already fragile defences. Before I knew it, I was telling her everything.

How Jamukha had tried to force me to lie with him in the furs after Temujin went to visit the Kereyids; how his touch aroused my body even while my spirit screamed; how I'd seen him in my spirit visions – betraying Temujin to the Taychuit chief after he'd been banished from our camp, and later with Whisper in the cave.

"I still don't really know how he did it without anyone finding out," I told her, sniffing back my tears. "But the Merkids told me they had thought of a way around my curses, which means something spiritual, Jamukha had Whisper captive, and Papa's dream said the wolf would lie with the deer . . ."

"So Jamukha is Jochi's father? And you invented this wolf-spirit called 'Genghis' to put Temujin off the scent?"

"There really was a wolf! Everyone saw it . . ." I blinked at my servant, unable to understand how she could be so casual about it all. "I told you, I can't be certain, and the last thing I want is for Jamukha to be khan! But he's Temujin's anda, isn't he? And my body knew whoever came that night, so it can't have been a stranger or a Merkid like Chilger. It was someone who had already kissed me, and apart from Temujin there's only one other . . . oh Heaven, Khoga! What have I done?"

This last part came out as a whisper so soft I could barely hear my own voice. I don't think Khoga could have heard – she was going a bit deaf – because she frowned at me. "Jamukha," she repeated. "Well, I suppose it's better than a Murdering Merkid – or a Terrible Tartar, for that matter. At least Anda Jamukha's a prince of our people with a decent bloodline."

I stared at her in disbelief. How could she joke about it? But then the way the spirits had tricked us all struck me as funny, and suddenly we were both laughing. Jochi, surprised, stopped crying and reached for the end of my braid. I scooped him up and cuddled him close.

"At least your father's a Mongol," I told him, as he gurgled and tugged at the wool that fastened my hair. "We'll just have to hope Jamukha has the sense to stay out of Temujin's way until his hunt for Genghis is over."

I should have realized the spirits had not finished with us yet. Jamukha never did have much sense where I was concerned.

- 11 -

YEAR OF THE OX

IN THE SPRING, Temujin took out his fury on the Tartars, leading his new army across the steppe to avenge Yesugei the Brave's death. With his victory over the Merkids and his papa's war banner to inspire the men, he won easily, executing the Tartar Khan and every male in the Tartar camps who stood higher than the lynchpin of a cart. In my heavily guarded yurt back at our camp, I was spared seeing this slaughter. But the tears of all the little Tartars he sent back for us to raise as Mongol warriors almost broke my heart. They made me think of little Jochi, who might lose his father in the same way if Temujin discovered the truth.

On Red Circle Day, we killed a hundred of our captured oxen in celebration of our victories and held a great feast so the Ancestors could bless my husband as the new Mongol Khan. My family were among the many who came to congratulate us, and Mama got a place of honour when our shaman shared out the meat. Papa gave Temujin yet more gifts of furs and horses and, to show we weren't poor any more, Temujin gave Papa some of the Merkid and Tartar gold.

Now that the killing was over, I could feel properly proud of my husband as he strode about the camp in his fine new clothes, grinning like a little boy. Altani and Orbei made a fuss of the baby, and Orbei clasped her hands together and said, "You're so lucky to be married to a handsome khan, Borta!" in her silly way. But I forgave her, because right then I did feel lucky to have my husband named khan at last, a healthy son suckling at my breast, my parents as guests of honour, and my friends with me again. It almost made up for the shadow of losing Whisper . . . almost.

I started to think that maybe the war I'd seen in my nightmares had already happened. I thought that now Temujin had been officially crowned khan, Jamukha would give up the few Mongol clans who had not yet come to join us and crawl off into the forest somewhere to hide. I thought that now we had made an alliance with the Kereyids and scattered the Merkids and the Tartars, none of the other tribes would dare raid us. I thought Temujin would eventually give up looking for the wolf spirit called Genghis and turn his energies to making peace. I thought he would come to love little Jochi as I did, make him his heir as the firstborn son should be, and forget the way he had been fathered . . . it must be true babies make a girl's spirit go soft.

I was still having Orbei-style fantasies of us all living

happily ever after when, only a few days following our celebrations, yet more refugees arrived from Jamukha's camp. Along with the good news that they had decided to join us, they brought more worrying information that the escaped Taychuit chief and his handful of remaining clans had made Jamukha their leader and were calling him khan.

This sent a shiver down my spine and put Temujin into a terrible temper. He'd been drinking a lot of airag during the celebrations, so I'm not sure he was thinking straight, but that's no excuse. He ordered the hostages we'd taken during the raid on the Taychuit chief's camp to be dragged before him, seized an axe and hacked off their heads. Khasar and Belgutei had to help him, because not even with the wolf's spirit in him could my husband manage to chop off several hundred heads, one after the other, without a rest. We heard the screams of the dying men from inside the women's yurt. They woke little Jochi, who started to cry. Altani and Orbei went very quiet. I don't think my half-sisters had been in a war before.

Temujin's mama sat stiffly, her expression set like stone. "It's Anda Jamukha's own fault," she said. "My son's only teaching him a lesson."

"But *why*?" Orbei wailed. "Why does he have to chop off their *heads* like that?"

"He's spilling their blood so their spirits can't return to haunt us," Lady Hogelun explained. "Then he'll send the heads to Jamukha's camp so his anda understands what will happen if he tries to challenge Temujin for the khanship. If you don't like it, you don't have to watch."

With Jochi's mouth silenced on one of my breasts, I hardened my heart and nodded. "My husband is khan now. Anda Jamukha must be taught his place like everyone else."

Altani glanced at me and quickly looked away again, perhaps seeing the pain in my eyes. But Orbei stared at me in confusion. "Borta, you've changed," she said.

"What do you expect?" Altani hissed. Giving my younger half-sister a warning look, she slid an arm round me. "Was it very awful in the Merkid camp, Borta? We heard how Temujin raised an army to rescue you. People are saying he should be made khan of all the tribes, not just the Mongol clans."

"Yes, we heard everything." Orbei instantly forgot about the executions. "How he changed into a wolf so he could run through the enemy camp unharmed and find you . . . I think it's so romantic! I hope my husband will rescue me like that one day."

"You haven't got a husband yet," Altani pointed out. "And you wouldn't want to be captured by an enemy tribe – tell her, Borta."

So far, I hadn't told anyone except Khoga what my captivity had really been like. Even after all the terrible things that had happened to me in the Merkid camp, my body still remembered the wolf's touch that night, and the memory made me flush. I became aware of the other girls' eyes on me. Then my arm gave a throb, reminding me of the price I'd paid for my stubbornness, and my spirit curled up inside me again. I must have gone pale, because Altani reached out to take the baby. Orbei bit her lip.

Old Khoga looked up from the milk she had been beating into curds, and her forehead creased in concern. "You're tiring Lady Borta," she scolded. "She needs her rest."

This annoyed me, because my body had healed and my spirit itched to do something useful. I had grown tired of being guarded like one of Temujin's treasures.

When the flap of our door lifted and a strange girl peered in, all dusty from riding and carrying her saddle bags, I was glad of the excuse to send Khoga away with the baby.

Temujin's mama greeted the visitor, while I sat and breathed deeply until the darkness in my spirit cleared. Then the girl gave her name, and my spirit twisted again.

"Borta, this is Khadagan from Chief Kiriltuk's old Alliance," Lady Hogelun said, careful to use the Taychuit chief's real name. "She's got some news she claims is for your ears alone. We'll leave you two to talk in peace." She beckoned to my half-sisters and led them out after Khoga and Jochi.

So I finally got to meet the girl who had helped my husband escape from the Taychuit chief's camp, all those years ago.

To remind her I was Temujin's wife now, I remained seated on the couch. Little Jochi wailed outside, upset at being separated from me, and Khoga hushed him. Not that I heard the baby's cries any more than I had heard the dying men outside. I was too busy looking at Khadagan's thick dark hair, her strong legs and wide hips as she set her bags down. Maybe she didn't count as beautiful exactly, but I had no difficulty imagining Temujin in the furs with her. I experienced a stab of jealousy as I remembered the kiss I'd seen them exchange in my spirit vision.

"Lady Borta," she said, looking curiously at me as well. "You're even more beautiful than they say. No wonder Temujin is so much in love with you he destroyed the whole Merkid tribe to get you back."

"Did you come in with the last lot?" I asked to cover my embarrassment.

She nodded. "My brothers wanted to take old Fatface prisoner and bring him with us as a gift for Temujin Khan, but it wasn't possible. I brought this instead." Khadagan fumbled in her bag. "Jamukha sent it for you. He says he's sorry and he never meant for things to happen like they did. He said you'd recognize it . . . are you all right, Lady Borta?"

"Where did it come from?" I whispered, my eyes on the pale object she'd brought out of the bag. At first I'd thought it was a horse's skull, but then I realized my mistake. Not the skull of a stallion, but the delicate skull of a deer.

Whisper.

"A cave in the Khorkonag Valley." Khadagan's words came from a long way off. "Jamukha said it's important, something about the spirits . . . he says he hopes you'll forgive him, and that you might agree to see him again now Temujin has regained control of the Alliance."

My body sat frozen, while my spirit whirled helplessly back across the years to the Merkid camp under the red moon. I thought the pain had faded, but the sight of that skull brought everything back, as raw and terrible as the night I'd shared Whisper's death. *Forgive him?* How could I ever forgive the traitor who had betrayed my husband and killed my pet – never mind what else he might have done to my body under the red moon? The last thing I wanted was to see Jamukha again, and any sympathy I'd felt for him vanished.

Khadagan held out the skull, pity in her eyes. "Lady Borta? Do you want me to take it to Temujin?"

I roused myself.

"No." My voice emerged as cracked and rough as it had done after my rescue. "But you can tell Jamukha I know who the wolf was that night, the one called Genghis." I took the skull from Khadagan's hands and stroked the eye sockets, the narrow muzzle. "And if he ever comes near me or my son again, I'll tell my husband everything."

Khadagan took the message herself, riding a fast white mare. She was gone several days. When she returned, she went straight to Temujin's tent, and whatever message she brought back for my husband from Jamukha, it ended the fragile peace between our two camps, once and for all. After our guests had gone home, Temujin ordered the blacksmiths to start making more weapons for battle in the spring. Then he gave me an embarrassed look and returned to his tent, from which Khadagan had yet to emerge.

The thing I'd tried so hard to prevent had happened. Temujin and his Anda Jamukha were at war.

- 12 -

YEAR OF THE TIGER

A BATTLE BETWEEN blood brothers is a terrible thing. Being shaman-trained, I knew the Ancestors would curse any man who shed his anda's blood. So I warned Temujin that if Jamukha died in the coming battle, it must be bloodlessly, or we risked destroying everything we had achieved so far. He gave me a strange look, and I wondered if he knew more about what had happened in the Merkid camp than I thought. But he just nodded, kissed little Jochi on the forehead and hurried out again to check on the training of the young horses.

My husband spent more time that winter with Khadagan than he did with me, but with my first baby to care for I had little time to feel jealous. When Jochi slept or Khoga took him off my hands for a few hours, I worked on transforming Whisper's skull into a violin. A deer's skull is more delicate than a horse's skull, so the work required patience and care. The fingers of my damaged hand were still prone to tingling and numbness, which made it a slow task. Then I had to learn how to play my new violin with my twisted arm. The other shamans watched my painful progress, but could not help me.

Nobody can hurry the spirits.

The magic returned to me like the first snowflake of winter, melting as soon as it lands on warm flesh, leaving behind doubt that it came at all. But my shaman powers returned more strongly with every pure note I drew from my violin, until I knew the time had come to talk to my husband about his anda.

You should have seen Temujin's face when I made him promise to let me decide Jamukha's fate! I don't know what he thought I was going to ask for. But whatever he did think, it must have been worse than what I actually asked, because he agreed right away. Of course, by then I had played my new violin for him and proved my power by summoning Whisper's deer-spirit into the tent.

His eyes flashed when I spoke Jamukha's name. "Can you really bring him here?" he asked, still staring at Whisper's spirit.

I nodded.

"Then do it," he said, his voice rough. "I'll give you one night with him, before I execute the traitor."

"Promise you'll do it the way I say?" I insisted, gripping Whisper's skull tighter – partly in triumph, partly in fear that the magic would fail me at the last moment.

"On my dead father's bones," Temujin promised,

and there is no more binding an oath on the steppe than that.

We cuddled a bit afterwards, and I refrained from mentioning Khadagan. I knew I'd have to get used to the idea of Temujin taking other girls into his tent now he was khan, but it didn't worry me as much as I'd thought it might. As he inhaled the scent of my hair, I knew neither Khadagan, nor any other girl my husband married to secure alliances in the future, would ever take my place as his first wife. It made me feel warm and strong inside, and I did not protest when he slid his hand under my clothes, its calluses hard against my flesh. But just as we were starting to get more serious, Boorchu came blundering in with some question about gelding the colts born that year, and we had to break things off.

Flushing, I rescued my violin before Boorchu could knock it off the pile of furs, and escaped to the women's yurt. I didn't want to hear about the gelding, and I had spirit work to do if I was going to bring Jamukha here to finish things properly, as I'd promised Temujin I could.

At the next full moon, I put on my warmest deel and took my deer-skull violin outside to sit by the glowing embers of our campfire. Belgutei was on guard duty that night with his lads, every one of them trusted warriors who had been with Temujin since Holy Mountain. They stiffened when they saw me. But when I smiled and raised the violin, they settled back to hear me play.

Whisper's spirit appeared at once. My pet looked beautiful – younger than she'd been when the wolf killed her, but not a fawn as she had shown herself to Temujin. Although snow lingered on the ground between the yurts, she had a sleek summer coat. I suppose spirits don't need to worry about the cold. Hoping she could travel just as easily through the snowdrifts, I closed my eyes and thought of Jamukha.

Smoke from the fire drifted my way, bringing memories of my childhood lessons. But this would be more difficult than when Papa's shaman had taught me how to send my spirit across the steppe to find my husband. As far as I knew, no one had ever made a spirit journey quite like this before.

Jamukha . . .

My spirit curled up tightly inside my body, and my damaged arm throbbed in memory. When I opened my eyes, Whisper was still there staring at me and trembling. I could see the glow of the fire through her ghostly body.

I took deep breaths. She wouldn't go if I acted fearful. "Find him," I said softly. "Don't be afraid. He can't hurt either of us now."

Belgutei frowned at me. Unlike Temujin, he couldn't see the spirit I was talking to, so he probably thought me crazy talking to myself. "Lady Borta, you shouldn't overtire yourself—" he began, getting to his feet.

I flashed him my shaman look, and he sat down again.

"Find him, little deer," I whispered again, raising the violin to play.

This time I felt my pet's spirit leave, like a shiver of ice across the back of my neck. I closed my eyes again and played faster, thinking of Jamukha when he had been sitting under Temujin's special tree staring at my belly. If I thought of him that day, when he'd been wary of me and I'd been safe in our camp, it helped blank out the other times when he had scared me.

I kept playing, all through the night, until my damaged arm ached and my fingers were numb with cold. *Jamukha*, the strings called across the steppe. *I'm waiting for you.*

Without the power to send my spirit out from my body, I had no way of telling where or when Whisper found him. I only know that she did. My pet came back in a trembling rush and entered her skull so fast, the violin leapt out of my hands and almost rolled into the fire.

"What the—!" Belgutei scrambled to his feet to rescue it. I opened my eyes to see the first light of dawn. Frost had formed on my deel. Shaking his head, Belgutei handed me the violin. "Lady Borta, I must insist you go back to bed! Temujin'll whip the life out of me if he finds you sitting out here in the cold at this hour."

He might do, too. He'd killed Belgutei's elder brother for less.

Belgutei's lads were rubbing their eyes, as if roused from a trance. It occurred to me then that playing a skull-bone violin to enchant my guards while I sent my pet's spirit across the mountains in search of our enemy might not be the best of ideas. But who was going to attack us before spring? Not Jamukha, that was for sure. He would wait for the moon's red circle, believing the wolf spirit would return that night to give him courage.

He'd be disappointed.

Spirit magic is very tiring, but I knew I'd done enough.

Jamukha would come. And this time he would be in *my* power.

That was the first battle I did not spend hiding in the women's yurt, terrified that enemies would overrun our camp and drag us all away as slaves. Out on the hillside, playing my skull-bone violin with the shamans, I felt powerful and strangely unafraid. Was this how my husband felt, when he rode into battle with his bow in his hand and his fierce young warriors yelling around him? I could understand how a man might miss such excitement in times of peace.

With the noise of the storm raging overhead and the wailing of the violins, I barely noticed how the fight was going. Horses galloped past, many with empty saddles, their coats wet with the blood of their fallen riders. Men yelled battle cries and screamed as they died. Lightning flashed and rain hissed down. Our campsite turned to mud.

Later that day, when his army had been routed and the last of his allies had fled, Jamukha's generals approached our camp under the white tail of truce, leading a bedraggled gelding with their unconscious khan roped across its saddle and secured into a makeshift cangue. My stomach jumped, thinking they had killed him. Blood matted his dark hair where they had hit him, and the man leading the horse was none other than my Merkid captor, Chilger the Athlete.

When I recognized Chilger, my twisted arm gave a throb and my spirit shivered with unwelcome memories. I hung back in the shadow of our war banner so they wouldn't see me. Water dripped from its dark tails down my neck as the men dragged their prisoner from his horse and thrust him to his knees.

This woke Jamukha from his daze. With our spears poking his back, he blinked groggily around our camp, maybe looking for me. I waited, my violin quiet in my hand, while Temujin's brothers disarmed the other men and made them kneel beside their leader.

No one spoke as my husband walked slowly down the line of prisoners. He carried his battleaxe, its blade dripping blood. The huge silver-blue wolf followed him, our banners fluttering through its body. I watched it warily, but the wolf spirit showed no sign of helping Jamukha.

Temujin's axe flashed, and Chilger the Athlete's head rolled in the mud, making the other prisoners flinch. "That's for laying your filthy hands on my wife!" he hissed at the twitching Merkid, who wet himself as he died. I couldn't help feeling a bit sorry for Chilger, even after what he'd done to me. He'd only been obeying the orders of his elder brother when he had shattered my arm with his hammer. At least he had escaped being boiled alive.

Temujin paused before Kiriltuk the Fat, whose stomach

had shrunk somewhat during his time as a refugee in Jamukha's camp. "You betrayed my father," I heard him say in a cold voice. "Death is too good for you." The former chief's flesh wobbled in terror. But Temujin gave him the same merciful blow he'd given Chilger, and Kiriltuk's head rolled too.

By this time, the other enemy generals had given up pleading for their lives and resigned themselves to their fate. "You betrayed your leader," Temujin told them, and they stared at the ground in shame as his axe swung again.

Finally, breathing hard, he came to his anda. The wolf bared its teeth as he raised his axe for the last time and asked, "Why did you do it? *Why?*"

"Just k-kill me quickly," Jamukha begged, his voice trembling along with his body. "Please, before Lady Borta sees me like this."

I held my breath. Temujin frowned, fingering the blade of his axe. Would he break his promise to me?

The blade flashed and buried itself in the mud beside Jamukha, making both the prisoner and me jump. "You're my anda," my husband said in a rough voice. "I cannot spill your blood without bringing the curse of our Ancestors down on our people. Lady Borta will decide your fate."

With a groan, Jamukha twisted his wrists against the cangue that locked them to his neck. "If you make me suffer, I'll haunt you until the day you die," he said, finding some courage at last. "Send my spirit to the Ancestors and finish this!"

Temujin beckoned to me. Though my mouth had gone dry, I parted the dark tails of our war banner and stepped out of its shadow.

Jamukha went still as I approached. His once-handsome cheeks were hollow, his braids stiff with blood and dirt. He gave me such a desperate look, my heart twisted in pity. But he could not meet my eyes for long. His gaze flickered to my hand, and to the violin I had fashioned from Whisper's skull. He stiffened as he recognized it. He was probably wondering if I still had the power. I hoped for his sake that I would have enough.

"Bring him," I said, and led the way into my yurt. Jamukha's guards hesitated, but Temujin ordered his brothers Khasar and Belgutei to escort him after me. They were rough, dragging the prisoner's knees through the mud, but I did not say anything.

"Leave us," I ordered, after they had flung Jamukha down in a heap at my feet.

They glanced at each other and hesitated.

"The prisoner might be dangerous, Lady," Belgutei said. "Temujin told us not to leave you alone with him."

"Does he look dangerous?" I asked, raising my violin. "Besides, I have this. Guard the door. I'll call if I need you."

They looked doubtfully at my violin. Khasar frowned. "Temujin said—"

"And *I* said get out! Or do I need to enslave your spirits too?" I gave them my shaman glare until they flushed and left, but not without checking Jamukha's cangue and giving the prisoner a final kick on their way out. I saw their shadows outside against the glow of our campfires and knew they would come if I needed them. But I also saw the shadow of the wolf sitting between them, and knew I would not need to call on human aid tonight.

Jamukha knelt at my feet, dripping blood on the expensive rug, watching me warily. He seemed unable to speak, and I wondered if the wolf spirit had got his tongue even as it had taken mine after my rescue from the Merkid camp. When I laid my violin carefully in Jochi's empty cradle, his nervous gaze followed it. I sat on the stool I used for nursing the baby and folded my hands in my lap.

"I should hate you," I told him quietly. "But since the spirits were involved, I'm going to give you a chance to explain. Tonight, there will be only truth between us. You know you cannot lie to a shaman."

Jamukha licked his lips. "Can I see my son?" he whispered.

"No," I said. "Jochi is Temujin's son now, and we only have until dawn. I want to know about you and the wolf. Talk!"

And so Jamukha, perhaps thinking it will save his life, tells me a story that almost breaks my girl's heart. But I am a girl no longer. Now I, Borta Khatun, shaman and mother of a new nation, must find the strength to finish what I have begun.

- PART THREE -

BLOOD OF WOLVES: JAMUKHA'S STORY

"WHAT NOW?" ASKS Fallow Doe. "The girl is a woman and can no longer run with the deer."

"Yes, what now?" asks Blue Wolf. "The boys are men and our work here is done. In the year of the Snake, these two swore to be blood brothers before Heaven. In the year of the Pig, they desired the same girl. In the year of the Tiger, they fought with arrows and brought war to the steppe. Now it is time for the two to become one so that the Mongol people can become strong. Tonight the girl will choose which wolf she lies with. Tomorrow the world will worship Genghis Khan."

- 1 -

YEAR OF THE HARE

IT SHOULD HAVE been me.

When the girl I intended to marry held out her sun-browned hand so that Yesugei the Brave's son could clasp it in his chubby fingers, a red rage filled me. The shaman bound their wrists together with a chain of flowers and brushed their knuckles with his white horsetail staff. Then he spoke the words that promised Dei the Wise's daughter to the boy still known by his baby name of Temujin.

Stars fizzed inside my head. There was a stone in my hand, sharp and dangerous as an arrowhead. I'm still not sure how it got there. I cast it wildly behind me and stumbled into the forest. If I'd stayed a heartbeat longer, I might have killed the heir to the Mongol Alliance, and the war would have started many years earlier than it did.

I don't know where I spent that night, while Dei the Wise's camp celebrated his daughter's betrothal and the two chiefs got drunk on the fermented mare's milk we call airag. Maybe I got a bit drunk, too. I don't remember that part, but I was sick as a sun-dazed marmot afterwards. Airag doesn't agree with boys too young to bend their bows, and I'd only just mastered mine that year.

I know I spent several nights out on the steppe without my horse, having nightmares of a huge silver-blue wolf chasing me through the long grass. I had a vague memory of following Yesugei the Brave when he headed home. I watched him join a party of travellers, who welcomed him with more airag, and that's where the memory fades. When I woke, three days later, my fingernails were crusted with dirt and blood. Blue Wolf only knows who – or what – it belonged to, but at least none of it seemed to be mine. Embarrassed by the thought of Yesugei's son seeing me in such a state, I washed myself in an ice-cold stream and began the long walk back to Dei the Wise's camp.

By the time I reached my aunt's tent, still shivering with the aftermath of fever, Temujin had gone. It seemed someone had poisoned Yesugei the Brave on his way home across the steppe, which made a shiver go down my spine as I remembered the travellers I'd seen him meet. Temujin had returned to his family to bury his father's bones, leaving Borta with her father until she was old enough to get married. With all the excitement, nobody had even noticed my absence. I found an abandoned flask of airag, downed it in one gulp and crawled into my furs to sleep off my adventure.

When I recovered (well enough, thanks to my aunt fussing), Yesugei the Brave was dead and Borta was promised to the new young leader of the Mongol Alliance. Why would she even look at an orphan like me?

No contest, you might think. But Temujin wasn't around. The spirits had given me, Jamukha of the Jadaran clan, time to change her mind.

- 2 -

YEAR OF THE DRAGON

ONE KISS. THAT'S all I wanted to begin with. Heaven knows I'd waited long enough for it, watching Borta grow from a skinny girl into a long-legged temptress. Maybe I should have waited longer, but the day the shaman joined her hand to Temujin's changed things. I had to let her know how I felt, before Yesugei the Brave's son came back to claim her and it was too late.

I chose my time carefully and waited until she was alone in the trees on the riverbank, where we'd have some privacy if things went the way I hoped. Her pet deer was with her, but I wasn't afraid of a deer. At first I thought it was going to be all right, and she'd swooned in my arms because she felt the same way I did. But then she had to go and scream, as if I were some enemy warrior trying to carry her off!

Of course, her half-sisters heard and came galloping to her rescue – and I suppose it did look a bit bad, because by then Borta was struggling in my arms and her clothes had been pulled awry. The older girl Altani half strangled me as she pulled me off her, so I didn't have a chance to straighten them. And by then Borta's silly pet fawn had returned and she was kissing the deer instead of me. Better than kissing Temujin, I suppose, but it didn't do much for my pride.

The other girls helped Borta back to camp, casting black looks over their shoulders at me as if I'd tried to cripple her, instead of merely caught her when she fainted. I followed at a distance, not wanting to get into an argument with her half-sisters.

We were nearly back at camp when I noticed the spots of blood on the leaves behind them. My heart thumped uneasily. I half hoped the silly deer had hurt itself running off into the forest like it did. No such luck. Borta was clutching at her half-sisters' hands, and I could see a trickle of bright blood running down one slender ankle. If I'd hurt her, that would mean trouble for me.

I hurried to catch up, meaning to find out how bad it was and beg her not to say anything to her father, but the flap of Dei the Wise's yurt swung shut in my face. Altani pushed me away, and her sister Orbei glared at me.

"See what you did, Jamukha!" the younger girl said. "She's bleeding! Dei the Wise will have you whipped for this."

I looked back at shadows under the trees, wanting to escape. But by then, the camp boys had overheard and gathered round, scowling and muttering. They had never really accepted me into their clan. I gripped my bow tighter. They eyed it warily. Half of them couldn't bend their bows yet. That gave me an advantage, but not much.

I'd resigned myself to a few bruises followed by an uncomfortable night or two in my forest shelter, when Dei the Wise lifted the flap of his yurt and came striding out. The boys backed off. But I could see from their chief's face that my punishment would be worse than any they might have thought up for me.

"Jamukha!" he said. "Put that bow down and come over here."

So I had to stand before Dei the Wise in the middle of his camp, my ears burning and everyone watching, while Borta's father told me exactly what he thought of me for taking advantage of his daughter in the woods. "What have you got to say for yourself, Jamukha of the Jadaran clan?" he said, when he'd finished.

I drew breath to explain. Then I shut my mouth, because I knew it would only give them more reason to hate me.

"She fainted," I said. "I tried to catch her when she fell, that's all."

My aunt, who had reluctantly taken me in when the Merkids killed my parents, folded her arms and shook her head at me. Dei the Wise sighed.

"Borta is promised to Yesugei the Brave's eldest son," he said. "Did you think that promise doesn't stand now Yesugei the Brave is dead? Even if Temujin doesn't return for her, do you think I'd give my daughter to an orphan like

276

you, with no brothers to protect her? We took you in when your parents died because we felt sorry for you, Jamukha. But I see by your squirrel fur collar you can bend your bow now, and your actions today show you're a boy no longer. I've no place in my camp for lads who think it clever to catch a girl in the woods and force her like a stag in rut."

I looked at my feet so I wouldn't have to see my aunt's disgusted expression. It had only been a kiss, but I knew she wouldn't see it like that, considering the blood. I wondered then if Borta might have hurt herself deliberately to get me into trouble, though I couldn't see how she'd done it, since I'd followed her all the way back.

"Jamukha?" Dei said. "Are you even listening to me?"

My aunt opened her mouth to add her view of the matter, and I could see myself being dragged off by the ear and thrashed across her knee like a small boy if I didn't say something.

I raised my gaze to look Borta's father in the eye. I'd been a prince of the Jadaran clan, before the Merkids raided us. In other circumstances, I could have been betrothed to his daughter instead of losing her to Temujin.

"I heard you," I said. "But I'm not sorry for trying to kiss Borta. She isn't married yet."

In the forest, a wolf howled sending a shiver down my spine. Dei the Wise must have heard it, too, because he glanced past me and his lips tightened.

"Very well, Jamukha. You can take a horse and your bow and some food for the journey, but from tonight you're banished from this camp. Go back to the Jadaran clan, and be thankful I don't have you whipped before you leave."

His words chilled my heart. Not that I much wanted to stay in his camp after today. The other boys would make my life miserable, and the girls would be worse. But to be sent away – not to see Borta again until after she was married to Temujin – that frightened me more than a whipping.

"Can I say goodbye to Borta?" I asked.

Dei the Wise's face turned purple. "Get out of my sight before I change my mind about the horse!" he said.

Borta's half-sisters spat at me as I pushed through the crowd to fetch my few belongings from my aunt's tent. I bared my teeth at them, and Orbei shrieked and hid behind her elder sister. Her fear made me feel a bit better. If I was going to be an exile, then I didn't have to crawl to anyone.

I took the best horse I could catch, and trotted out of camp before Borta reappeared from her mother's tent. If there were wolves nearby, I wanted to put as much distance between them and me as possible before dark.

The girls followed me as far as the river to make sure I left. I could see Borta's pet deer behind them, staring after me too.

"Better watch a wolf doesn't eat that fawn!" I called over my shoulder. I pushed the horse into a gallop so I wouldn't have to hear their reply.

- 3 -

YEAR OF THE SNAKE

I WANTED TO hate Borta for getting me banished. But the further I rode from Dei the Wise's camp, the hotter my desire for her became. So, instead of trotting back home to the Jadaran clan with my ears burning, I headed for the Alliance camp to find Temujin. I planned to stay with his people for a few years until things cooled down. Then, when he rode to claim his bride, I might get another chance to tame the wild deer-girl. She wouldn't get rid of me that easily.

A simple enough plan, you might think. Except, of course, Temujin's family turned out to be no longer with the Alliance. When I turned up asking for him, I almost got myself arrested. A fat old chief called Kiriltuk seemed to be in charge and was all for sending me straight back where I'd come from, but I talked fast and persuaded him I could be useful as a spy. In the end he told me where they'd left Temujin's clan, and we made a deal.

If I found Yesugei's family alive, and of that there appeared to be some doubt, I'd stay with them for a year or so and report back to him on Temujin's plans. In return, Chief Kiriltuk would support me when I was old enough to make my bid for Borta, and give me some of his warriors so I could protect her. It sounded like a decent enough deal at the time. Only – Blue Wolf's balls – the fat old fox never warned me what my new home would be like.

To say it wasn't what I was used to would be polite. Temujin's camp had been pitched in some Heaven-forsaken patch of forest up the wildest reaches of the River Onan. I got lost several times trying to find the place. The first snows caught me en route, and my horse slipped on the mountain trail and broke a leg. I had to fight off a pack of wolves for its meat, and they got most of it. When I stumbled across Temujin's camp (more by luck than judgement, I have to admit) my heart sank. A single much-patched yurt in danger of collapse, eight scrawny geldings that might have been silver-bay under all the mud, a handful of sheep with tangled wool, and that was it. An abandoned marmot hole would have been more appealing.

Temujin's clan turned out to be rather smaller than I'd expected, too. In fact it consisted of just Temujin, his three younger brothers, his two half-brothers, the two mothers and a baby . . . Temujin's sister, as it turned out, though it took me almost a month to realize little Temulun wasn't a boy, the way she screamed. Not surprising, really. The poor mite must have been hungry all the time with no men to hunt for their clan. The whole family seemed to be surviving on onions.

Obviously, the last thing they needed was another mouth to feed. Temujin's mother told me so, the first time she saw me. "Jamukha," she said in a no-nonsense sort of tone, looking at my squirrel fur collar. "I hope you understand that if you're going to stay with us, you'll have to help out like everyone else. We can't afford to feed hordes of guests who just turn up out of the forest."

I nearly said, "What about the hospitality of the steppe?" And, "How many hordes are going to find you all the way out here?" But I caught myself in time. Temujin's mother seemed rather fierce. I suppose being abandoned in charge of six hungry growing boys and a starving baby girl can make a woman strong. So I smiled my most innocent smile and said, "Of course I'll help out, Lady Hogelun. It'll be my pleasure."

At which she gave me a narrow-eyed look, as if she saw right through me, and for a heartbeat I was afraid she had the shaman magic that could see into a man's soul and discover his darkest secrets. But she had no real choice in the matter because by then I'd shared blood with her son.

From that day onwards, our two spirits were joined as one under the sacred bond of *anda*, and Dei the Wise's prophecy took on a whole new meaning. I should have known the Ancestors would have the last laugh, but it was the only thing I could think of at the time to persuade Temujin to let me stay. Our being blood brothers wouldn't stop me leaving when I needed to make my report to Kiriltuk, or so I thought. More fool me.

We spent that winter trapped in my anda's patched yurt by waist-deep snow. You can imagine how crowded it was, with the smoke filling the tent, the baby crying, the two mothers arguing over the best way to ration our food, Temujin's eldest half-brother Begter being a sting under the collar, and the younger ones squabbling over every little thing. It drove me half crazy, I can tell you! Several times I thought about stealing one of Temujin's silver-bay geldings and joining Kiriltuk's Alliance. Then I'd remember Borta's limp, soft body in my arms and remind myself why I had come.

Temujin and I escaped the yurt whenever we could, supposedly to play knucklebones on the frozen River Onan, but actually to practice with our bows and arrows. I'd already taught my anda how to bend his father's bow, which he'd been having trouble with when I turned up, but that only made a boy into a man. To be warriors, we needed to learn how to shoot a moving target from horseback, which is a completely different thing. Begter watched with a sneer as we rode off, saying he was too old for stupid games. Fortunately, he was also too stupid to realize what we were really up to.

We passed the days practising our shooting skills by going after game in the forest. To be honest, we weren't that good at first and spent more time chasing after spirits than deer. But Temujin's delighted grin every time he bent his bow made me laugh, and I almost forgot he wasn't my real brother. That winter, we got to know each other like andas should, hunting together in the secret glades, and talking half the night lying curled together for warmth in our forest shelter, as close as lovers.

Come spring, we finally managed to bring down a buck, and our secret was out. Temujin's mother decided pain-in-the-backside Begter should join us on our hunting trips, and our little holiday up the Onan ended in blood. There was no love lost between my anda and his elder half-brother, but I'm pretty sure Temujin wouldn't have had the guts to do what he did, if it hadn't been for the wolf.

- 4 -

YEAR OF THE HORSE

I'D SEEN THE big silver-blue wolf several times by then. It must have followed me after its pack finished off my poor horse on my way up here. The creature was definitely haunting our camp, maybe hoping to carry off little Temulun when Lady Hogelun's back was turned. It would have a long wait. Temujin's mother wasn't born yesterday. She carried the baby around, strapped to her back in a basket of twigs, while she did her women's chores. Besides, Temujin's little sister still had a boy's name to stop the spirits from carrying her off in the night. And that big brute of a wolf was, I felt certain, some kind of a spirit. Every time I caught its amber eyes looking at me, a shudder went down my spine.

"What do you keep staring at the trees for, Jamukha?" Begter asked, as we rode out in search of meat for our Red Circle feast. He had been jealous of my anda bond with Temujin from the start, but that year of the Horse he made it perfectly clear he was suspicious of me too, and latched on to me like a tick.

"If you want to hunt deer, it helps if you actually look for them," I snapped, making Temujin chuckle.

Begter scowled and slowed his horse to stop mine. "I don't know why you came here, Jamukha," he hissed. "But don't go thinking that because you're my brother's anda now, you can take *my* place in this camp. I'm the eldest around here, and one day when my mother remarries all this will be mine." He swept his arm at the trees and the flies and Temujin's winter-thin geldings with their ribs still showing through their patchy coats.

In my opinion, Begter was welcome to the sorry little camp and everything in it – except my anda's future wife, of course, when she joined us. "Actually, I think you'll find I'm a few months older than you," I pointed out.

He flushed and grabbed my braid so he could hiss into my ear, "You might be older, Jadaran princeling, but you're not as strong as me, and don't you forget it. If you're thinking of abandoning us in this forest, think again! I've got my eye on you."

He had, too. I knew I wouldn't be able to make my report to Kiriltuk without getting Begter off my back first. I considered putting an arrow into him during our hunt and claiming it was an accident. But Temujin flushed a huge stag, and it must have knocked me down, because all I remember was a blur of red mist that reminded me of when Dei the Wise's shaman had bound Borta's hand to Temujin's. The

285

next thing I knew, its carcass was draped over my horse's saddle and we were on our way back to camp, while Begter complained the whole way about me mutilating a perfectly good stag. I had no memory of killing the creature, but its blood was under my nails and splashed across my face as evidence.

Gorge rose in my throat. I decided I must have some sort of spirit-disease brought on by the red moon. Under the influence of it, I did things I didn't remember; things that left blood on my hands. I dared not admit this to my anda, though, in case he asked where I'd been the day his father rode to his death on the Tartar steppe.

"You'll have to put Begter in his place soon," I told Temujin, as the two mothers prepared the meat for the feast. "He's got his eye on your inheritance."

My anda sighed. "I know. But Mother's right, we need him to help us hunt. He's strong. He'll make a useful general in my army, once he learns to shoot straight."

"Only if you can trust him," I pointed out.

Temujin gave me a sharp look, and the anda scar on my thumb itched. I felt a bit hollow inside, to tell you the truth . . . me, talking about trust, while planning to make my report to Chief Kiriltuk just as soon as I could get away.

A month dragged by before I got another chance at Begter. Temujin was determined not to bring Borta to his camp until he could look after her properly, and Begter had been teasing him about his promised wife all day. He was being

286

deliberately crude, trying to embarrass my anda, when in fact I was the one doing most of the blushing.

Begter's boasts about what he wanted to do to Dei the Wise's daughter made me sweat under my collar. His descriptions were explicit, and every time I thought of Borta grown into a young woman, my groin stirred and I wanted her more than ever. But I kept my head bent over an arrow I was whittling and held my tongue, imagining that arrow whistling its way into Begter's eye. The wolf was watching us again from the far side of the river, and the last thing I wanted to do was pass out and make a fool of myself as I had done earlier that year under the red moon.

Then Begter made some comment about andas comforting each other under the furs. While Temujin hotly denied this, he whispered slyly in my ear, "Is that true, Jamukha? Is that why you ran away from Dei the Wise's pretty daughters and came all the way up here to rough it with us boys?"

Enough was enough. I finished my arrow and blew through the hole I'd made, which would make it whistle to startle a deer into freezing until it struck. It was a good arrow and I was determined not to miss this time. So I swallowed my anger. Calmly, I told Begter I was making the girls wait until I had more warriors to protect them.

This set Anda Temujin off talking about all the warriors *he* would raise to get his father's people back, which gave me an idea. I offered to go and fetch my anda some lads and check on Princess Borta on my way. I knew Begter would want to come with me – he'd stuck to me like a leech ever since our Red Circle hunt, more suspicious of me than ever. I planned on putting my arrow into him on the trail and leaving him to the wolves. But the spirits had other plans.

Before I could get Begter out into the forest alone, the younger brothers rolled into the clearing in the middle of some silly fight over a fish. Begter got heavy-handed with Temujin's brother Khasar, who had been wrestling Begter's brother Belgutei, and Temujin got upset enough to challenge his half-brother with his father's bow.

My anda handled things well, getting Khasar to back him up with the other bow, trapping Begter between them like a bear with a sore head between two hunters. Temujin's quiver lay out of his reach. It was a simple task to smear a little of my sweat on the arrow I was making so that, when I gave it to my anda and he aimed it at Begter's heart, the shaft slipped easily between his fingers.

I still don't know if Temujin would have killed his half-brother if the wolf hadn't distracted him. But after Begter had insulted my anda's promised wife, his manhood, and his anda in a single breath, who knows? Anyway, once I'd washed my arrow in the river no one was the wiser, and I finally had my excuse to leave camp.

As my gelding picked its way through the forest, I wrestled with my conscience, trying to decide how much to tell Kiriltuk. It occurred to me that someone who could kill his half-brother for an insult to his promised wife might just as easily kill his anda if he suspected him of spying. Besides, betraying Temujin to his enemies didn't seem like such a good idea now we were blood brothers. So I rode downriver to the Alliance camp just as fast as I could and told Chief Kiriltuk straight out.

I would not spy for him on Temujin's family any more. I'd done what he asked and roughed it in the forest for two years, but now it was time he kept his side of the deal and gave me those warriors he'd promised me. After all, I'd entered my thirteenth year and that made me a man. I didn't tell old Fatface I planned to use his warriors to collect Princess Borta for Anda Temujin – though I did tell him that Temujin had killed his half-brother so he would think that to be the reason I was running scared.

And how did Chief Kiriltuk thank me for enduring such deprivations and risking my life? He laughed in my face, told me he had no intention of giving any of his men to a spy who had broken cover like I had just done, and ordered me to run home to the Jadaran clan like a good little boy. My Anda Temujin obviously needed a lesson, and he'd take it from here.

To say I was furious he'd broken his side of the deal would be like saying it had only bothered me slightly when I'd woken to find blood in my mouth on Red Circle Day. I almost strung my bow and put an arrow in *him*. But before I could do anything quite so stupid, the undergrowth behind me rustled, reminding me I stood alone among my anda's enemies. Suspecting some new treachery of Kiriltuk's, I spun round in time to see a deer bounding away. I stared after the creature, certain for a heartbeat that I'd seen a long-legged girl fleeing through the trees after it.

I shook my head. I had Borta on the brain.

The fat chief laughed again. "Jumpy today, Jamukha! Don't worry, nothing will happen to you as long as you obey orders. After all, we might need you to spy on your anda for us again one day. A pretty boy like you seems well suited to the task."

His bodyguards leered at me. My cheeks burned. I clenched my fists, the confusion returning as I remembered Begter's words. *Andas comfort each other under the furs when there are no girls to be had.* But as Kiriltuk watched me in amusement, maybe expecting me to throw a childish tantrum, the fury inside me cooled and hardened. I would get my warriors, with or without his help.

I shouldered my bow and rode away from our meeting in what I hoped was a dignified fashion. When I was sure they weren't following me, I reined in my horse and tried to think. The way I saw it, I had two options – go back to Temujin's camp and warn my anda that Chief Kiriltuk planned to punish him for killing his half-brother, or continue with my plan to collect Borta and work out a way to rescue my anda later.

One thing was certain. I wouldn't be much help to anyone, let alone Anda Temujin, without some lads to follow me and fight at my side. Maybe I could persuade Dei the Wise to lend me a few of his warriors? He should know by now that I had done nothing more than try to kiss Borta when she'd accused me of attacking her in the forest the year after Temujin left, so the way I saw it he owed me an apology for banishing me. On the other hand, once Dei the Wise heard about Begter's death, he might have second thoughts about my Anda Temujin being such a good match for his daughter. And did I really want a bunch of her father's warriors hanging around when I next met Borta?

In the end I decided to do what Kiriltuk wanted, and headed to join the Jadaran clan for the winter. No sense in arousing his suspicions, and once my clan heard I needed an escort to take Dei the Wise's daughter across the steppe to her promised husband's camp, I ought to get plenty of volunteers. I'd train them myself until I knew I could trust them. Then I'd have my own band of faithful warriors to watch my back and help me guard Borta until I got her safely back to my anda's camp. It is a long way across the steppe with an ox-cart, plenty of time to make clear my feelings for her. And when we arrived, with any luck Temujin would be too distracted by Chief Kiriltuk's plans for him to think about marriage for a while.

- 5 -

YEAR OF THE SHEEP

PERSUADING MY CHILDHOOD friends to follow me turned out to be rather trickier than I'd expected. Since I'd gone to live with my aunt in Dei the Wise's camp, they had all learnt to bend their bows and shoot straight like Temujin and me. They'd already formed their own little war bands and were planning their own small raids. They didn't seem all that pleased to see me back, actually. Perhaps informing them I intended to be their prince again, straight out, had been a mistake. On reflection, I should have waited until I'd hunted with them a few times before I asked them to follow me. But they saw my leadership potential in the end. It just took me longer to talk them round than I'd anticipated.

In the meantime, we got news that Chief Kiriltuk had raided Temujin's camp and captured my anda. Apparently, he had put Temujin into a cangue and dragged him back to the Alliance like a common criminal to face trial for the murder of his half-brother Begter. The trappers who brought the news claimed Yesugei the Brave's son had begged Kiriltuk for mercy and acknowledged the fat old chief as leader of the Alliance.

I didn't believe the last part. First of all, I couldn't imagine my anda begging Kiriltuk for anything, not after all his brave talk of how he was going to raise an army to get his father's people back, so I felt fairly sure that was a tale grown in the telling. Secondly, it made my plan to collect Borta safer, for now there would be no danger of bumping into Anda Temujin at Dei the Wise's camp, which would have been embarrassing to say the least.

In the end, ten of the braver Jadaran lads agreed to come with me to collect Princess Borta. Worried about Kiriltuk sending someone after me with a cangue now he had captured my anda, I didn't stick around to see if I could talk any more of them into joining us. Instead, I thanked Heaven for small mercies and hurried my small band towards Dei the Wise's camp. I planned to get there and back again with Borta well before Red Circle Day, avoiding any trouble with the Tartars en route by travelling light and fast.

It felt good to be riding across the steppe again with the wind in my hair, especially with a bunch of eager lads at my back. I'd spent all winter worrying about what Chief Kiriltuk might do to my anda, so learning he had merely put Temujin in a cangue actually filled me with relief. On the way, I encouraged the lads to practise various tricks on horseback that Temujin and I had invented back at his camp. This resulted in a few bruised backsides, but I think I impressed them with my skills. I promised they could be generals in the army I was raising for my anda, which seemed to keep them happy.

As we neared Dei the Wise's camping grounds, though, their minds focused on only one thing. "How many sisters does this Princess Borta have, Jamukha?" asked Yegu, a big lad who had proved himself the best shot of all my childhood friends.

"Yeah!" said his younger brother Okin. "I hope there's going to be enough girls to go round when we get there."

"There will be," I assured them, thinking of Borta's half-sisters, and how it would serve them right for attacking me when I'd tried to kiss her, if my lads did decide to carry them off across the withers of their horses.

"Good." Yegu grinned. "About time I got myself a wife. And you say all the girls in Dei's camp are as beautiful as this Princess Borta's supposed to be?"

"Very beautiful," I told them.

"That's good." My friend mimed something disgusting, and the others chuckled.

"This isn't a raid to capture girls," I reminded them, a bit worried they might have got the wrong idea. "The whole point is Borta's father must give her to me willingly. Remember, she'll be queen of a new nation one day. So no funny business."

"Oh, don't act so high and mighty, Jamukha!" Yegu said

with a snort. "Girls are girls, princesses or not. And even khans are just men under the furs . . . or did your time with your anda wither you down there, as well as making you grow so pretty?" He leant out of his horse's saddle, grabbed my belt and tried to peer down my trousers.

"Get your hands off me!"

The red moon was close, and I felt tense and prickly. His words reminded me of Begter's taunts, the day Temujin had killed him for insulting Borta.

Yegu let go of my belt with raised eyebrows, and the others went quiet. With an effort, I calmed my breathing and took my horse into the lead. They had only been messing around. The last thing I wanted was for Yegu to turn around and lead them all back home again, leaving me stranded in the middle of Tartar territory on my own. I'd never get hold of any girl then, let alone my Borta.

"Sorry," I muttered. "But I'm serious. No tumbling the girls until you're asked, and leave the negotiations to me. Dei the Wise's people know me so they'll listen."

At least, I hoped they would listen and not shoot me on sight.

I urged my gelding into a gallop so we wouldn't have to talk any more. I could still feel the flush at the sides of my neck. Just because I cared if I kept my fingernails clean, and hadn't messed with any of the girls in the Jadaran camp over the winter, that didn't make me any less of a man, did it? I was actually quite proud of my restraint. In my eyes, saving myself for Borta made me khan material.

Thanks to me losing my temper with Yegu, we missed the turn to the river and got lost. Then I couldn't find Dei the Wise's camp anywhere – he'd moved it, of course, to find better grazing for his herds. We spent several days riding in circles and asking other travellers for directions, and on top of all that one of the horses put its hoof down a marmot hole and went lame. The spirits must have been angry with me. What with one thing and another, it was approaching Red Circle Day by the time we came upon a lush valley with Dei's tents pitched on the bank where the river emerged from the forest.

My lads whistled in appreciation, and I had to admit that by anyone's standards the camp looked impressive. Chief Dei had always possessed many herds, and his yurts were decorated with gaily coloured banners. His people, dressed finely in felt and furs, gathered round to welcome us and offer us the hospitality of the steppe. They didn't seem to recognize me, but I recognized Borta at once. My first sight of her, standing so remote and beautiful at the edge of the crowd, made my heart thud and my palms sweat. Heat flushed through me and centred you-know-where. If Yegu had pulled at my belt right then, he'd never have called me "withered" again.

Though my mouth had gone unexpectedly dry, I gave my anda's promised wife the speech I'd prepared so carefully as we crossed the steppe, about how I had come to escort her to my Anda Temujin's camp so they could get married. Of course, she must have seen through it at once – I only found out about her shaman skills later, and by then it was too late to make her trust me. She dragged her hand free, declared in a haughty tone that she wasn't going anywhere with *a traitor like me*, and fled the camp.

Fortunately, everyone else seemed as embarrassed by Borta's reaction as I was. Dei the Wise apologized for his daughter's rudeness and invited me and my lads to stay for the Red Circle feast – an invitation I almost turned down, thinking of the red moon madness that had overcome me last year. But to refuse his hospitality would have been even ruder than Borta calling me a traitor and running off into the forest. We could hardly neglect the ceremony of the Ancestors. Besides, dragging Yegu and the others back across the steppe before they had eaten would have been a sure way of losing my small horde for good. They'd been eyeing up Dei the Wise's fat oxen almost as eagerly as his daughters, and licking their lips at the promise of succulent meat ever since we arrived.

Borta's half-sisters Altani and Orbei were eyeing up my lads in much the same way, which made me smile considering how fiercely they'd protected their sister from me the last time I was in their camp. Even the previously unfriendly camp boys seemed more interested, once they heard I'd sworn anda with Yesugei the Brave's son and saw I now commanded some warriors of my own. I thought I might be able to talk a few of them into joining us to help rescue Temujin, so I accepted Dei the Wise's invitation and prayed I wouldn't kill anything under the influence of the red moon.

As we unsaddled our horses, I kept half an eye on the trees for Borta's return. But she didn't come back that night, although nobody seemed very worried by this. I remembered how it used to be quite normal for Borta to disappear into the forest with her pet fawn, and it seemed she hadn't grown out of the habit in my absence. I hadn't seen the deer when we arrived but that didn't mean it wasn't still around. I only hoped we wouldn't have to take the silly creature with us when we took Borta.

When the airag started to flow, my lads took it in turns to chat up Borta's half-sisters, while I watched the trees warily for signs of the spirit wolf. It did not seem to have followed me across the mountains to the Jadaran clan, and I hadn't seen it on our way across the Tartar steppe. But I had a horrible feeling it hadn't stopped haunting me. Worried about Borta out in the forest with the spirits on the loose, I grabbed her younger half-sister – plump, giggly Orbei – by the arm.

"Where can we go to be private?" I said.

At first I thought the girl must be too drunk to be of any use, the way she flushed and looked at me with her big eyes. Then she giggled again and led me down to a place on the riverbank hidden from the camp by a pile of boulders. Judging by the noises in the bushes, we weren't the only ones using this spot.

I didn't want her in that way, though.

"Tell me about Princess Borta," I said, keeping a good eye out for the wolf. "Where did she go? When will she be back?"

Orbei made a face. "Oh, don't worry about her. She'll be all right. She often runs off into the forest, you know that. She'll be with her stupid deer. She'll probably stay there all night."

"So she's still got her pet fawn?" I said.

Orbei nodded. "Of course! It's a grown deer now, though."

"Do you know why she called me a traitor and ran off like that?" I asked, thinking maybe their clan had been in contact with some of Kiriltuk's people, in which case I'd need to explain myself to Dei the Wise before he got the wrong idea.

Orbei gave me a confused look. "Because she's in *love*, of course. She's been waiting years for Temujin to come back and marry her. She's a shaman now and she doesn't like you very much, Jamukha, I'm sorry."

A shaman, who could see into a man's heart and know the truth. It made me feel a bit ill.

"But I told her I'd take her to Temujin's camp," I said, swallowing my nerves. "If she really is a shaman she'd know that's the truth. So why's she being so silly?"

"I know you did, but . . ." Orbei pulled another face. "Oh, I don't know! Don't ask me these questions, Jamukha, please. It's meant to be a secret, her father doesn't know she's been training to speak with the spirits . . ." She lowered her lashes and peeped at me from under them. "*I'll* not run away from you. You've grown quite handsome since you left us."

I felt like slapping some sense into her. Did the girl really think she could replace Borta in my furs?

On my way back to camp, I thought about going to look for Borta, but Dei's airag must have been strong. Turned out the only thing I shared my furs with that night was a muddled dream of a hunt with baying dogs and the usual blood and screams.

At dawn, I woke with a start. The screams belonged to Borta's half-sisters. Apparently, they had found Borta unconscious in the forest and had called the shaman to bring her spirit back to her body. I checked my nails for blood – still clean, thankfully. If the wolf had come and savaged Borta while I slept . . . but, to my relief, it seemed my anda's promised wife was none the worse for her night in the woods, and her pet deer was soon safely penned behind Dei the Wise's yurt.

I wanted to talk to Borta and find out if she'd seen any spirits last night. But after all the fuss, I wasn't surprised to learn that Dei the Wise had decided not to force his daughter to go with me.

In the morning, I lured Borta to the spot Orbei had shown me behind the boulders to say goodbye. I had a half-formed plan to threaten to tell Dei the Wise about Borta's secret shaman training, which I hoped might persuade her to come with me willingly. If that failed, I could always drag her across the withers of my horse and ride off with her.

But when it came to taking action, I couldn't do it. My red moon boldness of the night before had gone, and even the thought of losing Borta again couldn't bring it back. Knowing the green light in her eyes came from her shaman power unnerved me. Also, Yegu and the others were waiting nearby with the horses, watching us, so I had to do this right.

After her reaction on seeing me, I knew I was pushing my luck trying for a goodbye kiss, but – Blue Wolf's balls! – what's a red-blooded lad supposed to do, when the girl of his dreams has grown more beautiful and desirable than ever since he last set eyes on her? Then her silly deer escaped from its pen and spooked the horses, and I decided we'd better leave before someone got hurt.

I nearly wet myself worrying she'd tell her father about my finger in her palm, let alone all the other things she claimed to know about me. But she can't have mentioned any of it, because Dei the Wise didn't order me arrested. What was more, he seemed to have forgiven me for the misunderstanding by the river when we'd been children. Borta's mother even packed us some food for the journey back to my anda's camp, while Dei the Wise explained Princess Borta wasn't quite ready to join Temujin just yet, but he'd make sure she would be ready and waiting when my anda came to collect her himself.

Then he looked me in the eye and said, "Men can't fight

a prophecy, Jamukha." Which made my stomach churn, I can tell you, and I wondered if he knew more than I'd thought.

I found myself riding away from Dei the Wise's camp embarrassed as a toothless wolf with just the ten lads I'd persuaded to come with me to collect the girl I desired now more than ever. All the way back upriver, they teased me about not carrying out my plan to carry her off. Maybe, they joked, echoing marmot-brain Begter, I loved my Anda Temujin more than I loved girls?

I cared for my anda more than I cared for any of them just then, that's true. I clenched my fist on my bow and considered putting arrows into their backsides to teach them some manners. But that wouldn't help anyone, least of all my anda. Instead, I cooled my anger, turned my horse away from the river and headed up into the hills.

"Where are we going, Jamukha?" Yegu asked, still chuckling. "Aren't any girls up here that I can see."

I let them sweat a bit. When the wolves started howling and they began looking nervously over their shoulders, I explained. "Up over that ridge is Merkid territory. They murdered my parents so they've a debt to pay. We'll raid a few of their camps and see if we can get hold of some more horses, grab some sheep and goats as well for my anda's family to live off while he's away."

I can only think some red moon madness must have lingered in my blood. But my lads' eyes lit up at the thought of some real action, and it did the trick. They soon forgot about Borta and her sisters, and started to worry about staying alive instead.

We confined ourselves to moonlit raids over the ridge, targeting the smaller Merkid camps. It was desperately dangerous – several times we were chased by Merkid lookouts – but the terror kept me from thinking too much about Borta, and to my surprise we turned out to be rather good at raiding. We got several fast horses including a small herd of silver-bays that reminded me of Temujin's although I didn't make the connection at the time, some fat sheep (which we slaughtered and packed into food pits marked with stones for digging up later), and a couple of she-goats that provided us with milk. Although my head was fuzzy with fear pretty much the whole time, and I could never quite remember afterwards what I did in those camps, Yegu and the others soon stopped teasing me about my girl phobia.

We spent a bit of time afterwards looking for Temujin's family, but his little camp beside the Onan had been abandoned. I assumed Chief Kiriltuk must have decided to take the whole family back with him to the Alliance, which at least meant my anda's little brothers would get enough to eat. If we turned up there now, things might get awkward to say the least.

To let things quieten down while I thought of the best way to help my anda, I led my lads back to the Jadaran camp, driving our captured herds before us.

That was when we heard how Temujin had escaped on

Red Circle Night. Apparently, Temujin had changed into a wolf and disappeared into the forest, putting the fear of Heaven into fat old Kiriltuk, who had been too scared of the Holy Mountain spirits to give chase.

The story of the wolf – though obviously grown in the telling – made me shiver. Temujin had escaped the very night I'd been dreaming of spirits in his promised wife's camp! He was bound to hear about my visit there sooner or later. I'd just better make sure I got a chance to talk to my anda before Borta did.

- 6 -

YEAR OF THE
MONKEY

I SPENT THAT winter in an agony of indecision. Did I take my lads to the Alliance in the spring and offer my bow to Chief Kiriltuk, in the hope he might now help me get hold of Borta to prevent Temujin marrying her and fulfilling the prophecy? Or did I try to find Temujin's new camp and explain my previous year's encounter with his promised wife, before Borta got a chance to tell him her side of things? Any hope I'd had of bravely "rescuing" my anda from Kiriltuk's cangue and asking for Borta as a reward, had been ruined by his escape. I needed solid information, not crazy rumours about my anda turning into a wolf and disappearing up Holy Mountain with the spirits.

So, when the thaw came, I led my eager lads back up the River Onan. Their numbers had increased over the winter to almost a hundred – after hearing Yegu and the others tell wildly exaggerated tales of our raids on the Merkid camps, everyone wanted a bit of the action. I promised them we would do some more raiding, but at the same time I meant to spy out Temujin's new camp, see how many lads he had with him and if he'd got married yet. I still didn't know what I'd do if I found Borta in my anda's yurt, but I would cross that steppe when I came to it.

We took the long way over the mountains to where I'd left my anda's little clan in the year of the Horse, searching all the hidden valleys and steep-sided gorges on the way, but saw no sign of Temujin or his family. I began to worry afresh about my anda. My lads, however, had grown more confident with their increased numbers. When they spied a large Merkid camp not far over the ridge, they were determined to carry off some girls this time.

I made the mistake of asking what they thought we were going to do with all these captive girls, even if we managed to get hold of some without getting ourselves killed in the process. Yegu glanced at his brother Okin, their eyes glinting with mischief. Blue Wolf's balls, but I should have seen it coming.

"Maybe Jamukha's afraid of girls?" Yegu teased, casting a sideways glance at the others. "Maybe he prefers his anda in the furs?"

"I am NOT afraid of girls!" I yelled, going hot under the collar.

They were all laughing at me now.

"Come on, Jamukha, let's have some fun!" Yegu said. "We can't raid such a large camp without you to lead us."

"That's true," I agreed, pleased they recognized that much, at least. Truth be known, I did want to do something a bit more challenging than horse stealing that year. My lads would have to get in some practice against real warriors soon, and this raiding lark wasn't so difficult if you kept your head. "All right," I said. "We'll do it. We'd best plan this one carefully, though. That's a much bigger camp than any we've tackled before. The best thing would be to attack on a feast day after the men have been drinking."

"Red Circle's only five days from now!" Okin said, and a shiver shot down my spine.

"Exactly," I said as if I'd been thinking of this all along, when in truth I'd rather lost track of the days as we searched for my anda's camp. "That should give us time to make enough arrows to kill the Merkid sentries."

I ignored my sense of foreboding. After all, I'd got through Red Circle Night last year at Dei the Wise's camp without embarrassing myself too badly. And even though there were more Merkids to worry about, I had more than a handful of warriors with me this time. With any luck, we'd get the raid over with well before moonrise, anyway.

"Brilliant!" Yegu's eyes gleamed. "We'll get a girl for everyone, even Jamukha."

The rest of the idiots slapped me on the back and cheered, as if we'd already done our raid and come out of it laden with Merkid treasure.

As we whittled our arrows, waiting for the feast to get underway, more and more Merkid warriors turned up at their camp. It looked to me as if their entire tribe had gathered for Red Circle Day. From our vantage point up in the rocks, their yurts looked like mushrooms sprung up overnight in the grass. Their clan banners rippled in the wind. Their herds roamed the steppe, numerous as flies. Horses, oxen, yaks, goats, sheep . . . even a few camels. I hoped my lads would have second thoughts when they saw how large the camp had grown. But nothing I could say would talk them out of it.

That was how I found myself leading a raid by the light of the red moon on an enormous enemy camp with barely a hundred lads behind me. My head did not seem to be part of my body. It floated somewhere up near the stars. I watched us gallop towards the Merkid sentries, bows raised, the feathers of our arrows edged in red, galloping headlong to our doom. Yegu was right behind me, but the others seemed to be hanging back. I opened my mouth to ask what they thought they were doing, and saw an arrow sticking out of Okin's throat.

Yegu hauled his horse round with an anguished cry as his brother tumbled to the ground. The others pulled up in confusion. Merkid warriors, not so drunk after all, streamed out of their yurts and ran towards us. My gut twisted in terror. Then a wolf howled on the ridge, and the red rage came.

I wouldn't run from the Murdering Merkids!

"Come on then, you cowards!" yelled a voice far too fearsome to be mine. "I thought you wanted some girls?"

I set my heels to my horse and galloped into the rain of enemy arrows, all self-preservation gone. The rest of that night was a blur of screams and smoke.

In the morning, I found myself trussed up in a Merkid yurt with a cangue around my neck, my ankles roped together and tied to the cangue so that my knees were jammed up under my chin. Every bone in my body ached. I had blood all over me. I swallowed my terror and made myself lie still, trying to decide how much of it was mine.

"I think he's calming down at last, Elder Brother," said a wary voice.

A shadow crossed the sunlight at the door, and an older warrior's ugly scarred face peered down at me.

"Careful, my khan!" another voice warned. "Let me check the demon has gone." Out of the corner of my eye, I saw a shaman's white robe. His horsetail staff struck my cheek, making me yelp in protest. Then he stepped back and nodded.

"So *this* is the Mongol wolf who's been raiding our camps?" said the Merkid Khan, prodding me with his toe. "A pretty-faced boy!"

His insult jolted me the rest of the way back into my body. Fear dried my mouth, but I knew I had to say something. "I'm Jamukha of the Jadaran clan," I managed in my most indignant tone. "I'm noble-born. If you release me, my men will pay a good ransom."

"Your men?" The Merkid Khan laughed. "You mean that

handful of cowardly Mongol marmot dung who ran off just as soon as one of them caught an arrow? We chased them back as far as the Onan. I don't think they'll be rescuing you in a hurry, Jamukha. They're probably halfway home by now with their horses' tails up their backsides."

This might well have been the truth. For all his yelling, Yegu didn't have my anda's courage.

"Well, we have you now," grunted the khan. "So I suppose the raids will stop. The question is, what to do with you? We lost some good horses last year."

"Ransom me for your horses?" I suggested, beginning to think again. They hadn't killed me yet.

The Merkid Khan chuckled and rested the toe of his boot on one of my hands. "Oh, I don't think so, Jamukha. We'll soon get more horses from the Mongol camps. The only reason you're not dead already is because my shaman tells me you are possessed by a demon spirit, and I don't want it in my camp if we're going to war with the Mongols."

A chill came over me. I'd raided a Merkid war camp with a hundred half-trained lads at my back. What an idiot! The Merkids had probably already slaughtered my anda's little family. Was that why I kept seeing the spirit wolf?

I tried to get a proper look at the shaman, but couldn't without sending some muscle or another into a painful cramp. I glimpsed the Merkid Khan's younger brother, though, staring at me in nervous awe. He didn't seem much older than me, and I wondered if I might be able to talk him into releasing me.

Then the khan grasped my thumb and bent it back, sending my body into another futile struggle that ended in agonising cramp.

"An anda scar, Jamukha?" he asked softly.

I tried to nod, found I couldn't wearing the cangue, and croaked, "Yes . . ."

"So somewhere out there among that band of cowards is your anda?"

"No," I said. "My anda wouldn't have abandoned me in an enemy camp." Even as I spoke, I thought of the way I had abandoned Anda Temujin in Chief Kiriltuk's camp, and felt guilty all over again.

The khan glanced at the shaman, who said, "It's been known for andas' spirits to share the same body, but usually only after one of them dies."

Another chill went through me. What if they decided to kill me to test the truth of this?

The khan's eyes narrowed. "The dead boy doesn't have a scar like this one."

Poor Okin. I felt responsible for him. Then I got angry again, because if Yegu hadn't turned back to help his younger brother, the raid might not have gone so wrong.

"Okin wasn't my anda, that's why!" I took a deep breath for patience. Merkids are notoriously stupid, and I didn't want to antagonize them any further than we'd done already by raiding their camps.

"So who *is* this mysterious anda of yours, Jamukha?"

asked the khan, still speaking softly, bending my thumb back even further until a fiery pain shot up my arm. "Why wasn't he with you?"

"You don't need to break my hand!" I snapped. "There's no need for all this rough stuff. Release me, and I'll tell you whatever you want to know."

"No braver than his friends, it seems," said the khan with a chuckle. But my words had the desired effect. He released my thumb, and I wriggled it in relief. "Well, Jamukha? Who is it, then? Another Mongol coward, I suppose?"

"Temujin's no coward!" I told the Merkids about my anda, embellishing the story of his escape from Chief Kiriltuk's camp in the shape of a wolf. I also told them Anda Temujin had a huge army, and that once he discovered how the Merkids were treating me, he'd lead his lads down on their camp like a storm from the mountains and leave every last Merkid dead. This was as likely to be true as the wolf transformation story, but if my captors thought my anda had an army they might be in less of a hurry to kill me, and more inclined to ask for a ransom instead.

The khan tugged at his beard. He glanced at his shaman. "The wolf we saw last night?"

"Anything is possible on Red Circle Night," said the shaman.

"None of our scouts has seen any sign of a Mongol army," said the Merkid Khan, giving me a suspicious look.

"Temujin's hiding it," I said quickly. "He doesn't want

our enemies to know about it, so he's – ah – just waiting for the right time to call on his warriors to join him. As soon as he hears from my lads that you've captured me, he'll be here. So you'd best let me go, and then I'll tell him you've got too many men for us to risk attacking your camp, and persuade him to concentrate on going after the Tartars who killed his father instead."

I thought this rather clever of me, considering my uncomfortable circumstances. As far as I knew, Temujin had no plans to raid the Merkids so I mightn't even have to admit to my anda that I'd been here.

"Hmm." The khan tugged at his beard again. "It does tie in with some of the rumours we've heard about Yesugei the Brave's son. But you've a very loose tongue, Jamukha, and you don't seem the sort of lad who would dare attack a camp this size with a mere hundred lads. Strikes me it's more likely your anda might have sent you here to spy on us while we were busy feasting, only you found our sentries rather more alert than you expected, hmm? Maybe we should roast the boy over a slow fire to get at the truth – what say you, shaman?"

The shaman gave me an evil look and stroked his staff. "There are other ways of making him talk, my khan."

Remembering how quickly Borta had seen through my story last year, and she not even a proper shaman, I decided to come clean. "All right, if you want the truth, I raided your camps because Merkids raided the Jadaran camp twelve years ago and killed my parents. Temujin doesn't know anything about it. But I wouldn't have raided this one if I'd known how big it was. I didn't realize how powerful a khan you are, sir. If you let me go, I'll return to my anda and tell him whatever you like. I'll even spy on Temujin for you . . ."

"Ha!" the Merkid Khan laughed. "Do you think I was born yesterday?" His foot landed in my ribs, and pain surged through me again, making me bite my tongue. Trussed like this, I would have no chance if they decided to hang me over a fire.

"Give me a test, then!" I said, getting desperate. "Anything you like! If you kill me, my anda will attack your camp in revenge and a lot of your people will die. But if you let me go back to him unharmed, he won't suspect a thing. What have you got to lose? I've already spied on him once, for the Taychuit chief . . . I was the one who told Kiriltuk about Temujin killing his half-brother and where to find his camp."

The khan glanced at his shaman, who nodded. "He speaks the truth."

"Then you're a cowardly traitor, to rat on your own anda!" The khan kicked me again, harder than last time. His younger brother winced.

I braced myself to be kicked to death by this Merkid thug. But after a third kick for luck, the khan crouched beside me and bared his black teeth. "However, it's no more than I'd expect from a Mongol, and your desire to avenge your parents' deaths was an admirable enough reason for raiding us. All right, Jamukha, it's possible you might have saved your miserable little life. As it happens, I do have a task for you, one that even a cowardly marmot-eater of a Mongol like you should manage."

The one thought in my head was to get out of that Merkid war camp alive, and promising to spy on Temujin for them seemed the easiest way. Whatever they asked me to do, I felt confident I would find some way around it. Short of killing my anda, anything else seemed a fair exchange for my life.

If only I'd paid more attention to Mongol history, I might have realized the price I'd pay for my freedom. When my captors finally took off the cangue, they put me on my horse and gave me back my bow along with a single black-feathered arrow. The bastards had taken everything else, including my saddle.

The Merkid Khan gripped my bridle and bared his black teeth at me. "Right, Jamukha! Here's your test. Your Anda Temujin's late father Yesugei the Brave stole my young wife Hogelun when I was still a lad like you. I want you to tell your anda that our fires are as many as the stars in the sky so he doesn't get any bright ideas about raiding us. Then, when he gets married, I want you to bring his young wife here to us. If she's pretty enough, Younger Brother Chilger can have her. Otherwise she'll do as a servant. Do you think you can manage that?"

I don't know how I kept my smile.

*

315

If the Merkids thought I'd deliver them Borta in exchange for letting me go, they had another think coming. But if I ignored their request, what would they do when they discovered Temujin's "huge army" consisted of just my anda, his younger brothers, and me? I couldn't even count on Yegu and the others, not now I'd got poor Okin killed.

I'd ridden barely half a day into Mongol territory before I heard horses coming after me. Suspecting Merkid assassins, I put my precious arrow on my string and twisted round to take aim at them, rather awkwardly without my saddle to brace against.

"Don't shoot, Jamukha!" the leading rider yelled. "It's us!"

Yegu.

I lowered my bow and grinned at my friend in relief. He had most of my lads behind him, some of them riding double. I counted heads. Aside from poor Okin, they all seemed to have survived the raid. They were gaping at me as if I were a spirit.

"Well, don't just stand there," I growled. "Someone lend me a saddle, and for the Ancestors' sake get me some more arrows!"

Yegu leapt off his horse and hurried over to stuff half of his own arrows into my quiver. "Jamukha!" he said in awe. "We thought those Murdering Merkids had killed you, for sure. You had the battle madness on you . . . we saw you kill nineteen men with your bare hands before they got the cangue on you! How did you escape?"

"I talked them into letting me go before I killed the rest of them," I said. I decided not to tell them about my bargain with the Merkids, in case it got back to Temujin.

"We were bringing our spare horses to trade for you, Jamukha," said one of the others. "But it went a bit wrong—"

Yegu glared at him. "Later. Chief Jamukha needs something to eat – get a fire going, you lazy lot!"

That was how I found myself back with my lads safe on the Mongol side of the ridge, laughing and exchanging tales of bravery far into the night. Clean again, with arrows in my quiver and a full belly, I began to feel a bit better about things. I managed to embellish the story of the nineteen men I'd apparently killed with my bare hands to make me sound like a great hero who had made a daring escape. Even when my lads told me two fierce lads had made off with some of our horses, I didn't connect it with Temujin at first. My fright in the Merkid camp must have curdled my brain.

"We didn't know what to do, Jamukha," Yegu admitted. "If you'd been with us, we'd have seen them off no trouble. But we thought they might be Merkids, and we did steal their horses in the first place, I suppose." He frowned.

"Only two lads?" I said, starting to think again.

"Very *fierce* lads. About our age."

"This raid," I said. "It wouldn't have happened up near Holy Mountain, would it?"

Yegu nodded.

"You idiots!" I yelled, though I felt like laughing in

317

relief. "That sounds like something my anda would do. I'll bet it was Temujin! What did these two lads look like?"

But it seemed none of them could give me a proper description. It had been dark when the "fierce lads" had attacked their camp, and they'd disappeared into the night with the silver-bay horses. Temujin and his brother Khasar, I decided, with another wave of relief. My anda wasn't dead.

Nor, apparently, did he have much of an army.

"We were caught with our trousers down," Yegu said in a small voice. "I doubt they'd know us again."

"You'd better hope not," I told them. "Because you're going to show me where this attack happened . . . we'll pick up their tracks and if it was Temujin, we're going to join my anda for a while."

I'd come clean, I decided. Tell Anda Temujin about the Merkids wanting to get their hands on Princess Borta, and explain that he'd better not marry her just yet. I would offer to take her home to the Jadaran clan with me so my lads could protect her. She should be safe enough there. In fact, the Merkid threat might work out well. Borta and I would have all winter to get to know each other properly, snowed in . . . Blue Wolf's balls, but the Merkid Khan might even have done me a favour!

My lads led me back to where they'd been camping when they lost the horses. But if it had been my anda who had taken them, then Temujin had vanished like a spirit into the mountains again, his tracks disappearing on the stony ground.

I was a bit worried Yegu and the others might want to do some more raiding to replenish our lost horses, expecting me to lead them with my red moon courage and kill nineteen enemy warriors with my bare hands every time. But my lads' appetite for raiding had died with Okin. With the Merkids on our tails, and with no idea where my anda had made his new camp, I decided the best thing to do was to head for the Alliance. Safety in numbers, I reckoned, and also as good a way as any to find out what Temujin had been up to in our absence.

You can't hide a hundred lads, even riding double. Fatface's sentries spotted us coming and rode out to meet us. "Where do you think you're going, Jamukha?" one of them asked, not bothering with the niceties.

"Back to join my anda," I told them, truthfully enough. "I promised Temujin I'd get him some lads."

He counted my lads and scowled. "Looks like you're trying to raise an army of your own."

"Got to make a show of it, haven't I?" I said with a shrug.

The other sentry chuckled. "Looks like a pretty big show to me – you must be more scared of your Anda Temujin than we thought! He's not here, you know. He escaped."

"So I heard. We've been trying to find his new camp. I don't suppose you know where it is?"

The sentries scowled. "Up on Holy Mountain somewhere. Spirits are hiding it. But your Anda Temujin won't dare show his face down here again, don't worry. We taught him a good lesson last year. He's no threat to anyone now."

Chief Kiriltuk took a rather different view. He counted my lads, our arrows and our battle-toughened horses, and narrowed his eyes. "What do you need so many warriors for, Jamukha? I hope you and your Anda Temujin are not thinking of challenging me for the Mongol khanship?"

"Of course not," I said, hoping he wouldn't bring his shaman over to test the truth of this. I'd had just about enough of shamans and spirits for one year.

Kiriltuk glowered at me. "You've been raiding Merkid camps, I hear. Practising for when you've enough lads to raid my camp, maybe?"

"No . . ."

"You're a dirty liar, Jamukha! If all you wanted were a few lads to show Temujin, you'd not be bothering to train them on raids."

I considered myself a fairly accomplished liar by now, not a dirty one – not now I'd washed off all the Merkid blood, anyway. But the possibility that Chief Kiriltuk might try to stop me from rejoining my anda worried me, because the thought of Temujin tumbling Borta in the furs still burned like a hot coal in my gut, never mind the thought of the Merkids snatching her from him and doing the same.

"That was revenge for my parents' deaths," I pointed out.

Kiriltuk sighed. "I've bigger things to worry about than an unimportant orphan with a death wish! But thanks to your childish raids on their camps last year, I hear the

Merkids have ganged together under their khan. If we're not very lucky, they'll be galloping through *our* yurts next in revenge."

Childish? Didn't he realize how close I'd come to death on our last raid? I'd only survived this long because of the peculiar bravery that came over me when the red moon rose. But I dared not tell Kiriltuk about my red moon madness or my bargain with the Merkid Khan, or he might see me as more of a threat than Temujin. So I swallowed my anger and hung my head, pretending to be the "unimportant orphan" he thought I was. Besides, he could be right. The Merkids might well raid the Alliance camp now that my lads had stirred them up. I just hoped they would wait until we were well out of it first.

Chief Kiriltuk grunted. "At least you seem to realize how stupid you've been. All right, Jamukha, you can stay with us for the rest of this year, where I can keep an eye on you. Then once things have calmed down a bit with the Merkids, you can make up for your stupidity by finding out where your anda's hiding and what he's up to. Report back to me, and I might not have to punish you the way I punished Temujin. In the meantime, your lads can sharpen their fighting skills by training with mine – the competition will be good for them."

What could I say? I didn't have nearly enough warriors to challenge the Alliance on my own, and I certainly didn't fancy spending the winter locked in a cangue with the Merkids poised for an attack. So I thanked the fat chief for his hospitality and retired to the guest yurt to change out of my travel-worn clothes.

While my lads and Kiriltuk's lads threw themselves into the training games with as much fury as if they were raiding an enemy camp, I spent that winter of the Monkey chewing my nails and thinking of Borta and my foolish promise to the Merkid Khan.

Yegu and the others soon found girls in the Alliance camp willing to keep them warm through the snows, but none of the Taychuit girls' sideways glances or inviting smiles excited me enough to take any of them into my yurt. Their foolish giggles reminded me of Borta's half-sister Orbei, and I had to drive away the more persistent ones with the flat of my hand, which just made them squeal all the more and run to their friends to gossip about me.

The only girls I could tolerate that winter were the warrior girls who rode like lads, could shoot straight, and stayed unmarried as long as possible so they could fight alongside their brothers if we were raided. Khadagan was one of these. Tall and muscular, she had the sort of no-nonsense attitude I admired, striding about the camp with her waist-length hair in a messy braid. I made the mistake of smiling at her one day, and that evening she slipped into the guest yurt.

I groaned inwardly.

"Go away," I said. "I'm busy."

She folded her arms and studied me in a way that made me uncomfortable.

"What do you want?" I asked.

"You're going to join your Anda Temujin soon, aren't you?" she said.

Gossip got about fast. I shrugged. "So?"

"I've got a message for him," she said quietly. "Tell him it's from Khadagan – he'll remember me."

I rolled my eyes, too busy working out how to keep Borta safe to deal with her request. "I've got more important things to do than carry lovers' messages across the steppe!" I said.

Khadagan frowned. "You're just as rude as my brothers say you are," she snapped back. "I can't believe someone as brave and honest as Temujin swore the anda bond with you!"

I sighed. Obviously, I wasn't going to get rid of her until she'd given me her message, and I was slightly curious as to what it might be. "All right, what is it?"

She glanced at the door and lowered her voice. "I want you to tell your Anda Temujin that my brothers have been talking to the other clans, and we think old Fatface had more to do with Yesugei the Brave's death than he's saying. We don't trust him to be our chief any more. When he's ready, we'll support Temujin as our khan."

I blinked at her. She seemed deadly serious.

I laughed. I couldn't help it. "Make Temujin khan? By all accounts he's still hiding on Holy Mountain with his little brothers and an army of spirits!"

Khadagan flushed again. "But that's why you're taking

him your lads, isn't it? To help him get his father's people back. Or do you just plan to run off home to the Jadaran when you leave here?"

The thought had crossed my mind, as you know – but only after I'd got Borta safe. "I told you, it's none of your business," I growled.

She looked sideways at me. "I hear you never look at girls, Jamukha. I'm thinking you've got a girl back home, and you love her so much there's no room for anyone else . . . I'm right, aren't I? It's like that sometimes. But maybe you care for your anda, too. If so, you'll take him my message." She ducked out of the yurt before I had a chance to deny this, and strode away in the dark.

I frowned after her, wondering if it could be true that Chief Kiriltuk had plotted with the Tartars to murder Temujin's father. I wouldn't put it past old Kiriltuk, even if he hadn't actually done the deed himself. I felt a sudden surge of protectiveness for my anda. He'd only been nine at the time. At that age, a father's death can destroy a boy's whole life. I should know. I'd only been six when the Merkids murdered mine.

Then I remembered what Khadagan had said about making Temujin khan according to Yesugei the Brave's wishes, and closed the flap with a furious jerk. Is that how they all saw me? Faithful Jamukha, who would do anything for his anda . . . I decided, then and there, that if anyone was going to marry Borta and be named Khan of the Mongols, it would be me.

Kiriltuk obviously still didn't trust me, because when we rode out to rejoin my anda in the spring he sent the young warriors who had trained with my lads over the winter to keep an eye on us. They planned to tell Temujin they were deserters from the Alliance – which I supposed my anda might believe, after what Khadagan had told me. It was a pain, but at least meant we should be safe from a Merkid attack, because the new lads almost doubled the size of my horde.

The closer we got to Holy Mountain, however, the more uneasy I became. Spirits walked up here. Everyone knew that. What if Borta was already in my anda's yurt and had sent her pet deer to spy on me? What would she say when she saw me again, if she knew I'd been talking to our enemies since we last met? I led my lads slower and slower, jumping at every rustle in the bushes. Yegu and the others eyed me sideways, no doubt wondering what had happened to my previous year's courage.

I kept myself going by imagining the look on Temujin's face when he saw the impressive size of my horde. But when we finally found my anda's camp, following directions from a steady stream of lads who seemed to be on their way there too, Anda Temujin wasn't there.

A fierce lad called Boorchu seemed to be in charge, along with Temujin's little brothers, who were not so little any more. In fact, that overgrown idiot Khasar nearly put an arrow in my horse before he recognized me, which at least took my mind off the spirits. After they had welcomed us, they told us Temujin had given up waiting for me to bring him my warriors and gone to collect Princess Borta on his own. He'd taken Belgutei with him to do the talking in my place.

Two years of chasing spirits around the mountain, and I'd missed my anda by just a handful of days.

- 7 -

YEAR OF THE HEN

WE HAD LITTLE choice but to set up our shelters and wait, while Khasar and Boorchu eagerly told us their side of the story. I barely heard a word of it (which didn't matter since I'd already heard most of it from Kiriltuk's people over the winter, anyway). I was too busy imagining Anda Temujin and my beautiful Borta in their wedding yurt at Dei the Wise's camp. One thing I could *not* do now was take Borta back to the Jadaran clan to keep her safe from the Merkids, as I'd planned. I'd have to think of another way to protect her.

When Temujin first came into view, riding at the front of the pathetically small band escorting his wife's cart, my first thought was: what an idiot, to bring Princess Borta all the way up here, so close to Merkid territory, with just a handful of lads to look after her! But admiration quickly took over. He'd brought her safely across Tartar territory in the same daring manner as Yesugei the Brave had taken him as a small boy to Dei the Wise's camp on their search for a bride.

My anda had grown from a boy into a man since I'd left his camp four years ago. Maybe not much taller – he never would be as tall as me – but more muscular and *harder*, somehow. Riding with casual but alert grace, his gaze flicking from shadow to shadow, Anda Temujin looked ready to drive off every enemy on the steppe with merely his flashing eyes and his charming grin . . . that grin, at least, had not changed.

The moment my anda turned that grin on me, my heart melted and my groin tightened, and I knew my lads' taunts and Khadagan's words had more substance to them than I'd been willing to admit. I'd missed him almost as much as I'd missed Borta.

Temujin welcomed me with open arms and an innocent joy that made me uncomfortable. What if he recognized the warriors Kiriltuk had sent to keep an eye on us? But he didn't suspect treachery from me, his anda, and so he didn't look for any. He introduced me proudly to his new wife, while I held Borta's green gaze with mine, praying that she felt as embarrassed as I did and wouldn't mention our last meeting – and Heaven must have tied her tongue, because she didn't say anything. Then my anda put his arm around me and wrestled me into his yurt, where we did some catching up as eagerly as if we were still in our first year cycle, before settling down to a serious war conference with his brothers and Boorchu.

The talk was mostly about our old problem of raising an army to get Temujin's people back, and in that area my anda needed serious help. I now had over two hundred lads who would follow me, plus some more back home with the Jadaran clan I felt sure would join us next season. But as far as I could see, Temujin had only three warriors who would be genuinely useful in a fight: Boorchu, Khasar and, at a pinch, his remaining half-brother Belgutei.

Temujin claimed there were plenty more lads who would come when he called on them, which made me think of the story I'd told the Merkid Khan about my anda's huge army-in-hiding. I had a peculiar shivery sensation at the possibility my words might turn out to be true. But it soon became clear Temujin's "army" consisted of at most a few hundred, and I relaxed slightly. We'd be evenly matched if it came to a fight over Borta, yet we should have enough warriors between us to fend off any attack by the Merkids.

As the others argued about our next move, the biggest problem in my mind was how to get Temujin out of the way so I could be alone with Borta. The easiest thing would be to persuade my anda to finish his recruiting without me, since he'd have to leave someone to guard his camp while he rounded up his horde. If the lads who had promised to join him were scattered about the mountains, then this would take him some time.

Temujin, however, had bigger ambitions than that. He didn't want a mere few hundred untried lads at his back when he raided the Alliance camp. He wanted a full division of trained warriors to take over the Alliance and get rid of old Kiriltuk for good. My hard-won little horde clearly hadn't impressed him at all. Before long, he started bragging about all the mercenaries he'd buy with the impressive sable fur Dei the Wise had given him as Borta's dowry. Thousands of men, who would follow him into battle to avenge his father's death.

I couldn't think where he was planning to get all these mercenaries from. It would have to be from another tribe, since he intended to use them to attack the Mongol Alliance. I got a bit worried about him going to the Merkid Khan and discovering I'd been in their camp last year. To distract him from the Merkids, I said I hoped he wasn't going begging to the Tartars – only to have my anda laugh at me and remind me patiently, as if he were many years older than me, that we were going to raid the Tartars right after he got his people back from Fatface. That left the Naimans, the Oyirads and the Kereyids – and the Kereyid Khan had, apparently, been Yesugei the Brave's anda.

You learn something every day.

Of course the others all wanted to go with him. The Kereyids are a rich tribe, and even if they were poor their camp would be a lot more comfortable than ours over the winter. I watched the way Temujin's cheeks flushed with excitement as he outlined his grand plans. He'd definitely got more ambitious since I'd last camped with him, and I wondered how much of that was Borta's doing.

Eventually, they remembered me. Temujin cleared his

throat, and I knew what he was going to ask before he spoke.

"I'll stay and look after Lady Borta," I offered. I must have been blushing by then. My heart was beating faster than a trapped marmot's, and I felt my groin stirring at the thought.

Rather sneaky of me, I suppose, to let my anda think I was doing him a favour. But having Borta so close, and yet untouchable, drove me half crazy. I didn't know how long Temujin and the others would stay in the Kereyid camp, but even one night alone with Borta would be enough . . . or so I convinced myself.

I didn't exactly expect Borta to welcome me with open arms, considering the curses she'd screamed after me as I left her father's camp. I suppose I could have approached things a bit more romantically. But I was done with foreplay.

I hesitated long enough to check Temujin and his brothers had safely gone, chased Borta's pet deer out of the yurt, and told my lads not to disturb us for any reason. They eyed each other and grinned. A couple of them made crude gestures and Yegu teased, "Jamukha's got over his girl phobia, I see."

Borta didn't have her shaman powers any more, I reasoned, so I felt safe enough – until she turned those green eyes on me and said firmly, "If you touch me, Temujin will know about it."

I assumed she meant she'd tell him, but by then I didn't

care. All I wanted was a fierce tumble in the furs with the girl I'd desired since I was about seven years old, and I could always tell my anda she'd made the whole thing up. So I grabbed her, intending to throw her into the sheepskins, strap her down with my belt if necessary – but something stopped me, like a shadow passing between us.

A prickle went down my spine. I glanced round, expecting to see the wolf spirit at the door watching us – and while I was distracted, my beautiful Borta kneed me in the groin.

Blue Wolf's balls, but that *hurt*!

The pain shot not only through my body, but through my spirit too. Tears sprang to my eyes, and for several heartbeats I could not see, let alone think.

When I'd recovered slightly, Borta was looking at me with a strange kind of sympathy. "I warned you," she said softly. "I told you what would happen to the man who tries to take away my shaman powers."

That was when I realized the bittersweet truth. Borta still had her powers. Which meant my anda hadn't done it with her in the furs yet. Which meant I couldn't do it with her, either, or Temujin would know someone had taken them from her in his absence.

It seemed he didn't trust us that much, after all.

I hardly knew what to do with myself. Thank Heaven it wasn't the red moon, that's all I can say. When I left the yurt and her stupid pet deer shot in to take my place, I felt like riding straight to the Merkids and telling them they were welcome to the girl. I didn't, though. I cared for Borta more than that.

Soon afterwards we were trapped by the snows, and I came to my senses. Temujin had clearly decided to stay the winter with the Kereyids so there was no great rush. Borta still having her powers meant we had extra protection from raiders. Forewarned, and camping in such an easily defensible place, my lads should be able to hold off a Merkid raiding party, and the winter would give me more time to work on Borta.

- 8 -

YEAR OF THE DOG

THAT WAS THE most frustrating winter of my life! Borta resisted all my attempts to seduce her. I couldn't decide whether I admired her for being so faithful to my anda, or hated her for rejecting my advances. I never got so much as a kiss from her to warm my lips, and if she saw me coming she went out of her way to avoid me.

I soon regretted sending my anda off to the Kereyids once it became clear Temujin was in no hurry to return. But I made the best of it, taking my lads off hunting in the forest whenever I could, and shivering through the lonely nights in my shelter trying to decide what to do about the Merkids. The snows were melting and my time was running out. They would come looking for me eventually.

I knew my anda would be slow through the passes if he did get the Kereyids, and the one place I could not be was anywhere near Borta when the red moon rose. I might have controlled myself during the winter, but once the spirits got involved I had no doubt that would be the end of Borta's shaman powers. My anda would never forgive me as long as I lived – which wasn't likely to be very long, once he found out I had forced his wife.

So when the passes opened, I told Lady Hogelun and Borta that I was going to meet Temujin. Then I ordered my lads to pack up their shelters and led them into the forest.

"Where are we going, Jamukha?" Yegu asked, his eyes glinting. "Are we planning another Merkid raid?"

"No!" I snapped. "Not after what happened last time."

"Then where?" he pressed. "I thought we were supposed to stay and guard your anda's camp until he got back with the Kereyids?"

"Change of plan," I told him. "And if you spot a deer, chase it off."

I suppose I could have left some of my lads behind in the camp to look after Borta and Temujin's family. But that would have left me with fewer bows than when we had raided the Merkid war camp, and that hadn't exactly gone well for us. If we met the Merkids before we met my anda, I'd need every fighting man I could lay my hands on.

Besides, there was the question of who I could trust to look after Temujin's wife and family in my absence. Kiriltuk's rabble made it plain they were here to keep an eye on me and would have refused to stay behind, and I didn't want to leave Yegu and my faithful lads with Borta and be left with only Kiriltuk's spies to watch my back when the red moon madness came over me. Also, in my wounded pride, I wanted to teach Borta a lesson. Show her Prince Jamukha of the Jadaran clan wasn't going to stick around forever begging for her favour. I wanted to scare her.

For the next few days, I led my recruits up little-used trails towards the Merkid ridge, leaving small bands of lads at the lookout points with instructions to send a messenger after me if they spotted a raiding party. My groin still gave me trouble when I thought of Borta, and I could feel the red moon waiting for me like an enemy on the horizon. As my horse tripped over roots, I cursed the Murdering Merkids, the sly old fox Kiriltuk, my Anda Temujin, Borta and her pet deer, the Alliance warrior girl Khadagan, and everyone else who seemed determined to thwart my ambitions. Then I cursed myself for being enough of a fool to end up in such a sticky situation in the first place.

As the sun went down on the third day, I decided we'd gone far enough. I stopped my horse in a gorge surrounded by steep cliffs. The sunset turned the larches to fire, making a pretty enough campsite. "All right," I said. "We'll camp here for the night."

Yegu glanced at my face, but asked no questions and passed on the order. As my lads set up their shelters, I scanned the cliffs to check Borta's deer hadn't followed us. That was when I realized we were being watched by more than animal eyes.

Sweat trickled down my spine. *Spirits!* was my first thought. Then: *Don't be ridiculous, Jamukha. Pull yourself together. It's not the red moon yet. They're just men.*

336

The shadows I'd glimpsed vanished quickly behind the rocks. I squinted after them, undecided. Who were they? It occurred to me I had made so many enemies lately, I could take my pick. They could be Merkid scouts, Kiriltuk's spies checking up on me, Temujin's brothers returned early from the Kereyid camp, or even lads from Dei the Wise's camp come to check we were looking after their princess properly.

"Light a fire and post sentries," I ordered. "It's getting too dark to ride now, anyway. We'll flush them out in the morning, whoever they are."

That might have been the worst decision of my life.

When the sun rose, we found ourselves surrounded by three hundred Merkids led by their wily old khan. Heavily armed bodyguards flanked him. His younger brother Chilger hovered behind, holding the horses. The rest of the Merkids knelt among the rocks with arrows aimed at our hearts.

With an effort, I summoned a smile for the Merkid Khan. "There's no need for all those arrows up there. I was just on my way to find you. Let's go into my shelter and talk this over like civilized men, shall we?"

The Khan drew his dagger and put it to my throat. "Civilized men? This looks more like a raiding party than an escort to me. You're a lying Mongol snake, Jamukha."

Better than a dirty liar, I supposed. But not much.

I swallowed my retort. I didn't want them to realize I'd left some of my lads watching the lookout points.

"It's been a while," the khan went on, examining his dagger and watching me. "I hear there was a big Mongol marriage last summer – rumour has it your Anda Temujin's taken a wife now, but I don't see any girls with you. I don't suppose you happen to know where she is?"

Kiriltuk's lads glanced at each other. I willed them not to say anything stupid.

"Jamukha . . . we can take them," Yegu whispered, his hand creeping towards his bow. All my lads were tense as bowstrings, watching me with eager eyes, no doubt expecting me to lead them into battle as I'd done before.

But we were outnumbered and in a bad place, and it was too early for my red moon courage. I shook my head at Yegu and said, "I've really no idea."

The khan bared his black teeth at his younger brother. "You hear that, Chilger? Jamukha claims he's no idea where his anda's wife is, yet andas are supposed to share everything. I think this Mongol wolf is lying to us. What are you doing up here, Jamukha? Planning another raid on my camp? This seems a rather strange place for a Red Circle feast."

Enough was enough. I was losing face before my lads, who were no doubt wondering how it was the Merkid Khan knew my name. I wondered what had happened to my lookouts – surely they hadn't missed three hundred Merkids riding past them in the night?

"If you must know, Anda Temujin's gone to collect the Kereyid army," I told the Merkid Khan, staring him straight in the eye. "He took his wife with him, and we're expecting him back any day now. I rode up here to meet him. They might be up there on the ridge already with their arrows trained on *your* men."

It was gratifying to see him glance up. His warriors turned their heads to scan the rocks.

"The Kereyids?" The Merkid Khan frowned at me. "But why would they help the Mongols?"

"Don't you keep up with steppe gossip?" I smiled at him. "The Kereyid Khan was Yesugei the Brave's anda. He's my Anda Temujin's spiritual father, which makes him near enough my spiritual uncle. I don't suppose he's going to be very happy once he learns you're planning on stealing his spiritual son's wife."

This was better. Yegu and the others close enough to hear straightened their shoulders and gripped their bows tighter. I did have a wild thought of ordering them to fight, but it didn't look as if we'd get out of this spot with many survivors, and I'm not a complete idiot. Not until the red moon rises, anyway.

Chilger cleared his throat. "Elder Brother, if the Kereyids really are coming like he says, maybe we should go back . . . ?"

"Shut up!" snapped the Merkid Khan.

He considered me. Then, to my relief, he sheathed his dagger. "No matter, Jamukha," he said. "We don't need you to bring us the girl. I got tired of waiting for you to remember your promise, and I happen to know your Anda Temujin didn't take his wife with him. It'll be an easy

339

matter to follow your tracks back to your anda's camp, so we're off to get her for ourselves. It's more fun that way."

My heart started to thump. Would Temujin arrive in time to help Borta, if he had left the Kereyid camp as soon as the passes opened? Not with an army behind him, he wouldn't. And without a decent number of men, he and his brothers would be little use against such a large Merkid horde. I might lose my anda tonight as well as Borta.

Trying not to show my desperation, I met the Merkid Khan's gaze and said, "If you so much as *touch* Lady Borta, Anda Temujin will lead his warriors down on your camp like a pack of starving wolves! He loves her very much . . ." That might have been the biggest lie I'd told so far, but never mind. ". . . and he'll be furious if he gets back to find her gone. But if you wait a bit, Temujin intends to use the Kereyids to raid Kiriltuk's Alliance. He'll probably get himself and most of his lads killed. While he's busy doing that, I'll bring you the girl. She's nothing to me."

That should at least give me time to get Borta somewhere safe.

Kiriltuk's lads were muttering about my revelation that Temujin planned to attack the Alliance. I doubted they would stick around much longer, but I had bigger things to worry about just now.

The Merkid Khan tugged his beard and frowned at me again, as if trying to decide how truthful I was being. He indicated we should go into my shelter. I followed warily, my brain still racing. If he refused the deal, how would I

340

get us all out of this alive? The only thing I could think of was to delay him until the red moon rose and we had half a chance of winning this battle.

"I have a problem with you, Jamukha," said the Merkid Khan. "It's one thing to rat on your own anda, but quite another to be so casual about getting him killed. Want to know what I think? I think you and the girl have had a fight, and that's why you're up here while she's waiting all alone down in Temujin's camp for her husband to return."

I must have flushed, for he chuckled. "Ah, so it's true, then? I guess she must need taming – it takes a real man to do that, not a pretty-faced boy like you. Be sensible, Jamukha, and stay out of our way. Then you'll remain alive, and so will your anda's wife. Younger Brother Chilger will look after her, and I might let you see her sometimes if you're still interested in helping us – a spy in the Mongol camps could prove quite useful. Otherwise . . ." He shrugged. "A pretty girl in an enemy camp. I'm sure you understand I can't be responsible for what my men might do."

He walked around my shelter, pretending to be interested in my furs and my saddle. I controlled my fury and watched him carefully to make sure he wasn't up to anything sneaky. At least my lads were still alive. If the Merkids did raid Temujin's camp and steal Borta, we might have a chance of rescuing her on the trail.

But the Merkid Khan was wilier than that. When I had my back turned to the door, he raised his eyes to look over my shoulder. Before I realized the trick, something heavy crashed on my skull bringing an explosion of stars. Then nothing for a long while.

While I lay senseless, the Merkids kidnapped Lady Borta from my anda's undefended camp and disappeared back over the ridge. I led my lads back as fast as I could, hoping the ones I'd left behind might have regrouped and got the women and children to safety, only to find the messengers they'd sent to find me slaughtered on the trail by Merkid arrows, and the rest of them trembling behind the rocks. We found Temujin's camp in ruins: the sheepskins trampled in the mud, Borta stolen, Temujin's family, his horses and herds, all gone. Only Borta's pet deer remained, limping in circles and sniffing mournfully at the flattened tents.

Yegu reached for an arrow, but I caught his wrist and ordered my lads to get a rope on the creature instead. "No!" I said. "That's Lady Borta's spirit deer."

The silly thing had injured its leg, so we lashed it across a spare horse. Its fear-smell reminded me of Borta, and I started to think again. We had found no bodies at the camp, so it seemed Temujin had not yet returned with his great Kereyid army. I had a bit of breathing space. Maybe, if I played things right, we could rescue Borta before my anda got back and found her gone?

I laid a hand on the doe's ribs and felt its little heart pounding fast and hard. "Don't worry, little deer," I told it. "I'll think of a way to make the Merkids give your mistress back to us."

- 9 -

YEAR OF THE PIG

I RACKED MY brains, trying to think of something the Merkid Khan wanted more than he wanted my anda's wife. I offered him horses, which were about the extent of my riches in those days, but he just laughed in my face and said I had a cheek trying to trade Merkid horses I'd stolen from *his* camps for the famous princess of prophecy and mother of a new nation – by which I guessed Borta had told her captors all about her father's dream and unwittingly given them even more reason to keep her. The Merkid Khan even had the nerve to send a message back saying that, once he was sure Temujin hadn't made her pregnant, he planned to marry Princess Borta off to his younger brother Chilger so that the new nation would be ruled by Merkids, not bloodthirsty Mongols. Then, if I was a good boy and kept my anda out of his way, he might reward me with one of his daughters as a wife in appreciation of my efforts.

This made me clench my fists in helpless rage. I had no

doubt the Merkid Khan's daughters were all as pig-faced as he was. Even if they turned out to be as beautiful as Dei the Wise's daughters, no Merkid girl could ever replace Borta in my dream furs.

Unable to risk a raid on the Merkid war camp with my small horde, and not yet ready to face my anda, I sent a messenger to Kiriltuk asking for more warriors to replace the ones I'd lost to the Murdering Merkids. Then I moved my camp into the Khorkonag Valley, where we could defend ourselves if necessary.

That winter, I took in anyone who would join me – the reinforcements Kiriltuk sent when he heard about the raid on my anda's camp, boys from the surrounding clans barely old enough to bend a bow, warrior girls, old men – anyone capable of stopping an arrow so I could get into that Merkid camp and out again with Borta. Opening the flap of my yurt in the morning frosts to see my all my lads' shelters, our herds of horses snorting in the cold air, our clan banners rippling in the breeze and my sentries patrolling the valley, I almost felt like a real khan.

I sent out scouts to check on my anda and discovered he hadn't got the Kereyids as he'd hoped to last year, though he had collected a fair horde himself and was still busy recruiting – obviously he had the same idea I had of attacking the Merkid camp and rescuing Borta. Feeling a bit sorry for my anda, I almost took my lads to join forces with his. Then I thought of how furious Temujin would be with me for abandoning his wife and his family, and decided to wait until he sent for me . . . or sent me a declaration of war. Either way, I'd find out if there was any hope of us staying together after we got Lady Borta back from the Merkids.

He's my anda, I reassured myself. My spiritual brother. Temujin could not shed my blood, no matter what mistakes I'd made, or the Ancestors would curse him.

It took Temujin's brothers longer to find us than I'd anticipated. But when the snows started to melt, Khasar and Belgutei rode into the valley. They came alone, so I invited them into my yurt to impress them with my hospitality and take the edge off their suspicions with airag. They told me that a party of Merkid raiders had stolen Lady Borta, and Temujin was raising an army to wipe the Merkid tribe from the face of the earth, while I bit my tongue and pretended to know nothing – except that Borta had been snatched while I'd been riding out to meet them on their return from the Kereyid camp.

It seemed Temujin's efforts with the Kereyids last year had not been entirely in vain. He had secured their khan's promise of two whole divisions, if he could raise two divisions of Mongols to fight by their side – a real army, not just a few hundred lads for the quick snatch-and-grab rescue I'd been planning.

But it suited my plan. So I swallowed my misgivings, promised that I'd help my anda rescue Lady Borta, and sent Khasar and Belgutei back to Temujin with a message to meet me with his army on the ridge at the head of the

Onan on Red Circle Day. We'd attack while the Merkids were feasting and, more to the point, while I still had my red moon courage – though I didn't mention that part, of course. Instead, I impressed on Temujin's brothers how important it was that they weren't late, and Khasar and Belgutei rode off with big grins on their faces as if they'd talked me into the whole thing.

I should have realized that if friends could find us, then so could the Merkids. Towards the end of winter, two warriors I recognized from last year's raiding party rode negligently into our camp carrying the white horsetail of truce.

"Our khan sends greetings to Jamukha of the Jadaran clan," said one. The other, I noted, was busy making a count of my men and my yurts. "Temujin's young wife is proving rather less of a breeding prospect than we anticipated," the spokesman went on. "Our khan doesn't want to risk bringing her shaman curses down on our camp, so he says he's happy to give her back to you, as you asked, in return for your services."

This seemed rather too good to be true after what they'd said last year. There had to be a sting under the collar.

"Untouched," I specified. "If you've hurt her . . ."

The Merkids smiled. "Oh, don't worry, we haven't laid a hand on the girl! Chilger the Athlete's welcome to the crazy bitch. Word is her spirit lives in an animal's body and will shrivel any man who lies with her."

"That's right," I said, and tried to persuade them it

346

would be safest to give Borta back to me immediately. Then we might not have to attack their camp at all.

I didn't think it would be that easy.

"You've got the wrong idea, Jamukha," said the Merkid who had been counting my men. "We've heard your Anda Temujin is raising an army to rescue his wife. You've got a decent number of lads up here yourself by the looks of things. If you can delay your anda from attacking our camp until after Red Circle Night, and come to our tents alone to help us with the ceremony, then our khan will make sure the girl comes your way as a reward."

My thoughts began to race around in circles.

"And what happens on Red Circle Night?" I asked warily.

The Merkids grinned at each other. "Spirits walk, Jamukha, you know that. It's just a case of making sure they're on our side this year. We've got a special ceremony planned for Red Circle Night, one guaranteed to put an end to this prophecy that is setting fire to the steppes. All you need to do is keep your anda's army out of the way until the red moon sets – shouldn't be too difficult, surely? Then we'll kill Temujin for you, and the Mongol wolf will be as toothless as a newborn babe."

A cold sweat bathed my neck. "You think the wolf is my Anda Temujin, then?"

They gave me a surprised look. "Of course – who else can it be?"

I thought of how the Merkid shaman had claimed I was

possessed by a demon spirit when I'd attacked their camp two years ago, and shivered.

"What's the matter, Jamukha?" one of the Merkids teased. "Having second thoughts about betraying your anda? His pretty wife not enough of a reward for you? Maybe you'd prefer it if we kept the girl and let you have Chilger the Athlete instead?"

They were too busy chuckling at their own joke to notice my fist clench on my dagger.

"Fine," I told them, relaxing my hand with an effort. "No problem. Leave it to me."

After I'd seen them off, I crossed the valley to the cave where Borta's pet deer was penned. I leant over the rail to watch the doe, and the way it looked at me made my heart beat fast and blood pound in my ears. "Stupid thing," I told it. "If your mistress really had shaman powers, she wouldn't still be a captive down in the Merkid camp!"

I wanted Borta; of course I wanted her back. But not if it got my anda killed in the process. For the first time since we'd sworn the anda bond, I felt Temujin's rage burning in my veins as if it were my own. I'd send the Merkids their Mongol wolf, all right, just not in quite the way they had planned.

If I was to get Borta to safety, and my anda through this alive, I knew I would need to time things very carefully indeed. Anxious not to miss the red moon, I arrived at the meeting place with my division of lads early on Red Circle

348

morning and set up a temporary camp. I sent a messenger down to the Merkid camp to let their khan know I was on my way to claim my reward, and posted sentries to watch the road into the valley, and more sentries along the top of the ridge to watch the first lot. I still didn't trust Kiriltuk's lads not to run off back to the Alliance when the going got tough.

Then, feeling only slightly safer, I gave Yegu strict instructions to wake me as soon he sighted my anda's army, and retired to my shelter. I lay down with a damp rag folded over my eyes in an effort to control the battle rage that was swelling nicely inside me. The last thing I wanted was for it to come too early and be wasted.

Temujin was taking his time, but I couldn't sleep. I lay there all day, getting hotter and hotter under my shelter, thinking of Borta and how soon I'd be carrying her out of the Merkid camp on the withers of my horse with her soft, warm body pressed against mine. I think I had a vision of killing a hundred Merkid warriors with my bare hands while the battle rage was on me, and having Borta fall into my arms in gratitude. Once she realized I'd cared for her pet deer all winter, she might see how much I really loved her. Temujin, being a generous sort of anda, might even give her to me as a reward for helping him rescue her. After all, he couldn't really love her, or he'd not have left her untouched on their wedding night . . .

All right, so maybe the red moon madness had already

invaded my blood. I could even hear the horse's hoof beats under me.

Bor-ta, Bor-ta, Bor-ta, Bor-ta.

In my dream, I galloped into the Merkid camp and found Borta a prisoner in one of their tents. When she saw me, she changed into a doe and tried to flee. But there was a cangue around her neck so she couldn't escape. I remembered our first clumsy kiss back in Dei the Wise's camp, when she'd screamed for her sisters to save her. No, that wasn't right – she was screaming at me, asking who I was.

I hardly knew myself. Temujin's blood brother? Orphaned Jadaran prince? Alliance spy? Merkid collaborator? I tried telling her I'd come to rescue her, but she was beyond listening to anything I said. Even in my dream, I knew telling her my real name would be a bad idea if something went wrong. I thought I heard a whisper in my ear: "*Tell her your name is Genghis*" but when I looked round, expecting to see the scheming Merkid Khan, nobody was there.

Now we were alone at last, and Borta lay squirming beneath me. I broke into a sweat. Smoke bitter with shaman magic got up my nose, making my head spin. I tried to open my eyes but the dream held me captive, hot and hard.

The red moon rose. Something brushed against my spirit, like feathers. Then there was only the sweet, warm night.

*

When I woke, everything was strangely quiet. I lay under my shelter with the rag over my eyes, a breeze cooling my sweat and my lads talking in low voices nearby.

The relief of not waking up to find myself in a Merkid cangue kept me lying there several heartbeats longer, enjoying the peace. Then I warily removed the rag from my eyes and examined myself for blood. None, except for a few stains on my trousers that had probably been there before. I didn't feel sore, either. In fact, I felt more relaxed than I had done since the winter I so foolishly swore the anda bond with Temujin.

From the position of the sun, it was around mid-afternoon. My army seemed to be intact, their horses grazing nearby saddled and ready to ride, their quivers stuffed with arrows. No groaning wounded or piles of enemy skulls. No screams of my nightmares. No Borta cursing me with her shaman magic.

It must have been a bad dream, after all.

"Yegu!" I called, crawling out from under the shelter and stretching the kinks from my shoulders. "Any sign of Anda Temujin yet?"

My friend came running. There was a strained look in his eyes, which didn't quite go away when he smiled. "Jamukha . . . thank Heaven you're awake! No, I'm afraid your anda and the Kereyids aren't here yet."

"Never mind. There's still time."

Yegu frowned. "You think Temujin's still coming, then? Some of the lads think we should move our main force back to the Khorkonag Valley, in case the Merkids come up here looking for us . . . but I didn't know if we should move you in your state. Do you think it's safe for us to wait another day?"

My state?

"How many days have we been here?" I asked, my relaxed mood vanishing to be replaced by a terrible sense of déjà vu.

Yegu wet his lips. "It's two days after Red Circle, Jamukha. When you rode off alone to the Merkid camp that night, I thought you were dead! But the sentries seemed to be expecting you and let you past, so I guessed you must have a plan. Me and some of the lads hid behind the rocks and watched. When you came back out again, you were staggering about like you were drunk, so I took you up on my horse and galloped back up here double quick. You've slept for two whole days. You had some kind of fever – we thought they'd poisoned you. Don't you remember any of it? Looked like the Merkids were having a good Red Circle feast . . . better than the one we didn't have up here waiting for Temujin, any rate." He grinned, trying to make a joke of it.

Red Circle Night was over. My battle-rage had come and gone. I thought of my dream. A fever-induced nightmare, or . . . ?

"How many people did I kill this time?" I asked in a dull tone. I almost didn't care. My plan to rescue Borta and become a hero overnight had failed. Even if Anda Temujin turned up now with the entire Kereyid army, the Merkids would be forewarned of our attack.

"I don't think you killed anyone," Yegu said. "Nobody came after you, anyway."

"Lady Borta?"

He shook his head. "I think the Merkids must still have her. They were yelling about a wolf."

"And did you see this wolf, Yegu?" I asked gently.

My friend shook his head. "Not me. Maybe it's still down in the Merkid camp somewhere?"

"Or maybe they've already killed it," I said, making Yegu look at me strangely. Would that account for my fever? Was that what happened when your anda died? Did his spirit invade your dreams and take over your body?

I almost abandoned the idea of rescuing Borta, but my worst fears were unfounded. Anda Temujin turned up the next afternoon, grinning like a little boy. He had brought the Kereyid army with him as he'd promised, led by their khan no less, although by then he might as well have brought an army of spirits. He claimed he'd been waiting for the Kereyid Khan to honour the Ancestors and make his prayers before riding into battle.

Meanwhile, I'd spent the whole day imagining the worst. I had a sore head still from my red moon fever, so I'm afraid I took out my anger on him. There was a tense moment, when Temujin asked why I'd left his camp unprotected and defenceless against the Merkid raiders last year. But we settled our differences for Borta's sake and rescheduled our attack for moonrise.

I didn't know how I'd get through it, quite honestly. But when we charged down that ridge and streamed across the Merkid steppe in a yelling, whooping horde, it proved easy enough to haul my horse back behind the others. In the confusion of firing the Merkid yurts, and all the screaming and running, no one noticed me trot off through the wreckage in search of Chilger's tent.

I found it easily enough – I remembered the way from my red moon dream, which chilled me rather. I swung down from my horse afraid of what I might see. Our army had already been this way. The wooden frame had been pulled down and smashed, the furs scattered, the couches overturned. Chilger's standard lay nearby, broken in two.

"Borta?" I called without much hope. "Borta!"

She'd gone, of course, along with everyone else who could still run. I levered up the felt with the end of my lance to check underneath for bodies – and one of the lumps heaved upwards and flung itself at me. It had a fur over its head, and for a heartbeat I thought it was my anda, changed into a wolf like everyone claimed. Then the fur fell off, and I found myself face to face with a very frightened Chilger.

He nearly impaled himself on my lance before he recognized me. "Jamukha! Don't kill me."

Warily, I lowered the point. "What are you doing hiding under there?" I said. "What have you done with Lady Borta?"

"She's with the other women . . . the guards loaded them all onto a cart."

"Why aren't you fighting with the rest?" I asked, relieved to hear Borta was alive, at least.

Chilger gave me a hopeless look. "The wolf-spirit killed Elder Brother the Khan! It ripped out his throat! I'm afraid it'll come after me next. Please help me, Jamukha. Your Anda Temujin will roast me alive for keeping his wife in my yurt, but I never meant to hurt her, I swear . . . Elder Brother the Khan made me break her arm so she couldn't warn her husband of our plans. If you let me go, I'll not tell Temujin *anything*. Please!"

Another shiver went down my spine. I considered putting my spear through the idiot Merkid lad to save my anda the bother. I couldn't help thinking it would make things very awkward for me if Temujin found out the truth about my deal with the Merkids, even though I'd only made that deal so I might have a chance of rescuing Borta if the Kereyids didn't show up. The battle noises around us were fading. Obviously we'd won. There hadn't really been any question of it, not with our combined divisions and Anda Temujin leading them. I just hadn't expected to still be breathing at this point, that's all.

I thought uneasily of my dream.

"Red Circle Night," I said, my mouth going dry. "Were you at the ceremony?"

Chilger avoided my gaze. He nodded.

"What did I do, exactly?"

355

His gaze flew to mine and away again. "Don't you *remember*?"

"I've had a fever. Just tell me what you saw!"

Chilger gave me a sideways look. "We blindfolded Temujin's wife so she couldn't curse us. The shaman played his violin to keep her spirit captive, but I think we did it wrong . . . Lady Borta's spirit must have seen us, after all, and then the wolf came . . . Elder Brother panicked—" his eyes widened and he looked behind me.

I was so jumpy, I'd turned to look before I realized it might be another sneaky Merkid trick. I needn't have worried. The Merkids were finished, scattered like ashes in the wind. A small band of riders with bows slung over their shoulders were trotting our way: Anda Temujin's lads, by the look of them.

I gripped my lance and took a deep breath, trying to think.

So Borta had been blindfolded that night? Even if I hadn't been dreaming under the red moon, even if I'd ridden to join the Merkid feast and taken part in some crazy spirit-ceremony as Chilger claimed, she wouldn't have been expecting to see me in the middle of the Merkid camp. If I killed him, my secret would be safe.

On the other hand, Chilger probably wasn't the only one who had seen me in the Merkid camp that night, and it might be a good idea to leave Anda Temujin someone other than me to hunt down for Borta's kidnapping. Even if Chilger was captured and told Temujin about my part in the Red Circle ceremony, who would my anda believe? The Murdering Merkid who had kept Lady Borta prisoner in his yurt, or his faithful anda who had raised a division of warriors to help him rescue her?

I made my decision. Jamming my helmet on Chilger's head, I hurried across to a dead Kereyid and dragged off his breastplate. "Put this on over your shirt," I said. "You can take my horse. I'll get another."

Chilger obeyed with shaking hands. "Th-thank you, Jamukha!" he stammered. "I'll not forget this. I hope Lady Borta is all right—"

"Get out of here!" I whacked the horse on the rump before I could change my mind, and Chilger the Athlete galloped away into the darkness of the steppe, taking his secrets with him.

- 10 -

YEAR OF THE RAT

AFTER THE BATTLE, everyone started calling Temujin "khan", which made me grind my teeth in frustration. If we'd attacked on Red Circle Night, as I'd originally planned, it would have been a different story, mark my words! But during the raid, with no red moon rage to help me, I have to admit my anda with his crazy bravado and his "follow me" grin out-fought me.

My lads claimed they'd seen Temujin change into a wolf and tear out the throat of the ox pulling the cart that held Borta, and even the Merkid prisoners claimed they'd seen the wolf with Temujin. This did make me wonder a bit if the wolf demon possessed my anda when it wasn't busy possessing me, but that was silly. Rumours aside, as far as I knew up until tonight Temujin had not even been on a proper raid, let alone in a battle. And now – because he'd got the Kereyids at my suggestion, and I had risked my life to make sure the Merkids would be unprepared for his attack – he had destroyed the Merkid tribe, and everyone took that as a sure sign Heaven meant him to be khan.

I rode with my anda in the place of honour at the front of our army. But rather than making me feel proud, panic stirred my guts. My lads had mixed with his lads, until I could hardly tell which was which. Meanwhile, Borta rode in Lady Hogelun's cart, no doubt telling Temujin's mother everything I'd said and done back in our Holy Mountain camp before the Merkids had captured her.

I'd just about decided the only safe option would be to separate my lads from Temujin's and head back to the Alliance as quickly as possible, when news came from the women that the spirits had stolen Lady Borta's tongue so her body could concentrate on healing itself. Lady Hogelun said Borta's speech would return once her arm had mended properly, and meanwhile Anda Temujin should sleep elsewhere.

I relaxed a little. A broken bone would take at least a month to heal, and by then I might have a chance to think up some sort of plan.

Temujin moved into my tent, determined to talk about anything except his wife, which suited me. "We taught those Merkid pigs a lesson, Jamukha, didn't we?" he said with a grin. "Now we'll never be apart. When I'm khan, we'll ride together on white geldings with golden belts around our waists and share everything again just like when we camped beside the Onan – only with enough warriors this time to see off anyone who tries to raid us! It'll be fun."

Privately, I hoped it would be nothing like when we'd camped by the Onan. Onions and flies and a permanently empty stomach, I could do without. The victory had obviously gone to Temujin's head. But it *was* good to be back with my anda. We cut our thumbs again that night and renewed our anda vows.

And if I did it for the wrong reasons, I hope Heaven will forgive me.

The sensible thing would have been to leave before the snows came, but somehow I could not make myself give the order. The trouble being, I couldn't stop thinking of Borta in the women's yurt. The glimpses I caught of her when she emerged to squat briefly behind the tent – though torture for me – kept me in my anda's camp as surely as if Temujin had locked me in a cangue. While she remained nearby, I told myself there was still hope she might come to love me in return. And since she and Temujin hadn't sealed the marriage bond before her capture, maybe . . . just maybe . . . Borta was keeping herself for me?

Several times that winter, with Borta recovering in the women's yurt, I thought we might live up to the rumours of andas comforting each other in the furs. But Temujin's thoughts were a thousand steppes away, full of his plans to annihilate the Tartars once he'd got his people back from Kiriltuk, and crazier plans still – to lead his army east into the high mountains, where people lived in high-walled cities and were rumoured to dress in scarlet silk and have riches beyond our wildest dreams. His ambition scared me.

Then Temujin told me Borta was pregnant, which brought a fresh panic. I knew the child couldn't be Temujin's, because he hadn't spent a single night with his wife since we'd rescued her – so whose could it be?

I kept seeing Chilger, trembling under his flattened yurt, saying, "I didn't mean to hurt her." And then, even though she couldn't have known I'd been in the Merkid camp on Red Circle Night, I thought of what I might say in Borta's position. She seemed to hate me more than ever, probably blaming me for the death of her silly deer, when it had hardly been my fault if a wolf had broken into its pen while my men waited for Temujin on the ridge. What if she made up a nasty lie to get rid of me?

Blue Wolf's balls, but I must have been an idiot to stay as long as I did.

I spent more and more time sitting under our special tree, gnawing at my fingernails, while Temujin spent less. I was terrified of him finding out about my bargain with the Merkids but I missed him, too. His absence hurt almost as much as my frustrated desire for his wife.

When the branches parted one morning towards the end of winter and a rosy-cheeked, heavily pregnant Borta ducked inside, a rush of emotions tumbled through me. Joy that she was here at last, out of earshot of her husband's camp . . . terror that Temujin would find her under the tree with me and assume the worst . . . fear that the baby would come. While I tried to decide if it was a trap, she caught her breath. Then she looked straight at me with her green eyes and told me to clear out of the camp.

It took me a moment to realize she'd broken her winter-long silence. My panic returned, and I looked fearfully at the branches around us. My anda might be out there now, with his brothers and his fierce friend Boorchu, waiting to skewer me.

But no spears poked through the pine branches. No arrows hissed into the green shadows. I relaxed slightly. Temujin wouldn't put his wife at risk like that, and she'd come to warn me. Maybe she hadn't spoken to my anda yet? Since the Merkids had obviously taken away her shaman powers, I could probably invent a story to explain myself – but what would she believe?

Before I could get myself tangled up in another twisted net of lies, I asked her outright if she knew who the father was.

I should have known I wouldn't get a straight answer from someone who had trained with a shaman. She mumbled something about a spirit called Genghis, and the name stirred something deep inside me, although I couldn't remember where I'd heard it before. At the time, I thought Borta had gone a bit crazy after what the Merkids had done to her, and thanked Heaven she didn't seem to know much more about that night than me.

Then she accused me of killing her pet deer and betraying

Temujin, and we got into another silly argument that ended with her demanding to know what I intended to do when we reached the Alliance and I had to choose sides. She had a point. Kiriltuk's lads had been grumbling all winter about Temujin's plans to attack the Alliance, worried about their families back in his camp. When we got as far as attacking it, I wasn't at all confident they would follow me. If we won, Anda Temujin was bound to find out from someone there how I'd spied on him for the fat chief. And if we lost . . . well, I didn't plan on taking an arrow in the back for my anda.

So when the snows melted and Temujin, despite Lady Borta being so near her time, led us all on a merciless march towards the Alliance camp, I made my excuses and ordered my lads to stop early by the river. Anda Temujin wasn't happy about me refusing to fight, but neither did he stick around to talk me out of it. He had enough lads of his own now to take over the Alliance, and that's exactly what he did.

As it turned out, I was right about Kiriltuk's lads. Half of them ran off after my anda to rescue their families. But they didn't stay to fight for Temujin either. After the battle, they came running straight back to me with their women and children and the animals they had managed to save from their herds, full of spirit-tales about a huge silver-blue wolf rampaging through the camp.

I laughed at this old tale and told Yegu and his lads to let them in. "Was its name Genghis?" I asked them. But they just stared at me blankly as if I'd gone mad. Maybe I had a bit, by then.

Kiriltuk arrived towards the end, cowering in a cart like a woman. I didn't know if this meant he'd been the last to run away, or if his horse had expired halfway across the steppe from carrying his huge bulk. He had three of my anda's arrows in his backside, which made me laugh even louder. I told Yegu to pluck them out for him and bring him straight to my yurt.

Kiriltuk the Fat, former chief of the most powerful clan Alliance on the steppe, stood in my doorway wearing a torn deel and blood-stained trousers, red-faced and glowering at me. I remembered how he had told me to run back to the Jadaran clan like a good little boy when I'd gone to claim my reward after Begter's death, and smiled.

Time to enjoy myself.

"Sit down, Kiriltuk," I said, waving him to the couch. "There's no need for you to prostrate yourself before me – you'll only have difficulty getting up again."

"Pr-Prostrate . . . ?" He spluttered then seemed to remember he was in no position to argue. Still suffering from his arrow wounds, he declined my invitation to sit and said, "Jamukha, I'm grateful to you for giving my people refuge, but if you think that means—"

"You can stay," I said, cutting him short. "But this is my camp. I give the orders here."

"*I'm* chief of the Mongol Alliance!" Kiriltuk took a step

forward. Yegu prodded him in the chest with his spear, and the former chief collapsed on my couch with a groan of pain.

"Anda Temujin has taken over the Alliance now," I pointed out. "You can join me or not, as you wish. But if you leave, I doubt any of your clan chiefs will follow you. You're welcome to ask them."

I felt fairly sure I was on safe ground, since I'd already spoken to the refugee chiefs myself and given them valuable gifts from my share of the Merkid treasure. Kiriltuk spluttered a bit more, but even he could see things had changed between us. He could either leave with a handful of his people and spend the rest of his life in terror of Temujin hunting him down, or stay and accept my protection. I still needed something from him, so I smiled and told Yegu to get him some airag, which the former chief gulped from my bowl with shaking hands.

When I judged he'd drunk enough, I put one finger on the edge of the bowl and pushed it away from his lips. I smiled at him again, and the piggy eyes became wary. "Now then, let's talk business," I said. "About this promise you made to support me when I was old enough to make my bid for Lady Borta . . . I think it's time you honoured it, don't you?"

Chief Kiriltuk looked at the bowl of airag, at my yurt decorated with furs and Merkid gold, and at Yegu standing alert beside my door with his spear. "Lady Borta is Temujin's wife now," he said warily. "So it isn't that simple any more. I already gave you warriors so you could protect her, and you nearly got them all killed. What else do you want?"

"I want you to make me khan," I said calmly.

Kiriltuk paled. "I heard Temujin's people are calling him khan," he said. "The Mongols can't have two khans."

"That's why we must have a proper ceremony to make me khan as soon as possible," I said. "My anda's people are a bit confused, that's all. They'll soon realize I'll make them a better leader than Temujin, don't you worry. After all, I've had the right upbringing for it. And I'm sure you'd prefer me as your lord and master, rather than Anda Temujin and his so-called wolves, especially once he finds out you were involved in the plot to poison his father Yesugei the Brave."

This was a bit of a gamble. I hadn't managed to discover if there was any truth in Khadagan's rumours, and my spirit dream of ten years ago was hardly evidence. But Chief Kiriltuk paled even more. He drained the bowl, handed it back to Yegu and bowed his head.

"Yes, Jamukha Khan," he mumbled. "We'll have a ceremony, as you say. I'll speak to my shaman. Leave everything to me."

Obviously these arrangements would take some time if things were to be done properly, and we needed to put some distance between our two camps in the meantime. So I led the frightened refugees back to the Khorkonag Valley for the winter, where we had half a chance of defending ourselves if my anda got wind of our plans.

*

Seeing the blood and tracks in the mud outside the cave where I'd kept Borta's spirit deer brought back uncomfortable memories of my part in the Merkid Red Circle ceremony. There wasn't much left of the creature. It looked as if wild animals had fought over the carcass. Wolves, of course . . . but also deer slots and hoof prints. There were human footprints too. Someone had ridden up here while we'd been gone.

I felt bad about the death of Borta's pet, and she had reason to be upset with me. But it was hardly my fault Anda Temujin and the Kereyid army had been late on the ridge. I'd done my best and left it some food in its pen. I'd never meant to leave the silly creature unattended for so long, that's all.

I took the rope off the skeleton and stared at the scattered bones. A shiver went down my spine as the deer skull stared back at me, picked clean of meat. What if the shaman spirit-bond had not been broken by death? What if Borta could see me now and knew what I was planning?

I drew back my foot to kick the skull into the back of the cave with the other bones, but something stopped me. I bent down and picked it up. "Borta," I whispered, and kissed its pale forehead.

An icy wind stirred my braids. My heart thudded as I swung round, searching the shadows for spirits. But the pines stood dark and tall, creaking a little in the breeze. The cliffs were deserted.

Don't be stupid, Jamukha, I told myself. *It's not the red moon for ages.*

Shivering, I tucked the skull under my arm and took it back to my yurt. If I couldn't have Borta in my furs that winter, I'd have the next best thing.

- 11 -

YEAR OF THE OX

THE CEREMONY WAS set for Red Circle Day. I should have seen it coming, I suppose, but I was a bit distracted that spring. We'd just heard that Temujin had slaughtered the Tartars. He'd had plenty of experience leading his lads into battle by then, so I wasn't really surprised at his latest victory.

Rather more worryingly, my anda had sent out men seeking information about a "wolf" called Genghis. Obviously, Borta had told him all about that Red Circle night in the Merkid camp . . . but how much did she really know? I questioned the messengers closely. But the idiots seemed to think that this Genghis, whoever he might be, was some kind of ghost. According to the shamans, my anda was on a quest for his spirit animal.

I knew my anda's mind better than that. The only quest Temujin had in mind was one of revenge.

On the morning of the ceremony, I summoned Yegu to my tent.

"Keep a close watch on me tonight," I ordered. "If I show signs of being possessed by a demon, you must stop me from killing anyone, or they'll never make me their khan."

He gave me a sideways look. "How are we supposed to do that, Jamukha?"

"I don't know! Restrain me or something, but not so it looks bad. This is important, Yegu! Everything must go smoothly."

"We could tie you to your throne, I suppose," Yegu suggested with a frown. "You'll be wearing long sleeves. They'll hide the ropes. If people do notice, we could say it's part of the blessing. We'll have to warn the shaman, though. Shamans see everything."

A shudder went through me. But I trusted my friends. If Kiriltuk tried anything sneaky, my lads would soon put a stop to it.

So I said, "Good idea. Tell the shaman I'm worried about the Red Circle spirits possessing me."

He had little idea how close to the truth this was.

"What if the wolf comes?" Yegu whispered, glancing at the door flap.

Another shiver went through me. "Then everyone will just think it's the spirit of our Ancestors and take it as a good omen. Whatever you do, don't let me kill the wolf!"

Yegu still looked worried. "I'll do my best, Jamukha.

But when you get the battle-rage on you, I doubt even Anda Temujin could hold you!"

Come Red Circle Day, I couldn't even resort to my usual trick of lying down with a wet rag over my eyes, because Kiriltuk's women wanted to prepare and dress me for the ceremony. The giggling girls, squabbling over who would braid my hair, set my nerves on edge. I endured their attentions because this had to be done properly or my people wouldn't respect me afterwards. When they were finished, I gulped down three whole bowls of airag, hoping that might dull my red moon madness.

My people cheered me as I walked through the crowd to accept the blessing of the shaman. The girls who had dressed me nudged each other, trying to catch my eye. I remembered Borta's sisters, eying me in much the same way when I'd gone to collect my anda's wife from Dei the Wise's camp, which put me in an even worse mood.

I sat on a raised chair the girls had wreathed in flowers and gripped the arms so the sleeves of my deel draped them. I gave Yegu a nod. While the shaman started his chanting, Yegu knelt at the sides of my chair and surreptitiously wound the lashings tight around my wrists.

Two white horses were led before me, also draped in flowers – a stallion and a mare. The mare was in season, and the men could barely hold her. The shaman brushed the stallion's coat with his staff, and the two horses mated right there in front of me. I felt my groin stir and closed my eyes.

The stallion finished his business and came down to earth with a snort, and the men moved in with their knives. Blood sprayed my cheek. When I opened my eyes to see if it was over, I saw a shadow moving in the trees outside the ring of fires.

"Yegu!" I hissed, tugging at my bonds.

This had been a terrible idea. I could feel no hint of the battle madness, only cold terror. I imagined an assassin out there in the dark, sent by my anda to put an arrow in me.

"Yegu, untie me!" I hissed again, but my friend couldn't see the shadow, and ignored my request just as I'd ordered him to earlier.

As the red moon rose, my heart thudded faster. My head spun and stars fizzed before my eyes. The shaman approached me with the tail of the stallion, freshly cut from the carcass.

"Spirits of our Ancestors, bless Jamukha Khan!" he called, brushing the bloody horsehair across my cheeks. "Bless Jamukha of the Jadaran clan, direct descendent of Blue Wolf and Fallow Doe, Khan of all the Mongol people! Bless his sons and their sons . . ."

My sons . . . that would mean taking a wife, but Borta was the only girl I wanted, the only girl I'd ever wanted.

The shadow in the trees became a deer that looked like Borta's pet, Whisper. Its throat had been torn out by a wolf, and blood ran down its legs. Then the blood was somehow under my fingernails, and I could taste it on my tongue, and

I knew I'd hurt her, and my anda would never forgive me for that as long as I lived.

My ears roared, and the red moon turned black.

When I opened my eyes, the Red Circle feast was over. I lay in my yurt in my undershirt with angry burns around my wrists from the ropes. I didn't feel nearly as good as last year when I had woken on the ridge above the Merkid camp. My head throbbed and my mouth was full of grit. A blurred memory of feverish dreams gave me the panicky feeling that several days had passed.

Someone had left me a bowl of curds and some cold meat for breakfast, but no servants were around to help me. It seemed remarkably quiet. Maybe everyone was still sleeping off the feast. I drank the milk, then crawled to the door and warily peered out.

Relief filled me at the sight of my banner still rippling outside my tent. My horses grazed safely nearby, and my lads were on sentry duty down by the river as normal. But yellow patches showed in the grass where many of Kiriltuk's people had camped. A few carts stood by, piled with belongings, taking more families on their way out. Knowing that they were sneaking off to join Anda Temujin annoyed me, though there wasn't much I could do about it. You can't keep entire clans with you by force.

"Yegu!" I called.

He came running. "How are you feeling, Jamukha

Khan?" he asked. "Temujin's heard about the ceremony, and he's sent you some heads—"

"Never mind that! What happened after the moon rose? How long have I been asleep? Why is everyone leaving?"

Yegu pressed his lips together. "Not everyone, my khan . . . nearly half the families are still with us."

Only half? Worse than I'd thought, then. "Tell me everything," I said.

Yegu sighed. "I'm sorry, Jamukha Khan. You've been in a fever for three days. We couldn't stop them going. It was the talking animals . . ." And he told me this crazy story about how the animals in our camp had started to talk on Red Circle Night, telling people Temujin was meant to be their khan, and not me.

"The shaman said the ancestor spirits possessed them," he explained, shuddering a little. "They seem back to normal now, though, and everyone had been drinking so I wouldn't take too much notice of such spirit-tales, if I were you. Most of the lads think they were dreaming, and now you've recovered I expect the rest will stay. You're not the only one who's had a hangover . . . I blame the airag, myself."

Kiriltuk's women could easily have slipped something into the airag as they were making it, some poison like they'd slipped into Yesugei the Brave's drink eleven years ago on the Tartar steppe, that made people see and hear things that weren't there, such as shadows in the trees and talking animals. Obviously, my camp was still riddled with

Temujin's spies. But there was another explanation – one I didn't like to think about too much.

"What about me?" I asked. "Did I get possessed again?"

"I don't know, Jamukha Khan." Yegu avoided my gaze. "But I didn't see a wolf this time. We untied you when no one was looking and brought you back here. Don't worry, we told everyone you were communicating with the Ancestors so they'd leave you alone."

That, at least, was a relief. The ceremony must have been completed properly, and I hadn't killed anyone. I was khan, despite what the idiots who had gone to join my anda might think.

I rubbed my sore wrists, a bit worried the shaman might have seen through my lads' story. Then I remembered what Yegu had said earlier. "Did you say *heads*?"

Yegu coughed. "I think they're the heads of the prisoners Temujin took during his raid on Kiriltuk's camp. There were a lot of flies, but some of the men recognized their dead brothers. Anda Temujin sent a message with them. He said to tell you that if you want to see Lady Borta again, you're to come to the Donkey-Back steppe and fight him for her. Whoever wins will be khan of all our people, and whoever loses will be dead . . ." Yegu's voice trailed off. "Jamukha Khan? Are you all right?"

The deer skull I'd rescued from the cave hung above the door of my yurt, mocking me. My ears buzzed. My head felt as if someone had bashed it several times with a blacksmith's hammer.

Temujin must know about us. Borta must have told him. I knew I should give the order to move camp, make preparations for the coming battle with my anda . . . but all I could think of was Borta in Temujin's camp, guarded more carefully than his gold.

The way I saw it, the spirits owed me one, and the heads my anda had sent had given me an idea. I just needed a messenger who could get into Lady Borta's yurt alone, someone Anda Temujin would trust.

"Is that girl still around?" I asked Yegu. "The warrior girl who came to my tent that winter we spent with Kiriltuk's Alliance? Khadagan, I think her name was . . ."

Yegu gave me a lewd grin. I knew exactly what he was thinking, but by then I was past caring what my friends thought of my so-called girl phobia. "I don't think her family's left yet, Jamukha," he said. "It's a good idea to take a wife to take your mind off Lady Borta—"

"Send her to me. And pass me that skull belonging to Lady Borta's spirit deer."

Yegu gave me a puzzled look, but he was quick to obey and, despite my refusal to carry her message to Temujin five years ago, Khadagan did not need much persuasion to take the skull and my message to Lady Borta. Maybe the girl had been worried I wanted her for what Yegu assumed I did, and was just keen to leave my camp with the other deserters, but that worked both ways. If Borta accepted my peace offering and agreed to see me again, the last thing we needed were sympathisers of Temujin's spying on us.

The gift of the deer's skull didn't work out quite as I'd planned. Khadagan returned with news that Borta had given birth to a son, together with Borta's threat that if I came anywhere near her or her child, she'd tell Temujin that I was the wolf called Genghis. "We're not stupid, Jamukha," Khadagan added, giving me a hard look. "A spirit can't make a girl pregnant. This Genghis is a man. If you know who he is, you should tell your Anda Temujin before he kills every last red-blooded male on the steppe. None of us wants a war."

I didn't want a war, either. I knew who would come off worst. Borta had warned me to stay away, but – Heaven help me – I could not bear the thought of never seeing her again. Left with no other choice, I sent a message back with Khadagan saying I'd meet Anda Temujin on the Donkey-Back steppe on Red Circle Day with my army. Then I led my remaining troops higher into the mountains in case Temujin tried a sneaky attack before then, although I doubted he would. My anda was far too honourable for that.

- 12 -

YEAR OF THE TIGER

WHEN EVERYONE HAD chosen sides, I had just thirteen clans left in my alliance. With all those who had deserted my camp after my anda's declaration of war, Temujin now had an army at least ten times the size of mine. A ridiculous situation. My anda, who had started his raiding career up the Onan with only his little brothers and a baby sister, had been named khan by most of our people.

I needed to act fast, and the only way I could think of to raise more warriors at short notice was to go to the remaining tribes and form alliances with them. The Merkids and Tartars were history, of course – so I rode to the Naimans and the Oyirads and talked my tongue half off, persuading them to fight with me against my Anda Temujin. They had heard about the Tartar and Merkid massacres by then, so it wasn't easy. But I talked them round with excessive gifts of horses, furs and gold, ending up poorer than when I'd been turned out of Dei the Wise's camp all those years ago. In the end, in return for my sworn word on my father's bones that I'd protect them from my anda if the battle went badly, the Naiman Khan and the Oyirad Khan promised to bring their armies to meet me on the Donkey-Back steppe on Red Circle Day, when I'd promised my anda I'd meet him to settle things between us once and for all.

All this time, Borta's ghostly deer haunted my dreams. I even thought I saw it standing in the middle of the path on our way back through the mountains, where it spooked my horse and left me lying in the snow, much to my lads' amusement. They, of course, had not seen a thing and taunted me for wasting my arrows shooting at spirits. I knew then that Borta had cursed me, and there was nothing I could do except go through with this battle and hope to have a chance to explain myself at the end of it.

To my surprise, the Naiman army turned up on time, led by their chief in his battle finery. The sight of his waving banners, his horses with their bits jingling, and his hard-faced warriors jogging along in a massed horde, made me feel a bit better about the coming battle. The Oyirads, however, did not show.

"Maybe they got delayed, Jamukha Khan," Yegu said tactfully.

The Naiman Khan nodded. "It's possible. They've got to come through the mountains, remember. We should wait for them."

This made sense. Except, of course, the one thing I *couldn't* do was wait. Not if I wanted my red moon courage.

"And give Anda Temujin time to recruit more men?" I said in my most scornful tone. "His scouts will already have spotted your army riding in. No! We attack tomorrow, when the red moon rises and the spirits will be on our side."

"But what if they aren't on our side?" the Naiman Khan said, looking around doubtfully at my nervous troops. "We heard about the talking animals. It seems your ancestors think your anda should be Khan of the Mongol people instead of you."

Before his words could destroy what remained of my nerve, I jammed my heels into my horse's ribs and led my lads over the ridge to meet my anda's army. If this sounds like just the sort of crazy thing Temujin would have done, you're right. I'm not entirely sure where my courage came from that day. But Borta was down in that camp, and my heart had begun to race at the thought of seeing her again.

My bravery did not last long. When we rounded the cliffs and saw my anda's yurts spread below us, my mouth went dry. It's no exaggeration to say Temujin's camp covered the entire steppe. Dusk was falling by the time we got there, and I swear his fires outnumbered the stars in the sky. We drew rein and stared down the slope in silence.

"I think your anda's got a few more warriors than we thought, Jamukha," Yegu said.

"Take up your positions!" I ordered, before the Naiman Khan could back out. "We'll attack at sunrise."

I put Borta's deer firmly out of my mind and prayed the wolf would come to give me courage one last time.

*

That was the worst day of my life.

The sky grew darker and darker, until I could see no further than my horse's ears. Thunder rolled around the rocks. Lightning spooked our mounts. The killing went on below us, unseen, with screams and cries and frightened neighs. As the shamans' violins wailed, I started seeing spirits again – not only Borta's deer spooking my horse, but the giant silver-blue wolf ripping out the throats of my men. Instead of the battle rage, I felt sheer panic, which must have communicated itself to the Naiman Khan because his nerve broke. With the rain hissing down and thunder rumbling around us, he ordered his men to retreat over the ridge. Many of the fleeing Naimans galloped their horses straight into ravines they could not see.

I thought I saw Borta down below with the shamans, but I couldn't reach her. I slithered off my horse and huddled behind the nearest rock, drenched to the skin. I cursed the cowardly Naimans for running away, and cursed my own stupidity for relying on the wolf-spirit to help me, when clearly it had been on my anda's side all along.

Shadows raced past me in the gloom. I had no idea if they were friends or enemies, human or animal, man or spirit. Hailstones stung every exposed bit of my flesh. I gripped my bow and my last handful of soggy arrows, squinting into the storm, desperately trying to think of a half-decent excuse for when Temujin's men finally found me.

I didn't feel very much like a khan by the time the storm

clouds cleared to show us the steppe below littered with bodies. But at least I was still alive. I found one of my lads crouched miserably beside his dead horse and sent him down to Temujin's camp with a message. I told him to tell my anda I'd been forced into battle against my wishes by the Naimans, but I'd managed to distract the Naiman Khan from fighting by telling him tales of my anda's bravery and would talk peace if he would come in person to meet me. By then, the red moon should be in the sky to give me courage. I collected together a few more survivors while I waited for Temujin's reply, and we made an uncomfortable camp on the mountain.

Towards evening, Yegu arrived with a wheezing Kiriltuk and his remaining Taychuits, all of them covered in mud. The Naimans had apparently fled home terrified, telling everyone they met on route that Temujin commanded an army of spirits and could turn himself into a giant wolf. This old story made me groan, but I sent a couple of lads to see if they could find some stray sheep or goats. Between the flashes of panic, I knew we'd need meat to entertain my anda.

"He won't come alone," Yegu warned. "He'll probably bring his brothers to kill us all."

"Heaven will look after us," I said, clinging to my hope that Borta would talk Temujin around. "I'm the rightful Khan."

Kiriltuk scowled at me. "You're Khan of nothing, Jamukha! Thanks to that shaman storm, you've just lost half your army on this mountain! Temujin will have stolen the rest of our people by the time we get back down. The Naimans are not going to help us again in a hurry, and the Oyirads will stay well away once they hear the tale. Temujin will boil us all alive for this."

"He won't boil me," I said, my head still echoing with the wail of the shamans' violins. "I'm his anda."

Yegu and Kiriltuk glanced at each other, and the others began to mutter among themselves. I didn't like the way they were looking at me, quite frankly. But before they could say any more, the lads I'd sent to look for meat came back leading a horse with a dead sheep over the saddle and someone I'd never thought to see again clinging to its tail – the Merkid refugee, Chilger the Athlete.

Yegu and Kiriltuk went for their daggers, but I told them to relax. Chilger was alone and didn't look dangerous. When I welcomed him, they didn't question it. He wasn't the first Merkid refugee to have joined us. I suppose they thought I might have some sort of sneaky plan to get us all out of there alive – if only!

I set the lads to roasting the sheep they'd found and took Chilger aside.

"I tried your camp first, Jamukha, but Temujin's men were all over it," he told me in a hushed tone. "Then I met some Naimans fleeing across the steppe, who told me I'd find your army up here . . . is this it?" His voice held a note of fear as he looked at our bedraggled little band.

"I've more lads out on the mountain," I said, sweeping a vague arm at the rocks and keeping a wary eye out for Borta's ghostly spirit deer. "We'll regroup soon."

"I heard you'd been crowned the Mongol Khan, Jamukha . . . that's why I came back to offer you my spear, only it looks as if I'm too late." He looked round nervously again.

"Don't worry, Chilger, this is just a temporary setback. I am still khan. Heaven is looking after us." I drew myself up straighter and pointed to the sheep. "See, we've got meat enough for everyone!"

Chilger was too tactful to say this was because "everyone" consisted of so few, but I saw the contempt in his eyes. He glanced at the others and lowered his voice. "The lads who brought me here said you've invited your Anda Temujin up here to talk peace. Is that a good idea, considering what you did to his wife while she was in my yurt?"

A lump of ice formed in my stomach.

"He's my anda. He'll talk to me." Talking was the one thing I could always do better than Temujin. "But maybe you'd better make yourself scarce before he arrives," I added, remembering what my anda had said about Chilger the Athlete when he'd learnt whose yurt Borta had been kept in.

Chilger ran his tongue over his lips. "You saved my life once, Jamukha," he said. "So I'll return the favour. Temujin knows what you did that night in our camp. If you've got any sense at all, you'll flee into the mountains and hide yourself in the deepest chasm you can find before your anda gets up here."

The lump in my stomach had become an icy river. "What *did* I do?" I whispered, finding it hard to think straight. "I still can't remember very much of that night."

Chilger gave me a look of disbelief. "It's time to stop playing games, Jamukha! You're not even meant to be alive. Elder Brother and our shaman had it all worked out. They were going to kill you after you'd helped them take Borta's powers away, and then use her to lure Temujin into our camp so we could kill him too. But you were like an animal on Red Circle Night! I was terrified. We all were. You ravished Borta, and then you ran off and everyone said you'd turned into a wolf. We thought you'd killed her at first. Then her old servant told us it was just a spirit trance, but our shaman was having trouble with the ghost-stallion in his violin and couldn't do anything to help her. She didn't wake up until Temujin's army attacked our camp three days later. I thought you were brave, joining back up with your anda that night . . . you really don't remember what you did at the ceremony, do you?"

I could not breathe. The smell of the roasting mutton made me sick. "I thought it was a dream . . ." The echoes of the violins lingered in my head, mocking me. "So I was the wolf that night, after all?"

Chilger nodded miserably. "Our shaman had seen it possess you, so he knew you would come. And Borta's spirit must have cursed you, exactly like she said it would curse

385

the man who took away her shaman powers. Or why would you be hiding up here on the mountain on Red Circle Night with a handful of warriors like this? Temujin's been named khan of all the people who live in felt tents. There's no hope for us. We'd better leave right away. We might have a chance of getting away in the dark."

I stared at Chilger. "But Lady Borta never said anything," I whispered. "A whole winter we were camped together, and she never said a word! She told Temujin it was a spirit called Genghis."

I'd been the fool, to think Borta hadn't known it was me all along.

"That's because she didn't want you and Temujin to fight over her!" Chilger shouted. "Don't you understand? We never touched her before that night, so her son is probably yours as well. *Now* do you think your anda will talk peace?"

The mountain started spinning. The evening sun shining through the smoke of our fire, the eyes of my lads staring at me in horror . . . all reddened and blurred as if the battle madness was on me. Yet I could not move. My limbs had turned to water.

"So *that's* what you were up to on Red Circle Night," Yegu said softly, glancing at Kiriltuk. "We thought you'd gone into the Merkid camp to negotiate for Lady Borta's release."

My friend looked disgusted, as well he might. I felt a stab of shame at the way I had betrayed the only girl I'd ever loved.

"The Merkid's right," Yegu continued. "Temujin won't talk peace now. He'll hunt us to the ends of the earth. We've only one chance of persuading him to let our families live. I'm sorry, Jamukha—"

I never saw the blow coming. I think it might have been old Kiriltuk who hit me, but perhaps not. All of them proved cowards in the end. When I woke, I found myself tied facedown over my saddle wearing a makeshift cangue, and those who had so recently crowned me khan were leading my horse into Temujin's camp. Delivering me to the wolves like a lamb bound for slaughter.

Temujin personally executed the traitors who had brought me to him, beheading them with cold efficiency using his axe. I suppose that meant he must have disapproved of my generals' betrayal. But it could equally have meant he was showing off his strength and his power. If he was trying to scare me, it didn't work. On my knees and helpless before him, I had no courage left. If truth be known, I'd had none since the night I'd ravished Borta and the wolf spirit had abandoned me.

Trembling, I pleaded with my anda to swing his axe one last time and kill me too, before Borta saw me in such a pathetic state. I no longer expected any mercy from her. But it seemed she had asked her husband for the privilege of deciding my fate. So that night in the privacy of her yurt, locked in my cangue and tied to the tent post so I couldn't hurt her, I got a chance to explain myself, after all.

She wanted to know the truth and I was done with lies. They just get more and more complicated until you can barely work out what's true and false yourself. So I told her everything I remembered. I'm not sure it came out quite right, because the red moons blurred into one until I no longer trusted my memory. But she'd been shaman-trained, and nodded wisely at my tale of the silver-blue wolf and the red moon courage I'd possessed in battle but had lost towards the end.

"It's because you swore the anda bond with Temujin," she decided when I fell silent.

I was weeping by then, so uncontrollably that Temujin's brothers, who stood guard at the door, glanced inside to see what was wrong.

"The wolf possessed you so you could help my husband when he was in trouble," Borta went on, shooing them out again. "It used your body to make sure my son would be a Mongol rather than half Merkid, but it wasn't you in Chilger's yurt that night – it was a spirit of our Ancestors. My little Jochi will grow up to be a great general and help Temujin conquer all the tribes of the steppes. Now he's khan, my husband doesn't need you any more. He'll execute you in the morning."

"Please," I said. "Help me?"

Borta looked at me with pity, but I could see the shadow of disgust in her eyes that reminded me of her look when I'd trapped her by the river back in Dei the Wise's camp.

"Temujin's brothers want to make you suffer," she said

with a sigh. "But Temujin will do it the way I say. He promised. I can't save your life, Jamukha. But I know a way to let your spirit join us when the red moon is in the sky, if you want me to."

I stared at Borta through my tears. How could I bear to see her and my Anda Temujin together in the furs, even for a single night each year? It would be easier to join the Ancestors and forget I had ever sworn anda with the Khan of all the people who live in felt tents. But I did not deserve easy. I wanted to make up for my betrayal. I wanted to stay with Borta and my anda for as long as possible, to help them if I could, to just be with them if I couldn't. I wanted to see Jochi grow up.

"I want to stay," I whispered. "Can you do it?"

Borta stared back into my eyes, her face a blur surrounded by her dark hair so I couldn't tell if she was crying, too. She nodded and lifted the violin she'd made from my gift of the deer's skull.

"With this, I can."

She got to her feet and gently kissed me on the forehead, as she might have kissed our baby son, whom she wouldn't let me see. Then she lifted the door flap to let in the chill dawn air, and called for Temujin.

Temujin's brothers bend my body backwards over the woodpile to break my spine in the shadow of his war banner. Wolves howl in the mountains as its nine dark tails lift on the wind of my passing. Borta's violin plays faster, louder, calling my spirit out of my body and imprisoning it in the skull of a creature I betrayed.

If the shamans are right, there will be three generations of blood before that banner hangs quiet again with the white tails of peace. By the time our spirits are finally at rest, the ashes of our enemies will darken the moon, and the world will tremble at the name of my Anda Temujin, the mighty Genghis Khan.

HISTORICAL NOTE

The inspiration for this story came from a narrative known as *The Secret History of the Mongols* (Chinese: *Yuan Ch'ao Pi Shih*), which was based on a thirteenth-century Mongolian text probably written shortly after Genghis Khan's death. The version I read takes the form of an atmospheric prose poem ('The Secret History of the Mongols' by Paul Kahn, Cheng & Tsui, 1998), although the original Mongolian stories would have had an oral tradition.

At the time of Temujin's birth, rival nomadic tribes roamed the steppes of Central Asia – Mongols, Tartars, Kereyids, Merkids, etc. Each tribe consisted of clans based on family units, which could be quite large since all the tribes practised polygamy. Temujin's father Yesugei the Brave had stolen Temujin's mother from the Merkids, made a pact with the Kereyids, and united several of the Mongol families under one banner, including members of his own Borgjin clan and Kiriltuk's Taychuit clan, leading to the shift in power after Yesugei's death.

Temujin was proclaimed "Genghis" Khan, ruler of all the tribes of Central Asia, at a great assembly of the Mongolian people in the Year of the Tiger 1206. He went on to conquer the Middle East and much of Europe. After his death in 1227, his sons and grandsons continued to expand his empire until Kublai Khan unified China and founded the Yuan dynasty in 1271.

Because of his questionable fatherhood, Borta's eldest son Jochi never inherited Temujin's vast empire, which passed to her third son Ogodei.

Sometimes translated as "oceanic", the true origin of the name Genghis is still unknown.